MW01026550

PRAISE FOR

THE PERSIANS

"Half outrageous, compulsive, and shameless; half tender, loving, and funny: *The Persians* is a very brilliant, very special book."
— Jessica Stanley, author of *Consider Yourself Kissed*

"A captivating family saga, equally tragic and comic, *The Persians* is an unforgettable read with complex, chaotic characters you can't help but love."
— Josie Ferguson, author of *The Silence in Between*

"Glitzy, gutsy, and deliciously dark, a romp with serious things to say about misogyny, generational trauma, and losing your home."
— Samantha Ellis, author of *Take Courage*

"A witty and deeply absorbing saga of a family whose fate is intertwined with modern Iran's. I always knew epic Iranian families like the Valiats existed; I had just never met any. These five fierce, passionate, wounded women are at once tragic and hilarious, each voice meticulously crafted and singularly true."
— Dina Nayeri, author of *Who Gets Believed?*

"An irresistible novel about a singular yet wholly recognizable family. I fell in love with the women in the Valiat family: by turns feisty and foolish, wise and secretive, and full of so much love and longing it took my breath away. Sanam Mahloudji writes with such humor and zip that the heartbreak sneaks up on you. This is a remarkable debut."
— Edan Lepucki, author of *California*

"An epic of intricate and beautiful proportion, *The Persians* is exuberant, comic, and perceptive."

—Amina Cain, author of *Indelicacy*

"Filled with heartbreak, humor, and so much love, *The Persians* takes us on a journey to reshape our understanding of power, heritage, and ancestry—and brings a rare wisdom to the chaos of family."

—Vanessa Chan, author of *The Storm We Made*

"A wonderful multigenerational family drama with characters you really care about. I'm still thinking about them now. I enjoyed it enormously."

—Marian Keyes, author of *Rachel's Holiday*

"At once funny and profound, sprawling and personal, *The Persians* questions history's grip on our lives—is it possible to free ourselves from the past, and do we even want to? A gloriously engrossing debut."

—Tash Aw, author of *We, the Survivors*

"*The Persians* is an ambitious, glorious feat. Five women's voices become one irresistible whole in this darkly funny, richly satisfying, wonderful debut."

—Sarah Winman, author of *Still Life*

The PERSIANS

A NOVEL

SANAM MAHLOUDJI

SCRIBNER

New York   Amsterdam/Antwerp   London
Toronto   Sydney   New Delhi

Scribner
An Imprint of Simon & Schuster, LLC
1230 Avenue of the Americas
New York, NY 10020

First Scribner hardcover edition March 2025

SCRIBNER and design are trademarks of Simon & Schuster, LLC

For information about special discounts for bulk purchases, please contact Simon & Schuster Special Sales at 1-866-506-1949 or business@simonandschuster.com.

The Simon & Schuster Speakers Bureau can bring authors to your live event. For more information or to book an event, contact the Simon & Schuster Speakers Bureau at 1-866-248-3049 or visit our website at www.simonspeakers.com.

Interior design by Ritika Karnik

Manufactured in the United States of America

1   3   5   7   9   10   8   6   4   2

Library of Congress Cataloging-in-Publication Data
Names: Mahloudji, Sanam, 1977– author.
Title: The Persians : a novel / Sanam Mahloudji.
Description: First Scribner hardcover edition. | New York : Scribner, 2025.
Identifiers: LCCN 2024038241 (print) | LCCN 2024038242 (ebook) |
ISBN 9781668015797 (hardcover) | ISBN 9781668015803 (trade paperback) |
ISBN 9781668015810 (ebook)
Subjects: LCGFT: Domestic fiction. | Novels.
Classification: LCC PS3613.A3493338 P47 2025 (print) |
LCC PS3613.A3493338 (ebook) | DDC 813/.6—dc23/eng/20241015
LC record available at https://lccn.loc.gov/2024038241
LC ebook record available at https://lccn.loc.gov/2024038242

ISBN 978-1-6680-1579-7
ISBN 978-1-6680-1581-0 (ebook)

For my daughters

All the insouciance, all the gaiety is a bluff.

—Jean Rhys, *Good Morning, Midnight*

The PERSIANS

I

A SECOND FACE

BITA

FOR A WEEK IT was a nonstop party of drugs and cartoons until an hour ago when I bailed my Auntie Shirin out of the Aspen jail after her arrest for attempted prostitution.

In the white Suburban taxi that bulldozed across the uneven snowy roads, she poked her head out the backseat window, avoiding my questions. Finally, she turned around, her cheeks pink and alive, and yelled in Persian for me to stop meddling: "Foozooli nakon!"

Back at our hotel, Auntie Shirin marched down the third-floor hallway in her five-inch-heel over-the-knee boots. She passed 3E without slowing down. "Not dealing with Houman's kumbaya shit. Bita, my dear, my joon, I'm staying with you."

I hovered the key card over the lock, and my door opened.

Thirty minutes later she walked out of my bathroom wearing a big white hotel robe, and a towel around her head. The steam rolling out the door smelled of sweet chemicals.

Shirin removed the towel and shook out her hair. She lay face down on the king bed, on top of the cloudlike duvet. We'd dubbed my room Club 3M. Me, her son Mo, and all the dipshit kids of our parents' friends. They made mine the party room not because I was the life of the party but more the opposite—after Mom died last year we'd skipped the trip and could I really get into the spirit without a shove? For eleven years straight, since 1994, our friends and family had flown to Aspen from New York, L.A., and Houston, as if 1979 and the Islamic Revolution hadn't happened. As if we were still the most important families in Iran, descended from the great ancient lines, although this was America and nobody cared. The locals hated us. Not openly, but they did. I imagined them like that Pace Picante commercial, cowboys mumbling "Get a rope" when they saw us in all black, buying a thousand dollars' worth of caviar and champagne at the mom-and-pop market.

"Bita joon, fetch me a Fiji and a Marlboro Light." Auntie Shirin turned her head to the side, her cheek against the white pillow. She raised her arm and pinched at the air. "Be a good girl and do as your auntie says."

"Okay, sure," I said and rolled my eyes.

In Iran, before 1979, Auntie Shirin had chauffeurs and servants. Once she said to me, without an ounce of self-reflection, "Bita, even the chauffeurs talked about overthrowing the king. They drove me to the marches. They hated the Pahlavis nearly as much as me."

Her thick, dark hair splayed out across the white sheets, like ink spilling out on paper. She was a mess and I hated her and I loved her too.

I pulled a cool blue bottle from the minibar and got a cigarette out of the pack in my poofy ski jacket, stuck it in my mouth and lit it on a matchbook from the Caribou Club. The printed gold antlers of the muscular animal rose up in silhouette on the black cardboard. This was the club where my aunt was arrested for attempted prostitution. I inhaled deeply from the cigarette, watching the salt-and-pepper tip turn red, before passing it to Shirin.

"Here you go," I said, blowing out the first smoke.

"Good girl," Auntie Shirin said.

She brought it to her face, her deep maroon nails sparkling. She looked to the bedside table as if to say, Put the water there. So I did.

It was four a.m. and I was no longer high. Or drunk. Just tired and annoyed. I'd bailed Shirin out for ten thousand dollars and all she'd said when the cop brought her barefoot to the empty waiting area was "Thank you, Bita joon" and "I knew you'd answer. What a damn genius I was to call you first, my little lawyer-in-training. That was good practice for you. Houman would be going up the wall."

Then the cop handed me a large plastic bag of her belongings along with her boots, which even he knew better than to stuff in with her purse.

Now on her back, Auntie Shirin lay like a puddle soaking into the ground. The smoke rose from her lips. "Don't you dare knock on his door," she said, meaning her husband passed out in another room along the third floor.

I sat down in the tufted floral armchair next to the bed. On the TV, the newsman stood in a blizzard of white snow, in his black coat, breathing out white air. I pressed mute.

"They treated me like a common criminal. I'm disgusted," Auntie Shirin said and filled her throat again with smoke.

"Did they read you your rights? They search you?" I asked.

"Are you kidding? A horrible slob stuck her hand in my ass. I'm going to sue them, you know."

"Why don't we just focus on getting the charges dropped, Auntie? This isn't a joke—do you want a criminal record? Prison time? These charges can be serious. Think about your business—you're the face of Valiat Events, aren't you?" My voice grew high and slightly shaky.

She widened her eyes, ash building on her cigarette. "Mashallah, Bita," she said. "For an Ivy League law student, you're pretty fucking wimpy."

5

I looked away at the silent TV, the news always on. It was pretty hypocritical that she invoked allah, given that nobody in our circle actually thought of ourselves as Muslim. Although some ancestor once made the Hajj, circled that big black box and was known for doing so.

"You owe me," I said. "I could have left you shivering on a vinyl mattress until all the Persians came in and roasted you like a marshmallow."

"Attagirl," she said and smiled.

I rolled my eyes. "You're a jerk, Auntie. This is bad, even for you. At least you didn't go through with it. Right?" I pictured Shirin under a big blob of man, giving herself to him. "How did this even happen? Didn't he approach you? I don't get it."

"That pig. That stupid officer fuckface posing as a Dallas playboy," Auntie Shirin said, as she ashed her cigarette onto the floor.

"Do you think they targeted you?"

"For what? Being beautiful?"

I laughed and shook my head. "People from Iran are always a menace. One day we are hostage takers and hairy terrorists, the next we are a nuclear threat or a woman of ill repute."

She stared at me, daring me to continue, but I said nothing.

"He said, 'Baby, be my Cleopatra for the night. I want to be your sheik.' I've had it up to here with that shit. So I said, 'Okay, honey, I can be your Princess Jasmine, but it's gonna cost you. Gimme fifty Gs.' Bastard." Shirin narrowed her eyes, her oily black lashes folding together.

I laughed. "Where did you come up with that amount?"

"I'm worth twice that at least," she said. She stretched her arms out in a yawn, pushing against the headboard with her cigarette hand.

"Watch it," I said. Ash scattered behind her head.

Auntie Shirin dropped her cigarette into the bottle full of water.

"They're so uneducated," she said. "Everyone's a fucking Arab. They don't know anything about the Persians, that we were the greatest civilization on Earth. Let alone that our family in particular is something to behold. So then he said, 'Okay, baby, just walk with me to the ATM.' I'm no idiot. I know an ATM isn't going to give you that kind of money. So I said, 'You're full of shit.' He took out a checkbook and wrote me a check and gave me his entire wallet as collateral. I was going to do it, you know."

"It was a trap," I said. "But you're right. All they saw was woman with dark skin."

"What dark skin?" She looked at one arm and then the other. "No, no."

"Oh please," I said.

"This guy just wanted to humiliate me. He hates beautiful women."

I scanned the dining table. Ketel One, a mirror taken from the wall, rolled-up dollar bills, Gore-Tex gloves, torn-up ski passes with mangled wires, green soy sauce packets and used chopsticks from Sushi Olé. On the carpet, the shiny hard shells of kicked-off ski boots. Black-on-black Prada shopping bags. Half-drunk Fijis, red-lipstick-kissed necks.

"And those opium-smoking dumbasses," Shirin continued. "They won't find out. Let them play their silly games."

She meant the men, like her husband, Houman, and my dad, Teymour, who sat playing cards at their round table covered in green felt brought rolled up in someone's luggage. In their room, the air would smell of mixed smoke—sweet, earthy, and floral, crystal tumblers of scotch shining like stars against the soft, green sky.

"When you were in the shower I called Patty to see if she could help. Her old professor knows some lawyers out in Denver. I told her to be discreet. I know you wouldn't want word to get around."

"I don't need your lawyers, but fine, if you insist, I'll take their call."

"Don't do me any favors, Auntie," I said.

"And who's this Patty? Why would you call her so early in the morning? Shame on you."

"A friend," I said, tipping my head back and staring at the air vent. Gray dust clung to the slats, like petri-dish fur.

THERE WAS A KNOCK at the door. Then, more knocking. I opened my eyes. As I lifted my head, my neck ached.

"Go see who it is," Auntie Shirin said.

I wobbled over to the door, wiping drool from my cheek. Pressed my eye against the cold ring of the peephole.

"It's Mo," I said.

"Don't tell him shit. He can't take it," she said. "But wait." Auntie Shirin reached for the large Ziploc on the floor. Her married name—Shirin Javan—was scrawled on it in black marker. She shook it and junk scattered across the white bed. Matchbooks, makeup cases, phone, black purse. She hurried to refill the purse.

I opened the door. Mo plowed past me, straight to Shirin, whose head was back on the pillow. "The fuck, Mom? Where you been? I've been calling you all morning."

"The fuck what," she said. "Call it female bonding. Show some respect. You don't speak to your mother like that." She propped her purse up on the nightstand.

"Sorry, Mommy," he said. He bent down and kissed her head. He wore all black. His platinum Rolex shone in the bedside light. He was almost thirty, three years older than me. Mo short for Mohammad.

Mo and Shirin had the same beautiful dark moles on their faces, spaced like constellations, jet-black hair, fluid motions. Shirin smiled. Her makeup had stayed on throughout all this—eyeliner drawn slanted like cat eyes, mascara pulling her lashes up and away.

"I'm starved—can we eat?" she said.

Shirin swung her legs onto the floor and untied her robe. It opened up like a curtain and I saw her naked body underneath. She dropped the robe on the bed. I looked at Mo and saw that he was watching her too. Eyes full of love. Her boobs were round and stiff and seemed a separate thing from her body. Her tummy flat and tan, her pussy waxed into a razor-sharp V. Not like someone's fifty-year-old mother. I thought of the cop approaching her, kissing her. The only signs of age were in the veins that stuck out of her hands and neck.

"Can you believe you came out of this?" she said, looking at her crotch. "Best decision I ever made. One day I went to the toilet to take a shit, and there you were."

Mo raised an eyebrow. "Mom, no one else would think this is normal. Be serious."

"I am serious. It's a miracle you're not gay."

Mo laughed.

"Real nice, Auntie. I thought you didn't wanted to seem backwards anymore," I said.

"Talk to me when you have kids, Bita," she said. "No one wants that. My baby boy is a lady-killer." She gave Mo a kiss on his stiff, gelled hair then walked over to the loveseat where she'd dumped last night's clothes. A form-fitting black wool dress and her Chanel boots. No underwear. She put them on. Over it, she put on my black coat with the big fur collar. Her tanned skin shone. "Let's go," she said, smiling and grabbing her purse. "I could eat a cowboy."

As I zipped up my boots I saw the white powder already sliced into lines on the mirror. I leaned over, took the rolled bill, and snorted. Mo and Shirin did the same. I closed my eyes, breathed in and out. The inside of my nose burned and the bitterness leaked down my throat. I swallowed. And there it was throughout my body: the little flash of joy.

We walked out of the hotel room. I checked that the door tag read DO NOT DISTURB. At the elevator bank, a hotel maid was organizing her cart. Shirin acknowledged her and then, when she turned, snatched a handful of tiny liquor bottles and slipped them into Mo's coat pocket.

The three of us stepped out of the elevator onto the mezzanine carpeted in peach-and-orange paisley. Gold chandeliers lit up the room. A grand wooden staircase rose from the lobby and circled up to where we stood. The après-ski crowd sat on sofas and drank wine, ordering more rounds than they should. In that way they were like us.

We watched the guests down below, fresh off planes in cowboy hats and fur coats. I counted all the bleached blondes and Ken-doll haircuts. Bellboys rushed around with luggage. I spent my infancy on planes. Planes left Tehran daily with our kind, people who could bribe and smuggle their way out.

"When did you realize the Revolution was for real?" I asked my parents once. "Never," Mom said. We were more pro-Shah than we knew. When push came to shove.

"These Texans are making me sick. They're a couple cows and oil wells from being complete dirt," Shirin said. "Let's go have a drink."

We sat before the crackle of the mezzanine lounge fireplace. They'd really done it up this year—more than I remembered. Tinsel reflected in the mirrors. Christmas songs played on invisible speakers. I'd sung them all as a little kid in L.A. I'm sure Mo did, too, in Houston.

American newlyweds sat on the adjacent sofa. They Eskimo-kissed, twirled their wineglasses like they teach you at a wine-tasting class. Then they looked over at us and left. The fire warmed my body.

"Your mom would have loved this," Auntie Shirin said. "Seema was the biggest Christmas freak."

"Was she? She liked the cold air here, the cross-country skiing." *Would have. Was.* The words grated. Fuck cancer, that cheesy saying, and fuck how we distance ourselves from Mom, maybe to protect ourselves from death's entirety, distract us from its lack of a point. She'd been dead just one year and already I felt her fading from us. The little snow globe she'd treasured as a child—did it hold a pine tree? How can I remember her better? How would a real Muslim do it?

According to one of Mom's rare stories about her youth, my grandmother Elizabeth modeled herself after Hollywood actresses—like Elizabeth Taylor. Even before that Elizabeth's famous visit to Iran in '76, with all the seductive posing in front of landmarks. Our Elizabeth hated children. The children she hated most in the world were her own: her son Nader, my mother Seema, and Auntie Shirin. Elizabeth didn't want to be a mother. She told my mom at sixteen, the day she finally got her first period: "After you came out, bloody and screaming, my life was finished. I was finished." She liked to talk about how much her vagina stretched giving birth. Why wasn't her life over after Nader came out? Nader, a semiliterate bully who ate ants. Was one kid doable, not life-ruining?

"This is the last time I'm doing this dumb trip, kids," Auntie Shirin said, rubbing her shiny, dark nails.

"Why?" Mo said.

"It's more and more of us every year. Aspen is infested with us, and the people of my generation are so boring. The men pretend they're young. And the women act like my old naneh. The monarchy crawled up their asses and died. Roll me a joint, baby." She passed a bejeweled cigarette case to Mo and ordered us a bottle of champagne. I'd thought she was going to say it was no good now without Mom. Maybe she felt that too. I clinked my glass to theirs and then against the edge of the table as my hand wobbled. I waited for something to break. Shirin smoked her joint and nobody stopped her.

"Your fathers," Shirin said, inhaled and exhaled, "are such losers."

"You're so mean," Mo said. "Dad does good business."

"Hah," Shirin said. "In Iran, they *were* the economy." She looked at me. "Houman and your dad are now selling what? Fake Iranian teabags with inspirational messages?"

"Yo, the fake part is not their fault. Hello, sanctions," Mo said.

Suddenly, Shahla, Neda, and Leila appeared in front of us. Sisters I could barely tell apart, Houman's brother's kids. Thick hair blow-dried straight, perfectly arched eyebrows, sad sexy mouths. Like me but, if I'm being honest, much prettier. Black pants, tight sweaters, diamonds, fur earmuffs. Somewhere between ski bunny and Playboy bunny and Iranian Ivanka Trump.

"Oh, girls, sit down. Eat. Eat," Auntie Shirin said. "Looks like all you're on is Ritalin and coffee. I don't understand you girls. You eat, you just eat smart. Lunch, okay. Dinner is for pigs. For dinner you eat a nice salad and that's that."

Shahla, Neda, and Leila giggled and two of them flipped their hair from one side to the other.

"We're going shopping. I need a new dress for tomorrow," the girl on the left said, cocking her head. "Side-boob for real."

"Da-yumn," Mo said. "We got the hottest girls. I'll always say that."

I made a gagging expression, a finger in my mouth. "Incest much? Besides, you only date blondes."

"And you only date Harvard guys? Well, before your dry spell."

"That's different," I said.

"Oh, is it?"

I shook my head. But he was right.

"These Houston boys invited us to a party on Red Mountain," the one in the middle said. "We gotta look fi-yah, yo."

"Hmm. You know anything about these guys?" Mo said.

"Oh, suddenly you're our big bad protector? Shut up, Mo! No one's in it for the conversation. *Blaaah, blaaah, blaaah*," Leila said hoarsely. I knew her by her voice: the oldest, the wisest, the one who'd been passing out drunk on tables since she was eleven.

—————

"LET'S VAMANOS. IT'S FOUR," Auntie Shirin said. "Stores close early today." She put her hand in the air and waved down a waiter. Not even our waiter. "Check?" she said to some guy in a navy uniform. "Don't have all day."

The man rushed back to the bar. I was a little drunk and too tired to act sober, so I stretched out my legs noisily on the coffee table. "No more stealing though," I said. "They charge fifteen dollars for each of those mini bottles. For real, Auntie."

Shirin smiled.

I did like making her smile. "You're such a criminal," I added and watched her now ignore me.

Mo scrunched his brows. "Huh?" he said.

"Joke," I said.

When the waiter didn't return, Auntie Shirin stood up and walked down the stairs and, we could see, out the revolving glass door. She didn't turn back. Mo and I shrugged our shoulders and followed. For a few seconds, I was alone sealed in the glass chamber. The world was quiet. Half gone. Perfect.

Outside, I joined Mo and Shirin under the green awning. I zipped my coat up to my face, feeling jagged metal against my lip, and drew up my hood.

We walked over the melting ice and cobblestone. Cowboy hats bobbing up and down with shopping bags. Everyone buying last-minute Christmas presents, and now so were we. My eyes watered in the cold wind.

Auntie Shirin pressed the buzzer at the entrance of a jewelry store. "Are we just looking?" I asked.

A security man let us in and then resumed his position inside. He wore reflective sunglasses and a tight tan uniform, like a caricature of an '80s highway patrolman. He did not smile at us or even look in our direction.

"What shall I get you?" Auntie Shirin said to Mo.

"For what?" Mo said.

"A new watch? What about you, Bita?"

"I'm okay," I said.

"You're turning down jewelry?" Auntie Shirin said.

"Shouldn't you take it easy today?" I said.

"Saket," Shirin snapped.

An older woman organized boxes on the other side of the glass counter. She wore a long ivory cardigan, her dyed caramel hair pulled back into a loose bun, her posture perfect. I hated her right away.

The woman looked up. "Can I help you?" she asked.

"I'd like to see your men's watches," Auntie Shirin said as the woman approached.

"Wonderful." She twisted a key in the glass case, which held a miniature Aspen dripping in jewels. Diamond-stud earrings suspended with invisible string as snowflakes.

"Nobody needs another watch," I said.

"You know what? I'll take them all." Shirin glared at me.

The woman took a step back. "Oh my. Are you sure?"

Shirin raised an eyebrow. "What do you think?"

"Do you want the prices first?" the woman asked. She unfastened watches from the green-and-white felt mountain.

"Throw in that necklace too." Shirin nodded at an emerald choker that doubled as a gondola cable.

"You must really love Christmas," the woman said. "That green is marvelous for the season."

Shirin laughed. She shook her head. "You have no idea."

The woman stared at us. "I'll go wrap these."

"Throw them in here," Auntie Shirin said, pulling out the Ziploc from the Aspen jail.

The woman stared at the pile of watches and then at the empty plastic bag scribbled on in Sharpie. Her perfect hair and face powder reflected the overhead lights, giving her the glow of an angel. She looked back at Shirin and smiled, lips pursed like she'd never felt sorrier for anyone in her goddamn life.

OUTSIDE THE STORE, AUNTIE Shirin put on the emerald choker—an octagon, held on to her neck by a chainmail of gold. It glistened. She'd bought six watches. Spent over thirty thousand dollars. She swung the plastic bag side to side sharply as she walked.

"Where'd you get that bag?" Mo said.

"None of your business," she said.

The sun was out now, the clouds moving fast. The snow on the ground blinded me. I put on my sunglasses.

"Don't ever embarrass me like that again," Shirin said. Her boots sounded hard on the red brick.

"Embarrass *you*?" I said. "I was just trying to help."

"I don't need your help," she said.

"Come on, guys. Cool it. Let's get a crepe," Mo said.

"Whatever you want, sweetheart," Shirin said. "Give me those vodkas."

Mo reached into his pocket and handed the bottles to Shirin. She stopped, tucked the bag under her arm, untwisted one bottle's top, shot it. Did the same with the other two. She tossed the empties into a mound of snow. I considered picking them up, but what was the point.

The big Aspen mountain—what the locals called Ajax—ascended ahead of us as we approached the line extending from the red-and-white-striped crepe cart. I felt dizzy and hot. I looked at my feet on the uneven bricks. I remembered something Mom used to say: if someone says, I like your bracelet, in Iran you're supposed to offer it to them. Just like that. Of course I couldn't ask Shirin to pay me back the ten thousand dollars bail money. It would be against everything they ever taught me. Besides, the money belonged to our family.

"Hey hey hey, if it isn't my favorite people of all time," I heard. It was Uncle Houman, with Dad. They had red noses from the cold, their short beards grizzled. They wore big fur hoods and thick parkas, Moncler or Façonnable. Dad held a cigar in his hairy hand. "Where've you been, darling?" Houman said. "I didn't see you last night."

"You know. Defending our honor," she said, crossing her arms.

Uncle Houman laughed. "Just relax, honey. Seriously. Relax. Everything's okay." He tilted his head up to the crisp blue-and-white sky, drew his arms wide, and breathed in. "*Ahhhhh*," he breathed out a cloud of white vapor. "What could be more beautiful than this? Aspen, Colorado, with my beautiful wife and family?" He patted Dad on his back.

Shirin shook her head. "Come on," she said. "You're pathetic. This town is a shithole."

"Order me a chocolate crepe, will you, Bita?" Dad said.

"We've got the poker tournament of the century going on," Uncle Houman said. He patted Dad's thick coat again, like he was dusting a pillow. Dad coughed, stretching out his cigar hand.

Two police officers with mustaches walked past us, chocolate sauce crawling down the sides of the crepe plates in their hands. I watched them and watched Auntie Shirin watch them. One of them smiled at her and winked.

"Excuse me?" Shirin said, loudly.

The cops turned around. "Excuse who?" the other one said, chocolate sauce now dripping over his fingers.

"Don't you dare look at me," Auntie Shirin said.

"Now, now, Shirin joon. Relax," Houman said. "Sorry, my wife must have had a few too many."

"Dirty pig," she said.

"Hey," the cop who had winked said. "Watch it."

Shirin looked back at us. Nobody said anything. The cop stood, his feet wide apart. He shook his head and squinted at Shirin in the bright sun.

Auntie Shirin turned again and looked at me, then Mo, and then our fathers. "Wait a minute here. None of you shits are saying anything?" she shouted.

I looked at my feet. Please let her stop. I waved people along so they'd pass us in line.

"Now, now," Houman said again. "Let's all just have a Merry Christmas. It's fine."

Auntie Shirin clenched her fists. "Shut up," she said, suddenly quieter, her jaw clenched, too.

The cop stepped closer to her.

"Get the fuck away from me," she said. "I saw that face you made. You heard about the Cleopatra bullshit, didn't you? You know who I am, don't you?"

The cop scrunched his eyebrows. "Huh? I should arrest you right now for public intoxication. Want that?"

"I'm not drunk," she yelled. People in line behind us started to walk around us without asking, their heads turning.

"Really?" the cop said. Then he turned to Houman. "Control that shit mouth on her," he went on. "If it weren't Christmas Eve, I'd put her in jail right now." He started to say something to the other cop, who took out a notepad.

"Shirin," Houman said in a low voice. "What is wrong with you?" He grabbed her arm and shook it.

17

"I nearly fucked one of their guys last night," she said. Her words, a weapon. She steeled her face.

Houman stared at her and didn't blink. I'd never seen him so still.

"What are you talking about, Auntie?" I said. "Come on. Stop that."

"Mom," Mo said. He looked at her and then at the people watching us.

Shirin fixed her gaze towards the ski mountain.

"She's joking," I said.

Auntie Shirin let out a bitter, angry laugh. "Nobody defends me. Nobody sticks up for me. What. Do. I. Have. To lose?" she asked.

I stared into her shiny, dark eyes. "What are you talking about? You have everything," I said.

But I didn't believe this. She was miserable. Mom always said Shirin was the sharpest of all their friends. Even though Mom was the booksmart one, Shirin turned out the most ambitious and daring. Most able to shape the world to her will. I was supposedly smart too. But what good had any of these qualities done us? The Revolution fucked everyone up. Even Mo and me and the three Ivanka sisters. Even if we didn't really talk about it. What was wrong with us?

"Please, Auntie," I said.

She shook her head. "I got you idiots presents." She swung the plastic bag in front of the men. "But I changed my mind."

Auntie Shirin walked away from us. Away from the crepe stand and the lift-ticket booth. She didn't look back. She stopped for a moment when she reached the base of the mountain, where people had left skis punched into the snow. I waited for her to turn, but she didn't. She started walking up the mountain. I could feel her leaning forward and bending her knees. I could feel the hot tears on her face—or was that wishful thinking? Skiers shot down fast, right past her, inadvertently spraying her with snow and making her pause to brush herself off as she climbed. Then, next to the giant tower of the gondola, she stopped. Skiers below her now shook snow off their helmets and clicked off their skis. She looked up, craning her neck. Her arms reached out like she was submitting herself to the mountain. Surrendering. The plastic bag dangled from one hand, the light bouncing off it.

She was far away now and I had to squint. Auntie Shirin reached into the bag. Suddenly, she swept her arm in an arc across the sky. Then, again. Her hand at the bag. And then her arm across the sky.

Objects curved like boomerangs flew across the air, glittery against the sun. But none returned. The beautiful, useless watches.

I said nothing. I watched Shirin. I watched the mountain, letting my eyes travel past her, up along the slope leading to the top, obscured by clouds. The mountain looked both soft and sharp. Rock pierced through powder. I breathed in the cool, crisp air.

Tehran was very dirty, everyone knew. A city running on smog. The last time I had breathed its air, I was a baby. As a kid, I felt surprised when I learned Iran was mountainous, the Alborz mountains growing just north of the city. Embracing Tehran in its majestic, silent beauty. What kind of Persian was I?

And yet I watched Auntie Shirin, I watched myself.

SHIRIN

BITA AND MO DON'T get it, but their universe is plastic, a joke. IKEA, Zara, Americans with their "history." America, the history killer. They don't care about heirlooms. Antique furniture is despised—they call it "brown furniture." They want particleboard, veneer, MDF. No. When you evacuate, you take your jewels. All our Revolution stories involve jewelry. You take your jewels no matter if you like them. Before photographs or your poodle. Yes, we had a poodle, a big beautiful sloppy dog. I'm not ashamed to admit.

Instead of thanking me, Bita and Mo laugh when I offer them jewelry. They don't see that it's my greatest expression of love, faith in our family's continuity, our family a living creature needing heirlooms— jewel-hungry gem thieves, gluttons as all survivors are, ask Darwin.

We came from a great man, descendants—great-granddaughters in fact—of a constitutionalist, a hero fighter, a man who, according to all the stories of Mommy and of course that famous Persian history treatise *Choking the Great Lion*, gave his life for democracy in Iran. Babak Ali Khan Valiat. The Great Warrior, they called him. It was the early 1900s and he wanted Iran to be a secular republic with a democratically elected parliament. He nearly got us there but he failed in the end, or I wouldn't be telling this story.

How I love Bita and Mo both, and yet they watched in silence as the saleswoman at the jewelry store talked down to us. I'm sorry to say they don't know the meaning of family. It's not their fault: America is younger than my favorite ring, a Siberian amethyst, the rarest kind, dark purple that flashes red and blue in the light, like a code of its seriousness and truth, surrounded by emerald teardrops, playacting to be a flower sunk down into its leaves. A sneaky gem. When I wear it, and hold out my hand to admire its strong colors, ones found in nature and yet hard to fathom, I am my grandmother Banou Khanoum at her dressing table. The Great Tiny Boss, as she was known to all.

When living got too risky, when we self-imprisoned in our walled homes, isolated from our countrymen—yes, in those gardens you hear about, drinking pomegranate juice and eating pistachios, all that nonsense if it makes you feel better—it was time to flee. The protests increasing in number and size and violence, all those students from the villages. Early on, after they published that infamous story calling Khomeini a "mad Indian poet"—the spark that ignited it, as they say—and the Shah's men killed students protesting in Qom, even I demonstrated, waved a sign: DEATH TO THE MONARCHY. You see, I didn't agree with absolute authority. It wasn't enough that the Shah released some prisoners after killing hundreds. I had Marxists in the family, a Swiss university education! A friend even kissed Khomeini's hand in Paris—Khomeini, the great democratizer! Hah!

But soon enough, after that forty-day cycle of mourning they all talk about, the repetition of grieving and then the explosion of more protests and more killings, that Shiite periodicity, the mood grew even darker. The signs then read DEATH TO THE SHAH. THE BLOODSUCKER. Worse things, too, were said with those placards, words I shall not repeat

21

but know they involved orifices and actions upon the elite, including our family members. The Cinema Rex burned with the five hundred people inside. The Shah imposed martial law and sent in tanks and helicopters and gunned everyone down. All this has been said a million times. What's once more? People swatted like cicadas in summer. He rolled over the young and they grew more angry.

Mommy feared for us. She said, "Leave now for the sake of your children. Let it die down, then return in comfort. Take your jewels, mine, too, just in case these barbarians make us give them everything." Little did we know the future ahead, courtesy of our supposed saviors: mass executions, firing squads, beheadings, compulsory veil. An Islamic state.

My sister, Seema, scoffed. She didn't know something very important about Iranians like us. She thought we were superficial, lived in the world of the material, ignorant of deeper thought. Well, how is it that we have Hafez and Saadi and Ferdowsi and Farrokhzad?—yes finally a woman too. How is it that we have a lineage of the greatest poets on Earth? Really think about it. The language, the words, they're a side effect. It's that we Iranians know what is possible of the world. We see that it is capable of such glorious immeasurable heart-pounding beauty. But then again, most of life isn't like that.

Is it?

The rose and the thorn, and sorrow and gladness are linked together. This is probably eight hundred years old. I forget who said it, but it's important. Remember it. Some people say we don't even have a separate word for rose—it's just red flower—but we have something better: imagination.

These jewels, the Armani, a taste for the extravagant, Perrier instead of tap water—our valiant attempt to bring our wild vision of heaven as Earth to our everyday lives. Roses to the thorns. Even the less fortunate of us try—they care about having lush hair, impeccable shoes. More so. The Prada *Mahda*, as we say, the Chanel *Pahnelle*, the rhyming, it's all an act, pretend. You get the picture. The poets—those seers—aren't separate from me and Mommy. Or even Bita and Mo and Houman and the rest of the idiots. We are born artists, us Persians, born dreamers. Even if we express it in high finance or dentistry.

Seema thought our love of nice things was base—because we are insecure and want to fit in with the West. We want respect, legitimacy. I laugh at that.

The more makeup, jewels an Iranian woman wears, I say the greater her concept of beauty, the deeper she is, the more she hurts inside, the more incongruous her inner and outer lives. This is all that is left of beauty in the world! Have you never worn a bright color to lift your spirits?

Next time you see such an Iranian woman, look beyond your own distaste. I understand that distaste myself, you may be surprised to know. I wish everyone could be equally wealthy, I love all people, I have the utmost respect for the person who has to work to live, not just to shine brighter like me. No, think of such an Iranian woman and her distance from what she was originally: in her heart of hearts, an heir to millennia of culture, beauty. And yet, she, this woman, never had any real power. She was wife, mother, helper, whore. Those diamonds? They're all she has.

"It's overblown, this talk. We will stay," Seema said to Mommy the week before we fled Iran. We sat in Mommy's apartment, in her white marble bathroom modeled after what she thought a mosque for women should look like, as she mixed her hair dye in a metal bowl. Seema, with a newborn baby Bita on her breast, said nothing would come of it. She was not so sure this protesting would help the country, and soon, the military or SAVAK would take control. Things would get back to normal, then change could come slowly, responsibly. "Incremental progress, I am now convinced is the way," Seema said, who

SANAM MAHLOUDJI

had supposedly been a communist once, who as a kid would tell me the State should raise all children. "Give me my niece," I said and grabbed Bita as Seema rested on the closed toilet, doing those strange blinks of hers when she got agitated, then staring at her feet. "Of course the various interests need to be respected and listened to; we slowly need to become a true constitutional monarchy. Then, maybe we can be a republic."

Mommy threw her arms in the air. Channeling ancestors. "Vay vay vay, khoda," she said. The arms of her robe swinging with her fists. "If you don't go, I will die of worry. I will wear only black for your impending end of life. And if you don't die, I will never let you forget you disobeyed me. Never!" The wooden spoon in her hand flung hair dye across the room.

We laughed. Bita cried. A streak of goop ran down the formerly pristine wall behind the bathtub.

I knew it was a bluff. Mommy would never wear all black. If she taught me anything, it was that all black made a brunette look like death, a rule I didn't follow, of course. But if we didn't die, I believed her; she'd be angry for eternity, her ghost would sit in my brain like it was her own living room.

About Nader, her only son, she was almost Zen, though she wouldn't know what that meant: "He has no wife, no children, he rests easy. If he goes, he goes."

Our travel agent, Yasaman Khanoum, rescued us. She ran her own agency. See, we had jobs, us women, even then we were active, ambitious. Yasaman Khanoum sent us to Vienna first. Said that was safest. All attention was on Paris. Who was flying in and out. Then a short flight to France where we'd spend the autumn on the Côte d'Azur, in Cannes, and wait. And because we had money in the Swiss banks, we'd lie in the waning sun in gorgeous French string bikinis, nibble on

24

veal milanese and that nearly Italian Riviera pizza of the Old Port, and drink burgundy. Then when the fighting died out, we'd come home to Iran. Our travel agent extraordinaire had no doubt.

I laugh in Yasaman Khanoum's likely dead face now. We were fools, all of us. In the end, we left much earlier than most of our friends. The first to say goodbye.

"GET IN THE CAR, kids. We're leaving," I yelled up the stairs. Abbas Ghassem and Nanny and the kolfats were waiting for us downstairs, as if in a receiving line. Abbas Ghassem, bearded and dark, in all white; somehow the grease from the stove knew to steer clear of his apron on a day so solemn. Nanny, a woman I picked out of a dozen because she had maternal breasts and thin lips. The kolfats—we had one kolfat just for mopping floors. That one held a Koran up over her head, waiting for us to walk under it. The Koran on a tray along with a crystal bowl of water filled with rose petals. A book she couldn't even read.

"Go get the children," I said to Nanny. "Where are they?"

"Madam," Nanny said, looking not in my eye. "Mohammad is ready—he's just asleep. Shall I wake him?"

I laughed. "Khanoum," I said. "Do you not see that we are waiting for them?" Back then you could be rude to your servants. And you called them servant. It was more honest.

"Now now," Houman said, leaving his too-neat barely used office, the place where he made a phone call or two, pulling a wide tie from his pocket. Already at thirty years old he had the beginnings of his rounded stomach, and then a mustache like many of the men did, rolled cuffs, hairy arms, brown bellbottom suit sharply creased. He was just starting to wear his Polo cologne—the green bottle, gold top, the one he still wears, turning him into a stamp of manhood, a hunter in

25

leather treading through a wet forest. I used to smell it on his pillow when he was away on business, can you imagine, and miss him. What a dope I was.

"Shirin, they're nervous. Give them a break," Houman said, his hands wrapping his tie around his neck, folding and pulling cloth.

"And, Madam," Nanny said, always pronouncing it *Maahdahm* like I was some grand ballroom, a magic trick, ta-da.

"What is it, Nanny? Just say it." I grabbed a cigarette from her front pocket and she lit it with fingers that trembled.

"Niaz asked for Khanoum Valiat." She crossed her arms over her English-style uniform, her beige belted dress with round collar, brown necktie. I dressed my servants well. They were an extension of me after all.

"Well, she can't see Mommy now," I said, and inhaled. "Tell her I've packed all my valuables and she is one."

"I'm not explaining well. She's not here, Madam. She ran to Khanoum Valiat's."

"By herself?" I said. "How could she? What are we supposed to do?"

"Darling, we can't miss this flight—we might not get on another." Houman walked to me and squeezed my shoulders. "They say it's men like me who need to worry."

"Let me call Elizabeth." I grabbed the phone in the hallway. "Mommy," I said. "What are you doing? Did you think I wouldn't notice you've taken my only daughter?"

"Vay, Shirin, she turned up here and is begging to stay. She doesn't want to leave me or Roshani alone. What a good girl she is. Who taught her to be so considerate?"

"She wants to . . . stay? Mommy, who cares what she wants. She's six."

"Why are the daughters of my friends so much nicer to their mothers? Why is it that I have the rudest daughter? What did I do to deserve that? You know that Nasreen is watching little Bahar because her daughter trusts Nasreen with her children. Why should I get less? You explain that to me."

"Why not let her stay?" Houman mouthed behind me. "Elizabeth Khanoum will take good care of her. It's just a month, maybe two."

I turned to face him, and, seeing my expression, he stepped backwards to the front door, the one we secured five ways now—two dead bolts, a chain, sometimes a silver fork, a chair.

"Shirin? Where did you go?" Mommy asked.

I felt myself squeezing the life out of the curly telephone cord. The door before me was made of wood and wood could be burned down. "Fine. Let her be. She'll just miss a great holiday," I said to shut her up before I started to pick my eyes out. "But please be careful. And don't let her eat too much gaz and get fat. She won't fit on a plane seat."

I slammed down the phone and lurched towards Houman, waving my cigarette. "What happened to *it's too dangerous* here? Not when it comes to Elizabeth's favorite. Or is it being left alone she is afraid of; she's such a hypocrite."

In the car, I sat in the backseat with Mohammad and Houman. Khosrow, my favorite chauffeur, drove. He was the one who took me to the parties when I was a kid, who knew how to keep a secret, ignored the vodka on my breath.

We took the cheap car, the older Mercedes—cracking leather seats, a lifeless sandlike beige. We didn't want to draw attention. Our street was so quiet. Shirin Street, Daddy had it renamed when I was born. Khiaboon-e Shirin. Sweet Street, you might call it, too. My name means sweet, if you can believe that. I was furious at Niaz, but why was I already missing her? Her usual spot between me and Houman sunken in the smallest amount. My throat caught.

"This is nothing," I said, looking out the window. "Where are the people?" We turned a corner in silence, the trees flashing in the sunlight, twinkling, waving us goodbye.

Houman looked at me, hugged Mohammad on his lap, Mohammad who was crying for his sister of all people. "Neezee," he called out. "Neezee."

I tried to not hear him. "Khosrow? Do you know where they are?" I said, squeezing his seat.

"Yes, Khanoum." He looked at me in the rearview mirror. "They are out in the streets."

"Are these not the streets?" I was confused.

"Someday, Khanoum. Inshallah."

"What?"

"Sorry, Khanoum. They will come."

Maybe I didn't know his true meaning then—but what do you expect? I'm not all-knowing.

Nobody spoke. We turned onto bigger and bigger roads. Slowly, like a swarm of bees that you don't hear and then suddenly they are above you buzzing their hearts out, I saw and smelled them. The thick horse stench and noise of people. I can't ever forget it—it was like a Persian poem. See, I can tell the story like people want to hear it. The sweat on their faces, signs high above their hands, voices joined. It must have been a hundred, a thousand, a nation. Marching towards our cheap car. Or, cheap for us.

Men with their shirts opened up. The women not caring whether they were ladylike—screaming insults at the Shah. Bisharaf, they said, the worst word in our language. No honor. Wasn't there a more civilized way to handle complaints? This seemed out of hand. And yet there was a part of me that felt sad, excluded from this unified voice. It's true. Why would I lie?

"Get off this road," I said. I watched their angry faces, their signs pointed at us. "Turn turn turn!" I smacked the back of Khosrow's seat.

Inside Mehrabad Airport, off in a relatively empty corner, I stood with Mohammad in my arms. He had cried the entire way to the airport, even after we escaped the demonstration. My beautiful boy, already two years old, who would never disobey me. I covered him in kisses. One for your left cheek, one for your right. He was getting so big. "Hold on to me with your feet," I said. Mohammad looked at me with his big, dark eyes. No squealing with delight from my kisses. He was wearing a beautiful suit. Navy and pressed with gold buttons, a white shirt, his hair parted to one side. White socks pulled up to his knees, black shoes shiny and perfect. Like a little doll. My children were little dolls, even the ungrateful one. Damn that girl of mine, who does she think she is? If she were here, she'd make him laugh.

People ran towards the departure gates gripping large pieces of luggage, dragging belligerent, uncomprehending children, everyone rushing or else waiting together in clumps like hair on the floor of a salon. Some yelling, an old woman crying on her knees—playing her role just right. People eating on the floor, passing spoons of rice. What a time to eat!

I tried to block out the noise, which was impossible. Seema arrived with Teymour and Bita in a pram, hiding under a warm mound of blankets. Bita was three months old. An accident, a hiccup, as they say. Seema was absolutely unprepared for a baby. She wanted to be a career woman but was fired from her first journalist job at that communist magazine because she was pregnant. What was she thinking? Clearly she wasn't, and I told her so before Bita came out of her. Afterwards, there wasn't much point in reminding her, was there?

We stood up from the chairs some misfortunates had offered us, straightened our clothes. Mohammad felt heavy. "Did you bring everything important?" I said.

"Here we are, aren't we?" Seema said.

I squinted. "Did you bring the diamond necklace Mommy gave you?" I said, using Mohammad as a disguise for my mouth.

"*Shhhh*." Seema looked around, blinked a few times. She whispered, also behind Mohammad. "Not that nonsense again. Khob, hala, Mommy gave Nosrat the gardener everything, and she stuffed it all deep into one of those giant sacks of rice."

"She what?" I widened my eyes. I tried to pass Mohammad to Houman but the child gripped me harder, his fingers clawing at me. I squeezed back to shut him up a bit.

"She told Nosrat to take it to Auntie's gardener, Habib," Seema said. "She thinks nobody will suspect the gardeners passing a bag of rice and Auntie Katti won't be bothered. Living in that tiny widow's house alone, no government ties, barely even a working telephone. She'll keep it safe."

"And she trusts the gardener—two gardeners—to give it to Katti? To not take it for their own greedy fingers? What an idiot." Who knew if Nosrat could even find Habib with our absurd method of giving addresses in those days—cross the bridge, turn right at the white fence, ask the shopkeeper's son.

Seema raised her eyebrow. "How little faith. Habib and Nosrat are family. We have a history, we paid for their children's education, for god's sake, Nosrat's father's spinal operation."

"Look around you. If Habib and Nosrat were family—" I started to yell. There were uniformed officers forcing a family out of the airport while they wailed, and we stopped to watch. The announcements over the loudspeaker were incessant over the commotion. I saw a little girl smile, teeth gleaming, as she threw a red ball down the corridor, completely unaware. What if I've made a mistake leaving Niaz? Was

I blinded because I was mad at her? I whispered to Seema: "We're on our own. They don't want us in charge. They don't even like us. These assholes want to take over and believe me, they will take everything. You and your incremental progress." I stepped back.

"Oh, Shirin. Trust your compatriots. In the end, the people will win. All of us," Seema said.

I pulled her to the wall, with Mohammad the monkey hanging on to me. Soldiers marched towards us, and I wasn't even sure what they were marching for anymore. One glared at me. "First I was all for this change, these protests. Our bloodline demands it. As you know. The Great Warrior started it, maybe they'll finish it. But there's no room for us in their new Iran."

That sure shut her up. Seema nodded. Her poor lipstick was faded already, I could tell she had been crying from the dried streaks of powder on her cheeks.

"We are too much of a threat to any future new leadership. What would we get out of it except maybe our heads cut off. As a family they'll come for us. Of course they don't care about an old woman like Mommy."

"Well, good," Seema said. "Let others rule for a change." She pressed her lips together, tapped her foot. I watched the pointy tip of her shoe, the alligator skin shiny and glinting, demanding its place on the airport floor.

Mohammad, wriggling, let out a cry.

Seema flinched and held on to her breasts. "Ay, that hurts."

"He's not your baby." I laughed. "Seema, your breasts are broken."

Our men walked over with the luggage and pram. Houman motioned us along by making a walking cartoon with his two fingers pointed down.

"Wait," I said, making my own cartoon, holding out my hand like a guard. I went over to the large window. I think I knew even then.

It was a bright day, the sun yellow, shining and hot. No clouds. Niaz inside a building, sitting on a sofa with Mommy. I saw the mountains across from me. Men in uniform holding big guns stood in a line. The king's men who just a few months later would declare neutrality. What did they want? Did they hate the king too? Who would they kill first if they could kill exactly anyone? The answer would surprise you.

SEEMA IN THE AISLE seat, on the packed airplane, as we waited to take off, leaned over, ashing her cigarette in the metal tray. I sat at the window and we kept the middle for our purses. Those who place purses on floors cannot be trusted. We put Bita in her bassinet and Mohammad in the row next to us for some peace and quiet. We could see them but who wants to hear that ruckus constantly. Someone on the plane—I don't know, a grandmother—gave Mohammad a toy to play with and he was busy turning a little handle and looking inside a paper box. The activities that occupy small brains!

Seema pulled up her hand luggage—a Louis Vuitton monogram suitcase—and unzipped it on her lap. There I saw it: a small cushioned bag, covered in pink damask roses—the oldest ancient roses, the one we turn into gol ab, that the backwards Christians stole from us in their Crusades. A pink snap button in the center. I knew that bag. "Doesn't look like a dictionary or book of verse," I said. I peeked into it: the diamonds glittered, baby birds in their nest. Mommy's best pieces. "Liar."

"Oh, get over it," Seema said. "I'm just being practical." She snatched the bag away.

I still remember that damask bag on her dumb lap, the pink roses. Oh, how I love rosewater. Few people know that when the Shah finally left Iran on January 16, 1979—a date imprinted in my mind—on his supposed "extended vacation," people in the streets sprinkled each other's heads with rosewater. Rosewater! The way we do over graves.

"But, Seema, no," I said. "You can't have it both ways. You say we're too materialistic. *This* is why we are having these protests." I leaned over and shook the bag. "You're as bad as me, Khanoum with her crown jewels."

Seema looked at me, scrunched her eyebrows—always perfect, even more than mine. Straight and solemn, a refinement I'd never know. Isn't that how people are divided—the tactful and the coarse. My eyebrows arched, showed too much emotion. Like Mommy always said, Seema's tricked us to believe she was neutral, even-minded, fair. Even when she wasn't. I hated those eyebrows.

Seema looked down, smoothed the bag with her hand. The veins in her hands bulged. She shook her head and sighed loudly so dumb Teymour leaned back in his seat in the row ahead of the children. "Seema, are you okay, my love? Darling?" He reached for her.

I wanted to throw up all over the smooth airplane seats. I tried to make eye contact with Houman. A stewardess in a miniskirt and go-go boots walked past him, smiling. He smiled in return, released his fingers from the back of his seat. What a fool!

Seema looked at me again, those perfect eyebrows, but those eyes—dark, secretive—that reminded me of my childhood. Of home, now gone. She smiled, and her eyes reached out as if she wanted to rest her head on my shoulder and cry. A look I'd seen before in Mommy's car when we were girls. But I didn't lean towards her. I didn't even nod or smile back. Her nervous energy was gone, and all I sensed was pain. But I did nothing. Actually, I did worse. I turned to face the window and shut my eyes.

I SLEPT FOR A week when we got back from Aspen. Never going again, that's for sure. Those cops—I needed to smack the chocolate drool off their mustaches. How Houman and Teymour betrayed me. Even worse, Mo and Bita, who aren't the dumb men of my generation, doing nothing like I was nonexistent, or just a piece of tarte tatin without feelings of my own. They are weak. They don't know what it means to fight. I was born to fight.

None of them knew that two days before my arrest I'd sat down at Mezzaluna in the cold morning sunshine, dressed in my new Bogner one-piece, ready to crush some moguls, as they say, drinking my final espresso of the morning minding my own business. I was early, or Mo was late. Faranaz and her gang, Houston and L.A. Persians, sat down at a table on the other side of a wide planter. The combination of perfumes alone nearly killed me. They must not have seen me because I heard Faranaz: "Can you believe that Houston magazine—to put Shirin on the cover as if she's so special. She uses the Valiat name like it's a prize, to impress everyone, but that name is nothing anymore. They're nobodies." Then Manijeh of all people, Manijeh who I had taken out to lunch, said, "Too bad they're all in Aspen. I was hoping they wouldn't come back. Can you imagine Shirin's now the head of the family!" Faranaz added: "It really is a shame Seema's gone. At least she had some class." They all laughed. When I cleared my throat, they turned their heads and nearly choked on their biscottis.

I don't care about gossip. Who cares about these bored Iranian women who've followed me to Aspen because they actually adore me? They are jealous I have a real career. Ten years as event planner to the finest, founder of Valiat Events, and I get rewarded with the cover of *Houston Living*. Important magazine people insisted on posing me on a large executive desk, stockinged legs crossed, rotary phone handset at my ear. This chatter was the Evil Eye at work, of course. Their envy. Wanting to ruin my success. Do I care that we all went to Swiss school together and I was probably the first person outside their families to meet their children when they were born? Back in Iran, for each child

34

of a friend, I used to give a beautiful gold bracelet with their name engraved in script. And then they dare say I have no class, that my name is nothing? That my family is a bunch of nobodies?

Back in Houston, I instructed Houman: "Keep your son's empty bed warm with your sweating feet, your lack of care." I was not having it. His attempts at peace were cries for help—roses, lilies, chocolates stuffed in a heart-shaped box. When he came home with a gift certificate for a massage, I said, "Do I looked stressed? You think I want to hang out with those Russian hookers?" Another time, a basket of scented soaps shaped like Texas stars and longhorns. I said, "Do I smell bad? Am I a college girl?" What kind of gifts were these? Ungifts. Backhanded gifts. Insults. Pecan pralines—"Are you trying to make me fat?" White roses, "What now, am *I* dying or dead?" I threw them at his bearded face. I dumped the pralines in a pot, melted them, and poured them over his golf clubs.

Today, my business manager, Anthony, called. "Shirin," he said. "This is not good. People are talking about this arrest."

"Tony," I said. He looked like Anthony Bourdain, tall with a bad boy walk, and I'd always wanted to call someone Tony. "Tony, that's impossible. Nobody knew about it! I threatened my family with daggers if they said anything."

"Well, I've gotten a few messages from clients. Riani, the mother, called and said her daughter's wedding can't be mixed up in scandal. They want to know if it's true."

"I am not surprised about Mrs. Riani with that perky fake nose. If anyone is scared of a little fun, it's her. What did you tell her?"

"I said not to worry. That there is more to the story than she's surely heard. That all events will go on just the same with the same Valiat excellence."

"That's not enough. You need to feed a client like that some well-constructed lies. We need a PR strategy," I said. "Get Martin on

35

the phone. I need to have a proper story for her and anyone else who pipes up. And they need to hear it from me."

LATER THAT AFTERNOON, I was arranging flowers in the living room. Of course I'd gone to one of the Flower Row shops; they're all owned by Persian men. Because they know me—Manouchehr, Fereydoon, whoever they are, in their jeans and washed-out shirts—they know: None of that baby's breath. No white roses. I want tropical, birds of paradise, protea, the stranger the better. I like to be loud. I am here, my flowers shout at visitors. Let me dazzle.

Manouchehr or whatever his name was, the one with the gold tooth, had the nerve to snicker a little, a side smile. I noticed it and I said, "What's your problem today, Agha?" My hand on hip.

He gave me some kind of loose shrug. "Well, Khanoum, I thought one of your suitors might be the one buying you flowers."

Who was the weasel here, blabbing to even the manual workers? I nearly stuffed his mouth with my bouquet.

Mommy hates flowers—I think that says it all. What kind of painter hates flowers? Anything that could rot in front of her eyes, attract bugs, smell of outside. The most uninterested-in-nature person I know, this woman who owned more land than you can imagine. When guests brought her flowers, she made Nanny put them in the rooms she never entered, like the kitchen, the children's bedrooms. Although Nounou, my grandmother, the tender one on my father's side who lived with us, loved flowers, Mommy never gave her any. I used to steal them for Nounou.

I was deciding which way to turn the cut crystal vase—that matters, can make or break the look of the flower arrangement—and the phone wouldn't shut up. It sang my Gipsy Kings "Bamboléo" ringtone, which always brought me a smile—even the millionth time. As

I've said before, it is our true national anthem. "Martin, is it you?" I said.

"Hi, Mom." The ungrateful child spoke into my ear. Right away, my brief joy vanished.

"Niaz. Salaam," I said. Stupid Niaz. I didn't feel like talking to her. My child who couldn't even be bothered to leave a dying country to be with her mother. Sure, she didn't know it was dying then, at six years old, but she's old enough now and still hasn't expressed any regret for staying.

"I have some news," she said. "Guess who died?"

"No. Don't tell me. Mommy? No," I said. Impossible. The day would come, but it wouldn't be today of all days. Would it? They say it's the most mundane moments you need to suspect. I wasn't close to tears, however, and I started to think, what kind of heartless wretch am I, that my own mother has died and I have clammed up like I never knew what an emotion was, what loving someone—my own mother, at that—even meant?

"Mom! I wouldn't turn *that* into a game, are you divooneh? Think," Niaz said in her thick dahati Iranian accent, which she probably got from the working-class people she went to school with, but who knows.

I said, "Why do you call me 'Mom'? You're not American. Call me Mommy if you must, or Shirin, which we both prefer. You know I was basically a child when I had you. People wouldn't believe it if they saw you calling me Mom."

"Okay, Shirin," she said.

"That's better," I said.

On the other end, silence. Then the phone line sounded like crumbling papers, ears when they're water clogged, typical for a phone call with Iran. Was she rolling those Houman-like eyes of hers? She was just like him, despite the years and miles; she always saw the positive.

But then, she somehow found the time to belittle and backstab me, her own mother!

"You still there?" I said. "Ha-llo. Ha-llo." I tapped the mouthpiece with my nail tips.

"Oh, oh. . . . Let me, hold one, one minute, Mommy joon," Niaz said. But the child was not speaking to me. As if she has another Mommy. She was still doing this. I could see my mother's weathered arms reaching over Niaz's head. Pulling the handset, grabbing the cord like a tug of war. Taking over.

"Ay, Shirinac?" Mommy said. Her voice falsely sweet.

I groaned. "Yes, Mommy?"

"Shirinac. I don't know what nonsense Niaz is getting into. It's nothing at all. Basteh digeh, Niaz. It's nothing and it's terrible to talk like this." She went squawking on in that bird voice about how we were family, we all "love one another," much more than any of those Americans, how in Iran we knew the meaning of loyalty. I supposed I'd learned that from her. Then a long diatribe about people who'd wronged her. Nobody was safe—the grocer, her doctor, of course me. When she got to me it was more of a question in her voice—Would I care if she had died? Had she read my mind?

"Fine fine," she said finally. "Parvaneh jan." She paused. "Poor Parvaneh. She was much older than me though, so it's no surprise. They say she was sick a long time. But in your country, New York is a good place to die, isn't it? None of that driving everywhere. God willing she is free."

"Poor Parvaneh? She's the dead one? Ali Lufti's Parvaneh? I know you pretended to be friends, but you hate this woman," I said. "And you're the same age, Mommy."

"Oh stop. That's not true."

"Which part?" I said. "Which part is not true?"

"Well, she's much older."

38

The telephone crackled.

"Be careful what you say. Remember, we're not alone."

"Oh please. They don't care what you're saying." I laughed. "Ding, dong the witch is dead. Khob, since Ali Lufti's in New York, why don't you go visit him? Stay with Bita. Oh, Mommy, what will you do now? Maybe you can propose to him."

She slammed down the phone before I could continue. I was more elated than I had been in weeks. Being mean to Mommy was pleasure work. Deserved. The story was one of an adolescent crush, more legend than real, a joke. Ali Lufti, son of the family chauffeur. I laughed again. I knew Mommy would never go to New York, but actually what about me? I could go. The Persians are much better in New York. More sophisticated. They'll love me there. Eat whatever I squeeze out of my ass. And once they hear about my defection, these Houston losers will beg for me to come back and cast my light on them once more.

When I was a little girl, Mommy would dress me up and tilt her head. I was JonBenét Ramsey in her baby sexiness before that child was even an egg in her grandmother's womb. "No, no, that doesn't look right on you." "Oh dear, that is just funny. Your legs, no your arms are all wrong. Your head is enormous." I did not know anything then. I thought very simply that she was doing something of value—trying to make me look my prettiest. Always trying to improve me, a victim of my own bad looks and taste. And only frilly dresses, curled hair, makeup at nine years old would do.

It wasn't until Bita was in middle school and approaching me with banal questions like "Why am I so ugly, Auntie?" or "Will anyone ever like me?"—Bita who never even had a mother like mine—that I realized what Mommy had done to me.

When I decided hey, I have a brain, it was too late. The only person who always treated me as worthy of an intelligent conversation was Seema—and she's dead. Nobody else took me seriously and there was no room then for a girl to be both pretty and smart. Still isn't, despite what the young people pretend. Bita could be an exception, pretty but she pads down her looks. I tease her: Good luck with that, Bita joon. No act of vengeance against her looks is going to kill her attractiveness completely, poor thing. And Niaz, who knows what she's doing. A waste of a life, if you ask me. She had the chance to do something. Stuck in Iran to care for Mommy and be "true to her country" as they say here. Her country would kill her for a plate of torshi. Now what do they want with a girl with no credentials except her pre-revolutionary elite family? I don't have to tell you what kind of credential that is.

But forget these stories. What hurts me most in life is that Niaz. When she calls Mommy—*my* terrible mother—"Mommy" it kills me. I tell myself it's just an expression without meaning. Like "it kills me." But, in a way, Niaz is dead to me. I let Mommy keep my daughter. Those are words that are hard for me to think. But they don't kill me. Almost, but look who's here? You need the thorn to have the rose, as they say, if you want me to get poetic.

I picked up the phone and dialed: "Tony! I have good news—great news. I've done your job for you, and Martin's too."

ELIZABETH

THIS IS A STORY of a nose. That's how it starts. A tale told for years to any daughter or granddaughter, distant cousin, niece, or even shy boy who'd hear it. Told to the young and old. A warning. And a dare.

It was 1942 and Elizabeth was sixteen. Her nose was the biggest of the four sisters. So huge she was thought doomed. Presumed forever alone.

The nose, it started innocently enough above her eyes like all noses. If you stopped looking then, you'd be stuck on those mystery eyes—hard like an animal's. You might even forget to breathe. But that's not how anyone sees a face. You don't stop at the eyes. Even eyes like hers.

Elizabeth would draw her nose sometimes and it would make her cry. Bumpy, bony, and downward pointing. The tip made her think of a worshipper dipping his neck to prayer, an Olympian high diving into a pool. People are not that complicated, and they do not change. Neanderthal man was as vain as today's man. There is nothing as primitive as beauty and being attracted to it. Big nose equals no suitors, no love. At least if you're a woman. So much so that people, again usually women, pay masked strangers to sedate them, break their noses, miniaturize them. They hate themselves, and they hate their hatred. But they go on unreformed.

So there she was. Rich girl with big nose. But she was not alone. There was also Ali Lufti, the chauffeur's son, someone who without Elizabeth's nose would not exist in this story. Because in 1942 feudal Iran, if Elizabeth had an average-sized nose, she would have never even looked at a chauffeur's son.

Or would she?

The big estate could have been an English country house, except for how hot the sun was, how savagely it burned the stone. There, one famous day, Ali Lufti smiled at her.

She stood wearing her thin cotton dress, tied in a ribbon at the back, and tucked her hair—brown and shoulder length with big loose curls—behind her ears and watched his face. Tan and unpimpled, with a flash of mischief and curiosity in his dark brown eyes. His jaw sloped inwards and landed in a sturdy chin with a handsome dent in it. A chin that made her have that funny feeling. There he was. Staring into nothing, the empty steps, the swirling air, then staring into her.

He smiled. His lips moved apart, widening, narrowing. His teeth perfect, straight, and blinding. Yet wasn't he poor? How were his teeth so white?

See, it is foolish to think that the uglier one is, the less concerned with appearance. Sometimes the uglier people are the shallowest. The weakest ones, the most brutal. Elizabeth paid great attention to the surfaces of people's faces. The thickness of their eyebrows, a woman's penciling in of curves to evoke a certain personality. The creases that grew deeper in the corners of people's mouths and on their foreheads as they aged—especially if they were sociable. The noses and ears that never stopped growing.

She grew to be an expert on faces. And with the empty hours stretched in front of her, a girl in a Tehran manor alone with her thoughts, she took to drawing secret portraits in her bedroom. She started at age four, all from memory. As soon as she learned to draw a circle, she drew a face. Or as soon as she drew a face, she drew a circle. It is one thing to observe faces, it is another to imagine them anew, to give them life on paper. In doing so she made them her own.

For revenge, or to soothe her ego, when she drew anyone except her baba or Ali Lufti, she drew their teeth yellow. The color of old kitchen rags or bath soap or snot. She would do this and laugh, all by herself in her quiet, curtained bedroom. Sure, there's something sad about someone with an ugly nose to be so concerned with faces, looks, the physical. That is life—full of sadness.

That famous day, when Ali smiled and his teeth were just as she had drawn them so many times before, Elizabeth smiled back. Her world had shifted. Not a mere step, it gained a dimension. As did Elizabeth—after that smile, she was sharper, brighter, attuned like never before. She was suddenly alive. Ali, who was mostly alone, too, perched on a tree branch or hunched on the grass studying a piece of metal that belonged to a car. Before this day, Elizabeth had noticed him, watched his movements, but until today he'd never looked back.

The question remained why a smile from a near stranger could have such an effect. Conventional wisdom blamed her nose. But perhaps the nose is not just a distraction from but an obfuscation of the mystery of human longing. Why one soul wants another. It was not in the interest of a girl in 1942 Iran to feel, to want. But Elizabeth was not aware of where she was in history. Nobody is, really—for it takes a certain foolishness to move us forward. Of history she knew so little, only that there was a new king for reasons of war, one that involved many countries, but not her.

For Ali, she made her eyes look big like deep blue ponds, like egg yolks opened on a pan. She fluttered her eyelashes. She knew what to do. Baba had taught her. Not directly, but by watching the kind of woman he flirted with at parties, on the street, who he valued. Women who held themselves with shoulder blades nearly touching, chins jutting out, lower backs curved into a C. Who, when Baba told a joke, laughed with every muscle. Who looked ready to leap inside him. He was a man who loved women—certain kinds of women.

Elizabeth was Baba's favorite—despite her colossal appendage, or maybe because of it. He called her Elizabeth the Great, and in certain moments she did think of herself as such. Her name was itself great and uncommon in Iran—she was not named Shamsi or Nilou, no ordinary girl's name. She was Elizabeth, named after Baba's favorite English girlfriend. At twenty years old, he studied law in Paris; it was fashionable and forward-thinking to study in Europe and return "educated." They didn't consider their thousands of years of learning at home: the Cyrus Cylinder, hospitals, bricks, wine, backgammon, ancient refrigerators, ice cream, Omar Khayyam. Not then. No, by going to Paris, these Persian men were better suited to rule in the Western style. They could appease the Farangi. Be "civilized." Baba wore a three-piece suit, and in his right hand he held a monocle. The girls were the icing of such adventure—physical proof. And even more than English girls, anything French was the height of culture. Baba peppered his Persian with French phrases, a specific word, a pronunciation. *Ou est ma ceinture? Excuse-moi, madame. Viens ici.*

TEN MONTHS EARLIER, THEY were in the leafy courtyard of the summer house north of Tehran, with its stone turrets, where the family caravanned every year. For months the children slept outside on blankets made of llama fur laid out by the servants, and the women and girls of her family—eighty percent eyebrows, eyelashes, and hair—ate dinner on quilts under the glowing stars. Elizabeth, age fifteen then, sat with her plate of food on her lap, worlds apart from the deafening female chatter.

This was another of the famous stories. Little did she know they'd left Tehran early this year because there was word Iran could no longer stay neutral in a fight happening elsewhere. The British and the Soviets were bombing Tehran—supposedly the German influence was too strong. German residents needed to flee, and soon the Shah would be forced out, too, to be replaced with his son. But Elizabeth was not thinking of any of that. Her mind rested on wanting to be alone.

As close as she felt to her baba, these women in front of her were strangers. They treated her like a nuisance. Mostly they ignored her. Being the youngest, perhaps she really was an intruder. She demanded no attention or love.

This one evening, in the moonlight, Elizabeth's sister Katherine, who they called Katti, determined and lynxlike, her eyes shining, picked up from the canvas quilt one of the tall flickering candles and held it up high. Like all the other sisters, Katti had a small, elegant mushroom cap nose. If there was a bone, a hard fiber at the tip, it was all but forgotten, vanishing into tiny nostrils.

Katti leaned over and shone the candle on Elizabeth's nose then started to laugh. First a giggle, and at last a cackle. She stopped for a breath and said, "When Elizabeth walks into a room, first her nose enters." Katti pointed to the shadow of Elizabeth's nose swimming to and fro on the stone wall.

"Look at that, what a monstrosity!" the others said. "She's not Elizabeth the Great, she's Elizabeth the Nose."

Katti turned her eyes upwards and acknowledged the full moon. The rest of the group looked up with her. All eyes on the moon, then down at the nose on the wall. They watched the shadow—Elizabeth's nose—jerk forward. Maybe it was the size of the moon, the roundness

45

and fullness of it, or the way the shadow of the nose moved as if in response, but whatever it was, the group, all together, exploded in laughter. Katti and all the women and girls lying about the lush fabrics. The aunties and cousins, Anahita, Faranak, Sudabeh, there were so many. They laughed and laughed and cleared their throats and wiped away tears. In Elizabeth's ears, it sounded like one voice. "That's too good," said young Sudabeh and all the women looked at one another's noses and gave playful pushes and squeezes. Elizabeth swayed, looked down at her lap.

But Katti wasn't finished. With panache, she picked up a whole wet glob of greasy eggplant from a silver platter. Sweet and charred and sticky. And she let it hang off her perfect straight nose. She undulated her arms like she was in a dance and swung her head side to side. She jiggled in her seat—the bells sewn around the pillow ringing. The eggplant-nose swished round and round and dropped onto her lap. She screamed. The eggplant-nose sunk into the folds of her dress.

Every one of Elizabeth's female relatives howled even louder. Elizabeth's sisters, her cousins, even her mother. Despite the nose, they looked like Elizabeth: their thick shoulder-length hair, big eyes, expressive chins, red lips. Except for her mother with her tightly pulled-back hair. Hearing Maman laugh, Elizabeth's cheeks burned like hot iron. She rose, shaking, and brushed her dress with her hand, like it was full of crumbs or mouse shit.

And then she began to cry, as if she wouldn't ever stop. Tears poured out, warm but cool on her hot face. The women became silent watching her. Gathering their skirts, smoothing ruffles, sniffling. Back in her room she was going to draw all of their teeth green—not even yellow. But what would she do now, in this moment?

Elizabeth wiped her tears with the back of her hand, looked into each of her three sisters' eyes—Katti, Susannah, who they called Soosan, and Lily—as well as her mother's, and said, "Well, at least

Baba doesn't curse the day I was born. You'll see. You will all die broken and alone because you'll never have his love. Never!"

The candle, now back on a low table, wavered. All was still except for the sound of the leaves rustling and the chirping of night animals with yellow eyes. Elizabeth felt a wad of spit forming. She churned it in her mouth, and once it grew large, leaned over Katti's head, and pushed it out with her tongue. The web of mucus covered Katti's eye, pulling down towards her cheek. Viscous. Glorious.

Elizabeth didn't wait. They'd beat her later. Amidst screams and servants rushing over with pails of soapy water, she ran inside.

Baba would never have told Katti and the other sisters he hated them. He pretended he was a happy father. So why did the sisters believe Elizabeth? How did they know it was true? Because Elizabeth was Baba's favorite. They were all prettier, but still, he doted on the ugly one. Elizabeth did not know then that by the time she, the youngest daughter, was born, he had finally accepted his fate as a family man. That to live outside his narrowly prescribed world was impossible. With acceptance came peace.

Upstairs in her room, Elizabeth took out her sketchpad. The family called her Rembrandt, but more to embarrass. A compliment like that is a dagger. Worse than an insult. How dare she consider drawing human figures, a girl like that? Elizabeth had pictures of everyone tucked under her mattress, but she had never shown them her work. Beyond simply transcribing their physical attributes, she felt she was capturing their spirits—however unkind the person was to her. In reality he was short but Baba in her drawings was big and tall, with a soft round belly and red face, a bushy mustache. Elizabeth drew him fast, easily. Banou Khanoum, her mother, was the boss, his opposite. Diminutive and thin, she barely ate, never laughed except in cruelty. Her skin was thus perfect, a peeled egg. Her fine hair in a chignon. It was her quick wit and cunning, so they say, that convinced Baba to marry her. Elizabeth drew her slowly, precisely. Like she'd be burned on a pole if a line was misplaced.

But no, no, no. She wouldn't draw them tonight. Looking around her room—the summer room with its woven chairs and muslin curtains, she wanted something of her own. Elizabeth picked up her pencil. She'd never drawn Ali Lufti before, she'd never dared. A worker boy? What are you thinking, Elizabeth? The lone voice of the pencil scratched at the page. She started to draw him.

Ali Lufti's eyes were beautiful. Tailless fish that lengthened towards the edges. His eyebrows slashed straight across his face, a horizon, and met in the middle in hairs that moved both left and right like they couldn't agree on a direction. A distinguished nose—not big but not delicate. Strong and curved like a sail. Elizabeth touched her own nose. Tears filled her eyes again, but she hardened them so the tears would stay inside. Kept her face still.

His body was long, like an oar. His hair was full and brown, curls flung back. She imagined running her fingers through Ali Lufti's locks and resting her cheek on his head, smelling its musk. She breathed in deeply and for an instant smelled a thick animal odor, mixed with engine oil. How strange!

She continued with her work and made his teeth shine—perfect white rectangles, blank slates. Elizabeth put down her pencil. Forgetting that outside her room was torment, she was swept up in her daydream as if by a river current. She closed her eyes. Breathing in harder still, she was transported. Elizabeth became the hunk of metal she'd seen Ali Lufti handle. Something he'd touched many times. Gasoline and musk filled the air again, more potently. She grew lightheaded. She was the metal and Ali Lufti, those fingers, were caressing her, holding her and rubbing. Her leg twitched, startling her, and she opened her eyes.

Back in the room, the moonlight shone white through the curtains onto her hand. Her nose was now just a nose. Not a portal. She felt it—its bumps, the far-off tip. Elizabeth slipped the finished drawing into the back of her notebook and stowed it, with the pencils, under her bed.

Now that Katti, Soosan, and Lily had husbands-to-be attached to their futures, the attention was on Elizabeth. Maybe her nose made her less precious to give away. "Any day now," her mother would say. She'd be married off to some boring minister of this or that. Never to love, never to be less alone.

But what if she stopped obeying? What if Ali Lufti married her? Nobody had ever done such a thing. Elizabeth opened the window above her desk and climbed into bed. It was somehow cold. She kept herself in her day dress, and shut her eyes. She heard the sounds of her sisters and cousins chatting, plates clattering. She lay down and thought of Ali Lufti.

AFTER THAT DAY, AFTER her sister Katti thrashed her with tall sticks behind the summer house and told her never to speak to them again, Elizabeth drew a picture of Ali almost every night. Then she touched herself. She was oblivious that anyone else in the world had ever done what she did alone in her bed.

Her arm moved across the paper—her pencil outlining his chin, shoulders, deepening his eyebrows, and then those perfect beautiful teeth. She drew him wearing his uniform. Buttoned shirt, slacks. Long and barefoot. He'd caress the metal that was her body. She'd feel a fever and a chill, a tickle under her dress, and then with her left hand, Ali Lufti's hand, she'd feel herself. Now the metal was squishy and juicy and warm and it was like all her cells were reaching out to his hand. She'd been so shocked the first full time, she thought she'd gone mad. When it was over—because there was a clear, she didn't know what else to call it, finale—she knew, of course: Ali Lufti was doing this to her. He must be a wizard working his magic. What else was she to think? Unlike all her other portraits where only she controlled and molded the subject to her whims, when she drew him, it was two ways: he was speaking to her. She repeated it the next day, and the next. When she'd pull out her paper and pencil, it felt like jumping into the sea—the instant her hot body touched cold water—awakened, enveloped, eaten up as if by a large-lipped fish.

Was this story about magical masturbation really passed down through Elizabeth's family? Well, not in minute detail. But the daughters and cousins and nieces, and even shy boys and old aunts were told enough—evenings alone to draw, her legs stockingless, her mind pulled by a force—to imagine it.

THIS MAGIC WAS IN Ali's blood. This was why he smiled at her now for the first time, ten months after the Night of Eggplant. In front of the big house, he knew about her bedroom fantasies. That devious Ali Lufti. What did he want from her?

After the smile, she didn't know what to make of her life. But she was alive. Elizabeth left the house, a basket in hand, curls falling down her back. Sun gave her hair sparkle, a tint of red—the dark red of a ripe cherry, the kind grandmothers put into jam. She walked towards the place just outside the garage where the imposing cars were parked, the line of American cars like sleepy hippos. The pictures of Ali that she drew were in her basket, every single one. If she burned them, his power would die, she was sure of it. But did she want that? Did she want to give this up? She didn't know. But she had to do something.

Elizabeth's feet tickled in the hot grass. She wore leather sandals made from the horses' old saddles. She smoothed her long dress, the sleeves ruffled like a wave. A winged creature, she walked as beauti-

fully as possible and couldn't help but turn her head in his direction—
this was what she wanted. There he was, lying on the dirt, messing
with a giant steel underbelly.

A box of the cook's matches rattled in her basket. She made her
steps louder, crunched over plants and toe-tapped rocks. She whistled.
His dark head poked out from the car.

"Ali, come, baba," a voice said. It was Fereydoon, the chauffeur,
Ali's father. Ali dragged himself from the car, shirt grease splattered,
hands stained black. He sat and wiped his face with a dirty cloth.

Elizabeth, waiting to be noticed, looked over and then back at
her basket, then over again. Ali threw the rag into a pail and faced
her. He smiled again, a second smile. Instantly, Elizabeth whipped
away. She ran as fast as she could into the dark woods. Nobody
could guess where she was going. Neither could she. Elizabeth was
a clever girl—she knew unconsciously it would help to be lost. To
be this daring required disorientation, a sense of being someone and
somewhere else. Under a large tree, she dropped her basket, kneeled
onto the dirt, fanned out the stack of pictures. She didn't think, in-
stinctively knowing she'd change course if she lent space to her plan.
She had to move fast.

The orange of fire on the match warmed her face. She lowered
the flame to an edge of paper, watched the white sheet blacken, the
charred line rising diagonally. Eventually she needed to let go so her
hand wouldn't burn. But instead of dropping the lit paper upon the
rest of the drawings, at the last instant, her mind caught up. As the
paper was just about fully scorched and ready to eat up her fingers,
she tossed it into the nearby pile of leaves. She needed these pictures.

"Miss Elizabeth," a voice said. "Can I help you?"

She knew the voice as the one she imagined when she drew his
picture—but she had never heard it in real life. Elizabeth turned from
the growing fire.

"You're mad! Don't burn down the woods," he said.

"I'm cold, I just needed a little warmth," she said and smiled because it was nearly summer. She tucked the papers back into her basket as the small fire grew.

"You will burn us to cinders!" Ali ran off and returned again and again with buckets of water.

Elizabeth watched. His magic was alive. She could feel it, and she began to notice the strange sensations again. The ground around them was black and drenched.

"Are you satisfied? Did you enjoy your fire?" Ali asked.

"Yes," she replied.

"Don't do that again."

Her fingers felt into her basket, and she pulled out a paper. Without even looking at which drawing of the dozens she held, she dropped it into Ali's hands.

"That's me."

"Don't be ridiculous," she said. "It's just a cousin. A mean cousin, one I hate." She smiled.

"Well"—he crinkled his eyebrows—"he is my mirror. I hope you won't hate me too. Walk with me to the edge of the wood? I must get back." He folded the drawing into his waist.

She nodded.

The top buttons on his shirt were open, and hair whiskered out. That hair was dark and curled too—a smile, a comma. If only she could pull out a hair for herself, she'd put it under her pillow. They walked side by side, not a word between them, just every feeling on Earth that she didn't know a name for.

Nothing was expected of him, just to carry on the family occupation. As long as he did what he'd been told, there was no story.

"If you want to keep walking with me, you cannot be a chauffeur,"

Elizabeth said. The aristocrat in her was taking hold. She couldn't believe herself. This youngest daughter. She smiled, her nose curving.

Ali laughed and bit his lip. She imagined tasting the blood ready to gush out underneath. "What makes you believe I want to?" he said.

She held out her hand. He took it.

"First, you need to go to school. Baba will help—any son of an employee can go. Don't you know that? You need to work with your brain."

Ali held up his hands. Dirty and dark from the sun, calloused.

"You need land and a house and a way to travel."

"That's a lot of trouble for someone I barely know," he said.

"Are you sure about that?" Elizabeth raised an eyebrow. This was a look she perfected in her bedroom, studying the faces she'd drawn. She had never used it with another person. Finally, her tree was bearing fruit. The magic in her room was coming to life after all, and she had made it so. They stood at the edge of the wood another moment, then Elizabeth walked ahead.

SEEMA

A SILK SCARF BLEW against Elizabeth's neck, black cat-eye sunglasses, and bright red lipstick. If a cigarette wasn't dangling from her mouth, it was dying out in the dirty car ashtray she emptied by sticking her arm out as she drove and shaking it, who cares if the ashes flew into the backseat, into the faces of her children. I am watching her and now I try to find my bearings. I dig my bare toes in the wet soil, hold on to a tree trunk, but the thoughts knock me around like wind. What could all this want with a dead me?

It was 1964 and every afternoon, we waited outside the school entrance—a black metal gate now locked. We went to a school for the irreligious children of industrialists, Europhiles, those destined to lead based on lineage, as well as the inevitable quota of expats, officially named British International School. English was our primary language, even though we didn't trust the British who, like the Russians, turned us into a game.

My brother, sister, and I watched our mother's imposing vehicle grow larger before our faces. Elizabeth in her big, green convertible sped to the school entrance. Horn blasting—an angry trumpet. Kids and mothers, servants in black veils stumbled out of her way. Held their ears. And we were not future leaders, just ungrateful pests.

"Basteh, I don't have all day. Seema, stop fooling," Elizabeth would say. Nader, Shirin, and I rushed into the backseat. Elizabeth—I never called her Mommy—shoved and poked us on the way in with her gloved hand. I always got it the hardest—the glares and pokes. But why? I didn't know.

The seats were dark blue leather with pinprick holes up and down the sides, like Daddy's wing tips. Saeed Roshani, my Daddy, in his dress shoes, khaki suit, round tortoiseshell glasses, thin white hair, *Herald Tribune* under arm, off to kiss the butts of ministers, to a job that didn't get him respect or love from anyone, least of all Elizabeth. Elizabeth who said unless you're the boss, you're a slave.

For Elizabeth, to love Daddy—whom she called Roshani in front of us as if they were business associates—was impossible. I knew that even as a young child. Daddy was thirty years older than her. When they married, he was fifty-two. "Practically dead," as Elizabeth loved to say at parties, especially to the married men and the young uniformed waiters, with us listening under a table draped in cloth, mille-feuille on our lips. Even worse, he'd only asked for her hand after he was refused by Auntie Katti, her beautiful fair sister, sefeed-e-booloori—crystal white—with a small nose, long blond hair. Blond is a relative term. To a European, Katti's hair was brown.

In the backseat, I sat between Shirin and Nader. I was twelve, the middle child. Nader was fifteen, Shirin nine. Even then, I believed children should be taken from parents and raised by the State. I read this in a Communist pamphlet I pulled from the trash pit outside school and thought this sounded smarter than the royalists who cared about family lines and continuity.

The back of my mother's Jaguar. Scornful red lips. Shirin's jeers, tossing my books down the stairs. My weird ways. Nader poked me in the ribs. Elizabeth told me I was unwanted. She said, "Seema, you ate up my whole life and spat it out." But I was the smart one, the one with promise. Daddy talked to only me about history. Not Nader. Nounou braided only my hair. Not Shirin's.

On many nights, poking my head out of my room after bedtime, I overheard my parents speaking under the chandelier in the hallway—neutral ground. The crystal glass sparkling and their faces lit in the glow, spotted like leopards.

Elizabeth would say, "This child is too much. Too disobedient." Daddy would say, "At least she has a mind of her own. My strong-willed intelligent girl." Elizabeth shook her head, reviewing my latest naughty act—say, sneaking the pot of stew with lamb and yellow peas out to the peasants beyond the house so that Abbas Ghassem had to make us a whole new dinner. "The meat was tough—he had to scorch it for it to cook through in time. Tender lamb cannot be rushed," Elizabeth huffed.

"She is too much," she repeated.

Daddy raised his scruffy white eyebrows, considering her words, doubting with his silence. When I was younger, this had made me smile. Now I didn't care anymore. In my secret library of old books I stole from the houses of family, I read about the kings of Iran murdered by a relative. Usually by poison. Sometimes blinded. Throne usurped. I thought about this when I went to bed or was bored at school. If even the kings killed one another, the best of the best on Earth, what could you expect out of the rest of us?

After dinner, I changed into my nightshirt and ran up to the attic where Nounou joon, Daddy's mother, lived. Tonight, I didn't want to hear my parents' whispers. Nounou joon left her room only for meals and daily walks around the grounds. She weeded the garden and poured millet into the bird feeder through a funnel to catch rocks. She memorized the way light hit the bees nibbling on lavender, how the sound of wind changed depending on the surrounding trees.

"Dokhtaram, bia," Nounou joon said. Lying on her side, in her twin bed. I got in next to her. The coils creaked. Nounou wrapped her long arm, bony and strong, around me. She smelled like sheep's wool, hand cream, and peppermint. Unlike Elizabeth's mother, Banou Khanoum, who was already dead, Nounou had the ways of the dahati, the peasant. I let Nounou kiss my cheeks, brush the hair out of my face. I closed my eyes in her lumpy bed.

When I was five or six, Nounou gave me a sponge bath as I stood in the fountain in the garden. The sun reflected through the trees and Nounou hunched over me as everything in that watery world flitted. It was a second world—just for us. Nounou's body, rising and falling with her scrubbing, danced on the water's surface, and sometimes a leaf from the reflection would break off the tree, drop into the water, looking for its disappeared mate, not knowing it was looking for itself. Maybe moments like those are why my new world looks like this. But what is this empty country with no other people? Trees, water through a valley, the bright sun. Without others, it can't be a paradise, can it? Here I stand, wearing an old cotton dress, like something Nounou might have sewn. But Nounou is not here.

"Your mommy thinks her job was to birth you and that's that," Nounou had said during that bath. In the heat of the summer, Nounou used the big bar of soap from the kitchen and a rag to wipe me. For my toenails she used an old toothbrush, bristles that blackened with my grime. "Your mother is no mother."

Six years later, in bed with Nounou, I fluttered my eyes, unsure if the sound of animal feet scurrying and sliding across the roof was real. I was also unsure about the feeling in my growing body—my cells multiplying, skin stretching, bones lengthening. The room was dark. Faint starlight shone through the window cut from stone, high up, beyond reach.

The next day would be the worst day of my life and I didn't know it.

In the morning, Nounou was up and folding her white cotton nightgown into a rectangle. Her jar of cream open. She wore her black dress, ready to feed the birds and mend socks.

In my dreams that night, Nounou had died after falling asleep on her chair, needle and thread and Daddy's socks in her tight fist. In the dream I was stunned that a dead person could bleed. For our family, dreams weren't indiscriminate, especially if you remembered them. They came true, or sometimes, their exact opposite did. There was no one rule about it—this made dreams exciting, and also terrifying. We feared them.

Nounou pulled out the top drawer of her wooden dresser and placed the nightgown inside, spreading over it jasmine petals. I had watched her do this a thousand times. Was her breathing labored, was her heart straining, could I count her minutes?

She turned. "Seema, my girl," she said. "The morning has come to bite you." She sat on the bed. "My lovely pony. When I was a girl, I was just like you." She ran her finger down my edge. "I looked like you, too. Your narrow nose, your big eyes and lips. But if I was bad, I didn't get my dinner. You're too clever for that silliness."

Nounou tried to steer me by taking my side, being my friend. It didn't work but she kept trying. "Stop antagonizing your family." She dusted her hands.

I took a deep breath and said, "But my mother hates me and Nader and Shirin are idiots. I wouldn't care if they get sick with diphtheria or worse. Let them die."

"Look, you don't have to give in where it matters. Just give in where it doesn't," she said. "You need your family. In life and death."

I nodded, not sure if I understood. Nounou looked at me. She paused, as if by waiting I'd understand. When her youngest child, my daddy—who went by Saeed—was seventeen, Nounou took him and left her family in Mazandaran. Far north where people spoke Russian, had blue eyes like the sea. The family had no last name, so there was no finding them later. Nobody would say what happened—only that they left. She and Daddy made up a last name: Roshani. It meant light, or the one that's lit. After they moved, Nounou joon removed her veil, a lucky thing in those years that Reza Shah banned the veil and ordered women who refused to remove their headscarves or chadors to be beaten. Saeed impressed Tehran with his negotiation savvy—in part due to his bright blue eyes. He was a bachelor, an old one eventually, until he followed Katti, Elizabeth's sister, to her parents' home one day to ask for her hand. She was already taken.

Once, I asked Elizabeth why we didn't have cousins or aunts and uncles from Daddy's side and she said she didn't know what became of Daddy's family. That they didn't matter.

"Get ready for school, you'll be late. Your mother will kill me," Nounou said, shooing me out.

DOWNSTAIRS, NADER, THE IDIOT, ate cornflakes with Zamzam—Iranian Pepsi—instead of milk. Like he escaped from a family of donkeys. He wore navy school pants too short, a white collared shirt with a pocket for his rocks and twigs, mud-caked black shoes. His hair was curled and messy and he kept tucking pieces behind his ear so they wouldn't drip with Zamzam.

Nader looked up and squinted. Simple as candy but he was brutal, punching me in the face when Elizabeth wasn't looking. Pushing me down stairs. Even when I was a baby. He'd make a good soldier, they always said. I disagreed, he had no precision. No finesse. Too stupid to even be considered naughty. He once killed Nanny's kitten by drowning her in a pot of water while trying to give her a bath.

Dressed in my plaid uniform skirt, I sat in the kitchen and waited for Abbas Ghassem to set down my breakfast of stone bread, butter, and honey, with light-colored tea. "Merci," I said, looking up at his thin face, peppery stubble, gray eyes. He shut them and nodded. He hated me too.

Abbas Ghassem's father had been Elizabeth's cook when she was a kid, and it went on like this for several hundred years. He placed my plate between my hands and left. Abbas Ghassem drowned the bread in sugars and fats like Nader to one of Nanny's kittens. When I finished, I picked up my plate and licked it. Floral and pasty, honey traveled down my throat. I imagined bees, their fuzzy skins, brushing my insides, and sucked my tongue.

"Don't be disgusting," Nader said.

"Worry about yourself. Where's Shirin?"

"When did your face grow so fat? Nobody will like you."

"Die," I said and pushed in my chair, ran upstairs to the second floor. Into our bedroom, my bed untouched—sheets and blanket tucked tight by the maid. Shirin's bed, though, a mess. Sheets on the floor, dresses still on their hangers piled a dozen high. Shirin stood in front of the old foxed mirror against the wall, in a pink taffeta dress with ruffles around the sleeves and hem, turning back and forth.

"Get changed for school and come eat," I said.

Shirin looked at me in the mirror. She stuck out her tongue. "Get lost."

I remembered what Nounou had said. "Look, you want to be dressed, prepared to learn, you're smart. I know you can excel."

Shirin had learned standing in front of the mirror and pouting from Elizabeth. Even at nine years old, she attempted to look like an ingénue. Elizabeth got *Vogue* magazine shipped from Paris, and the two of them were study partners. Elizabeth telling her what was pretty or bland or in bad taste because the woman looked desperate. Shirin licked her index finger like Elizabeth to turn pages, examined pictures from the back to the front. Lick, flip, lick, flip, pout, twirl the hair. Shirin dreamed of a prince in a carriage coming to sweep her away.

"Hurry, Shirin. Change."

"You're just jealous," Shirin said and flipped her hair, which was darker than mine, as was her skin. Her face was sharper. Moles perfectly placed. I supposed she'd inherited more from the ancestors of Banou Khanoum, Elizabeth's mother. Raven headed and black-eyed. None of us looked like Daddy—the brown eats up the blue, dark is stronger than light. This is how we explained it.

"Maybe I am. I wish I were more like you."

Shirin laughed, surprised. But life was easier when a daughter fits into a mother's mold. I wondered what came first, Elizabeth's rejection of me, or me of her.

At twelve years old, my chest was nil. I needed no bra, had no period. Shirin, my younger sister, was going to have all these things at a younger age, and maybe even before me. Though I told myself I didn't care, I was lying.

FINALLY, EVERYONE IN THE car, Elizabeth swerved around corners in our neighborhood. Trees, houses, people walking. So repetitive it looked like a pattern, an illusion, not real life. Tree, house, person, green, brown. People are most like each other when looking through windows, noticing the world.

What was real life before all this was built? I liked to think it was the most beautiful place imaginable. Just soil, plants, sun, rain, the wildest animals. When wild wasn't wild because everything was wild.

Elizabeth drove on and the wind blew my hair. Big machines dug up ground, knocking down old buildings. In 1964, Iran was at the cusp of a new era, Daddy would say. Elizabeth smirked, oblivious that her new Parisian dresses, her way of life—that matched how wealthy mothers in America, in New York, lived—were a direct result of these changes. She had barely noticed when women were given the right to vote two years prior. Iran was becoming a superpower. Soon it would again be the center of the world—it was on the road to that kind of future. We were better than the Russians, the English. They said it, and I believed it.

Nader jabbed me in the stomach. I hit back. He yelled. I giggled.

"Saket," Elizabeth said without looking back. Swatted her gloved hand in the air.

We waited at the stoplight, engine revving.

A man and a woman stood at the corner holding hands. "Look at this man and his stupid girlfriend," Elizabeth said. She laughed, bitterly.

Shirin giggled. "Stupid people!" she said. A perfect parrot.

"But why is *she* stupid?" I said. The woman had great posture like Elizabeth. Dark haired, big painted lips. Hair in perfect curls. Waist cinched. The women were learning from one another, even if they couldn't have the magazines flown in from Paris.

"He is obviously from a lower class than her," Elizabeth said. "Do you see his shabby suit?"

I hadn't noticed, but looked more closely. His suit was a few sizes big. Baggy at the shoulders, too long at the sleeves. His shoes were brown and worn and cracked, not polished like Daddy's. No bulge from a watch around his wrist.

"Even if he does well, he'll always be that man. Nervous around money. Worthless."

"Wasn't Daddy poor when he and Nounou joon came to Tehran?" I said.

"Don't be ridiculous," Elizabeth said. "They were important up north."

THE PERSIANS

I saw Elizabeth's eyes in the mirror. Her sunglasses off, she squinted hard at the road. When the light changed, she drove us past the couple and I saw her studying them. Elizabeth lied. She wanted a husband and children—just not the ones she got. She said she could never forgive Daddy because he never gave her the blue-eyed child he promised, or because he was too old, or because she was his second choice. Was any of it true?

The couple now in the distance, I looked up again at Elizabeth in the mirror. She had a look on her face I'd never seen: she'd grown pale, her eyes frozen, like she'd seen her own ghost. But aren't we all exactly that? Each the ghost of an unchosen path.

At a small body of water shaded by a large tree, I bend down and swish around for those missing leaves I watched as a child.

SHIRIN

MARTIN CALLED AT LAST. "What took you so long, Marty? Who do you have on your roster more prized than me?" I joked. "I'm packing for New York right now, so this needs to be fast." My Louis Vuitton lay open in the middle of the walk-in closet.

"You've really knocked it out of the park, Shirin," Martin replied, but without his usual lightness. We liked to talk like we were on a team together, a very American thing to do. Martin, my German co-conspirator. "In all seriousness," he said, "this is very bad. Much worse than Tony told you. I'm fielding calls from ten different clients. All concerned to be associated with you. One is saying this is proof of your disdain for family values and even America because you act like you are above the rule of law. *Houston Living* said they're getting complaints because they put you on the cover."

"That's what's wrong with Houston. So old-fashioned. And so small. In L.A., this would just be one of many scandals. In New York they won't even bat an eyelash."

"So that's why you're going to New York?"

"I'm not going to let this destroy me. A good arrest can help the business. Look at the rappers, the hippy-hoppers." I dropped a handful of my bras into the suitcase.

"I'm not so sure about that, Shirin," Martin said.

"What are you waiting for then, Marty?" I said. "I told Tony we needed you to come up with a real plan. Why do I even pay you?"

"Of course. Absolutely," he said. "I'm sorry, Shirin. First we deal with the charges. I'm calling the top lawyers."

"My niece is helping me with that."

"The law student?" he said.

"Next point?"

"Okay," he said after a long silence. He knew better than to argue. "Two, we need people to trust you again. Otherwise these things can fall like dominos," he said.

"What things?"

"Businesses. Your business. We don't want a mass exodus."

"Oh, you're making too much of this. It will blow over and you'll see. They will see. I am still me and they know me! But okay. If you say so. Just write me up a fucking great script. And I'll make the necessary calls."

When I hung up, Houman, the big bear, walked into the bedroom and saw me packing. "My god, what are you doing, Shirin?" he said. His hands in the air.

"I'm going to New York for a little breather," I told him. "Get away from these ommol Persians, and to some Persians with sophistication. They will know I am to be cherished."

"Shirin," he said, and he actually lifted a stack of clothing from my bag and tried to force it back onto a shelf. "You have to let this pass. Stay put and it will be fine."

This is the last thing he should have said to me. Stay put? I do not do stay put. I do not hide. Well, I guess I did hide out in Cannes during the Revolution but that was a different situation. I yanked the clothing away from him, sending silk flying across our legs.

"Why do you hate me?" he said.

"I don't hate you," I said, pushing my pantsuits across the floor with my foot.

"And this with the police? Your boyfriend?"

"It was a joke and it took a bad turn. Is that my fault?" I said.

"Was it a joke?"

I didn't respond.

"At least wait and see what the next few months are like. Maybe the best thing here is some face time. You are amazing with your clients, Shirin. Please don't be rash. Don't throw away everything you've built."

"You're just worried that if I go I might never come back." And I left him standing in the closet.

NIAZ

MY MOTHER ABANDONED ME when I was six. My father, too—but he's a father and biologically blameless. We don't blame a male lion for killing a pride's cubs. Why blame a male person for leaving? That's how I thought. My mother left me with my grandmother, Maman Elizabeth. She left me with Baba Roshani, too, but, if we expect little from a father, we expect even less from a grandfather.

I ran to Maman Elizabeth's house that morning in 1978 clutching my little doll. Weaving between buildings, trampling on bushes, I needed my Maman Elizabeth. Who else would make my dolly her perfect tangerine baskets—starting with a whole tangerine, she'd peel away enough skin to make the form of a basket, then remove the fruit segment by segment. But the tangerine skins always dried out, stiffened, and split. Dolly would need replacements.

"Devil child! What are you thinking? You could have gotten killed," Maman Elizabeth said at the door in her skirt suit and low heels. "Your parents are leaving today," she huffed. "Well now that you're here, stay for tea while we decide what to do with you." She pulled me in by the arm. "Cook!" she called.

Two minutes later I sat at her low living room table, on the floor, drinking watered-down tea with a spoon and eating strawberries sprinkled with sugar. I fed a bite to Dolly.

The phone rang and Maman Elizabeth sat at her little table in the corner. "Shirin," she said. "Well yes she is, as a matter of fact. Hold on." Maman Elizabeth stood up and said close to my ear: "Niaz joon, be a darling and go ask the cook to prepare the meat for supper."

When I returned, Maman Elizabeth was off the phone and seated on the sofa. "Sit." She tapped the spot next to her. "Your mother told me to keep you for now. To make sure you're safe until they return. She is smart. She knows you're better off here with me." She squeezed me. "You won't believe what fun we will have. Rami and Pasur every day, all the gaz and chocolate ice cream you want."

My eyes widened. "Promise no rosewater flavor."

"Of course not. You are my treasure, Niaz joon."

I smiled. *A treasure.* I didn't believe it. My mother never called me that. She'd say I was like a doll, but dolls don't have real feelings. My mother was a treasure—to my father, to men who came to the house to deliver flowers, blushing under their mustaches.

But where was my mother? What did Maman Elizabeth mean? I felt a panic. Like the boat I was riding had just sprung a fast leak. Water gushed in. "Mommy left?" I said. "Why isn't she coming to get me? Is she angry with me?"

"Na kheir. Nothing like that." She hushed me.

I nodded but I wasn't so sure.

"Niaz joon" this, "Niaz joon" that. I craved that repellent comfort of Maman Elizabeth, letting her brush my frizzy hair until it was straw. We both had edges that softened and melted against each other. She was smaller than my mother but also wider. I submitted because she loved me and I wanted her to.

In the West, punks were smashing idols. It was Attar's *The Con-*

ference of the Birds in the twentieth century—the kids didn't want to be told how to be, they'd be their own masters. It was like that in Iran, too, except in 1978 Iran, when the idols were smashed, new idols rose, the likes of which the West could never have imagined. Neither could we, not really. In February 1979, Ruhollah Khomeini descended elegantly over Iran in his black robe, like a glorious bird, gliding down from Paris, the sun catching its feathery folds and blinding everyone.

The schools shut for the rest of the year. There were no secret classes or lessons at home. The beautiful tall blondes we called Miss Taylor, or some other confident name denoting both common origins and European power—Taylor, Miller, Farmer, Driver—all fled.

I sat with Maman Elizabeth in her apartment and watched the new revolutionary state on the news, everything black and gray. No color in the clothing or faces. Maman Elizabeth still insisted on wearing color but all around us, corpses. No children's programs, just the news. Even I knew his name, Khalkhali, the hanging judge. My mother left me here to see these things, to know these things. Sometimes I played with other children behind the building. Sometimes we still had birthday parties.

Before everything shut down, I'd gone to Tehran International School because my parents wanted me to have other vistas. In my last year there, a boy with long brown curls from a part of Tehran I'd never heard of had joined the school. His parents were maybe chapis—leftists. We all whispered this—we copied our parents. Kian was nice to me and made me laugh when he pulled my ponytail. Something inside me knew it was his way of talking to me because he didn't know how to otherwise. Now I was stuck wondering if he was dead, looking for him in the corners of the TV screen.

Outside our window, Maman Elizabeth, Baba Roshani, and I

would see soldiers walk by—I could tell they were just boys with mustaches. Once, they were pushing wheelbarrows full of books.

"They are taking books from the schools and burning them," Maman Elizabeth said.

I imagined the power of matches, these thin slips of wood, and the power given these boys. Trees burning trees. History burning history. Huge orange flames.

When schools reopened the next school year, mine was all-girls and all Persian language. Nobody I knew from before. Where had they all gone?

We wore a scarf as part of the uniform but it wasn't very strict. We let them fall around our necks. The teachers were not true believers in the regime. That came later. Still, the biggest change was in me—I had a second face growing on the side of my head. I felt it when I walked to my seat. It was my old face, my secret and true self.

One day, on the walk home from school, I saw Kian. Maman Elizabeth pulled me along as her pet as usual. He was bigger now, and instead of shorts he wore long pants. He also had a second face. Our two second faces watched each other secretly. Despite the honking and the rushing of shoes, and the shouting in the street, making sure none of the men in dark colors carrying guns noticed.

"Please, he's my friend. Can't he come over?" I said to Maman Elizabeth. "The girls at school hate me."

Maman Elizabeth smiled. "I doubt that but alright, Niaz." She approached his mother the next time we passed each other and invited them for tea. While they talked inside, I played with Kian in the alley behind our apartment. As if we were in the forest telling ghost stories, and not breathing in black clouds of exhaust, hearing skirmishes and wondering as much as our young brains could wonder what this new existence held for us, he told me his parents were having secret meetings at their home. His parents, including that mother who now sat across from Elizabeth, were Communists. I looked up at our kitchen window. Is that what they were speaking of too?

Soon after, Kian came for lunch alone while Maman Elizabeth sat at her telephone table in the hallway. Over bites of clumpy lubia polo, Kian pushed aside the meat on his plate saying it was too expensive and a symbol of the oppressor class. "People who escaped Iran, like your parents, are traitors and cowards. They should be executed," he said, slicing his neck with his slender finger. I didn't know what to think as invisible blood oozed out. I imagined my mother in a noose, neck floppy. After a year, I was already basing my image of her off a photograph in the living room.

"It's not their country anymore," Kian said.

Whose country was it, though, because it also wasn't Kian's parents' country. They were after all working in secret; I imagined dark rooms, fake names, outlandish wigs.

I knew I was supposed to be outraged that he called my parents traitors, so I launched a spoon of rice onto his wide-eyed face and stormed out of the kitchen. He didn't know my parents. Still, why did I want so badly to believe him?

My parents, for the three minutes a week we spoke on the phone, shouted orders. Even if they wanted to, Maman Elizabeth wouldn't allow any discussion of the new government, in case we were being tapped. To me it was always the same: "Be good, Niaz. Respect your grandmother, Niaz. Do your homework, Niaz. Make good grades, Niaz. We will come for you, but you seem happy, Niaz. Niaz. Niaz. So well taken care of. Elizabeth never paid this much attention to me when I was your age, she just dressed me—enjoy it. We'll call next Sunday." I began to hate Sundays.

To Maman Elizabeth, while I listened through the small round attachment pulled from the phone's back, it was: "Are you just feeding my child sweets? Are you making her learn? Do you want her to be fat and dumb? I won't forgive you if you ruin her."

I smoothed out my dress, examined my middle for any sign of growth.

THE RIDICULOUS MUSTACHIOED SADDAM Hussein bombed Iran, and there were beautiful, murderous flares in the sky and sirens in the streets, our whole building shaking. Maman Elizabeth plastered all the windows with a special tape to prevent glass from bursting inwards, in patterns so lovely I think of them as decorations from childhood. Designs of yellow stars and setting suns with their rays like accordions fanned wide, like big upside-down smiles. I was eight now and turned all these leaders and their minions into cartoon characters. Sweaty villains with swagger, cigars and big bellies, pompous military uniforms with bulging medals, black berets sipping tea in delicate glass cups. I also imagined them in floral dresses like my mother wore and caught in the act of something shameful, legs twisted, humiliated, fingers on lips.

What we called red alarm meant run to the shared basement. White alarm: emerge. Red was louder, scarier. Bombings happened at night. Never at school, at least then. The red alarm sounded exactly like a speeding race car in a video game, I later found out—or more accurately, from then on, video game race cars sounded like the end to me. Niaz, don't be afraid, I told myself. I had made up with Kian and sometimes found myself in his basement on nights I was eating dinner at his house—Maman Elizabeth let me go over as much as I wanted. Maybe she thought they were better at hiding.

I didn't know why my countrymen were fighting more people. But this new enemy was clearly demarcated on any globe—a whole other country, not inside the cat shape. Iraq taking advantage of an Iran in chaos. This was easier to understand than fighting within. Easier than Iranians hanging other Iranians in public, shooting students, getting rid of anyone who didn't agree with everything you said.

My mother called and said they saw on TV that bombs were dropping, but still she didn't offer to take me away. "America's confusing. The jokes are different. We're learning," the three of them said.

"Like how?" I pressed.

"Oh, we don't know. Nobody fights for the check. They sit on their beds in their outside clothes. Things like that. Be patient, Niaz," they said.

I said, "I'm happy here, I'm not leaving."

My mother was silent and then, "Okay, Niaz joon," as if I hadn't said anything important. Then she disappeared. Sometimes "joon" could mean its very opposite.

I turned nine and was furious all the time. Did I want to stay or go? These weren't choices I knew how to make. But there was a sense of pride, a superiority that I was here while they were playing Mickey Mouse dolls and eating Hershey's candy bars, cooking dinner not to air-raid sirens but to the hum of air-conditioning. Pride that I was part of a special group of people, from a country where we endured. I shared this unspoken attitude with Maman Elizabeth. It was in the way she only brought home enough food for two days at a time, rather than ever stockpile—forcing herself to shop, a defiant act and a denial that life had worsened.

Later, I learned that hidden inside this pride was the desire to protect myself: I was the baby on the doorstep. During this time the grocery shelves were sometimes empty. We lost weight—both of us, Baba Roshani, too—and I knew my mother would be pleased. The roundness of my cheeks hollowed.

The nice teachers of the early months were long gone. Every morning our new teachers examined our headscarves—now full maghnaehs—to make sure they were affixed properly. If there was stray hair, they pulled at single strands to inflict pain, and said god would get us. No more backpacks, they said. Backpacks were from the West. The evil West, the Great Satan, the snake.

Maman Elizabeth said to lie if my teachers asked me if she drank alcohol or played cards, to say nothing about my family in America. "It's even illegal to play a song, Niaz joon. Treat everyone like a rat!" she cautioned.

The other girls at school looked at me funny from under all their black as if they were born to live like this. As if I, the motherless, was the only weird one. They whispered as I passed. I wanted a partner in crime so we could put chalk dust on the ceiling fan and turn it on, poke the asses of girls with needles when they prayed, but I had nobody. One afternoon, we were supposed to play quietly in the schoolyard. It was May and hot and I couldn't wait until the summer vacation when Maman Elizabeth and Baba Roshani said if it was safe we'd drive to the Caspian and I'd get to play with the grandkids of their friends. Baba Roshani reading his paper on the veranda, Maman Elizabeth gossiping and playing cards for money.

I looked around me and everyone was occupied—girls sitting together playing games or circling the tree in the middle of the cement field. Our schoolyard wasn't much—like a car park without cars. Teachers huddled in a corner in conversation. I looked up at the sky and made eye contact with the sun. I hated it here. This sun even. My eyes burned and I looked back to the teachers, still busy. As quietly as I could, I tiptoed along the edge of the yard and then down the alley behind the school building. In front of me, up a few steps stood the big black dumpsters.

I was wearing my headscarf, which was wet and smelly and made me feel hot when I wanted to be cool. I squeezed my fists together as hard as I could and screamed. I grew hotter. I jumped up and down

74

and then, with another scream, yanked off the scarf and hurled it into the dumpster. With my flattened hair and sweat around my temples, I whipped my head side to side. I felt good and free. My ears bare, taking in air, unfiltered sounds, birds, car horns. Kian would be proud.

Breathing hard, I collapsed onto the steps. I had never done anything like this before.

"Who is that? What do you think you are doing?" a teacher yelled. Three black chadors marched towards me. I stood up bareheaded and crossed my arms, in only the uniform dress and white shirt.

"You can't do this. It is against Islam. You will be punished I promise you and not just by those you can see with your eyes!" Khanoum Morad, the religious studies teacher, said.

"Who's this child? Is that the one with the grandmother who thinks she's so special?" another teacher said.

Khanoum Morad laughed. "The one with the sunglasses in winter. What a tart of a woman."

I seethed. Khanoum Morad grabbed my arm. "Where did you put your headscarf? Put it on this instant and I will show you what decency is."

"No," I said and pushed her off.

Her face tensed.

"No!" I said again and when she lunged, I swirled saliva around my mouth and spat right at the space between her eyes.

With a quick slap of my face, I was kicked out of school. They said I was lucky they didn't give me a hundred lashings.

Maman Elizabeth had never wanted to hear about the daily goings-on at school. "It's too much to bear, this farce of an education and there's nothing we can do!" she said. But she saw what I saw. She lived what I lived. She'd stopped wearing lipstick in the first months of the Revolution after she heard the soldiers were grabbing women and cutting their colored lips off with razor blades. Without telling me, she visited the school, sunglasses on, lipstick perfect again, and convinced them to let me back in. She knew it was my only hope.

THERE WERE YEARS OF revolution and war but also celebrations, picnics, and contraband movies. By 1987 I stopped being of interest to Maman Elizabeth. I was fifteen. No longer cute. I hadn't brought her whatever she'd been looking for. After those early days of closeness, sitting together on the sofa, I didn't understand why Maman Elizabeth wanted me around—she was either alone in her room or out at her friends' houses, rarely ever with her husband who, apart from his daily walk, spent most of his day in bed.

Late one evening, I woke up convinced I had wet the bed because my pajamas were stuck to my pelvis, but in the moonlit bathroom, pants bunched at my ankles, I saw that my inner thighs were streaked red. The small room smelled like cold metal. I built a diaper from toilet paper wrapped around clean underwear. I hid the soiled underwear in a ball under my bed in the same box I kept the photographs my mother sent of Mo. Mo's face, my blood.

By then I was seeing my old friend Kian without Maman Elizabeth or anyone knowing. Bombings happened at all hours now, and sometimes we did stupid things. We'd meet in the side alleys between our schools and homes. I imagined Kian on a muscular horse, in all white, riding through the desert at the speed of light, coming to find me. I thought about the blood that came out of me every month. Red on white. The blood that drew me closer to him.

One afternoon, I went to his house, a cream-colored apartment building with a broken elevator, and greeted his parents who sat on the rug with other versions of themselves—serious, stern, agitated, foreheads creased. They were plain-dressed, the women not wearing scarves, and for the first time in my memory I saw a large group of women with all their hair hanging freely. It was breathtaking. I was in awe, as if seeing a scene out of a Romantic painting of sea nymphs, like the ones Maman Elizabeth once told me about at bedtime. All textures and weights, dark, wavy, flying carpet—like. I loved these women and their powerful hair.

Kian took me to the tiny kitchen for a snack, but I tried to listen to the other room. They called each other Brother and Sister. Passed information of jailed and tortured friends, those planning operations. I imagined they were gathering materials like household chemicals. It felt like a game.

"These father dog mullahs lied. They pretended because they needed our help. Now they kill us and won't share power? They don't want people to choose their own fate. They're as crooked as the Shah, foolish King of Kings," Kian mimicked the big ones, waving his arms.

He was, I couldn't help noticing, long-limbed and sleek like a deer. His eyes were light brown and he had freckles on his nose, his long curls a crown on his head. His neck was soft outside his sweater and I wondered about the curves underneath, the way they undulated. I imagined drinking juice out of the base of his neck.

"Remember how you used to get so mad at me?" he said and smiled. "You now see I'm right. Don't you?" His eyes twinkled.

I told myself: Don't answer his questions, Niaz. Keep secrets. Bleed between your legs and stuff the evidence in the photo box. Grow hatred for your American family, pronounced Ahmreekahee, like a strange squawking dinosaur, giant and vicious, thieving like their precious bald eagle. But don't tell a soul.

Mo on the phone was an idiot. All those TV ads, breakfast cereal and Day-Glo. Eleven years old. For years he was a toy commercial for G.I. Joe, playing commando soldier pow pow, pushing around little tanks vroom vroom, but he'd never heard a real bomb. How it sounded like it originated from inside you even if it went off two buildings away;

77

the way it made you fear dying unconscious in the middle of the night, that last wet drool on your pillow, the mental farewells said in the dark, just in case.

At night, I lay on my sweaty back in what would be a pitch-black room if not for the sliver of light at the bottom of my door because my grandmother couldn't sleep either.

ONE DAY, WITH A sudden buoyant feeling that not even this unending war could last forever, I said "I want to marry Kian" to my friend at school. Finally, I had a girlfriend: Shamsi with the green eyes flecked with gold; big, rosy cheeks; perfect marks. Her cloak longer than required. The stiff handkerchief in her coat pocket never used but ironed daily. "But why marry?" she said. "Vallah, you're sixteen. Don't you want to do something with your life?"

"What's that got to do with it?"

She laughed. "You're a fool, but be discreet and it's fine, I guess." She lowered her voice. "If you give him a suck or let him go in your butt, you won't get a baby. The other way, you'll have to get sewed up. But the doctors who do this are completely booked. You'll have to wait a year. And you definitely can't do that."

Is this what I meant by marriage?

At Kian's house, his parents were now gone more often than they were home. They'd been threatened, questioned, arrested, beaten. Their old love letters fed to starving goats. It was a miracle they weren't yet dead.

Kian's soft face had little hairs on it, growing at funny angles. Making announcements. His shoulders were broadened. He was still a deer with his long arms and legs, his wide-set eyes, but more buck. I had "rounded out," Maman Elizabeth said, but I hoped that wouldn't matter to him. Maybe he'd like me even more.

THE PERSIANS

I lay on his bed after school and lifted up my shirt halfway and waited. I was a show and my shirt was stage curtains. He turned, lifted his eyebrow, and smiled. "I can see your titties," he said.

I smiled. I could tell already this was a good idea so I sat up and pulled it all the way off. I wanted his full attention. I was becoming a treasure.

"I won't tell," I said. Magic words.

He sat down opposite me and I guided his hands over my chest. I was a teacher of what was unknown even to me. His fingers were still, so still, but warm. They softened. I took his other hand and placed it on the lip of my jeans. An invitation. He unbuttoned and removed my pants, slid his hand up my bare leg and pinched at my thigh. I made new sounds. The room spun and I went with it.

We kissed on his soft bed, our warm tongues playing with each other. He removed his trousers, revealing his penis. My first penis. It dangled from between his legs like the pendulum of a clock. Then, smooth and shiny, it rose like a sword, proud.

I pulled him to sit on the edge of the bed and sat on top of him but then guided him backwards. "This is better for us," I said proud of my knowledge.

Was his dick in fact a sword? A dagger, a knife? With him inside, we became two heaving starfish and the pain was excruciating. I was on the edge of consciousness. But, I'd already decided, I wouldn't stop it. I'd see this to its end. To what lived on the other side.

Time passed. The room flattened. The pain stopped feeling like anything different from me. It was me just as I was born. So I relaxed, pulled him in further. And then the plunging reached somewhere that finally, gloriously, pleased me—and each time it reached that place, the pleasing spread a little further along my limbs—like a current, a signal. I sensed it was trying to break free from a wall, a dam that kept it from rushing all the way through and out my skin. What was this wall?

I breathed and tried to let go. To just be a body. Two bodies. I lifted one leg and turned to my side, bringing him closer behind me. We were hot and wet and panting. Digging for treasures together. I felt a change in him now, too—he was responding and so I felt him more. I twisted my head and seeing him, behind me, deer boy with the long neck and broadening shoulders, his desire for me, I was finally set loose.

AT SCHOOL THE NEXT day, the girls talked about me in front of my face. I expected this somewhere inside my flowering brain but I'd ignored the warnings. I was ruined. But if that was true, why did I feel fine? I felt a power in their scrutiny.

At home, the doorbell rang. It was Kian. He walked in holding his head low, swinging his arms. I couldn't see his light eyes.

"Niaz. I did a bad thing."

"No shit."

"I told Babak."

"Idiot."

"I couldn't keep it to myself."

"Remind me not to tell you all the other dicks I've invited into my butt."

He blushed immediately. His face a plum.

"Some kind of Communist agitators' son you are. You want to go to prison? You want lashes? Look, you can either play their game or ours," I said. "We are meant to do this. Like animals. How else do people exist? Every single person in the world is a result of this. Well, except we used the wrong hole." I put a hand on my hip.

"We aren't animals. Animals don't feel love." He looked at me, his eyes big and dopey.

"You don't love me," I said. "I don't love you."

He looked away.

THE PERSIANS

Maman Elizabeth was doing her illegal doreh at Ameh Minou's house, or was it Khaleh Pari—who could keep these aunts who never visited straight? I held Kian's hand and brought him into my bedroom. For over a year, we did everything but the one thing we really wanted. I told him everything except the one thing I felt.

IT WAS THEN THAT I started calling my mother Shirin, and my grandmother Mommy. I didn't do this for a reaction. Well, maybe a little. Mostly I did this because I'd changed and I needed to mark it. I did it to be ironic. My grandmother was no mother either. I also heard Auntie Seema on the phone calling Maman Elizabeth just Elizabeth. I did it to join her.

The girls at my school stopped talking, as did the boys at Kian's; it was boring to gawk at something they themselves wanted. Shamsi's stern warnings didn't come true—that he'd discard me. I knew better, I knew my sway. Did I inherit this power from my real mother?

Kian was mine. After school, he brought me watermelon juice and stapled Communist pamphlets. He told me about the Tudeh Party, and before that the Persian Communist Party, how it started in the North, its ties to the Bolsheviks, the Marxists. I learned the history of these movements—the fight against forces who corrupted our Brothers and Sisters and impeded harmony, how Khomeini arrested and killed many of the old leaders. Maybe the heroic Writers' Association would be resurrected, he said, and we could help.

On the long-distance phone calls from Houston, Shirin and Houman talked about their swimming pool and tennis court. Mo, now twelve, was a champion tennis player, rising in the US junior rankings. That little yellow ball would bring him glory.

What would bring us glory?

I said, "Kian, the time is right to start helping. I'm ready to kill."

Kian laughed. "That's not what we're about. We're about changing hearts with debate, conversation. Labor laws. Minimum wage and
overtime."

"That can't be right. What about the poisons they collected?" I
quizzed him on darker fringe groups outside their core movement. The
possibility of kidnappings. "Can't we build a bomb? It's not very difficult. They'll never suspect us."

Kian looked away. "We are not as strong as we were," he said. "What
we're doing now is for morale." He turned back to me. "What—you
want to die?"

I shrugged.

I didn't know then that it would soon be the summer of executions.
People from all the leftist groups. They told the prisoners they were in
no danger. They asked them: "Do you believe in heaven and hell?"
They asked: "When you were growing up, did your father pray, did
he fast, did he read the Holy Koran?" This was a trick question. It was
only the son of a devout man who could be called an apostate. Some
say they killed three thousand, some say ten times that. Kian and his
family escaped to America before summer began. They didn't even
sell their apartment.

IT WAS 1992, FOUR years after the executions and the end of war. A
million Iranians dead. I was tired just like everyone else who was still
alive. They had exhausted us. They knew what they were doing. After
all that, who'd want any more trouble?

At university in Tehran, I studied math and science, the opposite
of politics or history because what was the point of listening to regime
teachers lie. The truth, if I even cared to discover it anymore, was my
job to unearth in private. What are nuclear bombs if not science? What
is election fraud if not math?

THE PERSIANS

Without Kian, all I had was my pretend mommy, and of course her husband. She was small like a cricket, on the telephone, talking all night at her little table covered in fine white linen, the machine shush of the rotary phone after she pulled each number. I now cooked dinner for the three of us, a combination of chicken, rice, and vegetables. Baba Roshani thanking me for serving his tray in bed, kissing my hand. Always the same chicken. I'd eaten so many chickens—a farm full of chickens. I took no pleasure in eating. From pan to mouth to gut to toilet. It was just something to make me fat or thin, loved or hated.

"Mommy, maybe Azar Khanoum can come less often now that I help with so much housework?"

"Niaz, you know your mother doesn't like it when you call me that."

"She's not here."

"Don't be rude," she said.

There was a question I still wanted to ask about my mother, but I couldn't even bring myself to say it in my head, despite the toughened meat of my heart. But it didn't matter anymore. Unlike my friends who idolized everything American, I didn't see what was so special.

In private, I started to write poetry. I wanted a new connection to language, to my subconscious. A gateway. I wrote one poem about a miracle baby conceived through anal sex, the mother still pure under god. Another about a young tennis champion, needing to win, serving a tennis ball with a grenade core. The themes were obvious.

PRETEND MOMMY, ROOTING FOR cotton balls in the bathroom cupboards, found a stack of my poems. I was red-faced.

She was shaking the small pile, sheets heaving to and fro. "But, Niaz, my dear, these are wonderful."

What? I seized up. These were my most inside thoughts. "You're not mad? You don't think I'm stupid and disgusting?"

She shook her head. "Art is all we have," she said. "It's the only thing that lasts." She told me a story about painting.

I couldn't speak. This little woman who sits on the same woven chair in her tidy skirts, in front of the same little telephone table, talking about the same few things—bowel movements, earthquakes, hair loss, and hijackings—was a painter? I started to cry.

"Now, now," she said. I felt her coming back to me.

I never knew why she wanted me to stay. I understood it even less now.

IN MY BEDROOM AT night, I wrote a letter to Kian and told him about my grandmother's painting, which she'd previously done in secret, and my poetry. How we spent afternoons working at the kitchen table. She with her watercolors; me, my pencil. I told him I missed his penis, when I meant his voice.

Addressed to Bethesda, Maryland. What funny words. Bethesda sounding like Bathsheba who married King David. Bethesda, Kian told me before he left, was a pool in Jerusalem with healing powers after being stirred by an angel. Maybe in Bethesda, Maryland, Kian and his family were healed of any pull to Iran. And Kian to me.

My first clue: he never wrote back.

WHEN MAMAN ELIZABETH AND I called my mother, Shirin, in America to tell her of Parvaneh's death, she laughed and said, "At last! Now Mommy can fly to New York and propose." Maman Elizabeth slammed down the phone. My mother can be a brute.

Afterwards, I call Mo in New York. "Elizabeth's an old woman,"

I say. The line crinkling. "Tell Shirin to be kinder. We won't have her around that much longer."

"You have no idea what's going on here," he says.

"What are you talking about?"

He tells me about Aspen and my mother's arrest. A cop. $50,000. "She's acting like she was teaching him a lesson. Don't tell Maman Elizabeth. Shirin's gotten it into her head to come to New York. It's crazy. I don't have time for this, Niaz. I have a gigantic deal coming up, a trip to Geneva. IPO city."

"This is what happens when you don't have real problems," I say. "Can't you talk some sense into her?" he says. "You speak her language." This time *I* hang up. The irony is cruel. In America, a charge of attempted prostitution is merely embarrassing. She probably laughed when they threw her in jail. Back in the old days, the ones Shirin has no idea about, a woman accused of spreading prostitution was executed by firing squad. She had been Iran's first female cabinet minister, a noble, hardworking woman.

And then there's Shirin. Alive and thriving.

She is so free, my mother. What does she know about me? In all those years, did she ever worry I'd be hurt, or arrested, or killed? Now why should I care?

II

WE LIKE POISON

BITA

JAMIE DIAZ'S OFFICE WAS on the second floor of a Harlem walk-up. A small waiting area led to a narrow hallway, a row of closed doors on either side. A clean smell of Windex and lemon. No receptionist, but the room had a tidy elegance, sconces and filigree. I knew therapists didn't usually have receptionists; I watched *The Sopranos*. A laminated card on the wall said not to knock, but to use the panel. I obeyed. I pressed the smooth button next to "Jamie Diaz, M.A., L.M.F.T" and it glowed a full moon. I stared at it for several seconds before looking out the window. I was glad to be back in New York.

When Jamie stepped out to greet me—fitted pantsuit, pointy heels—she looked more businesslike than I expected, which disappointed me. I'd picked her from a list because in her bio she referred to herself as a "nonjudgmental deep listener of humans," even though reading those words gave me a funny feeling. But, I wasn't looking for career advice. I wanted someone a bit like a fairy or angel or, I guess, a yoga teacher. I wanted someone different from who I usually encountered. Someone who could see me in a new way, could imagine something extraordinary in me.

After introducing ourselves, she asked, "Would it help if I asked you questions, or would you prefer to tell me what brought you here today?"

"My friend Patty is sick of listening to my problems. She said, and I quote, 'you should talk to someone.'"

"Okay. Well, before we dive in, how do you feel about your friend saying this?"

"Fine, but nothing that bad has happened to me."

"That's not a requirement," she said. Certificates hung in an array on the wall behind her, against a bland pastel landscape. On the low table between us, a box of tissues.

"Still," I said. "I haven't had the best time lately, but can't I get on with it?" Maybe her looking like a lawyer brought me too close to myself, wasn't letting me imagine something else either.

"It's a common misconception that the need for therapy is a weakness. We see it as an act of courage and I admire you for coming in today."

I wanted to roll my eyes, but I laughed a little and sat deeper in the chair, studied her concerned face. "Look, I'm confused, I don't know what's wrong with me or if anything is wrong with me." I waited for her to say something. When she didn't, I said, "My mom died." Boom.

She apologized as if it was her fault and then said some therapist stuff about losing a parent and being gentle with myself. I told Jamie she'd been a good mom. I looked away and my eyes met the box of tissues. As if strategically placed at this specific angle to encourage the expression of sadness, catharsis. To cement a kind of dependence on this fifty-minute block of time. I didn't want to tell Jamie that my hope to commemorate Mom by being with our family in Aspen had turned out badly. I didn't share with most people that I went to places like Aspen. I wasn't stupid. I knew it looked gross.

I told Jamie about the Buddhist books I'd read after Mom died in part to see if it would impress her, but I also said how the books made me overvalue "living in the present" to the point that if I wasn't making each moment count I felt guilty. We-only-have-this-life mantra, but to the extreme. I didn't tell her I thought Mom wasted her life. I knew that would make me look like a judgmental asshole, the opposite of Jamie—but it was why I read the Buddhist books, as protection, prevention.

"My mom kind of wanted me to go to law school," I said. "I'm doing this for her. She probably should have gone herself."

"What do you think she would say if you told her you were in law school for her?"

"I don't know. She'd shake me. Before she died, she said: 'Enjoy your life.' Which is easy for someone to say at the end of their life. It's not so easy to do."

"So she didn't say anything about law school?"

"I wanted to do something my family respected. Especially after what my aunt calls my 'lost years' after college. Jobs that went nowhere. I guess I thought law school would make me feel like I mattered. Or wasn't so selfish."

"Why do you say selfish?"

"That's just how I am. Hollow and spoiled and unlikable. That's how my whole family is. My aunt always says, 'We didn't come here for a better life. We left a better life.'"

I knew she wanted to ask what I meant about leaving a better life. And then I'd have to tell her about a hundred years ago, how our fame was deserved. My great-great-grandfather, a legit hero in Iran. A glimmering star. We had it all back then: a stable of ponies, what we now call personal chefs, the ear of every official. Now, in America, all we had was money. Nobody cared who your great-great-grandfather was, especially if they couldn't even pronounce your name, find you on a map, imagine touring your wonders or even imagine you having wonders to behold. They might pretend, but they didn't really care.

I didn't want to tell her about any of that. What *did* I want to tell her about?

"How are you feeling right now?"

"Now?" I was surprised. Maybe she wasn't who I usually saw in life.

"Check in with yourself. Take your emotional temperature."

I shut my eyes. Was I hot? Listless? I opened them. The room at first unsteady. When it settled, I spoke without thinking. "Sometimes I don't know who I am or what I'm doing here. I don't feel like me. But. What is me?"

I WAS GETTING READY to meet Patty. Primping. I looked at myself in the bathroom mirror, examined my angles. Not bad, but probably nothing to inspire anyone. Like all the Iranian women, I had big eyes and thick hair. I thought of how Maman Elizabeth drew portraits of family members in her youth. How would she paint me? What would she see?

For some reason I could be myself around Patty. With other people I pretended. I pretended my doorman apartment in Battery Park was rent-controlled and that I paid for it with money from summer employment. Pretended it mattered checks be split according to who drank more. I couldn't even be honest about these things with a therapist—a person I paid to listen. Oh god. Poor little rich girl—living a life I hadn't earned, and feeling guilty about it.

Around my family I was happy to stay in an expensive hotel but I acted like I was better than them, a law student unconcerned with such frivolities. Shaking my head at Auntie Shirin and Mo when they ordered caviar by the pound and left it uneaten, but still I went along for the fun, shared in that easy wellbeing. I hated myself around the Persians. Weren't we supposed to be mourning my mother? They said she was too smart for school, but I only remember her as a bored housewife.

I picked up my hairbrush and dug hard. It felt good to scratch my scalp. Tear at it. It had been impossible to think clearly during the two weeks I was in Aspen—it was a hostile takeover, a Shirin take-over. Without Mom to hide out with when she was tired of smiling around everyone. Back in New York, I was letting myself think about the future.

Shirin called me a "do-gooder," which sounded so boring. Was I boring? Of course I was—in part, I went to law school to "do good." But I did love criminal law. Why? The language of it? The words were cool: deterrence, retribution. Second chances. Did I like learning about lives unlike mine? Was it escape?

Sitting in class was a remote island from being a lawyer. Did I want to draft motions and spend my time researching case law on LexisNexis? Could I see myself standing up in front of a judge, in a suit, holding a pile of papers? Your Honor, may I approach the bench. Why not? Why couldn't I be like that? What would I do instead?

I left the bathroom and rummaged through my closet. Professor Jenilko, my criminal law professor, always had a snowfall of dandruff on his faded black polo shirts. He didn't care about sparkling, turning heads. His beard smelled like his last meal: pepperoni pizza probably. I found it endearing, lovable in him. He could get away with it be-cause of his brilliant mind. His sloppy appearance and his lack of self-consciousness. I dreamed of being that free. I pulled out a plain black hoodie and blue jeans, running shoes, and shut the closet door.

On Monday I'd be back in those sterile classrooms, the law school cafeteria with its outmoded gray tile floors, the pimpled student cashiers in their polyester blend blue aprons ringing me up. What was on my tray? A veggie burger, a red delicious apple, a water bot-tle made of plastic so thin it crackled in my fist. Walking through the quad past all those cheerful people, the healthy undergrads with big smiles and shiny eyes, thighs stuffed into bike shorts. The law students happily arguing with each other in the hallways, wearing their ill-fitting suits on interview days, dragging their rolly back-packs containing collections of colored tabs and highlighters. It was a weirdly hopeful place. These people believed there was such a thing as justice, and that they could bring more of it to the world. Wasn't I hopeful, too?

Patty called when she arrived and I put on my wool coat and locked up. She'd already graduated, but her public interest law firm let her defer so she could spend time in Jersey City caring for her mother after double knee surgery. Patty was born in New Jersey. Her parents came here from Colombia. They were normal, good people. Her mom was a pharmacist, dad a manager at a local bank. They clipped coupons and volunteered at soup kitchens and not just on Christmas.

"Hey, you," I said outside my building. It had been no Patty for a month. I smiled.

"She's back!" She rushed to hug me. "How you feeling?" She cupped my arms within hers. My wool pressed on her down and I wished I could melt into the stuffing of her coat.

"Weird," I said. "I talked about myself for such a long time with that therapist I don't want to talk anymore."

"Good. You're taking time for yourself."

I raised my eyebrow. She sounded like Jamie. Her hair, which was a lighter brown than mine and stopped at her chin, was now shaved around the sides. "Cute haircut," I said.

Patty smiled. Under her poofy jacket, she was wearing an oxford chambray shirt, buttoned to the top. Slim trousers. Natural color Jack Purcells. I never knew anyone who picked natural over white, it was like choosing your shoes to look sweat-stained, like they'd been sitting in a closet for thirty years yellowing, but I respected it—a clear and purposeful choice. Patty was full of those.

"I have some ideas about your aunt."

"Don't we all?" Before leaving Aspen, Shirin said she wanted Patty to represent her.

"I'm more concerned about one thing in particular. Is she a US citizen?" We were leaning our shoulders against the hard side of my apartment building as the usual people walked by—moms with strollers, dogs in sweaters, insane joggers in just shorts.

"Um, she has a green card. She never wanted to get citizenship. Despite my mom's urgings. Some kind of weird pride."

"Okay, so from my understanding the government can use certain crimes to revoke a green card."

"What?" I said. I pictured Auntie Shirin back in Iran. Antagonizing a mullah just for laughs. A nip slip? Oh god, she'd die. "Even if she's been here for years?" I asked. "I mean, she's kind of American by now."

"We'll need to research how long-term residency affects her status."

"Of course," I said. The thought of Shirin being deported gave me a little chill. An electricity. It was not entirely unpleasant.

"If they really want to fuck her over, I also wonder if they might argue it was more than just a simple attempted prostitution, which by the way in Colorado is punishable as prostitution. How much money did she ask for?"

"$50,000."

Patty laughed. "That much? Really?"

"She says she's worth twice that. The ego on this woman."

We agreed to go to the law library to look up the case law later. We crossed the street, heading to our favorite place that had all-day pancakes with real syrup and butter served by old-school career waitresses.

For a block or so my hand kept brushing up against hers. It was something about how I was walking. Maybe a bit looser, more relaxed because I had a friend, my only friend, with me for the first time in weeks. She did not pull her hand away.

SCHOOL STARTED. I TYPED notes on my old clamshell Mac, answered professors' questions. But after I zipped up my bag and went home Friday afternoon, all I wanted was my bed, which said climb in where it's cozy and you don't have to decide a thing. I stretched my arms and my legs out as far away as they could reach from one another. Pushed against the headboard. I sighed. It felt good. I yawned. Loudly.

I sat up and was lightheaded. Somehow it was Sunday evening. I looked out the window—blinking red and white lights. I blinked back. My phone rang from an unknown 212 number. Was it Patty at the library with new information and questions, or maybe just checking on me? I picked up the handset. On the other end, there she was, Auntie Shirin. As I listened I could feel her hot breath, sweet with cigarettes, as if she were blowing right into my ear.

"Why haven't you called me—the younger is supposed to reach out to the elder. We are all you have," Auntie Shirin said over the phone. "You're nothing without your family." It had only been two weeks since I last saw her.

She was in New York now. "I bought a one-way ticket," she said. "Houman tried to cancel it, can you believe that? He and Mo both contacted the airline and tried to convince them that I was a danger to myself. Me? A danger? I am my own woman, Bita. I needed a night at the Ritz to recover from the flight but tomorrow I'll come stay with you. You better have the place cleaned and get some coffee and real food because I'm not going to live like some poor college student. I'll need your bed. I'm not your age. My back is stiff."

"What about Mo. Doesn't he want to host you?"

"You know Mo. He has a big deal coming up. IPO, schmIPO. Said he's too busy for a visit. He's mad I don't listen to him. Just like his dad. But he said that if I organize a dinner he might introduce me to his new girlfriend. Lucky me. Probably one of those secretaries again. I mean, assistants." I could feel her rolling her eyes.

I let her talk and told her that we'd get her ready for the court hearing while she was here. Patty and I were working on it. But she didn't sound interested in that at all. When she hung up, I held the phone against my ear for a few seconds. I got up from bed. I knew she'd come.

ELIZABETH

SHE DREW ALI WHILE he sat still in the woods, and days became weeks became two years.

Elizabeth was eighteen. Her parents introduced her to suitors. She made faces. Raised one eyebrow, both eyebrows, none at all, embarrassed her baba.

All the while, Ali was the one she'd talk to, think about, and think about talking to. With him, she wasn't her nose. Her nose was for breathing. She imagined it: disappearing into a dot, into nothing.

"You're impossible," Baba said. "I can't keep sending them away."

"Then stop bringing them. I've made up my mind," Elizabeth said.

Baba shook his big planet-sized head. Rubbed together his meaty palms. "Let me get your mother," he said.

"Wait," Elizabeth said.

Baba paused. He pulled on his thick mustache, stroking the hairs. He tilted the axis of his head.

"I have something to say."

"Be my guest."

"I am your youngest daughter."

Baba kept tugging his mustache.

"Your reputation is set," she said. "You could kill Maman and it wouldn't matter." Baba raised his eyebrows. "You really could."

"Elizabeth, I don't care that I can kill your mother. You are getting married. A young girl like you, alone. It just isn't done."

"I haven't finished."

Baba crinkled his forehead.

"I have someone in mind. It's just that," she said.

Baba cleared his throat. "I am a very tolerant man. He need not match me."

"It's Ali."

"Who?"

"Ali Lufti."

"Who's that? What? The chauffeur's boy? Have you fondled his wee-wee? Oh, Elizabeth. Don't answer that."

"Oh, come on, Baba. Your British beauties? There is a thing called animal attraction."

"Sure that's one theory, but to weigh and purchase this, to bring it home? Of course I knew I wouldn't marry those English girls—they were entertainment. It just isn't done." He crossed his arms.

AFTER THE INITIAL SURPRISE, Baba was not worried. He knew that history and example were on his side. He also recognized a few truths about human emotion. Forbid it, and she would want the boy more. Say nothing and watch her fall out of love. She would come around and grow to hate both Ali Lufti and his love—even despise him for it. So he told Elizabeth, "Well, it's your life."

He couldn't have known this then but his decision to not say no became what he was most famous for, every future man in the family compared to this ideal. The ultimate show of power and influence over one's own was to never say no to a daughter, a son, or even a wife—not directly—but still be certain that they will bend to your will.

For Elizabeth, Ali soaked his hands, cleaned under his fingernails, shaved the minute his face started to develop a shadow. When he wasn't under a car, he wore new shoes. And unlike many of the workers, he knew how to read and quickly engaged in his education.

Baba told his wife nothing of his conversation with Elizabeth. Instead, he said, "I think our Elizabeth needs more time."

To Elizabeth, he said, "Don't rush."

Elizabeth hugged her baba. She decided not to tell Ali the news—she didn't want him to know she'd been won so easily.

Officially, Baba looked the other way when Elizabeth and Ali walked together with a picnic basket full of summer bounty. He congratulated himself on appearing modern. Still he sent Abbol Hassan, the cook, to keep an eye on them and break up anything irreversibly untoward. And just in case, he had a secret weapon, one he'd wield if events didn't proceed as planned.

"You are a gem—do you understand? You don't give a gem to an ordinary rock." Baba whispered this as he polished his own shoes.

Throughout the summer, Elizabeth walked with her small hand inside Ali's, noticed there was a fatherliness to a man's love, a being cared for. She felt Baba being slowly replaced on these walks. Now it was Ali who told Elizabeth she was clever. He even called her Elizabeth the Great. On one particularly bright day, after a long walk, they reached their picnic spot, a wooded place farther than Elizabeth had ever ventured, and Ali set down the basket, as usual. Elizabeth waited for Ali to clear an area for her, wipe it free of dirt and sticks. Perhaps put down his one good handkerchief.

Instead, he surprised her. Ali sat on a rock and tapped his fingers on the patch of earth next to him.

Elizabeth pointed downwards. "But the dirt." She was used to villagers laying their best fabrics on the road—ones they used to marry in—so her shoes wouldn't skim bare ground.

Ali laughed. "Oh come on, Elizabeth. That bit of dust won't bite. Aren't you even a little curious?"

Elizabeth shook her head. Suddenly she felt the import of her name. Elizabeth Valiat. The influence of her history. Still she swallowed and tried to play along. She recognized she was difficult, and not as adventurous as she imagined herself to be. Loving the chauffeur's son didn't make her so. "You're right," she said and made a show of pulling off her dainty shoes and pushing her feet into the dirt. "See," she said and clawed the soil with her toes. She scraped even more dirt with her fingers, the white crescents of her nails darkening.

The two sat together. Ali played with her hair. "You're an angel. My angel."

Elizabeth tried not to smile. For him, she curled her hair, had her facial hair threaded—her mustache, sideburns, every half strand on her chin and cheeks, thinned her eyebrows. She lined the rims of her eyes with kohl. Powdered her nose to reflect light and remove volume. She wore the yellow floral dress Baba had bought made of Chinese silk. Why did she do all this?

Ali said nothing about her dress, perfume, no words about her hair. Elizabeth had imagined one day she'd receive specific compliments from a man about her appearance, not just the unworldly devotions in which Ali spoke: my angel, my dove. Maybe he was still shy. He hadn't grown up around such ladies, so he was untrained. She had to forgive him this. He did recognize her value. Elizabeth opened the basket and removed bowls of dates and cherries, a jar of cucumbers, and a saltshaker. She laid all this out on the thin cloth the cook Abbol Hassan had packed. She bit into a cucumber to create a surface, tapped out a few salt crystals, and passed it to Ali.

"What a beautiful juicy cucumber," Ali said. "Greener than the longest grass." He took a big bite, and then another. Cut into a new one. He chewed with his mouth open. Somehow he was able to see the particular beauty of a vegetable.

Today, for the first time, his teeth were yellow. How could that be? Was it the light? Were her eyes finally telling the truth? It was her mind—she knew. It controlled how and what she saw. And then, he did not offer a single cucumber to Elizabeth. When he finished, he rubbed his mouth with the back of his hand.

Elizabeth passed Ali a linen napkin.

"I don't need that, don't waste it on me," Ali said and dropped it back into the basket.

Elizabeth observed all this as if for the first time—her mind paying deep attention to the differences between them, in expectation and restraint. In these two years, any doubts that threatened to surface she'd covered with her own handkerchief, so intent she was on being right. But now at this precipice, sitting in this farthest place, approaching the moment of announcing her lifelong loyalty to Ali Lufti, an opposing spirit came into being.

Yes, people who wiped their mouths on napkins were better. But why? She wanted not to care. Yes, she wanted his teeth to be white, but could she make that not matter?

Elizabeth grasped Ali's hand, sticky and sweaty, and squeezed. She wanted to love him, this man whose shining smile had moved her. Maybe her instinct to notice and draw his features, maybe this was the problem. Not her background, her origin, but the drawing. The art. Her focus on surface.

Back in her room at night, Elizabeth created new portraits from memory. She labored by candlelight, at a desk that was made with African rosewood that Baba had sourced. A fine wood, ideal for her work.

First, she drew Fereydoon Lufti, Ali's father. His bushy salt-and-pepper eyebrows. His beady black eyes. She sketched him fast with a light pencil, then spent the bulk of her time working over his face. Some things she had to invent. Did he have all his teeth? She drew his lips as curtains over them, giving him a large space between nose and lip that made him appear gentle. She saw how he looked like his son—with time, the smooth plane was layered with cracks and folds.

By drawing, she now understood, her love grew. Drawing Ali, or even his father. Wherever her pencil went, it was an instrument of love. Even when she depicted her mother. Making art gave her a different relationship to people—a better one. But, if she was always running to this other lens through which to see people, wasn't she running to be alone? Always alone? She was reminded of the way she conjured Ali the wizard to touch her—or how she imagined he had. And how she'd grown obsessed with a phantom. She felt a panic.

That evening she tried to draw Ali. She couldn't.

THE NEXT AFTERNOON, ELIZABETH sat in the central courtyard, a sketchbook on her lap. With her favorite green brush, she was painting the garden. Flowers in bloom, leaves swaying. The pool quiet—except for tiny insects circling, creating minuscule ripples with their wings. She saw colors, blue, green, yellow. But the nature bored her. It was all unthinking, unknowing. The natural world was chemicals and scents, instinct, sharp teeth, strange geometry. It was not her domain.

She rose and walked towards the garage. Ali was stuck under a car.

"You never talk to me about your mother," she said, loud so as to travel through steel.

Ali had no mother. But everyone has a mother. The story was she died in childbirth. Elizabeth doubted its truth. She wanted the full story.

"Did you hear me?" Elizabeth said. She crossed her arms.

When Ali didn't like a question, he asked another. His head slid out from under Baba's glossy brown Ford. "What's there to say?" Ali said.

"Did she work for my family?" Elizabeth said.

"Oh. Because everyone poor must be your servant?" He squinted at her under the bright sun and his look felt sharp, slicing.

"I did not say that."

"What difference would it make if I talked about her? Would you love me any more?" he whispered.

"Well. It's possible," she said, bending at the waist.

"I'm out of luck then," he said and disappeared back under the car.

Elizabeth straightened herself and walked away. She wanted Ali to follow. She knew very well that he wouldn't.

When there'd been a parade of suitors, there had also been the parade of their mothers. Ladies who wore big jewels past their big knuckles. Ladies with dyed hair that had been curled by a team of servants. These ladies—faces powdered, lips pursing whenever a smell emerged from the stables. She knew this type of woman. She knew how to manage around a mother like that. But did meeting these mothers turn her on to any of these men? No. Did it make them appealing? No. It wasn't the fact of the mothers. That is not what she wanted from Ali. It was the story that mattered. The image of her from his eyes. How one related to one's mother might indicate how one related to the world. But wasn't hers critical and cold?

"WE ARE VERY DIFFERENT," Elizabeth said to Ali. They stood against a stone wall. Ali had finished his studies for the week. "I think you won't like me if you shared a house with me. If you really got to know me."

After the conversation at the garage, he wasn't the man she'd drawn in her room. And it wasn't just the teeth. That sparkling smile was now a clown's grin. Those strong hands turned prickly and clumsy. When

Elizabeth first noticed this, she felt a black seed in her stomach—and ever since then, the seed grew and hardened with each day she spent with Ali.

She had all but given up her plan to marry him. Someone else wouldn't be so bad. She came from a proper family and she wasn't completely disgusting. The man, whoever he was, wouldn't be a monster. She'd need to open her legs five times for him—at most. She thought back to that string of suitors. There must have been one in that lot.

Still, she wavered. What if this was ordinary nerves. Ali would stand outside her windows in the evenings. Sometimes he brought an original poem. Other times, he just riffed. His voice was warm syrup. While everyone slept, he'd help Elizabeth climb out of her window. Together, they'd laugh under the moonlight. She enjoyed these evenings with him. There were moments when she even saw the old Ali.

At her request, Ali was learning about Plato. Elizabeth herself knew nothing of philosophy. They ended her book learning too early.

"You've never seen a perfect circle," Ali said one evening under a tree. "But you know what one is."

"Of course I've seen a perfect circle," Elizabeth said. "In fact I can draw one right now." She picked up a stick and bent over the soil.

"That's a copy of a perfect circle. It is not a perfect circle."

"I see, so there are no perfect people either," Elizabeth said. She did love how Ali made her think.

"You are perfect to me," he said.

Elizabeth scrunched her nose. "Don't insult me."

"Hair like the brightest sea, eyes of suns, your lips the deepest fruit," he sang.

"Don't ridicule me," she said. She liked being fussed over, and although this was nearer to the praise she was after, it was distanced with hyperbole. Ali seemed to be making a fool of her.

Still, Ali held her close and brought his lips to hers. In her anger, they kissed, sloppily, without restraint, inhaling each other for whatever each was worth.

Love and hate were not that far apart.

ALL DAY AND NIGHT, Ali read books or worked on cars. He had less time for Elizabeth. When she complained, Ali said, "But, darling. I do this for us."

"Well, I didn't know making money and buying a house would take so long."

Ali huffed. "I want to do something with my life too."

"Aren't you doing something now?" she said.

"No. Not yet," he said.

Elizabeth frowned.

"I want to change the world," he said.

"What does that mean?" Elizabeth said.

She knew how to be in *this* world. Not a changed one. How to be a daughter—not the prettiest or oldest—of an important family. And she knew how to draw—mostly faces. Recently, she had learned how to attract a boy she liked. But change the world? To transform it under her pencil was nothing. She looked at Ali with new eyes. She was half impressed and half alarmed. Baba went to school and never said the word "change." Even Baba fit into the world as it was. She had been too young to remember her grandfather, the Great Warrior, and she barely even knew the stories. He was surely involved in "change." But Ali?

ALI STARTED TO SHARE new ideas with her in the dark. Over candlelight in the garden outside her room. How the way it is does not have to be. Ruling class, peasants. These were words people invented.

Baba was growing impatient, but he let them have their evening talks. He would wander down the gravel path around the house and try to listen. He knew it would end soon. If not, he'd see to it personally.

Elizabeth scoffed at Ali Lufti's claims. "Of course that's not true. What else would your father be? Or Abbol Hassan and his descendants be, if not our cooks? That's too ridiculous."

"They could have their own future, and not be bred like livestock to serve the likes of you."

"Likes of me?" Elizabeth said. "But we're like family."

"You can just pack your bags. Don't you see?"

Elizabeth laughed. You arm them and then they turn on you. She blew out the candle. They stood in the darkened night, the moon not out, just the stars. She walked away in the faint glow. She didn't know how to handle these developments. After the end of formal schooling at age twelve, her learning was mostly limited to being a good wife and mother. She was taught to sew, knit, cook—even though she wouldn't need to. They were skills to harness if, say, all the servants came down with cholera. She was no good at any of it—pricked fingers on needles, burned her wrist on a pan of boiling water. Even her drawing was only to depict family members—decent portraits one or two would be proud to hang in their homes—and, if forced, a mediocre drawing of fruit, a prosaic country landscape.

The point was not to question or to change how things were. It was to follow the rules, play the game. To learn to love a man, to care for his children.

What else could she do?

THE NEXT TIME ELIZABETH saw Ali, he was not waiting in the area near the servants' entrance reserved for the help. He was in the central courtyard where Maman drank her afternoon tea. He was sitting right there—bold and defiant. In this moment, it did not matter that she disliked her mother.

"What are you doing?" Elizabeth said. Now he was not only confusing her, he was a snake. Full of venom.

"You know," he said.

"This is not allowed. Even if you are with me, for now."

Ali blinked. His eyes were sharp. He smiled—a smile she'd seen before—but he looked older somehow. "It seems you have decided about me," he said.

"I have?" she said.

Elizabeth hadn't decided a thing. But she waited and again felt the black seed inside her—its hardness, how it coincided with her whole body now in what seemed like permanence.

"Okay, yes," she said. "You've seen inside my heart. And I have seen what's in yours. Not an ideal love, just a poor copy. Goodbye, Ali." She left him on the bench and went back to her bedroom.

SHE DECIDED RIGHT AWAY she wouldn't tell Baba what had happened between her and Ali. In her room, she wiped her tears on her linen handkerchief. It was finished. Baba didn't need to know why. Elizabeth didn't even fully know despite her words to Ali, which she didn't entirely believe even as she spoke them. She'd say she was sacrificing her love for Baba. Out of duty to Baba, her family, her sense of what was right. He sat in Maman's seat! He wanted to overthrow them. She knew enough to know that appearing to obey her father was to her advantage.

On Sundays, after kabobs and rice that he buried under spoonfuls of deep crimson somagh, Baba loosened his belt and strolled through the garden with his cigar. He surveyed the flowers, called the gardener to snip this and that, correct an overhanging vine.

Elizabeth, out in the sunshine, wore his favorite dress—the yellow one with the white flowers. The same she wore for Ali. This dress complemented her thick waves, diminished her nose. Made her look more palatable. She believed this.

"Elizabeth, my princess," Baba summoned. Apart from a tribute to his ex-girlfriend, Baba also named her after the English king's first-born. He stretched his thick arm, squeezed her against his side. If he could, he'd suck her into him—absorb this child into this breast. Elizabeth knew that, and it was the comfort that a baby feels. She never wanted it to go away.

"Baba, I've been thinking," she said.

"Oh. Don't do that." He laughed.

Elizabeth smiled. The truth was she was tired of all that thinking. "I know I have a role to play. I don't want to disappoint you."

Baba held his heart through his suit jacket as if it were swelling— like a wave reaching its crest. He grinned.

"You are pleased," Elizabeth said.

"Well, yes. And you know, he knew he had a chance with you because of your nose. That's reason enough to disqualify him. He took advantage of you, Elizabeth. Don't you see that? Otherwise, he never would have dared. Foolish scamp." Baba shook his head—alas, this was his secret weapon, one he didn't need to use, but did now anyway. He couldn't help himself. "Besides, nobody marries outside class."

Elizabeth turned red. Baba the lion, big and fierce, the protector. Ha! It was *Baba* who was the snake. Not Ali. Ali loved her. Not despite her nose or because of it. Even if she had a perfect nose, he would have chosen her—just as she would have chosen him. Just as she loved him not because he was a chauffeur's son, or despite it. Even if the story had its origins in her nose and his standing, that was not why their first encounter had grown into love. It was not why Ali was making himself into a learned man. Not why she—in her best moments—wanted to break free of her narrow upbringing.

But was that true? Or was this why they were doomed—their entire love based on something so superficial? Her heart seized with this revelation.

"I hate you, Baba. I always have."

NIAZ

HI BITA JOON. THANK you, the cream is perfect. Now my skin is another story. Dirty air makes healthy skin the holy grail. And a good distraction— ask the women here. We are obsessed with treatments and salons more than ever, the mullahs be damned. I hear my mother is imploding, but why? Does she ever feel guilt or regret? I don't think so. Does she look at how she affects others? No way. If she ruins her life and career, if she goes mad, so be it. She's a grown woman. Her future is her business. Can you imagine if she were in Iran? Of course you can't—what do you know about Iran? Did you say your friend can represent her? Good idea. Keep it in the family. But you can't count on Mo to help—he'll just fake it; he knows what to say to act the good son, but he won't get his hands dirty. It has to be you. Call me back. But let's not talk about her—I've had enough of her for five lifetimes and she hasn't seen me in thirty years. Now I have to call Baba—he's losing it. Look at how she tries to rule us all. Is it like this with your mother—does she rule you from the grave?

SHIRIN

I MET HOUMAN ON a beach vacation in the Caspian when we were kids. The Caspian, where my ancestors originated, millions of years ago floated out of the sea, green web-footed marine creatures. Swam ashore to Mazandaran and Rasht and peopled it. Their gills shriveled up, they grew hair on their backs. The Caspian, its waters the source of everything, our ground zero.

Meeting Houman was meeting my past. Whenever I went up north of Tehran to Ramsar I thought of algae-wrapped sea creatures but what I saw, what was drilled into me every day at relatives' homes in our ancestral region, was the actual stupid black-and-white photograph of my great-grandfather, the G.W. The famous one. The one every family member displays prominently on whatever table, mantel, or wall will result in the most *oooh*s and *ahhh*s. I'd assumed one day I would display it too. So would every descendant of mine. The Evil Eye applies more to babies and women, not dead old men, so we didn't worry about proudly flashing his face.

I used to say to the younger generation: get the G.W. tattooed on your arms! Put him on your screensavers and wallpapers, whatever will get it circulating. Picture this: the Commander, our Great Warrior—the most serious-looking man you've ever seen—wearing a simple black fez, no tassel, and plain black coat. No one would doubt this man is special. Regal, even. So regal he refused the crown. So plain he makes you want to cry, rip your hair out. In the age of gold, of spangles on everything, he is a beacon of accessibility. He's just one of us! As they say. The magazines are such stupidity, as if Hollywood is anything.

So how could I be so angry with Houman? Enough to ignore his pleas for me to stay in Houston and weather out the consequences from my arrest together, enough to leave him for an adventure in New York without telling him when I was coming back? If I was. Easy. I cannot separate Houman from the G.W. I cannot separate Houman from the Valiats. So if they are telling me my family is nothing, that I don't have class, how would it help me to have Houman around? Houman who reminds me too much of my origins. Houman who thinks the cops were just doing their job. What use was he to me?

Even before this whole silly thing I had started to feel that I couldn't stay in Houston. It wasn't just the Manouchehrs of the flower shops. Picking up my dry cleaning, ordering petits fours at the Iranian patisserie, bringing in my racket for restringing, everywhere I turned, there was talk. I was getting bored of everything, even my business.

I call myself Shirin Valiat professionally, not Shirin Javan, because it's important people know I descended from greatness—I brought to every event the focus of great military might and the charisma of a constitutional purpose. I wrote bullshit like that on my brochures because it worked! I catered not just to the rich but to the adam hesabi, to people with purpose, the rarified kind. Significant people who needed wine tastings and looking at art to soften their social gatherings, who relied on me to find them suitable partners. And now, these evil-eyed women want to ruin me? These jewelry sellers? These real estate agents? These housewives telling us we're nothing? No thank you. Sure, perhaps my father, Saeed Roshani, was not truly the son of a feudal lord from the North—my parents' marriage not the coming together of two powerful families, just one side was great, but that is a little white lie. Who doesn't tell those?

Back to this photo everyone in my family hangs up—despite its lack of ostentation and despite it not being required the way those ridiculous Shah and later Khomeini and Khamenei ones are in Iran—in a preferred framing of twenty-four karat gold and a preferred size of double XL. Now this style is associated with bad taste, bandits like Donald Trump or footballer wives. But we invented this, and with us it has flair, superiority.

Back then I married the first idiot I met—the first who proposed. I met him at the Caspian and thought, yes. Give me your name. Erase my peerless Valiat with your unknown Javan. Done. Why not. Yes, Bita, your auntie was like that once. On his hands and knees on a towel, in a bathing suit with sand under his fingernails. I never thought it mattered, throwing out my name, everyone would always know who I was. Fine, technically I was Shirin Roshani.

Asking me questions about my early days in Iran, to which I responded with only what she needed to know, Bita stood next to me over the gas stove in her joke of a Manhattan kitchen—kitchenette they call it to distract you with something French—so I could burn the black hair off her arms. I insisted, wouldn't take no for an answer even though I'd just arrived and wasn't offered a welcome cigarette. She's as unlucky as me: the long hairs on her arms are thick enough to be visible in a mirror, say while doing the elliptical at the sports club, or going up a department store escalator where they haunt me. As a woman, I told her you don't want those moments where you're repulsed by yourself, at least not at twenty-six—whatever baby age she is—you are meant to be lovely at all times, and a thick pelt is not lovely.

"Give me your arm," I said. "Give it."

Bita, wearing some kind of dress that looked like a paper bag, dangled her left arm and relaxed it entirely into me.

"Hold it up, Bita. I'm not trying to collect arms."

"Auntie. This is really unnecessary." She shook her head. "But I love that story about Uncle Houman and you," she said, clearly not understanding my point. "I can see you as a Persian Annette Funicello, dancing on the beach in your yellow bikini. Are you sure you don't want to call him and make up? Let him help you? Go back to Houston?" She smiled, looking drunk or dizzy, the way these young people do sometimes when they are thinking. No poker face.

"Don't insult me. That was before my time, Bita. How old do you think I am? And she was not pretty with that nest of hair like a grandma and thick peasant legs. But fine. I don't care. Houman was the real beauty," I said and lit the burner, twisted Bita's arm over it.

"Really? Ouch!" She whined so loud I could smell her sour breath.

"Hold still. Yes. An Adonis. Ripped muscles, enormous smile. You'd never seen anything like that on the beaches of Iran. He would outshine all the girls and they knew it—they were terrified of him. You know when you're that young, looks are really all that matter, even if you believe otherwise. It's the hormones. But now look at him. He's like that Super Mario Brothers character you kids like. Fat, old, and foolish."

The air smelled eggy. Bita's hair shriveled up into tiny knots across her arm and I rubbed them off into the sink. "There you go. Ta-da." I turned on the tap to rinse the basin and then thought better of it. "You do the washing, Bita."

Bita pulled out the nozzle and sprayed the water around like a person who didn't know how to spray water, let alone clean a sink. Up, down, but not with the aim of getting everything into the drain. Seema never let her touch anything in the kitchen, for fear that she'd become a housewife too, but now Bita, poor girl, couldn't take care of herself. Thank god I was here to see it.

"Do you even know how to scramble an egg?" I said.

She smiled. "Auntie, you're so weird. I don't eat eggs. They're aborted chickens."

"What are these priorities? So you're pro-life for chickens? Let me do your other arm," I said. "Eggs have fed people for millions of years, and now suddenly, you have the answers?" I lowered the second arm onto the blue-and-orange flame. The hair singed in a path up her shoulder the way a fire burns along a path of gasoline. "Some skills everyone should know," I said.

"Ow!"

"Thin skin, just like your mother. Next time, just get some Jolen and bleach these," I said and raised her arm a millimeter from the flames—just enough to keep burning her a bit. "Houman was studying the Hollywood movies—he knew everything about Spencer Tracy, Paul Newman, Richard Burton. I thought what a waste of time, but still I threw myself at him. No, really, I fell right in front of him so he'd pick me up, brush sand off my knees. Such a temptress I was. I'd stand there and pour sand into my bathing suit, saying are you going to brush that off, too, and make his eyes dangle out of his skull. I was only fifteen. Barely out of diapers." I laughed. And if there was a man watching me now, I know merely my laugh at imagining my young self would tempt, would ravish. Don't let these men make you believe they've changed.

"Your grandmother tried to butt in," I said. "Told me he was not educated. He had a chemical engineering degree from Boston University! Okay, it wasn't Harvard. Nothing is. Not even Harvard. You know what I mean—look at you."

"I didn't go to Harvard," Bita said.

"Not the point. I almost told her that he did go to Harvard. But he's not that smart—she probably would have called my B.S. and slapped me in the face. I said to her, 'If you don't let me marry him, I'll marry the next man who looks at me.' She backed down like that extinct volcano she is, useless good-for-nothing. Still, even today, he's one of the best Iranian men. Which is not saying much. It says almost nothing, actually. So he doesn't cheat—these Iranian men, it is the one way they can get back at us for our rise in the world and their decline." I looked at Bita's arm, gave it a yank for good measure. "Finito, that arm is smooth as an ice cube. You're good for another four weeks. Then gorillas in the mist, here we come! Okay, how else do you need me to help you? Have you had your ass waxed?" I smiled.

"Shirin, stop."

"Fine, fine. Speaking of cheating, you know when your mommy got sick your dad thought he was to blame."

"Yeah, like she could catch cancer from his shitty behavior," Bita said. "Look, you've told me this bullshit before. I don't think she died from a broken heart. That doesn't happen. It's nonsense."

"Reality is not so easy to explain, Bita. There are mysterious forces at work. Cancer is often someone's fault. Internal pain needing a home, external pressure. Unexpressed feelings, toxic energy eats you up from the inside out. That's why you need to eat a lot of pineapple no matter what. I'm not exaggerating—the doctors all know this—they just don't tell you because the drug companies pay them. It has enzymes that cut through toxins and depression, zaps the cancer. Like that." I snapped my fingers.

"Stop. It was nobody's fault. Pineapples are not medicine and you know it."

"You believe you're going to live forever, you'll live until you're at least one hundred and three?"

"You know what? Just shut up, Auntie."

"Fine, okay. I raised you right. Don't listen to your elders. But sometimes I want you to listen to me. I'm not what I mean when I say elders. When are you going to take me out somewhere fun, Bita? It's not every day that I'm in New York. You need some realigning yourself."

"So the cancer was Dad's fault. He's toxic. I'm not taking you out, so I need to change. There's an enemy to blame. You get to say that about anyone. Like Niaz. She's toxic. But she's not toxic. A person isn't toxic. You call her that and then of course you can think you did the right thing with her."

"Who said anything about Niaz? Ungrateful child. Both you and Niaz, actually. You'll see—modern medicine doesn't count the power of the heart. But it matters. Weak heart, weak life."

Bita rolled her eyes.

"You who had a mother who listened to you. Why are you like this? Always cutting me down," I said.

"I don't know if Mom always listened to me. Her mind was elsewhere. Wasn't it?" she said.

"Anyways, are you embarrassed of me or something? You don't introduce me to anyone—you never have. I bet you don't tell any of your friends what you came from. Do they think we were just some refugees?"

"Weren't we?" she said.

"Refugees don't grow up in Beverly Hills."

"I think inherited wealth is a problem, actually," Bita said.

"Oh please. You know so little, you're still such a baby. You'll see. In life you make calculations. Like Houman. He was a means to an end, really. Once I got over his looks—which believe me, you do." I shook my head. "Looks aren't anything in the end. Not with a man—of course, we women aren't so lucky. After some time together, it's ambition that matters, and Houman lacks it. He is a kindhearted, golden-age-of-Hollywood-loving dimwit. A bit like Niaz, except for the Hollywood part, so you're right she is relevant to this conversation.

Men, my dear, just beware. They can steal your heart and then your bank account. So keep an eye on that inherited wealth of yours."

"I'm not looking for a boyfriend," Bita said.

"Well, why not?" I raised my eyebrow. "This is the time for that, Bita. They need to first meet you at your absolute best. And that is now. Not even next month. Your cells are dying."

THE NEXT MORNING I woke up refreshed. Bita's bed was no hotel bed but at least I was distracted. I found her in the kitchen microwaving some supposed block of food on a paper towel.

"Let's go spruce this place up," I said. "You're not living in a retirement home. Besides the leopard sofa I bought you, it has no pizzaz. They say leopard's a neutral now. Let's go to Bendel's."

Bita refused to indulge me with a department store but said since it was Sunday we could go to the flea market. She would let me get her a thing or two there.

"I don't want to eat with the plates of dead people," I said. But I gave in. After all, I'm just a guest here.

We took a cab at my insistence. "You think I was made to go on the subway?"

At this market, Bita started leading me around in circles. We must have looked ridiculous, like shivering mice lost in a maze. At least they were selling coffee in takeaway cups so I could warm my hands as we browsed. It was table after table of useless junk. Old makeup compacts, broken lamps, mirrors you could barely see yourself in.

"Bita, once you're a lawyer you stop pretending to be frugal. You'll make six figures and people won't bat an eyelash at your lifestyle. Trust me."

We stopped under an awning of some old guy selling military junk. Old medals and captain hats, disgusting torn-up boots. He probably had some Nazi stuff hidden for his special customers. I was glad he just sat behind his table and didn't talk to us.

"I'm not in law school to make a lot of money. I told you that." She blew into her coffee.

"Right. You'll see," I said, staring at the old boots. Could I get a disease from touching them, I wondered. "I'm sure they all say that," I said. "How many of your classmates actually pass up a good paycheck? Your mother was a bit like this, before you were born. But really— think of who you came from." I swept my arm across the junkyard.

Bita looked confused. "Auntie, I don't care about who we were a long time ago. That's not my reality. It has nothing to do with my actual life."

"How do you think you get to live your actual life?"

"You don't get it. I don't want to be like you. I don't want to do the things you do, or care about what you care about."

I laughed and threw what was left of my coffee into the trashcan in front of me. The white-haired man looked up. "That's an antique, lady."

I shook my head at him. What did he know about antiques. I squinted my eyes at Bita. "Very interesting that you are choosing to argue with me when I am in need!" I said. I may have raised my voice a bit.

She looked at me. Looked at the man. Leaned into whatever that contraption was and pulled out my coffee. "Sorry, sir," she said and stopped talking to me for the rest of the morning except a "no, Auntie" here or there.

"MARTY, BABY," I SAID, on the phone back at Bita's apartment while Bita shopped for groceries. "What's the score?"

"I have bad news. I spoke with what I'm calling our 'hot list' and they wouldn't listen to the talking points and they didn't want to liase with you."

"They? Hot list?"

"The Eskandarians, for one. They are calling up their lawyers to back out of their contract with us."

"What?" I shouted. "Whatever. I didn't need to plan their son's Sweet Sixteen anyway! I don't do parties for toddlers, or the children of toddlers."

"I'm barely hanging on to the Riani wedding, Shirin. They said in Iran your families were close for generations, and that is the one thing keeping them with you. And they appreciate your ties with the museum. They do love that location—they want 'cultured' and 'refined.' Remember?"

"Well, good. Tell them nobody in Houston except me could book a Saturday night in July at a real art museum in under six months' notice." I hung up. Thank god I was here. I don't know what I would do if I saw Khanoum Eskandarian at the sports club. Or good old Manijeh and Faranaz at the Iranian patisserie, they were always at the patisserie, now they'd be smiling, crumbs in between their veneers, thrilled that their Shirin's-family-is-nothing-anymore gossip was coming true before their very eyes.

Anyways, I didn't come to Manhattan just to get a break from Houston. Of course not. I have other things going on in my life. How could I resist the fact that Parvaneh, the wife of Ali Lufti, died somewhere between East Forty-Third and East Sixty-First Streets according to sources. Maybe I was also here to see him. To pay my respects, as they say. Surely at such a funeral everybody would be eating out of my hand in no time. And fine, maybe a part of me wanted to see what this famous Ali was doing.

When Bita came home with her jar of pickles and frozen pizza pockets, I scoffed at her disgusting food habits. "You ought to be grateful,"

I told her, "but maybe your wish is coming true, I suppose we are in decline."

"I didn't wish that," she said, acting dumb.

It's true, I told her. In less than a hundred years, we turned from the most fearsome warriors into utter wimps. Great-Grandfather, also known as the Great Warrior, the Greatest of Commanders, the Commander of Commanders, leading an army of thousands, owning the most land of anyone in Iran was the reason we were one of the most important families in Iran, some would say the most important. But alas, Great-Grandfather poisoned himself when the tide turned against him. And the tide *always* turns.

They were not ready for such greatness, the Iranian people.

He told his sons not to cry. Can you believe that? I asked Bita. "I am already dead," he wrote in his suicide note. I hate to admit that part, but sometimes it's the best option. The daughters, of course, were expected to ululate, beat their chests, throw themselves over his grave. His wife buried him with her own ox hands.

Bita nodded. "But why do we need to go over all this?" She was leaning against the counter trying to open the lid of the pickle jar, face turning red.

I pushed her away. "Because when I am gone one day, a long time from now, someone needs to be able to tell this story. Our future will depend on it. Here," I said, the lid easily coming off in my hand. "Let's hang that painting. It was by far the least depressing thing at that flea market of yours, and can you believe it was only twenty dollars? That's not even enough to buy a plain canvas this size!" I lifted the portrait of the aristocratic European woman I bought for Bita despite her protests. "I'm sure she gave alms to the poor," I said. "Hold it even," I snapped as Bita fumbled with the other edge of the gilded frame.

As we worked, I told her of the slow downfall. The years of property confiscated and swindled by two Shahs, which started even before the Great Warrior's death. No longer did we own half the country. This Great Warrior had a son. My grandfather, your great-grandfather—Houshang Agha. Baba Valiat. He was large and loud and generous and yet, he was no warrior. He got along with everyone, what a ham! Never said no. Wore three-piece suits, a pocket watch, gold-rimmed spectacles, his stomach bursting out of his belt—loved a good kabob and a compliment. He let Grandmother, Banou Khanoum, order him around in matters of the household—she was the dictator, the boss. Still he insisted on managing his four daughters without her, but that only proved the point. He was too domestic. Banou—who they called the Great Tiny Boss—would have made a better leader. She died when I was small.

"There, that's perfect," I said. "She's not as grand as a Valiat or even a Roshani, but at least you have something of substance in here." I admired the blues and grays in the painting's background, probably the river and sky of some cold city like Amsterdam or London, the ripples and ridges of the paint on the woman's long brown hair, her endless stare. "Too bad your grandmother isn't here to lend her expert eye to the quality of this brushstroke," I teased.

I didn't want to tell Bita it only got worse after Baba Valiat. The Great Warrior's grandsons—Mommy's cousins, the best of them Hormoz Khan and Keyvan Khan, were total losers, joining every get-rich-quick scheme around. It was a time for these schemes, the '60s, the '70s, when Iran thought it would be a global superpower, second only to the USA. They invested in massive building projects, machinery import-export, discotheques—but everything went bust. Hormoz and Keyvan lost all their money—really the Great Warrior's money—and then they lost all their wives' money, then their wives divorced them simultaneously, as if they hatched their plans together. They probably did! Hormoz Khan, the more decent one—it's always that one—took the Great Warrior's route and poisoned himself. We like poison in this family.

And what about the Great Warrior's great-grandsons? Hah. Like my brother. The epitome of idiots, Nader. Lives in Los Angeles, deep in Culver City, miles from the old MGM lot and the supposedly cool art scene, in a box on sticks, a dingbat apartment, where nobody can find him. He pretends he's not even Iranian. Goes by Nate, winning the contest for dumbest American name. Have you ever met a Nate with a brain? Don't answer that, I told Bita, because I told him this and he didn't care. An HVAC installer, he tries so hard, sweats as he pours his body into his work. But who wants a sweaty air-con guy? It's like a hairdresser with no hair.

"Auntie, you're so mean," she said.

Well, then I knew not to tell her what I thought about Mo. My Mo. The only great-great-grandson. Most of us aren't even having children anymore—what's the use? Sure I coddle and praise Mo, but he is too focused on his personal success. He was one of those kids who took their piggy bank savings too seriously.

So there's nowhere to go now, as they say. We have officially bottomed. But why am I focused on the men? Women have the fire in my family. But they are useless without power. Even worse, we get charred by our own heat. Look at Mommy. She was once strong. For that era, to have interests, like painting! To have a teenage crush—and on the chauffeur's son! But she sizzled on the spit. Some contend that I'm our last hope.

In Houston, after that Niaz called me about Parvaneh, I thought, that settles it. I stood up and walked over to my floral arrangement. I breathed in, and the flowers smelled like nothing, thankfully. Smelly flowers are so needy, so pathetic. It's enough that I look at you, isn't it? I took one last look at that outrageous bouquet of tropical flowers, in all the oranges and reds and half hues, and boom! Knocked the vase—crash—onto the marble floor. Shattered into tiny flashes of light. For a while I couldn't even focus—such a beautiful cacophony. I clapped my hands together. No way was I touching a single shard of it. That was it; it was showtime!

I knew right then I was bound for New York as soon as I could find a ticket, to the one place America really is. *What are you going to do in New York? Eat a bagel? I'll get you a bagel, I'll take you to a theater show! If you want me to*—I could just hear Houman sing out to me in his silly drawl. "Can you believe he tried to stop me?" I said to Bita.

"Yes," was all she said.

"Some things are broken and I need to fix them," I told him when he pushed me. "He didn't need to know everything. Neither do you," I told Bita. She rolled her eyes, of course she did.

And there I was on a flight to New York before I could change my mind. Called the airlines and told the woman on the phone—they're all in India but call themselves Marcia so we won't berate them, I don't blame them—"I am fleeing a domestic situation but I cannot elaborate, not here," I whispered as if my perpetrator was rounding the corner. The innocent darling booked me on the next flight. Except first class was sold out—that's why I came a few days later, I told Bita. At a time like this, we can't neglect ourselves.

It was hard to believe this husband of mine was the same man I first met in the Caspian. He fooled me good that Houman, and I refuse to believe, even though I contradict myself, that it was just my eyes that fooled me, caught up in teenage lust. No. He changed. But also, he was tied to my history. And beyond that he was a firestorm of plans back then: promised we'd be unstoppable, the stars of the Iranian elite. He was going to buy up all the good companies. Show up all the Shahrokhs, Rezas, Mitras, Shamsis—our parents and their friends were uncreative with names and so we all had the same twenty names—we Iranians don't do Saffrons or Pomegranates, Sailor Moons or Satchels.

And then, in a flash, the Revolution hit us and Houman rolled over. He now says tea is the next big thing. Tea! Convinced by your daddy, I told Bita, always so gullible. Tea is something your naneh drinks. It can never be rehabilitated the way coffee has—from Folgers to those eight-dollar concoctions that send me running to the toilet. Frappé, crappay. It's all about the origins—you get people to care about the past in the present. The coffee plantations—they give luxury tours now. But tea has no swagger. It's mothball soup. Earl Grey. Please.

God, I could use a good glass of wine. I'll order a case to the apartment. After all that talking, I told Bita I could use a nap.

The Revolution was twenty-seven years ago, and still we're living in an endless movie of *where do we go, what do we do?* It's easier to wait for someone else to figure it out. Maybe it's not Houman's fault he has no imagination—that was not demanded of young prince Houman in Iran. To be fair, think of how many bozos follow exactly what their parents do.

The door handle jiggled. Bita walked into the room and threw something at me in bed. "I wanted to give you a few more days to settle in but—"

"Watch it," I said. "What's this?" I picked it up off the floor. A letter, posted to me in Houston, opened and then Scotch-taped shut. I recognized Houman's messy scribble—he'd crossed out our Houston house and written Bita's address over it in a blue felt pen. Just thinking of his usual pen made me sick and also a little homesick.

I stared at the envelope. Sent by "Superior Court of Aspen." Double the postage and time stamps. I spun it to the floor as the UFO it was.

"You should open that. It's probably your summons. When do you want to meet with Patty? I bet you'll need to have an initial conference with the court—maybe they can do it over the phone since you're not local. Also, I don't want to scare you, but Patty is concerned about your green card."

"My what?"

BITA

"**WHY DO BAD THINGS** happen to other people and I think about myself? That's my focus ultimately. Me."

I told Jamie this in our second session. "You're human," she said. "We all do it."

"We're all assholes?" I said.

In our third session we started talking about my childhood. Of course we did. It felt appropriate since Auntie Shirin was here and seemed to be never leaving. She took up so much space. But I had a part in all that too.

"I remember the bad things the best. So predictable, right?"

"Go ahead," she said and wrote in her notebook.

"I was around eleven, sixth grade. In L.A. It was 1989." I told her how at school, there were a lot of Hollywood kids, but I didn't know that then. I didn't know who ran Paramount, I didn't know anything about *The Godfather* or whatever films fathered new gods. Like they could do no wrong—and of course their kids too, even if they were the worst kids, which they usually were. I was the only Iranian at school. We were early adopters, allowed entry into something special, supposedly.

THE PERSIANS

I wanted to paint a picture for Jamie, so she'd understand. I didn't want to lie. Not like Shirin who exaggerates everything. But therapy, I was learning, was a bit like performing. Telling a story, then attempting to make sense of it together.

"We were up at the top at Mulholland," I continued, "where it was like a desert. Chaparral and yucca, snakes and lizards but also a neon-green football field and every morning we had to pledge allegiance to the flag." I put my hand on my heart.

Jamie laughed. I was on a roll.

"America is such a baby, don't you think? We were all babies. The kids, the teachers. The only things that were old were the snakes. It was the end of the Cold War. There was Gorbachev and his big birthmark. That movie *Red Dawn*. I wasn't one of those kids who had regular nightmares of nuclear holocaust.

"There was one Black kid in my grade. Not one Latino. This was L.A. El Pueblo de la Reyna de los Angeles." I laughed. "Our classrooms were in temporary trailers spread across this big flat piece of land cut into the mountain. Our headmaster was a drunk, flirted with the kindergarten teachers. I have no idea why the school was so popular.

"My teacher, Mrs. Randall, had asked us to write about our backgrounds with the aim of showing how America is a melting pot. A patriotic assignment. Hardships that a family faced, especially in their origin countries—potato famines and whatnot, welcomed in America, and eventual success. It was going to be a lot about German, English, and Irish settlers, I guess. They probably wouldn't know very much. What were they going to say—we descended from Iowa? The Great Lakes? Yet somehow they talked about their histories in glowing ways, no matter what their backgrounds. Farmers, criminals, bus drivers. Mrs. Randall called it 'Family Chronicles.' Here I am, this little kid, thinking I was going to be successful at this because I had a very good story to tell. I interviewed my mom and dad and aunt and grandma—

none of whom wanted to talk to me. I mean, my family doesn't like anyone knowing their business."

Jamie watched me, smoothing her perfect skirt with her perfect nails—something I now relied on, enjoyed. It gave me space.

"My aunt said to me, 'Oh, Bita, we were like royalty without actual power. Like Princess Diana. Heard of her? Don't tell them that. Your friends won't like that. They don't want to know about our family.' My grandma said, 'I have many books of stories from my life—but they're not for telling.' My mom just went on about the former prime minister Mosaddegh and the 1953 US-led coup, the CIA. She was watching the news, her mint-green mask over her face, eating popcorn from that big ceramic bowl of hers. Looking like a skinned avocado.

"So I ended up writing whatever I had heard about how I came from this great man. Not about moving to America. But about my ancestor the Great Warrior. I was so naive. He was famous for fighting in battles sort of like the Civil War but for the future of Iran, during our Constitutional Revolution. When he and his army entered Tehran from the North on these big black horses, the people marched behind him and cried he should be king. They tried to crown him. But he believed in democracy so he refused. He said there shouldn't be kings, not even good ones. I was writing about how we were really pro-democracy people. Maybe unconsciously I thought it was my greatest chance of being accepted by my school, by America. Am I talking too much?"

"No, no. Not at all. Take your time."

I told her about the famous tapestry that captures his march to Tehran. "He's on his horse and people are surrounding him as far as the eye can see. The sky is dark with thick clouds. There are so many people. Thousands. They look like clumps of cotton—the cavalry in tall white hats.

"As a favor to the people, he accepted the job of prime minister.

And he traveled to France to learn more about democracy. But then there was a new Shah who didn't like my great-great-grandfather. And so they took his money from the bank and attacked his men. He went into a great depression and one day he poisoned himself."

"Wow. You knew about that at eleven? You were very young to be aware of so much."

I nodded. Therapy was an ego boost. "They didn't watch what they said around us kids," I said. "And they're dramatic. When they were upset about something, they'd say things like 'kill me now' or 'I'm finished' or 'bury me fast,' things the Great Warrior supposedly said. It seemed normal, I guess.

"I also wrote that by the time my grandma was born our family wasn't as important. I knew how much people liked a story of downfall. The Shah, especially I think the last one, took most of my family's land and gave it to the peasants. Still, as a child, my grandmother was like a princess. The peasants respected her grandfather, the Great Warrior. So they'd stand at the side of the road and sacrifice animals at her feet. Now she just lives in a regular old apartment in Tehran. She owns the land that her father gave her, a tiny fraction of what they once had, but she can't sell it. The corrupt government won't let her, and so it's not worth anything.

"I was proud of myself. I thought I'd done a good job explaining where we came from and who we are. I remember her so well, Mrs. Randall; she had this stiff hair, and these huge glasses. She read my paper, called me to her desk. And she humiliated me."

"How?"

"She said 'The assignment was to write a true story. This is all fiction.' She had seen Iran in the news, the embassy and the mullahs, all of that, and she knew there was no democracy there. She said this loudly and everyone heard. 'Bye-ta' she called me. I can hear her now. I had so much trust in her. Speaking of gods, I thought these teachers were gods. How else did she get to be a teacher in America? These kids, too, in my class with their blond hair, blue eyes, and French braids, they were everything I wanted to be. With their stupid ham and cheese sandwiches and Hawaiian Punch. Do you have any idea what I mean?"

Jamie nodded.

"Of course they didn't care about this famed history. I mean, she maybe told me it was nicely written and sounded like a fabulous tale, but that I needed to rewrite it and tell the truth."

"How did that feel?"

"Devastating. I was good at school and I could tell that my intelligence was something the other kids hated me for. Like, what is this weirdo doing getting better grades than us. It was like that for the Japanese girl too. Kanako. I just remember staring at my fingers and in that moment I even hated my thumbs. They always looked weird, astronaut shaped, like space helmets, and they were even more disgusting to me then. I ran to the restroom and cried." I paused. I looked at the box of tissues but I felt no tears now.

"Bita, that's a painful experience to have at a young age. That teacher was unfair to you. It makes perfect sense that you continue to seek approval from others."

I nodded.

"Did you tell your parents what happened?" she asked.

I shook my head. "How could they understand?"

"Did you redo the assignment?"

"I wrote what I knew Mrs. Randall wanted to hear."

"What did you write?"

"How when we first moved to America my parents bought little American flags at a gas station. On the Fourth of July we sat on the carpet waving them in front of the wood-paneled TV set. How *Saturday Night Live* and Bill Murray and *M*A*S*H* taught them American humor. Eating hamburgers at a Texas diner made such an impression on Dad. 'Why do they call it hamburger and then ask if I want cheese. Isn't that a cheeseburger?' Dad would say. He was so focused on stupid inconsistencies that nobody else noticed. I poked fun at us, put America first. I got an A."

"How do you feel about that, your new version?"

"Like I was putting on a show to get them to like me—but in their way." I looked up past Jamie to her wall of certificates. Was I doing that now too?

NIAZ, SORRY IT'S TAKEN so long to call you back. Things have been crazy. Shirin is still here. I don't know what she's doing. She thinks somehow New York will save her but I don't know what the plan is. She's going to fancy department stores and just sitting in the cafés waiting for rich Persians to approach her but they are not doing that! Remember when you said imagine if she were in Iran? Well, you must be psychic because my friend is saying there's a chance they could deport her. But Shirin is either in denial or too scared to face it. She yelled at me for ten minutes when I brought it up. Maybe you could tell her how her life would change dramatically in Iran? If only to scare her into getting her shit together, her story straight for the trial . . . if it actually goes to trial. The best PR in the world won't help her if she fucks this up. We're hoping they'll accept a plea for something lesser like public intoxication. Sorry, I know you don't want to be involved.

SHIRIN

"WE'RE GOING TO PARVANEH'S funeral," I said, balancing a cup of terrible coffee on my knee. It had been one long week of mostly sitting in Bita's apartment, rearranging her furniture and taking calls.

Martin and Tony had finally gotten me on the phone with Mrs. Eskandarian and Mrs. Riani. Individually, of course, but their message was the same. They did not want their names associated with mine. It was not good for their reputations, they insisted. "Shocker!" I'd said to Martin and Tony, mimicking Bita.

The Riani wedding was a lost cause, but with Mrs. Eskandarian the path was murkier. She'd implied contractual breaches. I told her that I was consulting with legal counsel myself and to think hard about whether she wants a party that will guarantee her son a revolving door of girlfriends for the next five years or not. In the background I heard young Cyrus whine: "But, Mahhhhhhhm." An average Persian mother cannot resist such a thing, so I knew it was just a matter of time.

The remaining clients would fall in line when a few of them went my way. Like Marty's dominos, but the reverse. And then there was Bita's friend Patty. She was still going off the deep end telling me maybe they'd send me back to Iran and that I better do everything I can to get the charge minimized. And then to not get convicted.

"Did you touch him?" Patty had said on the phone.

"You mean did I get my hand on that furry mountain? In a crowded nightclub?"

"I just mean did you lay your hand on him."

"I threw my drink at him."

"Are you sure it didn't slip from your hands? Look, this is all very serious and I get that you enjoy being outrageous but you want to make it sound like he really came on to you and you were the victim. Not the other way around."

I had gotten through a case of wine and a carton of cigarettes in under a week. Would having to go to Iran, "being removed" as they say, be the worst thing? I was suddenly toying with that, but I couldn't really believe it would happen. I've been too good a citizen for too long; well, I guess not an actual citizen. "America doesn't want to lose me," I said on the phone to silence and Bita's death glare.

But now, Bita, at the dining table, looked up from her laptop. "Parvaneh?" she said. "How do I know that name?"

I rolled my eyes. "Bita, we need to meet Ali Lufti. Let's go see what he's been up to."

She stood up as if standing would help her understand. "Why would you want to go to a funeral, and now?"

"You've never been to a Persian funeral before—your mom didn't have a proper one—you don't know what you're saying. A funeral is when the truth comes out, when everyone comes out of the woodwork. All the secret lovers, all the people the dead cheated with, or on. It's spectacular! A real shit show, as they say, and it's only a shame that the dead aren't there to witness. But I suppose that's the whole reason it happens. Nobody has any shame once you're a corpse. The shame melts away. This one better be especially good—she's been dead for over a month—can you believe that? Khatm is supposed to happen on the third day. Now they'll be ready for the extra juicy shit."

Bita folded her arms. "Okay, whatever. If it's such a shit show, do *I* have to go? I'm busy, Auntie."

"Busy doing what? I've noticed you've hidden your schoolbooks in my room."

"Have you ever tried therapy?"

"Darling, I might like the silly words they use but a therapist isn't going to help us. Your problems aren't because Mindy and the girls stopped sharing their potato chips with you when you were ten. They are deeper than that. You are like a thousand-year-old sick tree. You need a miracle."

Bita stared at me. "Worry less about what I need and focus on your case. You sure you don't want a more experienced lawyer? I mean, Patty is my friend but she's never practiced law before. She's totally green. Do you know what that means?"

"Yawn," I said. "Patty will be fine. I don't want any more attention on this than there already is. I don't need a Johnnie Cochran or a Kardashian mucking around. With them would come more looky-loos and swindlers. And that cop liked me. I know it. No bargains. This is like small claims court—sure, maybe with a ten percent chance of being deported. The real issue is my reputation; this little case isn't the main event. You don't think I've been through much worse than this?"

"You get this charge expunged, and you can fix your reputation. You get found guilty, it's over, Auntie."

"Of course, my little lawyer-in-training. Fine, let's do a face-to-face with Patty ASAP. But this funeral is important, too, and you are going. And listen closely."

"Yes, Auntie. What?"

"You may not think it now, but you may have the urge to say something cruel in front of these people. Do not indulge that desire. It might prevent other more interesting admissions. Go get dressed." I clapped my hands.

"It's now?" Bita said.

"We'll bring white roses. Get ones with tight petals, so they don't look too sexy for the occasion, straight as a stick, saw off the biggest thorns." I imagined a row of them lined up horizontally, dead bodies in shrouds.

SEEMA

SCHOOL WAS JUNK BECAUSE I was too smart for it. At twelve years old, I'd read Plato, Homer, Tolstoy, Shakespeare. But teachers are focused on behavior, and even the other children's mischief was uninspired compared to mine. Who cared if Jahangir didn't do his French conjugation homework, if Roya accidentally broke the teacher's desk. I stole the final exams and distributed them to the class because I disagreed with measuring us like we were in a race. It was a useless race, one meant to pit us against each other. I preferred people with oomph, by which I meant with purpose and a spark. Like a Kennedy or a Marx. Little did I know it was all child's play; all of it, Karl, Mao, John, Ringo, the revolutionaries, even Nounou—nobody knows what they're doing. We're all making it up, some of us better than others. I'd find out soon enough.

I raced to the attic as soon as I got home from school but the big door at the very top was shut, so I knocked. "Nounou, Nounou joon, I'm back!" I called, out of breath, overdoing my panting for show, but there was nobody to notice except myself.

"Let me in," I said.

Nothing.

"Let me in, or I'll have to break the door," I said. "You know I don't care if you're naked." I called as loud as I could.

Still nothing. I turned the knob and pushed. It had been an entire school day, eight boring hours and I didn't remember anymore the morning of lingering in Nounou's bed. My dreams of Nounou dying weren't in my thoughts.

The door to her room creaked open. I waited for Nounou to come towards me. Nothing. I scanned the room, took in its edges, and smelled wool, hand cream. Her windows were shut, which was odd as she believed in airing out a room during daylight hours, no matter how cold. She'd wear ten layers and catch frostbite over living in what she called an improperly ventilated room—"a dungeon" she'd say. "Why would I want to breathe dead fish? It's like drinking your own urine." She had oomph and was the opposite of every other adult who spoke of almost nothing except for drafts—they were all terrified of drafts. Now I walked around in circles.

"Nounou joon, where are you?" I can hear my little girl voice now: "Koja-yee digeh?" Digeh made it rude, but I was impatient. I walked over to the private bathroom and heard running water. My feet grew wet. I watched as my gray socks blackened, the water creeping towards my heels.

"What's going on? Nounou?" I called.

My feet heavy, as if flippered, I lifted one then the other. Nounou once let me bathe fully clothed, my dress clung to thighs, sucked onto me. I liked the feeling as much as I hated eventually peeling the dress off, its fabric reaching back to grasp at me, heavy, wanting.

"Nounou?" My voice resonant in the hollow.

The lights were flickering and the old bathtub was overflowing. Where was she? I flopped back into the bedroom and to the far side of the bed—the only place out of sight. On the floor, below the small table, there she lay. Nounou joon, in her black mourning dress, her head tucked into her knees. A large object hung off the edge of her bed: the big metal lamp—wrapped by its cord around the bedpost, then around Nounou's neck.

The funny thing is, I didn't scream. I crouched down and shoved her body. She was so heavy, as if waterlogged. She spilled over onto the rug, spreading out. The dead have no shame. Her eyes were open, the whites expanding, mouth slack. Her silver hair a thin fishing net over her face. The black cord twisted across her neck like a slash.

I am amazed how easily an image comes to me that I tried my whole life to protect, that I put a barrier around. When my mind would approach it, starting down the path of finding her body, the lamp cord, I'd push it away. So it was always half experienced, half shadow. But then, also, this image, this moment with Nounou became mine, a part of my deepest core, my special secret. One I feared but also loved because it belonged to me. Us. That last moment together. Like I had been part of the decision. The plan whispered into my ear.

Then all at once, I was overtaken by urgency and stumbled downstairs in my drippy wet socks, leaving a trail. I saw Abbas Ghassem, the cook, and told him what had happened. He put his hand on my mouth until I stopped. Then he walked over to the kitchen table, mumbled into Nanny's ear; she froze midstitch over a pillow and then the two rushed to Elizabeth's bedroom, dragging me with them.

Elizabeth stepped onto the landing screaming about her interrupted work. Green paint covered her fingers. What was she painting all this time? We never saw any of it. I held my ears as Abbas Ghassem explained until all together, the three crowded into me. In a circle, they yelled, waved their arms. I pressed my fingers hard over the stiff nibs of my ears until I felt blood pumping inside my head.

"What are you imbeciles doing? Go find her!" Elizabeth shouted. They looked at one another and left as one.

THE NEXT THING I knew, my face was having a bath. I was lying on Big Dog's bed, which was an old folded-up blanket in the corner of the kitchen floor. Big Dog was licking me all over. Had I passed out? I didn't move. I let the dog go on, have his disgusting fun. His tongue rough sandpaper, his warm saliva cooling my face as it evaporated. Abbas Ghassem walked into the kitchen holding a big broom and Big Dog shot off in the other direction. He shoved me on the shoulder with his slippered foot, and then with the broom. At the stove, he hugged a giant metal pot in his arms, lifted it off the fire. Abbas Ghassem was not burned by hot things.

"Dinner is ready, Miss Seema. Luckily you were asleep so you didn't destroy the meal. For once." He snickered and shuffled away.

"Where's Nounou?" I called. "What happened to her?" Maybe I dreamt it. I laid my ear on the cold hard floor.

LATER THAT WEEK, I overheard Abbas Ghassem rehash the whole story with the little Armenian maid, the parts I'd missed, as if Nounou's death were a television show they'd seen. After she yelled "Go find her!" Elizabeth herself, with the cook, Nanny, and the maid now in tow, ran to Nounou's room. At first they, too, missed her, and Abbas Ghassem threatened to beat me with his wooden spoon for playing another trick on him. "And I would have enjoyed every second of it," he said. But then Elizabeth tripped over Nounou at the far end of the bed. She fell over the corpse and broke a fingernail. In between cries related to her nail, she instructed Nanny to resuscitate her. "Go on and make her breathe again. What do you exist for? Hurry!"

Abbas Ghassem detached the cord from her neck and neatly arranged the lamp on the table. Nanny blew into Nounou's mouth. Nothing happened except Nanny nearly fainted from her effort. Just like heartbeats, everybody has a limited amount of air in their body, they say. Some use it for talking, Nanny used it for disciplining children, I used it to power my brain. "Breathe, Nanny, breathe," the others yelled. The little Armenian maid, apparently a genius among them, spoke up and said, "Let's call Doctor Borzadeh." "Great idea," they shouted back.

Doctor Borzadeh rode over on his bicycle—with his dark bushy mustache, his twinkling eyes, his pink cheeks, he howled when he saw what they had done with Nounou, which was to put her face down on the rug with her air passages blocked. "If she wasn't already dead, well, you people surely finished her off!" He hopped back on his bike and left them to blame one another.

Next the group called Daddy. Elizabeth was not allowed to call Daddy at work, as a rule. Both my parents were so insistent on their privacy from the rest of us—and from each other. This was around the time they started sleeping in separate bedrooms, an arrangement I thought I'd like if I were unlucky enough to ever marry.

So, when Daddy picked up, he whispered in a tone he used when angry that Elizabeth was a no-good distraction who had no respect for him or his work. Elizabeth promptly hung up, swearing she'd never speak to Daddy again.

"Cook!" Daddy said when he phoned back. "What is this nonsense about? You would think my mother has died! And how dare she hang up on me?"

"Can you believe he guessed it," Abbas Ghassem told the little maid with a smile he was trying to control. "Makes you wonder if this was planned. It's too perfect." The maid pursed her lips. "I wouldn't be surprised. They're ruthless." The two giggled and together they continued reliving the day. Elizabeth ran up to her room and shut herself inside. The useless turtle. Daddy came home, his face sewed tight, marched straight to Nounou's attic. A minute later, too little time to have even picked her up off the floor, he returned downstairs and sat at the telephone table as if he were making business calls. The telephone was too important a machine; it required solemnity, composure, detachment. An avoidant's tool for a task that begged for heart. He made a dozen calls and planned the next day's funeral. It was a point of pride to get a call from a family at its most vulnerable, an insult to be spared. A person most notified of the demise of others was one to admire.

LYING ON THE DOG'S bed, I wiggled my feet. They were dry and in giant wool socks. Were these Elizabeth's socks?

With Nounou dead, I was now truly alone. My siblings were nothing. My father loved me but he was always too busy. My mother hated me.

I shut my eyes tight, squeezed until I felt my eyelids suck into my face. It felt good in a way, like those wet clothes on my thighs. A hug of my eyes. At the same time, I clenched my butt. I stiffened my neck, curled my toes inside the scratchy socks. This was the time I started doing all that. I don't know how to explain it. It was a response. It made me stranger and even more alone.

Sitting up against the kitchen wall that day, I thought of the kings who were poisoned. I pictured them sipping a goblet of poison stirred into wine like syrup. That's how I would do it, but in the comfort of my own bed. None of this tying a cord around my neck, collapsing onto the floor. Nothing so degrading.

I squeezed my eyes some more.

The idea that Nounou joon wasn't happy had never entered my supposedly advanced brain. It was more surprising to me than her death. Of course she was going to die—she was old. People don't live forever, I knew that. But her unhappiness killed her, not her age. That was the revelation. I wasn't too young to consider other people's unhappinesses. I knew of Elizabeth's, Daddy's, my own. But Nounou? She was happy. She fed baby birds in the garden out of her own mouth. She sewed dresses for all the girls in our extended family. She sang songs in Russian that only she understood and danced to Persian folk songs. What did Nounou lack? What is to be happy, what does it look like if not like Nounou? Does it require romantic love, being known, having influence? Nounou had none of that. For some, isn't it enough not to be sick and starving? Isn't it enough to be a person, cared for in material needs, left alone with her thoughts, nothing demanded of her? Obviously not. It was then that I knew my life was in trouble. Before that my unhappiness was just kid stuff. The kind I assumed I'd grow out of.

AT DINNER, WE WERE silent. Daddy had a big success at work and the cook had prepared his favorite fesenjoon, a stew for a celebration. He served it anyway; why let the elegant sweet and nutty sauce go to waste? Maybe it was a celebration. Daddy home early after all. Elizabeth smiling in ways I never had seen before. Like she was playing hostess to a party of murderers. "Please, welcome, have a seat, a drink, don't kill me," her face said. The maid and Nanny were given the night off for their bravery—a first in our household. Nader poured Zamzam into his stew, and nobody protested. Shirin picked up the serving spoon and filled her plate for the second time, and then a third. Elizabeth didn't call her a cow.

I honestly didn't know a lamp cord around the neck could do it. I suppose we find ways. The man without a lamp uses a fishing line.

The woman without a poisoned drink slits her throat. The body gets what it wants.

Daddy kissed my forehead before he sat down at the head of the table. I wiped brown sauce off my lips. I needed to show him I was strong. That I deserved the kiss. That Nounou strangling herself wasn't some kind of problem that needed to be dealt with outside the usual family way. That, as Nounou told me, I could give in where it didn't matter. I was sure Daddy had made up a lie to tell his friends about how she died. *Of course, she died peacefully in her sleep. You know how it is at that age, the body stops.*

The phone rang. Nobody budged.

"I'll get it," I sang. Ready to perform my daughterly duty, show Daddy my worth.

"No. Nobody answer it," Daddy said. He rose, lifted the handle of the black plastic telephone and dropped it back onto its base. He pulled the cord out of the wall and climbed upstairs again.

A FAMILY OF WASHERS was upstairs in the attic. What was Daddy still doing there? It had been an hour since he left us at the dinner table. Their job was to clean her, prepare her body for burial. The family was a man, a woman, and two grown daughters. They'd brought their own buckets, towels, and soap. They needed four hours. Elizabeth insisted they be gone as soon as humanly possible.

I wondered how it compared to bathing a live body. Whether Nounou's body felt cold, if it had blown up and stiffened yet. I'd read about this process. Who would clean her bottom and breasts—and would the man hide his eyes, or was this a time to see flesh as just a thing like anything else?

Nounou's room did not know she was dead; the large beams still hung overhead and the animals scurried around in the walls, their sharp little claws scratching the wood. Were they expecting Nounou to open her drawer and rub cream on her hands? Push the windows wide open even in the cold? What would they think when the breeze never came?

And what of the baby birds?

And what of me?

At the dining table, Shirin perched on Elizabeth's lap. Shirin was the only one to ever sit on our mother's lap—even when Nader and I were infants it was Nanny's job to be the warm vessel. Still, it was rare; I hadn't seen their bodies linked in years. As if it were the most normal thing in the world, Elizabeth played with Shirin's curls as she drank her glass of vodka. And I could almost feel something inside her recoil from Shirin's touch.

The old stories, the traditional ones Nounou told me, say that for at least a year Nounou would not be fully accepted into the world of the dead. She would need our strength and support, our remembrance, to make it there, to protect her from evil spirits. By this, death brings the family closer.

Here, in this new empty country, my back straightens. How long have I been here? I sit at the lip of a pond unknown to me, arranging leaves according to size. Then again by color. Then again by beauty. I have nothing but time here. Is this what Nounou meant when she said, "You need your family in life and in death"?

"Aren't we supposed to be fasting?" I said then to Elizabeth and Shirin. "Praying? Doesn't she need us to?"

Is my family holding me, are they giving me their strength? Is this limbo of their making? This country is not my final home. I saw Bita, Teymour, and also Shirin at my bedside just before my death. I beheld their faces. Are they failing, my family?

Elizabeth scowled. "We don't follow those ancient ways." She snapped her fingers and Abbas Ghassem came to clear the table. "I'm going to my room," I said. Instead I walked up to the attic, knowing which wooden boards to skip so I wouldn't be heard. The man—the father—was standing outside Nounou's door. Dead flesh was still flesh.

The women were packing up their tools at the far corner of Nounou's room with Daddy watching. I imagined them different looking from regular people—extreme stature, elongated, see-through skin. But they were ordinary. Except all dressed the same, in plain brown clothes without buttons. I imagined their shirts sliding off.

White towels stuffed into buckets, I didn't look to see if Nounou soiled them. Bottles of clear solution lay on the ground. Various sizes and shapes of brushes, combs, unfamiliar metal implements. Some families did this ritual themselves—we were too modern.

Nounou had taught me that after death her soul would linger around the family for three days before starting its journey. I wondered where it was. Nounou, the body, lay on the bed wrapped in white cloth, only her face meeting the air. The room smelled of ladies' perfume and grass. Candles were lit on the two night tables. The lamp was dark.

I don't remember the three days I lingered.

Daddy and the washers spoke. He handed the mother a pile of money. She refused. Daddy kept pushing the money towards her, and in the end he folded the bills and inserted them into her coat pocket. He also gave her the final dress Nounou had worn. The mother bowed and the family left.

I had never seen Daddy cry—would he now? I closed my eyes, but all I saw was the blood glow. I squeezed until I hurt.

Daddy grunted, "I know you're here."

I walked out of the bathroom.

"Sit," he said.

I settled down on Nounou's bed, next to her feet, which moved gently, up then down.

"Not there you idiot." Even then, his voice was caring.

"Sorry."

I moved to a wicker chair in the corner. Daddy sat in the chair next to me. His arms, the way they rested on each other, reminded me of thick cuts of bread.

"Here." He handed me a small blue stone with writing carved onto it. "You are to put this under her tongue."

I hovered over her. I smelled camphor—like mothballs but woodsy. Nounou's tiny red Koran lay on her chest and I felt relieved Daddy was heeding ritual. I pulled open her mouth and lifted her tongue. It was still wet and soft, like something I'd find in the garden. Her eyes were also covered in the white cloth. I wondered if they could see anything at all. I did as told and sat back down.

"Listen carefully," he said. "You are the smartest one. I will tell you this once. I won't repeat it. You are not to share this with anybody, including your mother. Do you understand? One of you needs to know. Because I won't be here forever."

I nodded. I looked at the lamp.

"Your great-grandfather, the Great Commander or Great Warrior, as they deem him"—Daddy spoke in a low tone—"he was not great to everyone. He killed the men in my village. Handed their stuffed heads to the king. He was a double dealer that man, a secret king lover. He was no great commander." Daddy laughed in anger. "Your great-grandfather was a scoundrel and a murderer. Like anyone with power."

"Don't say that," I said. "The Great Warrior loved our country and people."

"Yes, yes, that's what you've been taught. Only a few people know the truth. It's written in books, in plain sight, but everyone ignores it. His suicide was just a way to distract us. One day you will understand. Don't trust anyone who anoints himself great. If he were really great, we would just call him Babak," he said.

"If this is true," I said, "he didn't kill you, Daddy. Why not? You're alive, aren't you?"

"You know who he did kill?"

"No," I said.

"My father. He was loved and they murdered him."

I breathed in and couldn't smell the camphor anymore, though I knew it was there. So Daddy married a woman descended from his father's murderer.

Daddy stared out the window. "You think my mother lived with indignity because I married your mother? I say she was victorious—in the end who conquered who? She was healthy, well cared for. Didn't she tell you?" I watched Daddy's face contort. "Didn't she sing you songs and teach you to sew?" He looked at me with hungry eyes.

You don't believe it yourself, I wanted to say. I said nothing.

He stood up. "I can never forgive her."

"She was happy," I said. A person saying that black was white.

"Good, good. That is what we will say. There was no discord. Remember, Nounou had a weak heart." He turned around to Nounou. "Open the windows to let in some fresh air," he said and pulled the lamp by her bed out of the socket—just like the phone—and carried it under his arm out the door.

After he left I stood over the bed. I watched her, waiting to see her body move, for her to sit up and, like always, tell me a story. What use was life if it simply stopped one day? I pushed her body. You can't even talk to me anymore. I pushed again. It moved only due to my force. "Talk," I said. I hit her head. Her mouth.

Shouldn't her soul be floating around somewhere? "Where are you, Nounou?" I said. "I know you're here." I looked up in the rafters.

I wanted smoke to be over my head in the shape of her. To form a long trail and curl across the room. I wanted her to test me—to tell me, smiling, with those large black gaps of her missing teeth shining, that

149

of course she killed herself because of this horror and that I needed to defend her. To tell the world.

But she didn't come. "I'll give you sunflower seeds. I'll give you anything," I said to the roof. Nothing. The candles on the two tables flickered. How could she have loved me, with the blood of a killer inside? How could anybody?

BITA

"YOU CAN'T WEAR THAT to a funeral. It's an insult," Auntie Shirin said.

"You said we hate this woman," I said.

"Doesn't matter. There are rules."

My clothing was spread across the living room, which now served as my bedroom because I'd given Auntie Shirin my room. I had no choice—if I hadn't, she'd have told the whole family I treated her the way American adults treat their parents. I'd basically have put her in a home, thrown her out with my garbage.

"Auntie, I won't know what to say to these Iranians."

"These Iranians are human beings. You talk to them like a human being."

"Next time, give me more notice." I flung the magenta sweater she rejected so it landed half on the coffee table, waterfalling onto the floor.

Auntie Shirin gave the sweater a look. "Really, Bita?"

I shrugged. One's twenties is not the time to be neat and clean. I needed messes, adventure, near-death. I had a long way to go. "What do I wear then. All black?"

"You need to look like death, but chic. Don't you have a black suit? What is wrong with you?" she said and went back to my room and slammed the door. "We leave in thirty minutes. Chop chop," she yelled from the other side of the wall.

Black suit. I had the navy one for law firm interviews. Never worn outside the Brooks Brothers' dressing room. I peeled it out of its nylon case in the hallway closet.

Thirty minutes later, Auntie Shirin returned, twirling her large black cat-eyed sunglasses, face full of makeup—white powder, black mascara, red lips—hair like a movie star. When did she have the time to curl her hair? It had looked nothing like that thirty minutes ago. I stared at her. I was always stunned by her beauty, those dark eyes and all those glistening edges. She made sure her hair color never had even a glint of red under the light, which she saw as cheap and silly, receptionist hair.

Auntie Shirin smirked. "You look like a bank teller."

"Shut up, Auntie."

"Didn't I ever teach you how to wear a suit?" she said.

I looked at her outfit. "No law firm would hire me dressed like that, Auntie. How are you dressed for a funeral?" I said. Shirin wore a tight-fitting blazer with gold buttons barely fitting across her chest, a Madonna-like bustier, pencil skirt, sheer black tights, and Louboutin heels.

"This is showing my respect," she said. "You are saying, I just left work at the bank, and didn't bother to wash my face."

Despite these comments, I was relieved by her appearance; it said to me everything was right in the world. Shirin woke up in the mornings, spent two hours in front of a mirror, examining pores, spraying hair. Like the comfort I took in looking at photographs of people taken a hundred years ago, so well dressed in wool suits and stiff hats, leather shoes with hard soles. It gave me confidence in their lives. I remembered how it was the same with Jamie. I found it oppressive at first, and yet later felt like I needed it—her careful outfits, her effort.

"People will be judging you by what you wear. Your brain doesn't matter there. Let me help," Auntie Shirin stood in front of me and opened my top buttons, fanning the collar out so that my neck was exposed. She rolled the sleeves of my suit jacket. "Hold on." She went back to her room and returned with a skirt so short it was more like a wide belt. "Change that for this." She shoved it at me.

"Wear the leather booties. You're young, no varicose veins, you don't need stockings," she said.

I pictured the seam women used to draw down their calves with eyebrow pencil. Both sexy and heartbreaking. I didn't feel like an argument, so I left the slacks pooled on the floor.

She wrapped a long gold chain twice around my neck and stood back and smiled at her work, arms folded. I felt mildly choked. "There. Now you look ready to grieve. Let's vamanos," she said. In the mirror, head tilted the same direction as my hips, I looked like a nerdy call girl.

THE FUNERAL WAS AT a French bistro on the Upper East Side.

"Who has a funeral at a restaurant?" I said.

"Who do you think? Persians," she said.

We sat in the cab. I'd let her do my makeup and it felt strange being dressed for a club but headed to see a dead person.

"Do you know anyone who's going?" I said.

"There wasn't an Evite, Bita," Auntie Shirin said with some exasperation that felt unfair given the circumstances. "They're all probably old enough to need a funeral themselves. Your dear auntie just wants to make an impression, which will be automatic, and speak with Ali Lufti. I hear he keeps to himself—hangs out with Americans. I'm sure they're more accepting of his background or else they're pretending—Americans don't like to admit their undemocratic ways."

"Does Maman Elizabeth know we're going?"

Auntie Shirin laughed. "Are you kidding? Apparently she's barely keeping herself together in Iran. Washing machine broken so she's soaking her clothes in the bathtub."

"Why doesn't she get it fixed?"

"Old age? Grief? Who knows. No money? But she won't let me give her any."

"Hmm. Why isn't Mo coming with us?"

"Bita, enough with the interrogation. You'll tire us both out before we even get there. Save your energy; usually, I don't speak for a full two hours before a big party. Three for a funeral because there's always more talking at a funeral. We don't have the option of dancing or drinking too much or blowing them off—at least not without looking disgusting. When I die, make sure everybody is miserable. I don't agree with all that American nonsense about having a funeral be a celebration—I want people sad, crying their faces off, ripping out their hair, and if I can hear from my casket, I do not want laughing. People are ridiculous these days. I want weeping, bodies prostrating themselves over me. Okay now, no more talking. We need our energy."

She clicked the cabbie's window with her nail tips and pointed to her box of cigarettes.

"Anything for you, angel," he said over the speaker, watching her in the mirror.

She grinned and lit a cigarette and blew it out her open window.

I looked out mine, listened to the engine until we arrived.

Shirin paid him from the back and he winked. Outside, she straightened her blazer and then used her finger to wipe up along the bottom corners of my eyes. "Your cat eye was drooping. Anything in my teeth?"

I shook my head without looking, and she grabbed my arm.

"Don't fuck with me," she said. "This is not a joke."

154

"You have some invisible spinach in there," I said, putting my finger in between her front ones. They felt slimy.

She slapped my hand away.

AN OLD MAN WAS at the door. He was thin with a stately nose, thick eyebrows, and a head full of silvery curls. He wore a black suit with a gold medal on the pocket. I could tell he had been very handsome when he was young. He knew it too.

I smiled and he smiled back, eyes sparkling. He had strong teeth. I tugged at the hem of my skirt.

"Good afternoon," Auntie Shirin said softly, squeezing his hand. "My condolences. If it's not a bother, we are the children of a friend of Parvaneh Khanoum's. Our mother is in Iran, sadly. Could you please show us our dear Agha Ali Lufti?" Shirin said, all in Persian.

The man smiled and nodded. His cologne fumes were strong. Had he doused his entire head? "Shirin?" he said. "I'm so happy you're here." He spoke in a soothing near-British accent.

Auntie Shirin looked surprised. "Do I know you?" I laughed because for a second he did look familiar, like when someone from a distance appears to be waving to you but isn't.

"Oh, you look just like a Shirin I know," he said. "Please take your seats. The ceremony is starting. I can show you to Agha Lufti afterwards. Please." He winged his arm towards a row of empty chairs.

"Come," Auntie Shirin said to me. She bowed her head to the man.

As we sat, Auntie Shirin spoke, "What a creep. Did you get a whiff of that? Not a funeral smell—more like a *coucher avec moi* one."

"Come on. He seemed fine."

"He probably thinks I'm here to put my claws into Ali Lufti, the poor old bastard. I tell you, Bita, out of the woodwork."

In the small dining area, the tables layered with crisp white cloth were moved to the edges of the room. Drinks and food sat sweating, separating, wilting. Artists playing waiters stood in the spaces between and behind the tables dressed in black suits with white shirts. Rows of seats faced a podium and an explosion of white flowers, embellished with Parvaneh's name scrawled in big loopy letters on wide velvet ribbons. The "P's" were curled out at the ends. It had the air of a graduation ceremony, which in a way it was.

The seats were all full except for the last two rows. We sat in the back row, which was empty except for us. No one was trying to hide, or no one wanted to look like it. The audience was mostly old and in all black. A few children. One very small girl wore white, dressed for the wrong occasion, or not—maybe children are supposed to be in white, to set themselves apart. So far from death, usually. A cluster of younger women adorned themselves like Auntie Shirin: red lipstick, perfectly coiffed hair, quilted Chanel purses. Several men wore nearly identical black leather jackets, one cut like a blazer, but most wore regular suits.

"What Persians are these?" Shirin rolled her eyes.

In one corner, an entire congregation of non-Iranians huddled as if quarantined, though which way the disease moved was unclear. I had a feeling it went both ways. They were well-dressed but differently: below-knee-length skirt suits, double-breasted navy blazers with gold buttons, the women blond, chins up like they were all related to the Kennedys. Unlike the Iranians loudly talking and giving each other wet lip-sticked, perfume-scented kisses, they were not moving at all. They sat, thin lips stiff, pink skin, hands folded over laps, watching the empty podium as if at any moment someone would pop out of thin air and start the show.

This was my first funeral since Mom's. Hers was small, at our house. Maman Elizabeth didn't even come—she was too distraught. Niaz stayed with her in Iran and maybe it was better she didn't see Mom, or at least Mom's casket. But where was Parvaneh? Shirin sat staring off into the giant white bouquets as if discovering Jesus or Mohammad—except he had no image—in a cloud.

At the front of the room, a tiny old man stood and smiled. Then as quickly, the smile vanished when he woke up and realized where he was. He shuffled off to a few laughs.

"I knew that wasn't him," Shirin whispered. "Mommy would never have gone for *that*."

"Where's the body?" I whispered.

Shirin cackled. "Bita, we're not at the burial. That is intimate and has to happen within a day. Her body's eating itself now. This is the thing when people stand and talk. You don't have to know her to come to this. This is for the public. For show." Shirin kept looking around, angling her chin, shifting in her chair—as if she was trying to lure people into staring at her, to gawk and admire, but nobody was taking her bait. "I'm not impressed with these people at all," she said.

The curly-haired man from the entrance approached the podium. He thanked everyone for their support and said Parvaneh would be touched by the large attendance.

Auntie Shirin sneered. "Bastard."

We forced ourselves through a dozen or so people giving speeches. First adults about my age—the grandchildren—read from folded printer paper.

"Maman Pari was the most selfless person I knew. She never once asked me for anything. She only gave." Or: "Oh, her cooking, I'm hungry just thinking about it." Or: "When I turned sixteen, she gave me her favorite ruby necklace." Bullshit like that. Either it was true, which made her look pathetic, or more likely, it was untrue and they were liars conspiring in the myth she created around herself. It was their way of pretending to honor an old woman but really asking for our pity.

Then her peers delivered what were clearly not prepared speeches—

but these women had experience with funerals. By now they were naturals: "Here we go again," amid flowery weeping. One woman with thick legs and a colorful silk scarf added that she and Parvaneh weren't speaking at the time of her death. She tugged on the scarf. Explained how Parvaneh had betrayed her by not inviting her to a party at her house, but that all is now forgiven and that she bet Parvaneh wishes she hadn't left out her oldest friend. That sometimes it was too late, as it was for Parvaneh. There was mumbling in the audience: "Is this a time to settle scores?" I heard. A boy grandson, who looked like Mo with his gelled black hair, slunk from his seat and pulled at her scarf until she, all false smiles, tottered off.

Several more old women spoke, all looking more hungry than sad, sneaking peeks at the spread on their way to the podium, disappointed and disassociated, speaking so close to the microphone that we heard every mucous-filled breath. "We *meess* you, Pari joon, we *meess* you." It was bad acting. Or, good acting in movies made real life seem poorly done. It was like that when Mom died—at her tiny funeral too. Shirin who read her speech from notecards, wooden like she'd never been before.

The room got hotter. The rustling and discomfort spread. Old people whispering like teenagers. It had gone long enough for everyone to think about their own deaths.

When I was ready to run to the bathroom and hide until the end, Ali Lufti took the microphone again.

"He doesn't look devastated," Shirin muttered. "Big surprise. That's why it's important that your husband die first. Never forget." She pinched my side.

"Ow!" I wanted to unwrap the chain and throw it at her. "I'm sure he's sad, Auntie. He just doesn't feel like crying in front of everyone he knows."

"Thank you so much," he said, looking out into the rows. "Thank you thank you. I don't know what to say. This is extremely difficult. Of course we will all miss her. We are destroyed yet humbled. Roohesh shad." He bowed his head and walked off.

"That's it?" Shirin said. Everyone was rising, lining up for the lunch.

"Of course I won't die first," she said.

"I hear the food here is normally delicious," a man said to a woman as they walked, arm in arm. "Let's hope it's the regular fare and not some cheap funeral buffet."

"Shhhh," the woman hissed. "We deserve to eat well after that. Don't worry. The restaurant has a reputation to uphold."

"Don't even think about it, Bita." Shirin shoved me. "We're not eating. We talk to him and split."

"I could use a snack. Come on, Auntie," I said.

"I'll be sick if I have to watch these people chew their cold pasta." She grabbed my hand. Ali Lufti was talking in a circle of men. When they saw us approaching, the men each took a step back, like a dance troupe. "Please, be our guest," one said. The rest joined the chatter: "Don't let us get in your way. Don't mind us. We are nobodies. Just a couple of old guys. Mister Nothings."

Listening to them was embarrassing me. I wondered why they did this.

"See," Shirin whispered. "They don't even know who I am. They think I'm a girlfriend. Or you too maybe, looking so sexy."

"Shhh," I said.

"You can stay," she said to the old men, with a hint of flirtation. "This will only take a minute."

The men looked disappointed, but then stepped in closer.

She turned her head and her demeanor. "Agha Lufti. My condolences. Again." She nodded, slow and grave. I had seen her talk like this in Houston once before when speaking to a friend of Baba

Roshani's. But then, she smiled in a way that let me see her real self bleeding through. Shirin, breaker of rules. She lifted her eyebrow, tilted her head. "You. I know you, Agha." She used the formal "you" but pointed at him. I looked at her finger, lingering. "You knew my mother when you were a boy," she said.

The man smiled. "Yes. Hello, Shirin. You're even lovelier than your pictures."

Shirin squinted. "What pictures?"

"Your mother sent me a few pictures over the years."

Shirin folded her arms. "Oh, really? I don't believe this. Why would she do that? That good-for-nothing—"

"And you must be Seema's daughter. My poor girl. Her life was too short. You are just as beautiful. Come, come."

I stepped closer to the man. For the first time glad to be wearing the outfit Shirin had chosen for me, the chain hanging off my neck, so unserious. Ali Lufti pulled me into a hug.

"Long long ago," he said, motioning to an imaginary distance, which when I looked was the HVAC vent on the ceiling.

I tried to wiggle gently out of his arms. Shirin scowled so I stopped and let him hold me.

"You see," he said, smacking his lips. "I was a dear friend of your grandmother's. She was a princess when I was a student." He looked at Shirin and then turned to his circle of men. "Gentlemen, this is the family of Saeed Roshani and Elizabeth Valiat."

"Valiat?" one of the whitest-haired men said with a cruel smile. "You can't mean the descendants of the Great Warrior?"

"Oh, not that again," Ali Lufti said.

"The Great Murderer more like it," said another man, dark with round tortoiseshell glasses.

"Sorry, Khanoum." The first man smiled at Shirin. "If we can't tell the truth at a funeral . . ."

"Now now, Hamid. Those old tales are so passé. How dare you be this shameless in front of these beautiful ladies," Ali Lufti said. "Do you forget? We have a lot to thank him for."

"If you were from ten or twelve families. Come on, Ali. You can't be serious. Pardon me, but how as a young idealistic man, one foot dipped in revolution, did you attach yourself to that evil masquerading as good? It was bad enough they were your employers."

"Leave him be," another one, bulkier than the others, said. "It's not the time." He pulled up his pants by the belt buckle.

Ali Lufti looked over at Shirin. He took a deep breath. "Just ignore them. Look . . ." He walked closer to us and we backed away a few inches. Softening his voice, looking in Shirin's eyes, he said, "Why don't you and your niece come to the house for tea. That will be better for everyone. We can talk. But thank you for coming, my dear." He clasped Shirin's hands with both of his. "May the memory of my dear Parvaneh live in you, as in us all." He leaned his head down and kissed her hands as he cradled them.

Shirin smiled, her face exposing something new—a kind of anger mixed with confusion, an emotion I couldn't read, perhaps a sentiment I'd never seen in her before. Gratitude? "Of course we will."

"I'm famished. Let's eat ice cream!" Ali Lufti turned and said more loudly to his friends, clapped their shoulders. He then looked back at me. "You must try it before you leave," he said and grinned, a fool with a sweet tooth. I smiled out of courtesy.

WE SAT IN A cab headed back downtown. I noticed I was holding my breath for long stretches. Shirin lit a cigarette without knocking on the cabbie's blurry plastic screen. He twisted around while pressing on the gas and shouted, "Lady, what the hell?"

We lurched forward.

"You want the fare or not? I'll give you double."

He exhaled. "As you wish."

"Shirin," I said over the cabbie honking his horn at everything, "what were they saying?"

"Nothing," Shirin said. "Haven't you ever heard of jealousy? Coming from nobodies, all of them. You heard them. They can't stand it when someone around them has real history. No great man didn't kill people. Whoever the Great Warrior killed, I am sure there was a fantastic reason."

"So he did kill people?"

Shirin shrugged. "Probably."

"What, so now we're the descendants of a murderer? And he, this murderer, is where we got our wealth?"

"Life was more complicated then, Bita. Don't act so surprised. If I had planned that funeral, you would have seen caviar, chilled vodka, the works. Those men were secretly impressed with me, I know it. Wait for them to tell their wives. And their bosses. Can you believe they were serving ice cream in the winter?"

NIAZ

DESPITE WHAT SOME MIGHT see as bravery and confidence, inside I was always that baby on the doorstep.

At university, I had even fewer friends than before. The girls didn't even look my way. It was always the guys who noticed me. For this, I liked them better.

In my chemistry study group there was a guy named Morteza. He was the opposite of Kian. I would learn that many people choose lovers in this way, by reacting, the pendulum swinging, maybe it was to try and forget, and also not forget. While Kian was soft, lithe, light in color, Morteza was dark, stocky, built like a bull. He had thick eyebrows and a square chin, a shot-putter's legs.

Guys and girls were taught in separate rooms. Later it became separate rows. But they planned group study dates. It was an easy way to flirt. Parents and guardians bought the story for the most part and opened their homes to these rituals. The roles to fill were notetaker, teacher proxy, assistant interrogator, and several pawns to present answers. But when the mothers were in another room, the students winked, pinched, tickled, nudged. They kissed.

Somehow I was invited into one of these groups—I knew it was not any girl who invited me. Maybe Morteza. I had held his stare on the campus plaza once. I was sitting on a bench reading a book. Unlike all the other girls around, talking and laughing, I was alone. He drank his tea and watched me. I can't know for how long. When I noticed, I watched back.

"You can manufacture the feelings you want," Morteza said now, across from me at a table. Our science books were wide open. "If you're sad, or depressed, take this powder. If you can't sleep, take that one. God would agree." How did he know to tell me this? Couldn't a person like to sit alone?

Morteza was studying chemistry so he could make MDMA. His cousins in Miami, who'd been to all-night dance parties, told him about it. "It makes you forget the bad and feel the good," he said and unfolded a paper scribbled with instructions I didn't understand, diagrams of molecules, arrows connecting them.

"I don't want to feel anything," I said.

"I don't believe that," he said. "I promise it'll change your life."

The girls at the table, all with blowdried and highlighted hair, dark-lined lips, eyebrows cut sharp like knives, now looked my way.

MORTEZA—WITH HIS BIG SMILE and promises—had his way of finding drugs even if he didn't yet know how to make them.

A group of students took over an empty apartment near school. All its walls painted blue. It smelled like paint and cigarettes, and when the windows were open, car exhaust. We didn't have study sessions with nosy mothers watching anymore. We told our families that the apartment belonged to Homa's parents, only there was no Homa.

"This is not taryak. It won't make you a sleepy loser," he said next time. We sat together on the smooth sofa in the Blue Room. Tannaz and Siavash from school were fucking in the bedroom with the door locked. Surrounded by blue, I felt like a fish underwater in a tank. This didn't feel like home, and I was glad.

I wanted the drug. My heart beat faster as the rest sat at the dining table playing cards. Morteza slipped his thick fingers into mine and with his other hand pressed a tiny pill to my dry lips. My mouth opened and he dropped it in. I tasted its bitter outer layer before he handed me a cup and I swallowed the pill with a gulp of homemade vodka. He watched, then took one too. "May it nourish your soul." Morteza said the phrase uttered before a meal, as if we were eying a platter of sabzi polo mahi.

Niaz, breathe, it's okay. You're safe. After a half hour of fidgeting, sitting on my hands, humming a song, there was a moment when it all stopped. Then something. A lot of something. An intense feeling of wellbeing, of being awake, like nothing I'd known before. The substance moved through my spine, my brain, carefree, dreamlike, in waves that pulsed. Anything was possible.

MORTEZA AND I WERE each other's guinea pigs, experimenting on each other, seeing if a pill would bind us. The last time I'd tried to attach myself to someone, I failed. No matter how much I licked his body, he left for America. From the start my mother didn't let me get too attached, like she knew all along if she let me drink milk from her tits she might be mine forever. Only Nestlé formula for me.

This time would be different.

Morteza wanted to know what and how much would ruin me. Secretly, that's what everyone wants to know about everyone. What and how much will ruin you. And between lovers, the hopeful answer is *me* and as little of me as possible. He didn't admit this, of course not. If I asked what he wanted, Morteza would say, "I just want to know, when will you start having fun?"

I wanted my mind to be free. Wasn't that the point of this drug?

Morteza smiled with his rectangular black eyebrows, soaked into the sofa, and tipped his head back like a Zippo lighter, an object the boys all wanted, it being American. Flashy, optimistic, wholly unnecessary. His big, warm body in bellbottom jeans and an unbuttoned-at-the-top denim shirt, chest hair spilling out, jangling silver necklace and rings, his ponytail. He took over whatever he touched, made it his. Like with me, he pushed against me, wanted to wrap me up. But I pushed back.

Where we sat together on the Blue Room sofa was where everything happened from now on. The hair on his chest swirled and took me in. His big, warm superfluousness. What could I say? I wanted it. But still I tried to protect myself from failure by choosing someone like him, someone I laughed at.

"Do you feel it?" he said.

I answered by showing him my bellybutton. Just like that, I lifted up my top. It's round and deep with a hood at the top. He showed me his: T-shaped, flesh poking out. I said my bellybutton is deep because I'm here to take things in, and his protrudes because he is there to give. Like a cathode and an anode. Lying on the sofa, on top of each other, I tried to fit his bellybutton into mine. It looked like fucking.

Morteza was a feeling machine. He wanted to feel good, thus he took drugs. While on drugs, he wanted to feel the drugs, thus he danced. He wore a jar's worth of pomade on his hair, a hard shell, glistening like a plastic motorcycle helmet, ponytail squeezing out on one end. He shaved his arms with my pink razor. Favored tight shirts that showed his contracting muscles—he was a young Popeye.

We sat back up and he dimmed the lights and played me the KLF's, "What Time Is Love (Pure Trance 1)." Smuggled from Germany or England, I don't know which. He had cousins in Berlin and London. So many cousins. The music entered my ears. It had a physical presence, which was the only way to think of it. A digital hammer punching me softly, and I considered getting up but I didn't. Public dancing was illegal and I'd never danced at home. Morteza got up, cracked two glowsticks, and handed them to me. Reluctantly, but feeling loose, I stood and closed my eyes.

I was very high now, my whole body throbbing. Hearing the menacing theme of the song, I thought of a police chase. I felt myself playing the lead actor, hunting the weak, the frail, obeyers of the regime. The tables were turned, and the police were the purveyors of fun. I was moving my body in this room, tossed back and forth by these strange blades of sound. A persistent unending beat. I was a machine of the music but also human. The music was a machine but it housed, revealed, and trickled feeling and soul. I opened my eyes and started to whip the light of the glowsticks into circles and squiggles, following the trails as they interacted with the sound. On and on we went. Like maybe we would never stop.

"Wow," I said after. I felt the quiet, the darkness of the room. It was quieter and darker than any room I'd been in. Morteza smiled. My life had changed.

AT BLUE ROOM PARTIES he performed just for me, thick shoulders in his stretched jean shirt, and twisted the sticks—he was a gymnast, a breakdancer, a dervish. I couldn't help but fall for this clown. Glowsticks pointed straight at me, then behind his neck, then shaping flowers of light. He was my personal spectacle. "If more people did X, we'd have world peace," he actually said once.

I was moved by people with strong, sincere beliefs. I laughed still. I took his drugs, listened to his music. To see if it would make me more like him, which I believed would help me. In the yellow light, an interior dusk lit with candles and other young people, I told my life story to strangers. The whites of our eyes glowed like tigers'. We grinded our teeth, we shivered, held hands, and rubbed shoulders in bending centipede lines. I massaged sweaty T-shirt backs. Sometimes I danced. My movements flowed out of me in echoes. I had never spent so much time with so many people. Not until the next day would I realize my jaw ached, and I didn't remember the names of any of my new best friends.

In the beginning, I said "I was abandoned at six," and watched each face transform into a circle of pity. They didn't care that I was left with my grandmother who fed and clothed me, paid for my gasoline, ordered my braces. My parents left me and took my younger brother. Chose him. That mattered to these strangers who knew too much about me because I let them.

With these Blue Room parties I was an event planner long before Shirin. But I was more. I started to believe that we were creating hope, a new religion. We called ourselves "Hippy Irooni." The Hippy Irooni eluded the United States because they were never fighting real monsters; no one took away their right to speak. In Iran no one except the Shahs had that right. Only the kings could say anything. And now the Supreme Leader. So no. *We* were the ones who need peace and love—not the Americans.

On a phone call a few years later, Bita asked me: "Don't you know that 'the land of the free' isn't free for all?"

She was right. Niaz, don't be so provincial. You're embarrassing yourself.

I WOULD SLEEP AT Morteza's house and tell Maman Elizabeth I was staying at my girlfriend Tannaz's to study engineering. Maman Elizabeth was no fool. She nodded, made sure I packed my toothbrush and hand towel, placed them on the table by the door in a small case. Soon, I found condom packets folded into the towels.

But then a sickness, like something from my past saying not so fast. These drugs made me knobby-elbowed thin, like the fourteen-year-old European models in the illegal fashion magazines. I touched my shoulders, which felt like knife edges, looked into a mirror at my sunken eyes. I finally looked pretty. Soon, as if I was never a Hippy Irooni, the side effect became my entire reason. Ecstasy was as much a replacement for food as it was a mask for the dangerous truth of my own drug-free feelings. It happened fast.

Maman Elizabeth said: "Bah bah bah, Niaz. You look stunning." She hadn't complimented my appearance in years. "Come, aziz, and play a round of cards." She invited me to sit with her. What did she want?

"Twenty raisins, one yogurt, and all-day tea" was a menu I recorded in an old notebook of poems. I logged my intake:

One apple, small. Cored.
Bread and cheese, two bites each.
Dolmeh, three, spaced across a day.
Tea, black, endless pool.

I felt not only poetic and intelligent, but also spiritual, attaining higher states of being. I was beyond food, transcendent. Body fat was fluff, for those with no willpower or ambition.

At home with Maman Elizabeth when Morteza was busy, I was mad I even had hip bones; my silhouette wouldn't curve inwards like those European models. I would never be like them unless I sawed off bone. So I panicked. I stuffed myself with khoresht, wet meat, tahdig, rosewater ice cream. Mounds of food down my throat. It exited in explosive shit.

Being too happy was scary. Had I ever been that? Happy, calm. Just meant that loss was around the corner.

My period stopped and so did using condoms. Morteza didn't question me, of course not. He wanted no barriers between me and his penis. He wanted me to be as close to him as physically possible without cutting himself open and putting me inside him. He called me his "life force." He looked at me with those big apelike arms dangling by his sides, his giant eyebrows, and I thought, why am I fucking this idiot? And yet, there I was, and I even thought of those arms and eyebrows as mine.

ONE AFTERNOON, WEARING SOME new twelve-year-old-sized leopard print pants in the kitchen, I absentmindedly ran my hands over my thighs and then ass, to dry them off when washing dishes. My butt was a flat tire.

"I would die for this figure, Niaz. You got all the thin genes of our family. I suppose it's only fair given all the rest." Elizabeth seated at the kitchen table, engaged in her habit of shuffling cards for no reason.

As she shuffled, she continued, "The fashionable women in this world look just like you. Move to America, to Hollywood, stay with your Auntie Seema, Niaz joon, and be an actress, no problem! You don't act. No problem! Acting is secondary there, there's no art—it's about the look, the bones that are so beautifully lit on film. Niaz joon, just tell me, how do you starve yourself? Because, please, let's be honest, you are starving yourself. Aren't you? It can't be natural. Teach me. No matter what aerobics I do now, I retain this puff in my face. See?"

She pinched her cheeks, creating a constellation of pink blotches.

"An actor is a blank page. That's not me," I said.

"Oh really, Miss Ideas. Who are you then?" She kept squeezing.

"Come on. Stop hurting yourself," I said. "Throw out those magazines."

"This is nothing," she said, rubbing her cheeks. "I'd slice off an arm to be like you. Donate a kidney. Our family, unless we go to extremes, we have round bottoms and hips and never-thinning faces."

I thought of my fantasies of bone cutting.

She threw the cards onto the table. "Help me, Niaz joon," she said.

She was serious. I knew from pictures that Seema and Shirin were more Marilyn Monroe than Kate Moss, but they were both beauties. Sure, my grandmother was chubby the way a healthy woman was chubby—she had hips and thighs, large jiggly breasts. Women are meatballs, not dental floss. Not that I cared or accepted this reasoning. What was good enough for others was not good enough for me. But mine was not that different from a million other weight loss regimens.

Maman Elizabeth lit a cigarette and, neck bent, watched the tip redden as she took a puff and then the smoke when she exhaled. "Smoking's the best way to stay slender and beautiful without trying too hard. It's a lie that it damages the skin. I haven't seen it. Did Audrey Hepburn ever look ugly? Our exiled Queen? Revolution and war was the best thing for my figure, but that's over. My problem now, Niaz joon, is the rice—I can't just have one scoop. Cigarettes or no cigarettes. Who can stop at ten spoons of rice—rice is made to be consumed, to expand in your belly and form a nice comfortable coating in the lining of your organs, to love you. Like no other. No person. Nothing." She coughed and laughed at the same time, wiped her mouth and offered her box of cigarettes.

She didn't know better; she thought she saved me. I didn't want her to punish me by taking away the afternoons we sat together at the kitchen table making art. Me, poetry. Her, paintings. So, I accepted the cigarette, the first invitation into her adult world. She'd liked the cute little girl me, and now maybe the grown me. Not the one I'd been in between. Soon the entire kitchen was sheathed in smoke, and I lit more cigarettes and drank tea until my throat was scorched and I could barely see her face.

"What's your secret?" she repeated.

"Rice doesn't love you. But I take a pill that does, and it makes me love, too, it turns on my feelings for good. When it wears off, I crash, I'm suicidal, but the thing is, then my appetite is still gone for days. That's my trick, Maman Elizabeth. I don't eat when I'm the extreme version of happy, I don't eat when I'm the extreme version of sad."

"Shame on you." She slapped the table. "You're taking a magic potion and not sharing with me? Me, who feeds and clothes you," she said, exhaling. Smoke clouded the room and she held out her hand.

"Like I said, it has some side effects," I said.

"I don't care," she said, her hand at my nose.

From my pocket I drew two small dusty pills and dropped one into the middle of her palm. She threw it into her open mouth, swallowed some cold tea. I took the other one.

After a few minutes, she said, "I feel nothing. This is stupid. And worst of all, I'm hungry." She got up and took a plastic bag of herbs out of the refrigerator. She chopped onions and mint and parsley. After twenty minutes, she swung around and faced me. "Khob. I need to sit." She smiled. Then she really started talking. And she's already a talker. I chewed the inside of my cheek and tasted blood.

"Oh, Niaz, I feel *good*. You know what good means?" Her eyes rolled around her head and she sunk farther into the chair. Together we sat, and she rubbed the table back and forth. Discovering it.

"Me too. Normally, invisible chemicals control your behavior, but with drugs you control the chemicals that then control your behavior."

"Bravo, Niaz. Always so smart," she said and took my hand and we walked to the old sofa. She played Shohreh's "Omadi" on her little tape deck. I was impressed with her instincts. We sat back and listened. The flute was like ancient birdsong. A rolling beat dropped in. It was a song from before 1979, of course it was. She didn't listen to anything new. Shohreh's beautiful plaintive voice was begging, needing, loving. Maman Elizabeth did a Persian snap, both hands in the air. Her bracelets jingled. She stood up to dance. I swayed my shoulders and watched.

She was wearing a red tracksuit with white stripes down the sides that Auntie Shirin sent her through a cousin—did she send it as a joke? Maman Elizabeth looked like a tomato, but as I watched her dance, she was a flower in bloom, full of secret attractions. She played games and lured people with her nectar. When she was serious about exercising, which was almost never anymore, she put on a clear plastic visor over her roosari, along with this tracksuit, and her old white Dr. Scholl's and black socks, draped herself in her manteau and speedwalked the streets. I was in love with her, this surprising woman, as she danced in circles.

"Niaz, I was wrong," she said, undulating and waving her arms. "You are an actual fool for not eating food. It's because you are young. How is it that these young tasteless people want Mars bars and McDonald's and American candy! Yeck! No wonder you can give up food so easily—you don't know what food is! You've forgotten! See, people are pigs. Rosewater, saffron, walnuts—these are flavors of the gods. Not peanuts! Peanuts are the simple cousin of the walnut. You put salt on them and you can eat them forever, but walnuts have depth, bitterness, texture, and they look like your vagina!" She giggled. "Saffron is a true spice that transforms, remakes. Aren't I right? Do you see? Will you give up on your fasting? You can't be an artist and starve yourself—those are opposite inclinations."

Back at the kitchen table, she straightened the deck of cards in her hands.

"Wait, what am I talking about? Just kill me already. I am talking too much."

She shuffled the cards midair and they landed in a neat pile. She did it again, faster, then slower. We were hovering, then we were sitting. In my brain, the sound slowed down to the flip of the single card, the beat. I heard a drum machine, closed my eyes, nodded my head. I opened my eyes to Maman Elizabeth slamming her hands down onto the table so hard that she knocked off her glass of tea. It hit the tiled floor and shattered. The sound was loud and beautiful, cascading. Maman Elizabeth's pupils were huge, taking up her entire face. We looked at each other. I laughed and she laughed too. Between the two of us, there was a vapor of feeling, a wire of meaning. The drumbeat of the cards pulsed in my veins even as the cards sat right in front of me, motionless. Our messages reached each other without any effort and created a new thing outside ourselves. I'd never felt this way with anyone. Not Kian, not Morteza, not Shirin. Not anyone.

Suddenly, a person was a different possibility. I reached out my hands and we grasped each other. We held on. I was wading in a warm pond of our making, face up to the sky.

"I like food," I said slowly, smiling. "I just don't love it. You know? It's boring. It's structured by need, and there's more to life than wake up, eat, shit, and sleep."

"Oh, Niaz, is there really? Food is life." She shook her head. "Sure, I complain about my weight—a woman's curse. But I would never really give up food. It would be worse than giving up my children."

I laughed. "When was the last time you saw your children?"

"You are my child," she said and let go of me. "Look. Be honest. I know you have a boyfriend, and I don't care. What do I care? When I was your age, I had a boyfriend too."

"My age?" I tried to catch her gaze, warming up my hands on the table, pressing them down until the heat of my flesh absorbed into the wood and then traveled back out into me, a beautiful circle of energy. "I thought that boy, what's his name, was long before Baba Roshani.

174

When you were a girl in your little sundresses?" I hummed as I enjoyed the wood table.

"That's when it started. I was a teensy-weensy beautiful girl of sixteen. A little younger than you and—"

"Don't, please don't. I don't want to talk about Morteza."

"That's a good strong name. A peasant family?"

"Mommy!"

"No, that won't do. You won't call me that when I tell you this. You won't even call me Maman Elizabeth. Light me another cigarette."

I held out the lighter until she puffed smoke. One for myself too.

"Niaz, I am about to tell—"

"I'm ready."

THE NEXT MORNING, YESTERDAY was a dream and my memory a trick. Maman Elizabeth was whisking eggs and drinking tea, sucking rock candy.

"My head's a volcano. What did you feed me?" She scowled. "I'm not your playmate. Don't do that again. And forget everything I said. I made it all up. You hear me? Everyone likes a good story. You want eggs for breakfast or not? I'm only making them once. I'm not your maid."

"Yes, please." My stomach dropped. We both had headaches but that was all that we shared. The special mist between us had vanished. I knew there would be repercussions to being her confidante. I should have told her not to tell me.

I sat at breakfast, chewing rubbery eggs, sipping lukewarm tea, and fantasizing about what could have been. My grandmother without her restrictions. Me without mine.

"You can't swallow a pill and make your problems go away, Niaz. You'll get addicted, maybe you already are. I insist you stop this poisoning! At once. Even if you look like a Hollywood starlet." Maman Elizabeth said this from the kitchen counter, refusing to sit for breakfast. She'd removed her tomato tracksuit and wore a long wool skirt, a buttoned shirt, leather wedges so tight her bunions looked ready to burst through.

I nodded, crushed.

"And I'm sick of this fashion of revealing emotions. It's no good, Niaz. You feed your bad energy by focusing on all your miseries, you never get over them. You are too obsessed with misery, my darling. You must accept and move on. Accept and Move On. A.M.O. That's how I do it. Forget the past. Focus only on the future." She folded her arms across her chest.

She had a point. But if she hadn't told me about her past last night, would I even know her?

ELIZABETH

AFTER THE ARGUMENT IN the courtyard, Elizabeth didn't see Ali for five years. She married Saeed Roshani, the kind of man she was born to marry. Thirty years her senior, nearly dead. A man, despite his blue eyes, she could almost ignore. Their only sex happened once per month, when her weather changed, and only in order to make a child. That was the beauty of it. It was predictable. Yet after five years and sixty-three penetrations—there was no baby.

She improved at sewing and never drew her first love again. Drawing and painting were threats to the choices she'd made.

Ali, meanwhile, moved the pieces of his life along the board. He found support in the circles of knowledgeable men—"philosophers," they called themselves. Men who sat around and discussed important affairs. He was now one of them. What love? What hurt? Ali had his own students, questioned how the country was governed, and men listened. He learned to assume he was smarter than other men, as then they generally believed it.

Elizabeth overheard shards when Baba talked to Fereydoon, his driver who was Ali's father. Ali's success, his promise. Did Baba do it for her benefit—but why? When he spoke of Ali, Baba's voice was changed: a new question mark, an intrigue, something she wanted not to hear.

Elizabeth was always bored. Good girls weren't bored. They busied themselves with the tasks of life, dull duties that occupied their hands. But not Elizabeth. If she died tomorrow, nothing would be lost in the world, and this pained her. She blamed Ali for this feeling. In the mornings, she would lie in bed longer than proper. Long after Saeed left for work. The sun and her thoughts warming her body. Oh, the way Ali ran his weather-worn fingers, the fingers of a brute, through her silky hair. The contrast between soft and rough excited her those early days, made her crazy—and her old husband, Saeed, was a baby lamb.

Ali Lufti was still inside her.

On Thursdays, Fereydoon's younger brother, Mehdi Gholi, drove Elizabeth to the bazaar and walked behind her as she shopped. He did her haggling—for caviar, silk sleeping masks, French porcelain—and she'd nod and point like a queen. He knew never to walk in front of her, or to touch her—not even to lead her away from a cheat or crook. On the way to market, Elizabeth sat bored in the back of her father's maroon Chevrolet, staring out at the unknown world. What if she stepped out and never came back? What if she vanished? There was so much time for thinking, it was agony.

She bit her tongue whenever the urge arose to ask about Ali. Today, her tongue fought back. "What ever happened to that boy of Fereydoon's?" Elizabeth said, trying to sound as uninterested as possible. She yawned. She was a bad actress. But in those days, even the Shah was seen driving around Tehran with women who weren't the Queen, and the Queen, it was rumored, had her own distractions.

Elizabeth met Mehdi Gholi's eyes in the mirror. The second his look registered in her brain, she turned away. She needed to appear more innocent.

"What's his name again?" she said.

"You've forgotten?" Mehdi Gholi said. "Most common name in the universe, but a most uncommon creature. You were friendly, Madam. His name is Ali."

"Oh? Do you know where he lives?"

"I *am* his uncle." He laughed. "Of course."

"Take me there, why don't you? I have a business proposition for him." She paused for a breath. "Baba knows all about it. Nothing to wag on about."

Mehdi Gholi said nothing. He turned the car around, glided through the streets. Elizabeth knew she should be thinking: What are you doing you idiot woman? Instead, she felt calm—like a small, white cloud. In five years, she'd come to believe the story she told Baba as truth: that she gave Ali up out of duty. And now, still childless, she questioned this duty.

"Give me an hour," she said outside Ali's building.

"What if he can't see you on short notice?"

These men kept tabs on her. It never ended. In the end, she would show them. "I'm not worried," she said and slammed the car door.

ELIZABETH WANTED TO FINISH what she had started. She didn't know quite what that meant. It was 1949. The war was over, but what was that to her as an Iranian woman in a garden? Big, angry countries with artillery fighting for pieces of the world. She knew only that the Germans were now fallen and the men were talking more of America. Yes, there'd been food shortages, rising prices, a riot about bread. Millions died from the occupation. But her life was the same. She was protected.

She pounded her knuckles against the big wooden door, then looked behind her. Mehdi Gholi waved from the maroon Chevy. The home was surrounded by a white stone wall—tall, indicating wealth. Ali had things to keep private and secure. Though thieves were rare when the price was supposedly amputation, a hand chopped off. What was the punishment for what she was about to do? She knocked again and the door creaked open.

No servant? No more steps to view the man of the house? She was prepared to climb a treacherous ladder or tell more lies, but there he stood. Ali Lufti. His beauty shocked her. In five years, his face had turned golden brown—healthfully charred, his cheeks covered in rough hair, his chin more angled, teeth blinding white, eyes like daggers. Hair aflame. She'd wanted his beauty to crumple, but he was even more himself. Elizabeth could barely look at him.

Ali wore a white shirt rolled up to his elbows like he was about to gut a fish. He was barefoot. His trousers were undyed linen. This was studied casualness. He wanted to be seen as "of the people." Elizabeth opened her mouth but nothing came out. He also said nothing. She brushed past him and walked inside, her heels echoing on the creamy stone floor. She'd dreamed of this a thousand times. He watched her and smiled. Maybe he dreamed of this too.

The house was dark, chandeliers unused, but light erupted from a room at the back. Elizabeth dropped her purse on the cold stone and walked across a grand reception into the room. There was a rumpled bed—that was all she saw. The raw silk sofas and oil paintings, the polished wood on the way in, she saw none of that.

She turned to him. "Ali. You made your bed for me. How chivalrous." She laughed.

"Always," he said.

"This house . . ." She waved her arm. "You can't be alone, can you?"

"Depends," he said. "You?"

She raised her eyebrow and took two steps closer. Ali stood still. Keeping her eyes on his, she unfastened her mink shawl and let it tumble to the floor. She kicked off her heels. Her dress luckily had no difficult closures—one by one, she slipped off its straps, pulled it to her ankles, and stepped outside its circle. Elizabeth stood bare in her silk brassiere and matching panties, the garter belt that grabbed at her tan stockings. She tilted her head and smiled at the man in front of her. She displayed herself to him, like goods at the market. He watched without a word as she lowered herself onto the bed, elbows propped, legs wide. She watched him back. Not shy about these things. Not anymore.

"Make me a baby," she said. She wanted him completely, their invisible parts to claim and colonize one other. It was nothing she'd felt before. Five years ago, she was just a child. Elizabeth closed her eyes, smelled the musk of his bedding. Ali shut the door and locked it. She watched his shadow crawl across the bare wall. He took the key and started tickling her with it, cold and hard between her legs.

In her ear, she heard old Saeed say his usual, "Don't forget to breathe. It won't work otherwise." She yelled: "Get this damn key out of me. I have enough sex with the foreign object that is my husband, thank you."

"Fine," Ali said. He removed the brass key.

"When I was a girl, you controlled me like a puppet when I drew you. I thought you were a wizard."

"Strange woman." He laughed, pulling down his trousers and throwing off his shirt.

With Ali inside her, Elizabeth stared at the ceiling and tried to feel everything, a first during sex. His penis against the outside-most part of her insides. The hair of his chest brushing her chin. What is supposed to be pure is created from an act of merging body parts that smell like urine, that live next to shit. Suddenly she saw that this is what made it beautiful. The creation of something sacred from the mundane, the un-holy. With her husband the mundane never moved beyond mechanics and slime. Right then, Ali so far inside, she thought, this was what made real art beautiful—the spirit that is created from the ordinary, everyday muck. Bad art remained just dried paint. And then for some time, she stopped being able to think. Her body, her mind submitted to feeling. Rising up her torso, descending down her legs.

Once she took the helm, she started to see things that were not there—she saw dolphins diving in and out of the sheets, which were the choppy sea. Above her on the ceiling, the sun shone. Currents swam through her legs. What a strange dream his part rubbing against hers constructed. Then the vibrations began, and they went on and on, stopping and restarting, until she could feel nothing at all. Afterwards, they rolled away from each other. She was soaked full of sweat, tears, semen, her blood hot and coursing right under the skin. She had never been happier or sadder.

She looked at him. "All those years, you never said anything about my nose. Why?"

"What's there to say? I like big noses."

Someone was pounding on a door. Elizabeth opened her eyes wider. They lay on their backs, their limbs now crossing like seaweed, lazy, salty, and wet. Reality returned. She sat up in the bed.

They had a secret.

BITA

AUNTIE SHIRIN TOOK OVER my entire apartment. First it had been her rolly suitcase and handbag, the clashing designer monograms. But then, a breezy purple fabric masking the venetian blinds in the living room, candles cropping up—the giant kind that cost a hundred dollars each—large ornate mirrors, leather floor poufs.

When I came home from school she'd be lying across the leopard print sofa, the one piece of furniture she bought for me when I moved to New York after college. Her feet would be up, toilet paper woven through her toes to keep the polish from bleeding. A mint-green clay mask covered all but her eyes and mouth, a towel wrapped over her head. A cigarette burning in a soap dish. She took so much care of herself.

"You have one good piece, and the rest of your apartment will reflect that sophistication," she had said. The sofa was now her office and it smelled of her too. Chanel perfume, face powder, leather. "Why do you insist on this drab pseudoliberal American goody-two-shoes life?" she'd say. However much she was taking over my space, I wasn't letting Shirin crowd my thoughts as she'd done in Aspen. Not here, not in my home. It was becoming obvious to me that we had entirely too much stuff. The way she'd just throw my clothes around the room to find something suitable for me or, on occasion, for herself. How she left her wineglasses on every surface—ones I never used. Purple rings multiplying on side tables. I started to donate some of my clothes. Shirin didn't even notice, especially with all the crap she was bringing in. "Wouldn't living with less help me see better?" I'd asked Jamie.

She shrugged. "What are you hoping to see?"

AUNTIE SHIRIN WAS WAITING for me, hand on hip outside Frankie's, one of those fancy fake diners with homemade Pop-Tarts. "Come, let's eat. It's freezing. Why's your hair wet?"

We were sitting at a table when Patty walked in. I waved.

"Well, well, well," Shirin said, Patty still out of earshot. "The famous Patricia. Has she been too in demand to see her favorite client in person?"

I rolled my eyes. "Call her Patty. And she's been trying to see you in person for weeks, you know that."

"Patty is a silly name," she said. "If she's working for me, I can't call her Patty."

"What about Tony and Marty?" I asked.

"I'm allowed to change my mind." When Patty got to our table, Shirin reached an arm out and presented the top of her hand like the Queen of England. Patty took Shirin's hand and moved it up and down. Shirin went along limply, then snatched it away.

"Have a seat," Shirin said. "I'm starved. Let's order one of everything. So, Patricia." She smiled.

Patty ran her now-free hand through her hair, which had a soft wave in it today.

Shirin cocked her head. "I have to get the most pressing question out of my mind. Bear with me, Bita. Is there ever a moment, Patricia, when you taste pussy that it reminds you too much of your own?"

"Auntie! This is not an okay thing to say."

"No," Patty said, perfectly calm. "Each pussy and, I've heard, dick, has its own unique qualities. Like a fingerprint or a snowflake."

Shirin laughed. "Now that is fascinating. I may have to try. I was always concerned it would be too familiar."

I frowned and looked at Patty. "I told you."

"You'll do, Patricia. For some reason I can barely ask Bita the weather without upsetting her. Waiter," she called out then turned to me. "There is such a thing as a healthy curiosity. You know, it is easier for the lesbians."

"Just ignore her," I said to Patty.

"I can handle it."

"Don't be rude, Bita, I'm right here."

"So what was your line of work before getting into the prostitution business?" Patty said, straight-faced.

Shirin laughed again. "Please. You have no idea how bored I was before I started Valiat Events. I don't do 'full-time mom.' There's no need to sit on the floor and destroy your manicure. Children need a nanny."

Patty smiled.

"Auntie. Not everyone can have or wants that," I said.

"You groan too much, Bita. Watch yourself. It's unbecoming, always shushing me. Telling me I'm bad. That's not the way to make friends in this world." She switched back to Patty. "Nobody wants to change diapers for their lives. Not even the nannies."

A man with an orange beard came to our table.

"A round of drinks—bloody marys, extra spicy, extra olives," Shirin said. "We are celebrating a new partnership."

"No, Shirin, we really need to talk with clear heads. Three coffees, please. And I guess some of those Pop-Tarts to share?"

The man saluted me and walked away. I put my napkin on my lap and ran through Patty's résumé—Legal Aid, summer associate at white-shoe firm, CPA. I could tell I was boring Shirin and let Patty take over.

"We've engaged a local lawyer to help as that's required. Our first telephone conference with the court, which you decided not to join, was quite a doozy. After a further review of the police officer's transcript from that evening, the prosecution has decided to add the charge of assaulting a police officer because of that drink you threw."

The waiter placed the coffees and Pop-Tarts in front of us and Patty continued. "You haven't taken the deportation scenario seriously, but you need to start, especially with this assaulting-a-peace-officer charge. It's a small risk, but you know how doctors talk about a small risk of something catastrophic? It's like that."

"Well, so, let's operate." Shirin smiled. "What if I have to go back to Iran?"

"Auntie, come on. Your life would be ruined."

She raised her eyebrow. "How is it not already ruined?"

I looked at Patty. "She's being dramatic. She doesn't believe that."

"I know you're pissed at this police officer," Patty said. "I just want you to control that anger when we appear in court. I think they are punishing you by adding this new charge. Bita told me you had an altercation with some other officers the day after the incident? At a crepe stand? That couldn't have helped. I really want to try to get you a plea."

"I don't want to plea. I'm innocent," Shirin said. "And I'm taking the stand, no matter what. They have to hear me."

"Well, I have some concerns about that, but hold on a moment." Patty looked down at her notebook and then rubbed her hands together. "So, let's go over this law together. If you were a US citizen, this wouldn't be an issue."

"No one has ever bothered me about not being a citizen before." Shirin put her coffee mug to her lips and drank.

"The thing is, Shirin, a green card can be revoked if a person is convicted of certain crimes, such as something called a 'crime of moral turpitude' or an 'aggravated felony.' After such a conviction, the government can start deportation proceedings. You are possibly guilty of both. Prostitution falls under a crime of moral turpitude, for sure, but you have two factors in your favor. One, you've had your green card for almost twenty years. This law I think applies mainly to people who've had their status for five years or less, but I'm checking that. Two, in Colorado, prostitution—attempted or not, doesn't matter—is a class 3 misdemeanor with up to six months in prison. Again, I need to do more research but I believe since it is not a felony, it isn't serious enough to warrant deportation under federal law. And immigration judges often waive prostitution as a removable conviction. But even if it isn't enough to deport you, a prostitution conviction might mean that if you left the country, even just for vacation, they might not let you back in."

"Ever? That can't be. I have an important trip to France this summer. Oh, this is good." She nibbled on a Pop-Tart.

"Well"—Patty raised her eyebrow—"that's why we need to beat this charge. It could also make it hard for you to renew your green card."

Shirin nodded.

"Potentially the biggest risk we face—"

"I face."

"You face is related to throwing that drink. Like I said, a green card can also be revoked if you're convicted of an aggravated felony. Assaulting a police officer in Colorado is a felony with a potential prison term of two-plus years."

"Two years?" Shirin said.

"Yes, and it expressly includes actions like"—here she read from her notebook—"throwing certain liquids such as blood, urine, or toxic or caustic substances at a police officer."

"That's disgusting, I did no such thing."

"They can argue that your vodka martini was a toxic or caustic substance."

"Please, it was completely watered down with ice."

"What's good for us, for you, is they would have to prove you knew or should have known he was a police officer and that you intended to harm him."

"Of course I didn't know he was a cop! Well, I mean, I maybe threw it when he told me he was a cop and said I was under arrest!"

"Okay. So we need to be very careful here. They still have to show that you intended to harm him."

"So I should say I didn't throw my drink?"

"No. You shouldn't lie."

"Really?"

"Well, did you throw it *at him*?"

She huffed. "I don't know. I was mad. Maybe I just wanted him to feel bad about tricking me. Of course I didn't want to injure him. I more smashed it on the table." She struck our table with her mug, making Patty and me jump.

A FEW DAYS LATER, Auntie Shirin came home and without removing her coat, she reclined on the sofa and rested her boots on the cushions, not noticing that the coffee table was gone. Or at least not commenting. When she took out a cigarette, I simply shook my head.

"We're having tea with Ali Lufti," she said. "I need more distraction, fun, and seems I can never escape tea. Advance notice, Bita, I'm giving you that. What would work for you next week, can you consult your calendar?"

"Just this once, okay?" I said. "How's Wednesday at five?"

"THE ONE WORD WE can't say today is, you know what," I told Patty after another evening of going over case law.

"The Persian word for sweet?" she said. I had taught her.

"At least for a few hours, I beg you."

Patty had arrived at the coffee shop in railroad overalls, a chunky beanie rising high above her head. I had been spending more time with Patty than ever before. So what if the main reason was Shirin, the time still added up. Since I got back from Aspen we had been trying all the pancakes in town.

"These ones are nine grain and the size of a big cast-iron pan," I read the unbleached paper menu.

"Sounds like we can split one?" she said. When it came steaming hot to the table she knew without asking I'd want the butter and the homemade blackberry jam on top. I inhaled the nutty and fruity aromas as Patty smoothed jam over our pancake with a big steel knife, then cut it in half, quarters, then eighths. I picked up my fork, opened my mouth, closed my eyes.

The texture was the best I'd had—crunchy on the outside, soft and fluffy inside. The taste of wheat so strong like we were standing inside an old flour mill, the jam slightly tart. I opened my eyes and Patty was doing the same, eyes closed, chewing. As we ate, we talked about which actors we liked best—Kate Winslet, Jenny Shimizu. We talked about *Foxfire* and *High Art* and Dana Scully. Funny words like *zinfandel* and *boogaloo*. Favorite flowers.

"I love fuchsias, our neighbor grew them when I was a kid," I said. "She was one of those real gardener ladies, with the green gloves and the big hat and clippers. Growing what no one else did in Los Angeles. They dangled like pink and purple ballerinas."

"She sounds gangsta." Patty did a dainty dance in her seat, waved around Edward Scissorhands and we both giggled.

———

ALI LUFTI LIVED ON the Upper East Side down the street from the funeral bistro.

We stood outside his apartment, one of those squat, never-changing
prewar buildings where people with taste and culture lived. Which war
I never knew, just that the real estate term meant he was legit in certain New York circles. You had to interview to live in these places, purchase the right dog from the right puppy mill—oops "breeder"—that
kind of thing. Money was only one prerequisite.

Auntie Shirin lit a new cigarette as we stepped out of the taxi. "Why
did you have to start a new one? I'm freezing," I said.

She frowned but tossed it on the ground, stamped it out. "Looks
like he's made something of himself. Guess the joke's on us. They said
he did well, but I was thinking well for a chauffeur, say, a studio apartment by the highway."

"What does he do again?" I said, looking around. The street was
too quiet. A lone uniformed housekeeper passed by holding an Hermès
shopping bag.

Shirin ignored me and walked up to the doorman, smiling. Without
asking our names he motioned us towards the elevator at the end of a
marbled hallway. I could see why a place like this might offer a sense of
wellbeing even greater than what we were used to.

A skinny, suited elevator operator pulled shut the heavy door and
interior accordion gate. He sat on a tiny stool in the corner. On the P for
penthouse level, he let us out. We walked onto a lush carpet.

"Which number?" I asked.

"There's only one apartment here, dummy," Shirin said. "We're in
his hallway or whatever. Bita, I cannot get over this! How has the news
of this not traveled back to Iran? Of course, he's of a different crowd."

We stared at the double doors at the end of the space—they were a rich, dark mahogany. On either side stood lion sculptures that looked to be made of solid gold.

The door opened—a maid in full uniform standing barefoot on more marble. She did have well-cared-for feet, flawless ruby red nail polish. Waving us in, she asked us to remove our shoes. "You can leave them in here," she said, pointing to a closet behind the door.

Shirin scoffed but took off her Louboutin boots. The maid held out a pair of blue plastic booties that looked like small shower caps. "You can use these."

"You can't be serious," Shirin said.

ALI LUFTI WAS SEATED in a room that looked at once like it was designed for a prince, and also by an absent-minded inventor. It was wall-to-wall gold and tapestries, crystal chandeliers and mirrors. The largest, most exquisite Persian rug I'd ever seen. Large brocade curtains cocooned it against the outside. Dozens of framed maps on the walls, old and peeling. One table full of vials and labeled petri dishes, microscopes, scales and beakers. Another abounding with blueprints, stacks of note-books, and ribbons of printer paper, the old kind with perforated edges punched with holes.

He sat cross-legged and barefoot on a velvet chair, drinking orange juice from a tall glass, back straighter than an ironing board, scrutiniz-ing a page of the *Wall Street Journal*. A pipe was burning on a crystal ashtray. I glanced at my blue booties and then returned to his bare feet. They reminded me of my own, long and narrow. There was some-thing of the artist about him in all this. Like Maman Elizabeth. But he seemed to have achieved some kind of dream life.

I peeked over at Auntie Shirin but she did not make eye con-tact with me. She, too, was studying his feet. Ali looked up at us as we approached, put his orange juice on the table. He grinned. After introductions, minutes of air-kissing and over-the-top compliments, we all sat. He on the velvet chair, us on a large tasseled sofa. He gripped the fibers of the carpet with his toes as he spoke. I tried to carve details into my brain, breathed in his sweet pipe smoke.

He offered us orange juice from a large pitcher and we toasted and drank. When he put his glass down, the tip of his upper lip and edge of mustache remained wet. He brought a white napkin to his face and dabbed it, gingerly but swiftly, and when he lowered his hand, his smile returned. I had never seen anybody but Maman Elizabeth wipe their lips quite like that. I was about to speak up and tell him so.

"My dears, I am so pleased to see you again," he said.

I could tell Shirin wanted to say something but was uncharacteristically holding back.

"I wonder," I said and cleared my throat. "Do you still practice law? Or are you busy with—" I looked around the room to decide what to describe.

Shirin pressed her nails into my side. "Oh come on, Bita. Ali Lufti doesn't want to get into all that," she said. I pried her fingers off me.

"No, no, it's fine," he said, stretching his legs out. "I am not a man who can work in an office anymore. Play that game. I have never been. See, I was raised under the body of a car. I tasted motor oil before I had my first sip of tea. It's true." His smile was disarming. His eyes sparkled. "I was getting into trouble, even as a baby."

"But how do you live—?" I said, trying not to look around the room.

Shirin glared at me.

"Aha!" He pointed his finger at Shirin. "For your mother, I worked hard. She sent me to school, and for that I'm grateful. Earlier, I had grand ideas—big political ones for Iran. But sure enough, I also learned how to grow a pot of money. It's like fixing cars, once you know the basics. Besides, what could I do after the mullahs stole our

Iran? My philosophizing meant nothing. Instead, we ran here. What else was there to do but make money? You think these Americans want to hear from an old Iranian like me?"

I noticed a book on the table next to him with a cover photograph of George W. Bush.

He followed my gaze. "You don't like him," he said.

"He's a warmonger who hides behind religiosity and naivete," I said.

"Bita!" Shirin snapped. "Look, Ali joon. We—Bita included if you can believe it—don't want to waste your time. You probably want to know why we're here."

"What do you mean why you're here? We're old friends."

"Of course," Shirin said. "We also want to—I'm curious—"

"Shirin joon," he said. The lightness drained from his face. He lowered his head for a few seconds then shot up. "My wife just died. Sure, after eighty years of life, it isn't sad, it's almost welcome. Even this old chap wouldn't turn death away, wouldn't begrudge it. But, you see, I had always thought I would die at the same exact moment as Parvaneh."

"I don't believe that!" Shirin said. "Impossible. People are too selfish. You're no exception. Everyone wants to be the last. To have the upper hand, the last word. To feel like the healthier and stronger one. Isn't it invigorating that you're still standing?"

"Well, I don't know." He twitched. "Khob. Maybe a little."

"Your maid with the charming feet has you occupied?" Shirin said.

"Na kheir, nothing like that," he said.

"You acted strange at the funeral, well, of course you would act strange at your wife's funeral, but that carrying on about my mother. Calling her a princess. And what was all that about having pictures of me? If it was just a little childhood crush, why would she have sent you such things?" Shirin took a sip of her juice.

"I might ask you, why would you come to my Parvaneh's funeral?" Ali Lufti smiled.

"I told you I wanted to pay my respects. Is that not allowed?"

"All the way from Houston?" He raised his eyebrow.

"I'm here on business." Shirin gave me a look that said don't chime in.

"Oh, okay, well sure, you wanted to pay your respects to the wife of the man who used to work for your mother's family. Do you do that with the former cook's children or the maids? Do you even know their names?"

"Agha Lufti, fine. Maybe I thought you could tell me something about my mother."

"So you did come with something in mind. An agenda, if you will."

"Yes, fine."

"Well good. I'm glad you admit that. Why don't you just ask *her*, the great Elizabeth? Don't you know her better than me? Who am I?"

"I've known her my whole life and she's never talked to me about this."

"About what?"

"You know. Stop playing coy with me."

"Ditto, Shirin joon."

"A few times I thought I saw something in her face when your name was brought up in conversation."

"Shirin, my dear, you have to understand back then people couldn't always follow their hearts."

She snickered. "Of course they didn't. But that didn't mean they would dream of their chauffeur's son. Did it?"

"That's true." He crossed his arms.

"What did you do to her, Ali jan?" she asked, her voice louder.

"Do to her?" He looked back at Shirin. "How could you ask me that, Shirin? Don't you know that we were involved? Isn't that clear?"

"Involved? When you were children?"

Ali Lufti laughed. "You could say that. But how is my poor dear Elizabeth? I hear she is suffering. Is that true?"

"Spill it," Shirin said, ignoring his question. "If you don't, I'll haunt you in your sleep I swear it on Bita's life, Agha Lufti."

"Okay okay, Shirin joon," he said. "We saw each other for years as children, yes. And then, years while we were both married. I never meant to betray my dear Parvaneh. Here, they call it an affair."

At that Shirin stood up, orange juice in hand, and threw it in Ali Lufti's face.

I sat, stunned. His cheek dripping.

AFTER WE LEFT ALI Lufti's house, me apologizing to him and his maid, Shirin yelling obscenities, I told her on the sidewalk: "So throwing drinks is like, your thing now? What on earth is wrong with you?" I said I had to go study and left her standing in front of Ali's building. I needed some space.

Every time I saw Jamie, two things happened: I started to know myself better, and my old world felt flimsier, more fake. It was coming undone and Shirin didn't see it or even care. I was a person in this family. I was a person apart from it too. I walked towards home in the cold, rehashing our last session.

"What is it based on, this supposed family of mine?" I had said to Jamie. "A country that doesn't exist. One I don't even remember. Would my ancestors recognize me as theirs? A nice apartment and an expensive handbag isn't an actual connection to the past."

"Well, didn't you once say your grandmother loves Chanel?" Jamie gently joked. "What matters is if it holds meaning for you. How you feel about the purse. Its spirit." This was about as woo-woo as she got, sermonizing about high fashion.

"Lately I've been asking myself real questions. If I had to make my own money to do it, would I travel with Shirin? Would I live the way I do? Maybe I've been conditioned for too long to want any different."

Jamie had nodded and said, "These are all interesting questions, Bita. But I want you to consider why you think people who need to make money are making purer choices. It may be that they're more ambitious or hungry."

I stopped at a coffee cart and asked for a white coffee with two sugars. I held on to the warm cup, its familiar blue-and-white Greek design and the words WE ARE HAPPY TO SERVE YOU. I pulled up the plastic tab and drank.

When I returned home, I got into my bed, which Shirin of course hadn't made. The raised princess-and-the-pea sleigh bed she made me buy a few years ago. "You need a proper bed with a proper head-board," she'd said. She'd kill me if she knew I was using it, that later she'd be sleeping in my sweat. I didn't care.

SHIRIN

"SHE BETRAYED US. YOU believe this woman? Shouting about safety, marrying well, reputation, and look!" I said. "She goes ahead with a disgusting affair with her boy chauffeur? Nothing looks so pathetic to these Persians as falling in love with the help—especially if you're a woman! No wonder they are trying to down me." I flipped the pages of my *Cosmopolitan* so hard it created a small breeze.

"What are you talking about? No one is trying to down you, whatever that means. You're being paranoid," Bita said.

I scowled. Of course Bita didn't know about the conversation I overheard at Mezzaluna so I couldn't exactly defend myself on this point. But also Nasreen in Tehran, Maman Elizabeth's best friend, called me last week. "Shirin joon," her voice like a whiny cat. "What is being said about your family? I hear hubbub here, hubbub there. First you are in the news? You are in the magazines, then you are in jail? They are saying you've destroyed the family name. How could anyone say such things?"

I saw her toothy smile across six thousand miles. Her big chin and sharp eyes. She was loving this. I warned her to keep her mouth shut and that if she told Mommy a word I would personally call the Islamic Republic and out her as a nonbeliever.

Bita and I sat in the empty waiting area of the salon, which smelled like Lysol wipes and cheap hair products. A-ha's "Take on Me" was on the stereo. Followed by "Rio" of course. A good salon played songs we all knew to get us relaxed, doped up, the ones our bodies could hum to brainlessly. I'm sure we'd hear "Say You, Say Me" and "Lady in Red" later. I was a genius at predicting the next song. It was in my bones. When the hell was this appointment going to start?

Trying to amuse myself, I tore off the magazine pages with the top five ways to make the men in your life beg, even though I could have written it, and folded it up, stuffed it in my leather shopper.

My niece just sat there like a glob, useless. I wasn't surprised.

"Bita," I said. "Say something. You come along with me, you make conversation like a proper person. Can you believe your grandmother ruined her reputation for some cheap thrill? Our reputation?"

Bita, world-famous lump, looked down at her magazine, *Salon Times* or something with ten terrible angular bob haircuts a page. I knew she was thinking about what I did in Aspen, what might happen to me. Reputations aside, I was beginning to understand why Elizabeth was such a shitty mother: she had been a lovesick fool. Silent Bita sitting there trying to find something smart to say—she was like that. Holding back, refusing to share her unrehearsed thoughts. So unlike her dear auntie. I groaned loud enough to startle her. She stared at me with those big, dumb eyes.

"Fine. Don't talk. You wanna know the truth, Bita? I envy her. They said 'No,' and she said 'Fuck it.' Can you believe this shit?" I laughed and swung my legs straight out, posing left then right, pretending to admire them. They were shiny and blemish- and spider vein–free, but I wasn't in the mood exactly.

"Isn't this freeing for you personally?" Bita finally said. "I mean, maybe it's okay not to control the story? Takes some of the pressure off, no?" She smiled, as if ding! with that smile I'd give her a stamp of my approval. No way.

"*Freeing? Control the story?* What bullshit. Don't try to talk like me. No, I don't envy her. She didn't follow through properly. She still didn't do what she really wanted and then took it out on us," I said. "And what do *you* know, Bita joon, about letting things just happen? You are one of the most calculating people I've ever met!"

Bita gave me one of her holier-than-thou looks and sighed. Like if only I were as enlightened as her. Of course Mommy didn't go for it. Suddenly, the terrible thought. "What if she got pregnant? What if . . . What if that's my real father? What if I'm, oh god. Half chauffeur?"

"Well, I've been thinking that might be possible."

"What? Why are you over there thinking such things and not telling me? It's not possible. It's entirely impossible. Unthinkable. Of course you wouldn't understand. There's no way. I can't have that. Daddy was a businessman, his father was a, well, I don't know, nobody knows thankfully. There's a difference between that and the help. And what, she thought she could do whatever she wants with no consequence?"

"How do you know there haven't been consequences?" Bita said. "And fine, if you say so, it's impossible. At least unlikely." She put down her magazine, crossed her arms.

I was fuming. "With some nerve Mommy always told Houman his family was iffy. Iffy! A step down from us. Ha. And guess what? *I'm* the step down, maybe bastard daughter of the chauffeur's son. Now that Parvaneh has croaked, you better believe this story will start making the rounds." I shook my head. "This news about Mommy is a nuclear weapon. This is what we will always be known for. We are a joke. Period." I poked Bita—the lightest touch, really I wouldn't even call it a poke, yet she held on to her arm like I'd maimed her.

"Maybe this affair sustained her. What if they really did love each other? Or do you care more about what strangers might think?"

"Isn't it obvious?" I gave a snort. "And what was his 'I hear she's suffering' bit? Is this something more? Did you tell Mommy about Aspen? If you did I am going to—"

"Allo, allo, dokhtar-am!" a voice emerged from one of the treatment rooms. Bita and I looked at each other and we both rolled our eyes in a temporary truce. "Sorry, darling, to keep you wasting away on account of me," the woman said, clopping over noisily in her Dr. Scholl's clogs. "Ahkhhh! Shirin joon, please velcome. Bita hadn't told me you would be here too!" After endless click-clacking, she stood in front of us, hands on her hips, looking at Bita like she was a naughty child. "Never mind. Shirin! It's always a pleasure to see you. How's Houston? You must have enough on your mind with all those high-profile court cases of yours! Don't sue me oh-kay! Evah! Na baba! And what about our most handsome Houman joon? He always makes me laugh so much when he comes for his—shhhh! Don't worry. He makes me promise not to tell anyone. I understand the men these days. They want to be clean but they don't want to seem fussy. Zohreh knows." She sucked in her stomach, tucked her low-cut T-shirt that clung to her leathery breasts further into her crotch.

So that was her name. Zohreh. She extended the last word of each sentence like it was made of goo that wouldn't let her voice go. I read between her lines: lifting and lowering her eyebrow pretending to be innocent, she was saying, even though I'm an aesthetician in drugstore hair dye, too much makeup, and no bra, I am better than you for not living in that shithole town with that shithole culture, not having such a vain husband, and not getting arrested for attempted prostitution whatever the true story, although we both know you'll always be my superior. After all I'm the one with a wastebasket full of your torn-off pubic hair. And it's only because of what we were in Iran; with each year that passes after the Revolution, your hold on us grows smaller. Soon it will be zilch.

Zohreh squeezed the sponge in her fist into a ball. Of course her disdain for me extended to Houman. These women weren't idiots. They all knew his type—the wealthy, pseudo-new-age Middle Eastern womanizer who quotes *The Secret* and Lee Iacocca in equal measure and acts like he's the second coming of Aristotle. Who spews this drivel of endless positivity to every woman in his life: housekeeper, hairdresser, sister, wife. It's so you get tricked into thinking the greedy are good. As if all anyone needed to live our lives "fully," as they say, was to believe in ourselves. The worst kind of man. At least we both were in agreement there.

"Hello, Zohreh joon. We are all fine." I flashed her my best limp smile. "I can't lie, though—you kept us waiting long enough. Without even a stupid tea. Hire some cleaners so you don't have to be on your knees scrubbing between clients," I said. I need my time respected.

I looked to her reaction for any anger. But some faces are good at hiding true emotion, like a brick wall, no Botox needed. You need an eighteen-letter passcode to know the truth. Never mind. I knew she hated me and was going to make me suffer in that damn room and I welcomed it. I deserved it. Why not? Know-it-all diva that I am. You think I don't know that about myself? Ha. Of course I do and I was thinking, yes, give it to me, make me suffer. Rip my skin to shreds. Just leave it hairless, baby. Maybe it'll help me forget all this shit for an hour.

I stood up, straightened my clothes, and motioned to Bita. "Bita, you come with me," I said.

"I'm good."

"Absolutely not," I said. "Come. Spend time with Auntie. Call it female bonding. Remember that? I didn't fly all the way from Houston to be neglected." I smiled. "I know your mommy took you with her every time. You begged her to take you. We can pretend. I'll be your mommy. You know I had no girl to do that with."

"Auntie, stop." But she followed me into the white box of a room like I knew she would. Why can't they make these rooms more pleasing? Nail up a bit of art—something French with a little class. A Degas print, a ballerina. I looked around. White table, dirty towel with old brown wax stains. Yellowing 2003 calendar from a car repair shop— a large close-up of a motor. Ugh. These mechanics were everywhere. Dead wall clock. She wasn't even trying. The magazine rack was empty except for some junky free newsletters.

"I brought my own towel," I said and shoved one of Bita's bath towels into Zohreh's hands. I folded up the paper bag and stuck it in my shopper. "I'm not catching lice or god knows what other little creatures lurk in these crevices."

Zohreh shook her head. "No no, I can't accept that, Shirin joon. We sterilize everything, the tools, bed, towels, everything. So we aren't the Four Seasons, but you won't get a better wax anywhere west of the Karun River." She laughed.

I laughed back but kept my towel arm extended. She looked at the towel like it had rabies even though it was perfect, clean, one hundred percent finest Turkish cotton. I waved it in her face while giving her my death stare.

"Fine, fine. My god." She put her hands up in surrender. You have to demand what you want with people, it's the only way. I stripped and tossed Bita the pile of clothes, my La Perla, my bag. "Bita, don't get my shirt wrinkled. Spread it out over you and don't move." She sat there now adorned in my finery and went back to her magazine.

I lay down naked, the way I love to be. I've never been shy with my body, thanks to all the poking and prodding and judging Mommy did when I was a little girl. I never got away from her watchful eye. You have a good body, you put it on display, but be careful. You are sensuous, use it, but just to get your way, what you want from them. She didn't say any of this outright, of course—I watched how she moved, dressed, spoke to men. Even in the Islamic Republic, many of the women I know do this still. Just indoors. Outside, it's done with the eyes. Here, in America, forget it—no one uses their eyes.

To think all that time she was using her body to have sex with a chauffeur!

I clasped my hands. "Okay, my dear Zohreh, do my bikini, but properly. I don't want anything crooked and I don't want to look like a six-year-old."

Zohreh nodded. "No, no, I don't do those kind of waxes. It's against our policy." She made an abrupt X with her pointer fingers, cheap gold bangles jingling.

"Policy?" I said.

"We do High Back, Low Back, Rectangle, V-Strip, Air Strip. But we never do Full Monty. Na kheir. We are 110 percent against. Fully opposed. See?" She pointed to a poster hung up in the corner. Cartoon sketches of different waxes in a grid, with a red circle and line through a large bare pussy in the largest center square. "This is your menu, Khanoum. Read it and weep." She snapped her chewing gum.

"What is this, Baskins and Robbins? Thirty-one flavors?" I said, sitting up. "What should I get, Bita? Something curvy, with squiggles?"

"You mean sprinkles?" Bita smiled.

Zohreh picked up a stack of white muslin cloths and fanned them in my face.

I swatted her away. "Stop that right now. Enough, Zohreh jan! Pussy can't be that complex." We all laughed. We were having fun.

"Khob, Shirin jan. Lie down and I'll give you something you'll remember. And *he* will never forget."

"Okay okay, enough. You're like a used car salesman," I said, as I lay down and willed my eyes shut, sucking in the smell of hot honey wax.

"Then what's the used car in this scenario?" Bita cackled.

I opened my eyes for just a second to give her one of my famous looks for good measure. Bita was beaming from her dumb joke.

And so, Zohreh walked over with her stainless steel butter knife dripping with that honey, muslin strips resting on her shoulder, and the waxing commenced. There are parts that are almost nothing—the backs of my calves, say. During those, the feeling bores me and I can forget where I am. I closed my eyes and felt my mind slipping off the stiff bed.

Then I remembered. "I just can't get over it, Bita. She owed us a modicum of honesty. Look—ayyy!" I said as a chunk of fur flew off my ankle. The ankle hurts. "Zohreh jan, that last bit really pained me. Will you be a dear and fetch me a glass of iced water. Do you have crushed ice? That's my favorite. And you might as well make this a full-body job." I cleared my throat and watched Zohreh's V-shaped ass leave.

"Auntie," Bita said. "Why are you so rude to everyone?"

"Bita, you ungrateful pest, listen to me. We only have a minute before she returns," I said. "Look, no matter what, we stay together, us family. We support each other. Family is gold, Bita. Your family is gold." I whispered, "Even if your grandmother is a low-class prostitute."

Zohreh returned with one of those old white mugs with advertising down the side. At least she'd given me the crushed ice. I took a big drink and Zohreh got right back to work.

"Ouch, khoda! Zohreh, take it easy a minute. Pretend you don't hate me!"

Zohreh nodded and dabbed wax onto my toes. She was meticulous, giving me a little break, thank god. I loved getting those tiny toe hairs removed—it was like icing on the cake and just a pinch. Then she lifted a leg higher than was comfortable.

I groaned.

"You should just ask her," Bita said.

"Just ask her?" I yelled after Zohreh pulled a strip from between my ass cheeks, both my legs sky high. "We are not *The Cosby Show*, Bita." My eyes said be careful. We couldn't have Zohreh understanding any more of our predicament. "I have to be in Aspen again soon, remember. How am I going to deal with that, and now this? It's too much."

Zohreh clacked over to her pot of wax, stirred it with her knife. I knew she was paying attention. "Now don't you start," I said to her.

"Look," I turned back to Bita. "Not me, not her. You ask him privately. You can be my shield. He won't be able to lie to that fake-sweet face of yours, you brainless overeducated fool."

Bita looked at me with the stillest eyes I've seen yet, stood up, spilling all my clothes onto the disgusting pussy-hair-ridden floor. "I don't need this," she said and walked out. She wasn't brainless, my dear niece. Why did I call her that?

Zohreh shook her head as she pulled another strip from my ass. "Bah bah bah. What was all that fuss about? These kids won't listen to us, Shirin joon. America has given them nerve. The nerve of a lifetime."

"Pick up my clothes will you, Zohreh? It's not about nerve. They don't know courage if it smacked them in the face."

When Zohreh finally pointed to my bikini line, I pulled up the skin just above it, tautened it. The silver heart on her choker swung from her neck. As she spread a knife of wax, she blew and cooled it. A wind. The wax melted into me, found its home. I took a breath and held it. I heard the rip—an unzipping sound—before I felt the twisting burn. This time, it was excruciating. "Aaaaakhhhh." Zohreh pressed down on my bikini line. She held it until it didn't hurt.

AT BITA'S, I OPENED the door and there she was on the sofa, reading a book. Like nothing had happened. Like we were best friends. I could play that game, too.

"I see you're sorry for what you did," I said.

Bita shrugged. "I'm not sorry and I did nothing."

Whatever. I gazed out at her Manhattan skyline, directly facing the old World Trade Centers. Still an empty pit. What a place to live, I wanted to tell her. Bita rented it dirt cheap in 2002 after firemen used the empty lobby to store the dead body parts, the teeth. In her wasted years between college and law school. Nobody wanted to be down here. It was a war zone. Bita said maybe it was like Iran during the Revolution. I laughed in her face. The scale, she has no idea about scale. She doesn't know what millions of people in the streets looks like.

I turned around. "Fine. You win," I said. "We ask him together. Then I will know what to say to that damn mother of mine."

Bita shook her head.

"Don't you feel any sense of duty to your auntie? Are you helping me or not?" I stared at her. I wanted to slap her. Shake her. Everything you are is because we gave it to you. You are nothing without us.

"Why don't you take Mo?" she said.

"Stop asking me about him. I don't know where he is this week. Dubai? You know how he is. Always jetsetting around, wheeling and dealing. Sons are useless when it comes to these family intricacies. Thank god I have you."

"Fine," she said. "I'll go with you. If you stop talking to me right now."

"Good girl."

THE PERSIANS

———

IN THE LATE AFTERNOON, I lay on Bita's sofa in my new robe. I was impressed with how my bikini wax was shaping up. A whole week and no new hairs. I was soft but not prepubescent as she had shaped my hair into a flirty triangle. Zohreh is that good—she can give a bikini wax personality. I squeezed Lubriderm onto my hand and rubbed it into my thighs.

"Auntie," Bita called from the kitchen. "Why don't we set up another meeting with Patty this week? A strategy session. Remember, the trial is March twenty-first, just a month away. We're running out of time."

"Fine. I'm starting to think it's sexy to be an ex-con," I said and picked up my wine. "Too bad I did nothing. Nada. Nothing that isn't done thousands of times worse every night in that Caribou place. Nothing that the dirty cop didn't want."

"Remember, it was a setup," Bita said, coming to sit next to me.

"I don't care. He wanted me. I saw it in his eyes."

"Look, you probably just need to act remorseful and maybe you'll get a few weeks in jail. A year or two if they convict you for assaulting the cop. It's Aspen, how bad can it be? Probably pretty sexy, right?"

"Is this reverse psychology? I am not putting on one of those orange jumpsuits. Maybe we ask Ali Lufti what he thinks. He has experience with the law. And obviously some kind of influence in this country. Maybe he'll make a call and I'll just get community service."

"Auntie, he was a political dissident in Iran like thirty years ago. He hasn't touched the law here. And I don't think he knows anything about PR or publicity. Besides aren't you mad at him?"

I shrugged. "Whatever. If this daddy Ali can help me, maybe I won't stay mad at him. Those country bumpkins won't know what hit them." I finished my glass.

I'd had lunch that day with a few of the most famous New York Persians. And can I tell you it was not something to write home about. They were no better than Persians anywhere. In fact, they were worse; in their matching blond haircuts they must all patronize the same stylist—I bet a slender and doting European. We sat down at a restaurant near Central Park. "Party planning, oh, that's sweet, Shirin. We only concern ourselves with charity galas here. We contribute to society. Culture. It's different here. It's serious. Did you really sleep with a police officer for $5,000? Was that performance art?" Vida and Soraya and Elaheh said. No mention that it was their finance husbands who made their charity balls possible. On the phone with Martin and Tony, I told them, "Maybe it's the younger ones I need to meet. The hip kids." I could feel them shaking their heads.

I HAD CALMED DOWN somewhat and phoned Ali Lufti, who was very pleased to hear from me. As he should be. I told him Bita and I needed to see him again. I didn't say why.

Because it won't do for an Iranian man to be entirely led into the fire by a woman, he invited us to lunch. He insisted. We met at some French brasserie Le Petit Cochon a block from his residence. They welcomed Bita and me, the host bowing at each of us, the black-suited waiters lifting our coats with two fingers, dusting our seats with feathers. I smelled fresh baguettes, butter sauce. They were so snooty with their peasant food, their frogs and snails.

Ali Lufti was already seated, drinking his orange juice, but he stood as we approached. Graceful and proper; even weasels can look refined. Mommy would like this restaurant with its French, or more likely faux French, waiters, white tablecloths, the way the waiter presented a bottle of wine like it was something special and rare and not old grapes.

"A round of your best bait!" I said, loud enough for the tables around us to stare, and laughed.

"Shirin, you are terrible," Ali Lufti said, smiling. "I've taken the liberty of ordering for the table."

"Look," I said after a few inane words, fifteen or twenty minutes of nonsense. "I think we understand each other. I gave up on politics, too, long ago. What's the big point? None of it matters—who you're for, against—so why not have a little fun while your blood is warm? *You* know what I mean. I mean, look at you."

He smiled sheepishly, sliced his butter into minuscule sections, and spread it carefully over three small slices of baguette.

"But never mind. Poor Bita's still at that idealistic age. I believe she has a question for you. I'm sure it's nothing, but—"

Bita cleared her throat then looked away.

"Cat got her tongue," I said. "Well, first, one quick question from me. I have a minor legal case back in Aspen I need to deal with."

He nodded. "I love Aspen. Such beautiful mountains. Yes, darling, I have heard of this minor matter, as you say. I trust you are handling it?"

I made a face. "Seems everyone is bored lately to be talking about nothing," I said. "You have seen a lot in your days. Much worse than this amusing little diversion. Don't you think the Persians might ultimately look favorably upon this? See me as in vogue, in so many ways? Victim of social injustice, defender of prostitutes? Our bodies, our choice!"

He shook his head. "Maybe if you were twenty, dear. Every generation, the kids rewrite a few rules. But, they can't for you. I would urge you to think of your family's history and take due care." I had been thinking big picture, but he was thinking the big picture of the big picture. Maybe this man wasn't such a steamrolled dinosaur?

"Listen," he continued, looking at me and then Bita. "Let's put Aspen aside for the moment. It was callous to assume you'd take my relationship with dear Elizabeth lightly. Like some tossed-off cuckoo. Shirin, I've heard much about you over the years. But now that we've spent some time together, I see you're more than the stories say."

I scoffed. "Oh please. Stop it, Agha Lufti. I'm just a one-trick pony."

"Not you, Shirin. And don't call me agha. Neither of you. That's much too formal. Bita, darling, what can I help you with? I am here to help. We didn't end things well last time," Ali Lufti said. "More wine?" He looked up and the waiter instantly shuffled over to our table and poured out the wine that sat in front of Ali's nose.

"Ask him." I narrowed my eyes at Bita. He nodded at her and dabbed his face with his starched white napkin.

"Okay," Bita said. "Agha, I mean, Ali joon, what I really want to know . . . Excuse me for asking but, we really just, we need to know . . . Did you and Maman Elizabeth ever, could you have, um, had a child? Together?" She scrunched her face like she was watching a car about to crash.

Ali Lufti leaned back in his seat and crossed his arms, observing us with a new curiosity. He stared, his face thin and angular, his white curls cropped close to his head, blue tie like a flash of sea. He made some throat-clearing sounds. I could barely watch anymore. Shaking his head, he said to Bita, "You're good. Very good. I'm impressed. I suppose it's time. She's dead, my poor dear one, she's not coming back. There's no reason to lie." He lifted his hands and flicked his fingers out like sunrays. "Poof. There it goes. Just like that. The whole mirage." He glanced at me and then looked down at his lap.

"Is that a yes?" Bita said.

"Be quiet, Bita," I said, annoyed.

"Don't be upset with us, darling Shirin," he said.

"Agha." I paused. "And yes, you are agha again. Was there more than one?"

He blinked slow and long. "We didn't think it through. We were young. Single-minded. But this isn't a game, I know. You're good, I'm good, all that nonsense. This is all our lives. Mine, and yours and yours," he nodded at each of us as he said the words. "And your mother's."

I looked at Bita and then back at him. I squinted. I knew this face. I've known it my whole life. How did I miss it at the funeral? How did I not know right away?

"Oh my god," Bita said. "What are you saying?"

"Khob. Tell her, Agha Lufti," I said. "Tell this girl who doesn't understand the kinds of secrets us Persians keep our whole lives, and for what?"

"No, it's okay. I get it," Bita said.

"What possessed you to make babies with my mother? Do you know how many lives you've ruined?" I stood up, I don't know why. "We weren't your toys to make and then discard. If you really loved her, you would have let her live her life without you. Instead you made it impossible for her to forget you."

Of all people, I was defending my mother.

Ali just looked at the table. He, the giver and the taker. But why did I feel that he had somehow just killed us all? Poof, as he said. My head dizzy, my throat throbbing, I had to sit back down. I felt my bones all like separate objects—and I looked at him, eyes still on the table, and wanted to rip off all my parts and give them back to him. They're yours. You have them. You deal with it. All of it.

"Perhaps I should have let her tell you," he said eventually.

"How can I expect anyone to ever respect me when scandal is baked into my bones? Did you hear that, Bita?" I sighed as loud as I could. "You never really knew Daddy so what do you care? One old man for another."

"Auntie, that's not fair. I care. I care a lot!" she said quietly, tears in her eyes.

Ali Lufti nodded and held his hand out towards mine. "Please, Shirin."

I looked at my father. I looked at my hand. I no longer recognized it as my own.

NIAZ

ONE WEEK BEFORE I graduated from university, Komiteh officers raided the Blue Room and the copycat Blue Rooms all over Tehran, smashing everything. The Blue Room was over and nobody got a trial. I was not caught, but that was neither a miracle nor even luck. It was the result of a large bribe given by the connected parents of a peripheral classmate who felt debt for the neural pathways I opened. Others weren't so fortunate. Hormoz, Hayedeh, and Farrokh, who gave their parents' abandoned basements for Blue Room parties, were thrown into prison and sentenced to twenty-five years. Rokni, our MC, received ninety-nine lashes. Oranous, who worked the door, paid a fine and took on a new identity as a rural farmer. Alidad, our connection to the best bootleggers, vanished. Dozens of parents offered cars or homes as collateral along with their children's promises of shunning such parties forever. None of it was a surprise. The remaining got married, left Tehran, died of their own will. As a people, we are great at suffering. We love to suffer. My small group of comrades proved no different. There were no more Hippy Iroonis as far as we were concerned. Dead or alive.

In the Islamic Republic of Iran, they know that rules on fun, or as they call it "morality," are needed to uphold the Islamic regime. Let the people feel free and it's all over.

At Morteza's apartment, deflated, I tried to read. My jeans halfway hollow, legs knocking around inside, just like I'd always wished. I don't want to be controlled by what my body needs, I'd told Maman Elizabeth. But without that, what was I? Was I human? I yearned for the simple days of physical need. Longed for my brain to stop interfering. I wanted to eat when I was hungry, sleep when I was tired, come when I was horny. I turned on the television and lit a cigarette, lifted my head to the ceiling. Why couldn't I just enjoy myself? Or like Morteza used to say—when would I start to have fun?

Morteza, the college dropout, now said "don't do as I do," and sold home-cooked ecstasy and video cassettes he copied from an ironically turbaned man who peddled them out of his white Paykan trunk. Danny DeVito in *Twins* was a customer favorite. Schwarzenegger or Stallone, even Van Damme: bestsellers. Morteza had two pagers clipped onto his baggy jeans—a drug one and a VHS one. We were quieter now, safer.

In his kitchen, mostly chemicals and tools: beakers, eyedropper, embossers, small plastic baggies. His refrigerator was littered with crumpled papers filled with final bites of hamburgers. He didn't exercise. He didn't dance—after the raids exuberance lost its appeal. No more parties, no more music, no more philosophy. He traded his tight shirts that highlighted his muscles for big T-shirts to drown his growing gut. He said, "You don't understand, princess. Some people need to make a living."

I considered telling him about my night with Elizabeth—the humble origins in my history, too—but why bother. He was trapped in his own fishbowl. I thought, A.M.O. as Maman Elizabeth said. Accept and move on, Niaz. So I grabbed my things from the table—book,

cigarettes, the silly expensive lighter he gave me when we first met—
and walked out the door.

IT WAS 1994 AND I wasn't finished. I taped onto my bedroom walls
old magazine clippings depicting Mohammad Mosaddegh taking
meetings with serious figures from his makeshift metal cot. "If I sit
silently, I have sinned," he had famously proclaimed. I was encouraged by this neurotic champion of the people, already dead nearly
thirty years.

I could be the forgotten daughter and a hero too. I was not just of
the people. I *was* the people. It was in my blood.

I picked up my degree in civil engineering and tossed my textbooks
into the dumpster outside Maman Elizabeth's apartment. I received
fine marks despite snoozing in class—the others didn't believe I was
naturally smart, so I was mistrusted. Was I a stooge of the government
sent to monitor my classmates, or an outside disrupter? Spy was the
word on the tip of everyone's tongues. Spies were everywhere. The
classmates whispered.

Mohammad Mosaddegh was bringing Iran to democracy in the
1950s. The democratically elected prime minister—founder of the
pro-democracy National Front—who handed the people unemploy-
ment compensation, sick pay, freed peasants, taxed landlords. Despite
being the descendant of a Qajar king—or maybe because of it. The
people wanted more. The Shah felt threatened. And then Mosaddegh
did the big thing that made him a "danger" to the West, that gave the
West the cover to cry red. He nationalized the oil. The oil that everyone wanted—that the British controlled through the Anglo-Persian Oil
Company, later renamed British Petroleum, or BP.

The CIA killed it. Of course it did. Paid mobs. Bribed officers. A
jailed leader. A Shah who installed the United States' puppet for prime

215

minister. Mosaddegh's closest associate executed by firing squad. The coup that changed the Middle East. This story repeats itself. An American story. As American as apple pie. Hawaii, Guatemala, Dominican Republic, Brazil, Republic of the Congo, South Vietnam, Chile, Nicaragua, Afghanistan, Iraq.

In school in the Islamic Republic, the tale of Mosaddegh was a warning against foreign intervention, the dual satans America and Britain. It was no hero's tale. There was only one hero in the new history books: the Ayatollah. But Mosaddegh was a hero to me.

So I made a flyer. I used one of the old magazine photos of Mosaddegh from my bedroom wall along with my handwritten words. His long, narrow face, nearly bald head, sloping shoulders, gray wool pajamas. He was my sullen philosopher king. I drew on him eyeliner, feathery mascara, and red lipstick, and covered him with a rose-patterned headscarf. His bed I turned into a bedlam of ornate Moroccan pillows. The old man Mosaddegh transformed into a charming diva. I took great care to draw into the pillow covers colorful repeating designs in gold and green and purple—geometric and floral, resembling the patterns I saw around me all my life.

I looked at this creation and laughed. What was the point? It was desecration, but in a way it was elevating women, wasn't it? Or was it demeaning women—it was only a woman who took to bed?

Underneath, I'd written these words:

Join the New Intimacy—
A Movement for a New Iran of the Mind.
No Mullahs.
No Bazaaris.
No Revolutionaries.
No Hippies.
No Shah Lovers.

THE PERSIANS

No Spoiled Children.
Deep thinkers welcome.

A friend at a copy shop made me three dozen black-and-white photocopies. Because the copies lost their color, I hand-painted the lips red and hit the streets. If it were America, I could have passed them to anyone who struck my fancy. But this was Iran. Informants spied on the coffee shops, just like they did at university. I stuck to the familiar—my friends and friends of friends. A more flirty type might have driven down Jordan Street aka Nelson Mandela Boulevard aka Africa Boulevard and slapped a flier onto the windshield of a car containing a handsome face, but I wasn't that type.

What was I doing? I wanted to be a poet but was I a promoter? I ate kuku and ice cream and lavash and I kept it down. I waited for my prize, but found it nowhere.

I invited the pliable and inquisitive, the young but not too young. Old but not too old. Using nerves and charm. I handed them a flyer and whispered what was not printed anywhere: a phone number in order to find out the address and exact time on the day of the party. I didn't want ninety-nine lashes. But I wouldn't commit the sin of sitting in silence. Already in my head I saw some kind of idealistic intellectual orgy: mustachioed men, top-hatted women, smoke too thick to see through, voices too curious to ignore. I made phone calls from payphones. Dozens a day.

I secured a partially furnished space in an abandoned apartment building for little more than a promise to invite the landlords, a married couple, Iraj and Giti, who dealt in exotic Saharan animals, roving illegal forest parties and drug weekends in Shemshak. A two-floor apartment with a balcony, long velvet couches, and floor cushions. What made this possible was the identity of the true owner—Iraj's father and notorious Islamic Republic official. The connected lived in a different country. Running across the length of the apartment, I spun around in circles in my socks. I was doing this. Only twenty-two, but look at me.

I called on DJs, dancers, philosophers. Raised money through rich friends. I paid off the Komiteh, the precursor to the morality police—I learned my lesson after the Blue Room—and used mattresses to ensure noise wouldn't seep out the windows. A band of women in flip-flops and gray rags arrived to mop and sweep and shine.

From the academics in my address book, I requested five minute talks on topics such as transsexuality, temporary marriage, the movement to abolish hymen repair, the absence of a nonderogatory word for gay. Even Rafsanjani, when president in 1990, spoke about the god-approved temporary marriage—a way for Islamic law–sanctioned sex outside marriage. Was it just a loophole for prostitution, for the patriarchy? The lengths they will go to keep up their illusion. But more importantly, I wanted my guests to talk of art, culture, growing a garden in the mind. I invited writers, designers, filmmakers, but also a waitress whose table I sat at for years who snuck me extra sabzi khordan and political pamphlets, a taxi driver I'd trusted to move contraband.

For weeks I was on the move, on the phones, making deals for goods and services. I was sneaking notes. I was the center of a whirlwind of activity. And I had to keep it almost imperceptible. Quiet like a creature on the bottom of the sea preparing for a fireworks show, one that could be seen even from space. If you knew where to look.

I smuggled into the apartment homemade vodka made of raisins and barberry. Cigarette cartons by the dozen. I distributed cigarettes evenly among crystal bowls. I asked friends to donate hashish and psilocybin. I wanted something unexpected and gorgeous to take root. I hadn't heard of anybody doing anything like this in Tehran. Not in the mountains, not in the country. Sure, there were party people. We liked to party, us Persians. But this New Intimacy was more than that. If the wrong person got word, I'd be charged with spreading corruption on Earth, waging war against god. The result: instant death.

Twice my phone rang and when I picked up, there was only breathing. Then a dead line. Was that the warning? Could these be my last breaths?

I STARTED TALKING ON the phone with my cousin, Bita. She was in high school, sixteen, and Seema said over the line, "Niaz joon, I want you to know each other." Auntie Seema's voice, quiet and clear. So different from Shirin's husky theatrics.

So I said to Bita over a fuzzy connection, I wish you could visit. See Iran. Me too, she said. I knew she didn't mean it.

On a later call, I asked, "What do young people care about in America?"

"Fitting in, being the same," she said. "We fight with our parents to dye our hair green, but then we all have the green hair. We wear the same flannel shirts. Still, we're carving a path from the past, together."

"What about Mumia Abu-Jamal?" I asked.

"I guess."

Maman Elizabeth would give me a look whenever I started talking about our government. "Shhhh," she hissed and looked out the window, following the telephone wires from inside to their possible conclusions.

I pitied and envied Bita both. Young Americans smoked marijuana without fear of death, snuck out bedroom windows, pierced tongues, refused meat, slept with their teachers. Then they entered the world renown of Harvard University and acted like oversexed compassless children. They knew so little. Still, entire departments of the world—purveyors of film, music, politics, money—were dedicated to wooing just them, privileged American teens. And the rest of the world followed like trained idiots. It made me angry that people who needed nothing were given even more. But that is the world.

Maman Elizabeth said, "Don't tell your mother you're spending so much time talking to Bita. She'll be jealous."

Shirin hadn't called me in months. It was hard to believe she'd even care.

I SAT IN THE quiet of my first salon-to-be, the room lit entirely by the light from votive candles scattered across surfaces. I burned esfand to ward off the Evil Eye, whispered to the Zoroastrian gods. Unlike the Blue Room, this was our culture. I wore a black feather cape over a shiny black bodysuit, black mask, my hair long and wild like an untamed jungle. Perfect red lips, red boots.

People arrived. Women in silky veils who disclosed beautiful faces. Men with stubbled cheeks. They kissed me and sat in circles on velvet cushions. There was speaking and laughing. The music hummed. Rollicking sounds of setar. I listened for words. Sufism. Iranian traditional medicine. A mystical seance in a central circle led by a woman shrouded in burgundy. I was too much a hostess to dive into any one water, so I walked around the edges. I counted fifty heads, no, more. A couple hours in, a woman approached me, gliding like a fish. I had never seen her before. I worried, was she a spy, a henchwoman? The DJ had half the crowd dancing to a revolving beat. Smoke rose to the ceiling, leaving a haze.

The woman said, cigarette holder in hand, "Is all this"—she gestured a circle—"your making?" She had to shout to be heard and we were slightly dancing together as we spoke. She clutched my arm to steady herself. Drunk, this was no government goon.

"Of course, who else?" I said.

She laughed. "Well, Khanoum, thank you for your efforts but don't you think these are the concerns of the idle? The privilege of those who can afford it? Iranians want a ruler to help them live, not discuss useless topics. They want shelter, food, safety, health care. This"—she motioned again—"is for the rich and lazy."

"I invited a taxi driver," I said.

She curled her lip. "But would you bed one?"

"Why are you here then?" I asked.

Grabbing my hands, she whispered. I felt her hot breath. "I'm rich and lazy," she said. "Can't I criticize myself? We should be sick of indulgence. If you want to do something real, go into slums, go into villages. Ask them what they want. Go on. Ask them."

Slums. Villages. Hah. I'd never been to a village. I'd barely been outside Tehran. Who would take me? The woman stared at me and then kissed me on the lips. Slowly. Somehow I let her. My body shivered. I closed my eyes and invited in her tongue. A kiss was a kiss. I loved a good kiss. But her lips pulled away. I opened my eyes and she was gone.

I pushed through the crowd, searching for her. People were huddled in groups, dancing, talking. When I got tired of looking, I stumbled upon my friend Fereshteh, who was chatting with some day laborers, or men dressed up as such. How did they get here? I wanted to show them to my new friend. I asked Fereshteh for mushrooms. A mushroom grew in the ground—in nature. It was lovely on its own, real without my efforts. Fereshteh dropped into my palm all that was left from a plastic baggie. She winked at me. I chewed up the twiggy mess and chased it with one of the worker men's vodkas.

I drifted off, like a branch sliding down a river. I asked the DJ—a beautiful man with a mustache—to play music that reminded him of home. A minute later, he dropped the needle on a track of American house. The crowd surged. But I got into his face and argued. Didn't

221

you hear what I said about home? I continued until he brought out a stack of Iranian records. I picked Googoosh, and Maman Elizabeth's favorite Shohreh's "Omadi" with its almost silly flute and strings, her voice of aching love, which I told him to play next. Why these old tunes, I wondered. I went into a corner of the room and sat on a cushion. The sounds of the party competed with my loud heartbeat. I felt the sex people were having in front of us and in their heads. Everything in the room brighter, more technicolor. The people lit from within.

FISH WOMAN REALLY GOT to me because she was what I woke up to the next morning in a sea of debris. I thought back to Kian and his failed Communist revolutionary parents. What would they do? What would the Great Warrior do if he were alive today?

I also thought about what Ali Lufti would do. My real grandfather. It took being high on ecstasy for Maman Elizabeth to tell me her secret. Son of a chauffeur. What would he think of my parties? Would he laugh? Would he agree with Fish Woman?

I didn't tell Maman Elizabeth about the gathering. She wouldn't understand. Too dangerous and for what, she would have said. The next week, at tea, I asked, "Did the Great Warrior really give up every cent for his belief in democracy?" The story went that he relinquished all his money voluntarily but was triply rewarded by the government for his selflessness.

Maman Elizabeth laughed. "No, no, that's a lie; they took it from him and gave him back a pittance. He was their pawn." She went to the bookshelf and picked out a burgundy book. It was leather covered, edged in gold. "Read this."

I ran my finger over the embossed title: *Choking the Great Lion.* It was only ever published in English and luckily my English was decent.

At night, I flipped through the pages. In photographs, the Great Warrior, Babak Ali Khan Valiat, was always the tallest of the men he stood near. This was not a coincidence, I'm sure. Maybe he drew the shortest ones closest to him. He had small beady eyes, never a smile. The book said he had a persistent cough, the appearance of nervousness. He was temperamental. The author—an American lawyer raised in Iran—was shocked when they met that this man was known as a military mastermind. I asked myself questions: Did the Great Warrior believe his precious democracy benefited the poor? Did he care if it did? Nothing in the book suggested he worried about anything other than himself and his so-considered noble power.

I thought about this nervous, moody, uncomfortable leader. Whether he would have been happier, better served doing something else with his time, how sometimes we don't do the things that suit us best. Planning the salon was exhilarating, but was I suited to host it? Sure, I liked being five thousand feet underwater with a blast of light cutting across my seafloor living room, but I wanted to be doing backflips for myself—not arranging a spectacular. I didn't like to walk up to one person, walk up to another person, worry whether they were happy with their drink, the conversation, crowd, level of high, room's temperature. Or was this feeling, wanting to hide, just because I'd been challenged?

I was temperamental. Like the Great Warrior. Great-Great-Grandfather. I found a chapter that touched on a controversy: the cruelty of the Great Warrior, his treachery. Although to the people in power he was highly principled, he had early on used murder to secure his standing. He entered villages opposing his authority and wiped out the men. Entire villages in the North, like Masou, according to *Choking the Great Lion*. I knew of Masou, the village of Baba Roshani and Nounou joon. And Nounou's missing husband—the one who disappeared and nobody ever explained why.

223

"Of course I know about this. You think I'm stupid?" Elizabeth said when I asked her. "For some, marriage is for reasons other than love. I was Roshani's revenge. So what. Eventually Nounou couldn't handle living in our house. But I was fine with it. *I* didn't kill her husband."

"I'm not surprised the Great Warrior did this," I said to Maman Elizabeth. "Look at what the leaders do today. But did Baba Roshani trick you? Did he confess that your grandfather killed his father before you married?"

She shook her head. "I tricked him too," she said. "I needed him too."

I asked Maman Elizabeth about villages. "Don't go to the villages. It's all peasants with no education, eating beans and wearing those old-fashioned clothes. Women spend their entire lives making meals, washing clothes, scrubbing floors. I own hundreds of villages. What use are they? Remember what I say: A.M.O. Accept and Move On."

SOMETIMES ADVICE IS BETTER ignored. Not wanting to draw attention, I removed the diamond earrings Maman Elizabeth passed down to me when I graduated from school. I dressed simply: gray trousers, a dark green poncho, black scarf. As I sat in the crowded train car, there was barely enough oxygen for every mouth. The windows were black with exhaust. I was hot, my underarms wet. When I arrived, I walked in a desolate field for what felt like miles. I was not used to all this space around me. Dirt, wide open land. As if I'd landed on the moon.

But then, I saw people. Bunches of them. Clustered. On the steps of buildings made of red clay. There were groups of women, all with delicate scarfs—wispier and more jubilant than in Tehran. They looked like fun pieces of cloth, thin, translucent, pastel, colorful stitching. Not like the law. More like culture. As I walked closer I looked at the women's faces, wrinkled and darkened by the sun and time. They watched me. I didn't have a plan; I was just there to see. A warm breeze swept through the gathered women and their scarves blew up like sails. I approached them. "I'm visiting," I said.

They laughed and looked at one another. One woman removed her scarf and handed it to me. Had I appeared to want their scarves? I smiled and removed mine to give to her, but she refused. I tried and tried, but she remained unmoved.

"Wear it well," she said in an accent I could barely understand. Her hair was white and glistened under the sun. Her head bare. Maybe they don't patrol here. I nodded and kept walking. Because of how the light bounced around, the faraway buildings looked not like buildings, but rather like a soft mass of orange. Like piles of turmeric.

It was cool inside a building whose wooden door was open. I spoke to more people—they were welcoming. No baby had been born in this village for fifteen years. I smoothed my new scarf with my fingers. What did the women do here? What did the men do? They were all old and dying. Soon, this village would be dead, too, the buildings and the sky all that remained. I thought of Nounou's missing husband, my murdered great-grandfather, his body left in Masou. All that happened there was he died early. They live. They die. That's it.

But, no, he was killed. And the murder reverberated in Nounou—and now, maybe, in me.

I NO LONGER THOUGHT that a party could be a transformation. Still, I threw party after party. It was almost a retaliation, a fuck you to Fish Woman that lasted eight years. Some parties had themes. Like spring. Like the color blue. Many were in places more removed than Tehran, where it was safer. The mountains, ski resorts. I took more drugs.

Rented and then gave up my first apartment. Lied to Maman Elizabeth about almost everything. Disappeared for months. She kept my room clean and gave me a warm meal whenever I returned. She told Shirin she had lost me. I was twenty-two, then twenty-four, and then thirty. There were adventures and mistakes, sometimes both in one.

What kept me going was this: the villages. The patrons started giving me money to keep my salons afloat. Every time they wrote a check, I funneled part of it to the villages I visited. I was making a difference, had a purpose. This was what I was waiting for, a way to fight. When Kian told me the history of the Communists and I horrified him by saying "Who can I kill?" I had wanted to know what would bring me glory. "I can plant a bomb and shut down a ministry," I had said. I was jealous of Mo and his tennis—the yellow ball, those golden trophies. Now I didn't care about glory.

I had learned something interesting about the women in the villages. The ones Maman Elizabeth, a woman with little education herself, denounced as having no education. The ones who cooked all day. These women, sure, they couldn't read. They didn't use Nivea on their hands. But they weren't miserable. They needed education, especially the younger ones, and health care, work training, mental health counseling. In other words, they needed money.

I called it the Zan Foundation. All the money went to the women. One morning, some of my most loyal patrons, people who wanted to feel necessary and intelligent, knocked on Maman Elizabeth's door. I answered. "No, we'll stand right here," they said when I invited them in. They crossed their arms and accused me of stealing their money. "We don't believe you, Niaz," they said when I denied it. "Come with us"; they pulled me. They wouldn't listen, wouldn't hear my explanations. They said, "You have cheated us. You are a thief." They were right. They were wrong.

THE PERSIANS

At the police station, however, they couldn't say why they had given me money. To throw parties seething with drugs and sex and freedom? No. Instead, they claimed I had "acquired wealth illegitimately"—code for brand her an enemy of the state. They urged the police to investigate. The policeman with his grim face, rough and pockmarked, said, "For now, go home."

When the authorities summoned me back to the station the next day to answer questions, I confessed all to Maman Elizabeth. I told her where I had to go, and that maybe I wouldn't return right away. "If I don't come home tonight, I'll need your help," I said. She yelled, "Why are you so stupid?"

"No, no, no, I didn't do that." I denied everything. Channeling money illegally. Being a spy for the United States, England, Germany, and Israel. Trying to tarnish the reputation of the Islamic Republic. Being a prostitute, promoting prostitution. They didn't care, they threw in every charge. I sat at a desk across from four officers and two women in chadors. They put me under arrest, twisted me into handcuffs, and said unless I admitted how I had gotten my money, I was facing lashings, prison. A long sentence. Shame on my family, now and in the future and for all eternity.

An officer with a big beard and a tight grip pushed me down a corridor, stale and hot. Around the third bend, all alone, he stopped us. I heard the hum of some machine, his breath one head higher than mine. He yanked me back, spun me around, and stared into my face. Then down my body. As he breathed through his nose, his ribs in a stained shirt expanded against me. My knees weakened, but he held me up by grabbing me by my scarf at the neck and he lowered his head to my face. Forehead to forehead.

I froze. His unbrushed teeth—strong and sour. His eyes were still and hungry, but there was a hint of fear. Was he scared of me? Of what

I might "make" him do? I stared back. He shook his head in disgust and relaxed his grip. I crashed backwards to the hard floor. He laughed as I rubbed my shoulder. There, there.

"What are you doing on the ground?" he shouted. He dragged me up and then through a door. The two women from earlier took me to a bathroom, stripped me, and gave me a rough uniform which included a matching headscarf. They crammed me into a cell smaller than Maman Elizabeth's bathroom with thirty other women. Circles had darkened under their eyes, their mouths seemed fastened shut. They had nothing to give. I had nothing in return. All night, I sat with my knees pulled in, like a ball. I was too scared to sleep.

Maman Elizabeth didn't wait for the morning to decide whether to help. She knew better than that. Charges would appear and then disappear the next day, only to be replaced by other accusations. Because there was no room to lie down, I would sleep—I had to sleep—while sitting up or leaning against one of the other women, inches from our own excrement, which collected in buckets we were made to clean out once a day. The loudspeaker played recordings of propaganda and the Koran. A young woman painted little papers with tea using a brush made of her own hair. One afternoon, a week after I arrived, they released me to Maman Elizabeth. Just like that. A fate that many others in my position would never share. I felt too guilty to look at the other women—why me? But I knew why. I held my head down and let an officer lead me outside.

On the way home, Maman Elizabeth behind the wheel with the engine sputtering, said, "I gave them a piece of my mind. They've never heard a woman like me, Bita joon."

I could just imagine. But I knew she had given them much more than that. What finally got them to let me go, she told me later when I wouldn't stop asking, was a deed to several thousand acres of land, her house up north, and a big chunk of her bank account. And a promise to keep me out of trouble. She looked at me, proud and weary.

I never threw another party. I owed her my life.

"YOU KNEW, DIDN'T YOU?" Bita says on the phone.

"I did."

"Why didn't you ever tell me?"

"I'm pleased Maman Elizabeth has had something for herself."

"But, Niaz," Bita says. "It's not just hers. They should have told their children."

"To what end?"

"Maybe it would have helped my mom to know."

"Don't use your dead mother like a weapon."

Bita groans. "Ali Lufti implied something's wrong with Maman Elizabeth. Is she okay? She doesn't know about Shirin's arrest, does she?"

"She doesn't tell me anything. But yeah, she's not herself. She's skipping her weekly hair appointments. Her nails are unpolished and cracked."

Bita tells me that Ali is richer than all of us together. A businessman in a New York mansion. I reluctantly agree to tell Maman Elizabeth that the secret is out. I have not spoken to her about this since that night on ecstasy fourteen years ago. I invite myself over for tea.

MAMAN ELIZABETH OPENS HER door. Slower to answer now. Her signature scratchy skirt and wedge mules. Except no makeup. No jewels. Hair undone.

"I am glad you are here, Niaz. I might want to go to the States."

"Does it have to do with Ali Lufti?"

"I do have children there, you know."

"Children who have a new father."

She looks up from her tea, raises her eyebrow. "Oh. He told them? Well, what do they want from me?" She pauses. "Haven't I suffered enough?"

BITA

HI, NIAZ. I'VE BEEN thinking about Maman Elizabeth's secret life. Okay. Maybe given the times that was necessary, but in 2006 it isn't. Not really. What would happen if I lived exactly the way I wanted? What world would crumble? Maman Elizabeth could have just married her Ali if it weren't for money and class. Could the Great Warrior's money be a curse? On Maman Elizabeth. On the rest of us. What if you thought in the back of your mind that you'd always be saved by it? Instead of saving yourself, you give that job to the money.

PATTY CAME OVER FOR another meeting with Shirin. I brought up a cardboard carrier of coffees and passed them out. We sat at my dining table, Shirin in her bathrobe and slippers, her hair in curlers. Patty was taking notes on a steno pad, an extra pen tucked behind her ear.

"So, Shirin, as long as you are clear to the court on what happened—which was not an actual attempt to commit prostitution—I really do believe you will be fine and found not guilty, no matter all that complicated law we last discussed. Do you understand?"

"I knew you'd exonerate me." Shirin smiled.

"We think that the officer was possibly racially profiling you," Patty said, hands knitted across her cup.

"Yes, that's what Bita says I should say."

"Only because it's the truth," I said.

"I'll say it if you think it will work," she said.

"Great," Patty said. "The optics for that are bad. So, yes, do focus on the profiling. Let's pretend I'm the prosecutor: Ms. Javan, is it true you asked Officer Clement for fifty thousand dollars? According to him, you said quote 'Okay, honey, I can be your Princess Jasmine, but it's gonna cost you. Gimme fifty Gs.'"

"Did he record me saying that?"

Patty raised her eyebrow. "No, he didn't record you. He's an undercover police officer, so he's trained to write down the details of your encounter afterwards."

"Look. He called me Cleopatra! She's a queen. Albeit an Egyptian queen. If you're meeting with a queen, you come bearing gifts. I said it will cost you. I wasn't asking him for money to have sex with me. If I found him attractive after he gave me the money, then maybe I would have had sex with him because I wanted to. Maybe," I said.

"Don't say you might have had sex with him. That's going to confuse everyone. Just stick to how you see yourself as very desirable and deserving of gifts. That's what happens between men and women in your culture when there is courtship. And say more about the race stuff."

"Fine," Shirin said. "He wanted to be my sheik. First of all, I don't know anything about sheiks. Do I look like I'm in a harem?"

"Focus," I said. Patty shot me a grateful look.

"I'm sick of this. Can we move on?" Shirin grabbed her coffee and took a swig like it was a cocktail.

"The key issue—the only one really—is whether you solicited money in exchange for sex," Patty said. "'In exchange' are the operative words."

"Maybe I did, but I was joking? He should have known that. I was mad about his Cleopatra comment," Shirin said.

"Okay, this is entirely different from the gift theory."

"This is more true," she said.

"Why were you mad? I mean besides the whole you're-not-an-Arab thing. Why did you care so much about what he said?" Patty asked.

"I thought he liked me," Shirin said.

"This is good," Patty said. "Is that true?"

"Unfortunately, yes."

"Okay, I think this will work. Personally even I believe this more than your gift explanation. You emphasize that you felt discriminated against, and that you thought he was harassing you—calling you Cleopatra—because you are brown. Which upset you because you did like him. So you implied he was some kind of a pimp. By demanding money you were trying to insult him back. Like, two could play at this game. You had no intention of taking his money in exchange for sex."

"I'm not brown. Look at me. For the record. But fine, I'll say that if it ends this."

"You're not white," Patty said.

"Maybe in America. To these uneducated classless country bumpkins who've never read a book, who don't know where the word Aryan comes from, and that without us they'd still be sacrificing each other to some goat deity. That I'm better than any of these Puritan farmers. When do they understand that, and when do we get to sue that officer for sticking her hand up my ass?"

"We don't," she said. "They're allowed to do that here."

III

OPERATION AJAX

SEEMA

IF I COULD TALK to Bita right now, I would say the things I didn't know before I died. Like: Don't trust anyone who tells you how to live. Those advice-givers are the people you must hide your ears from. Wearing a happy mask, big smiles as they grab your wrist and say, "To be happy do X, not Y." X and Y are anything, sometimes they trade places. Work or play? Be or do? Confess or lie? Kill or be killed?

Nounou, my beloved one, said, "Be nice to your siblings. Respect your parents." Then she killed herself. Why listen to such a person? These people are usually one loose thread from suicide, from ruin. Run away from them. No one knows you but you.

Sixteen years after I'd found Nounou dead on her bedroom floor, begged for her ghost in the rafters to talk to me, we were in Los Angeles, or rather New Tehran. Later, some businessman named the neighborhood around Westwood Boulevard "Tehrangeles." A silly word like Bollywood. New Tehran is more dignified. I'll always call it that. We came here to stake out a new life. We weren't after a neighborhood of Iranian music cassettes and kabobs, beauty salons and rinky-dinky visa application outfits. A silly name begets a silly concept.

In New Tehran, it was me, Teymour, and baby Bita. Teymour I

had married a few years before the Revolution. I was young, twenty-three, and he was so different from my family. He'd wanted to hear me talk. Gave me books as presents. Faulkner. Camus. De Beauvoir.

"I want a career," I'd told him, in the car going to the movies before they all shut down.

"You'll have a career. We're the same, you and me," he'd said. His thin serious face, his wire glasses made me trust him.

Then near the end of 1977, while settling into my first proper job, I got pregnant.

"You must stay home with your children. That's your contribution," my boss, Bahman Kamrani, editor of the communist magazine had said. I'd been there three months. Maybe he knew my heart wasn't in it, that I'd taken the job because it was the only one I could get. Something had changed in me, my stomach for violence, for any movement that thought it was the answer to everything. I became a realist. Marx lived off wealthy patrons; J.F.K. was a womanizer. These people with oomph I had worshipped all disappointed me when I learned more. Maybe Bahman could sense all that. Or maybe he was a sexist pig.

I told Bahman I could keep working, that I didn't have any children yet. As he handed me my final paycheck, he shrugged. Later, so did Teymour. A man, I learned, might say anything to woo a woman. I could have left him then, but I stayed. Teymour loved me. No one else but Nounou and Daddy had. A few months after that it was the Revolution and we fled Iran.

In New Tehran, Teymour worked at an office right on Westwood Boulevard. I stayed home with Bita and kept house. I was no longer a career woman. Who was I kidding; my three months as an associate journalist at an Iranian radical newspaper was not going to help, was not a résumé. Iranians had just taken Americans hostage in their embassy, shouting "Death to America."

I cooked for the first time in my life. It was not good. Nobody

THE PERSIANS

died—of pleasure or of poison. But I had to play that role—there was no one else. If you had some money but no connections, we were told real estate was the way to go. So Teymour looked into investments while I prepared beef stroganoff. Chicken cutlets in gravy. At first, I refused to cook Iranian cuisine. Refused to carry on the burden of my people. All that washing of herbs. Entire days of peeling and chopping. That poor Abbas Ghassem, the cook I tortured as a kid. I wanted to make what was new for us. Chili. Hot dogs. Peanut butter and jelly. It was hard for me to embrace the new culture, but I wanted to try.

In New Tehran in 1980, Café Luna was the only place to get a decent cappuccino, and this mattered to us. Cars zoomed by and the Iranian women we knew sat all afternoon in the hot sun under useless wobbly umbrellas, cigarettes dangling in hand, lotioned thighs greasing the plastic chairs. It was always cloudless at this sister latitude. We spoke but we said nothing, our babies crawling between our legs picking at the pink, mint green, and sky blue gum hardened on the concrete, as cigarettes ashed on their soft heads and gold jewelry sparkled on their mothers' wrists above. There were two types of us—the Names and the No-Names. I call them No-Names because they did not leave a name behind in Iran. We, of course, were the Names. But in New Tehran, the only people who cared about the Names were the No-Names. The Names thought *everyone* would care; in the beginning the Names thought even all the Americans would pay attention, that we'd be worshipped yet secretly murderously despised in America, just as in Iran. But, no. The Names were nothing without our No-Names. We needed them.

Of course, I know this class-based rhetoric is oppressive. I would have scorned this in the past. But, as I said, I was no wide-eyed theoretical baby anymore. I saw society for what it was.

Here are examples. Siavash, the deliveryman from Darband Restaurant on Santa Monica Boulevard, with the kuku sabzi so green

239

and fragrant that it made my head grow its own herb garden as I inhaled, wouldn't even let us pay for our meals, not a cent. His mother had been Daddy's secretary in Iran—I had to wonder whether "secretary" came with additional duties. Once a week Siavash, blue-eyed, stood at our door, sweating at the temples, with our bag full of kabob and refused payment. It was a whole scene. He refuses. I get mad, or rather, pretend to be upset. He laughs me off. I get madder, fake-smoking out of my ears. He waves me away. As he turns around, I stuff a hundred-dollar bill into his dirty back pocket. He acts like he doesn't notice that a strange yet beautiful Named woman is sticking her hand in his pants. Repeat next week, and on it goes.

Negeen, my favorite waxer at La Jupe Rouge on Westwood Boulevard, a thinking woman's waxer, just a bit sexier than an undertaker, meaning very. Quiet, solemn. Minimalist linen dresses, shoulder-length frizzy brown hair, a taste for French existentialist literature and Chinatown mary janes. I ask myself how many thousands of Iranian women's bodies had she touched before mine? But the deeply held love, oh the love. Just like all those women in Tehran who administered pain to me with such passion over the years, a cigarette in one hand, which became a Sartre paperback in Negeen's case, and a sharp implement in the other.

And because the call of herbed rice was finally too loud to ignore and I needed to make my own, Amir, the Iranian grocer down the street from Negeen. At Super Shanbeh, named after the famous Tehran supermarket, Amir Agha knew exactly what I wanted before I even tapped on the counter. I suspected he thought I added the "Agha" in pitying mockery but I was sincere. He was a gentleman with me. Sniffed the meal I was planning the second I pushed open the grubby glass doors and entered the unevenly air-conditioned aisles. Weighing, parsing chunks of parsley, cilantro, chives—his hands whipping through the herbs. Bagging fenugreek leaves even though he knew I'd throw them out the minute I left due to my iconoclastic interpretation of the holy ghormeh sabzi. A controversial choice borne of the desire not to smell of fenugreek for a week.

It did occur to me that maybe the No-Names' respect for us was insurance—if the Islamic Republic failed and we all returned, did they want us to remember them?

The non-Iranian No-Names' relationship to us Names was simpler, as they just assumed us to be of great importance. It was better to serve an Iranian princess than some Beverly Hillbilly.

Gary McGary, my American Ken doll physical trainer with dinner plates for calf muscles. I didn't know his last name so I invented that one for him because it made me laugh. It made him laugh too. Esmerelda, Gloria, Caridad, and most recently, Rose, the continuous stream of Filipina housekeepers who occupied the jail-cell room next to our kitchen. Twin mattress on a metal bed frame on wheels, old antenna TV set, no desk, no bookshelf. God forbid these people read or wrote, it never occurred to me to provide the necessary setup. I was so self-involved. We ran through these women like boxes of Kleenex.

After the Revolution, we Iranians were extreme in our disconnect. I can only talk like this, be so honest, because I'm dead. How could I have wanted to kill myself those early years in Los Angeles? Well, sometimes I did. I had no one. The served are no better off, at least not the thinking ones, no less dejected. With superior access to pills, weapons, penthouse apartments from which to jump. Nowhere to go but down. I'd say we have an advantage in the road to suicide, people of my type. Zarin, a childhood friend, alone in her Paris apartment, dead of eighty-two sleeping pills. Mitra off the ledge in Beverly Hills with only an Hermès necktie around her waist. Houshang, a former best friend to the Shah's youngest son, lay in a pool of blood, a gun at his tuxedoed side. Mehdi, Fati, Setareh, a medley of cokeheads. Of course, this is not taking into account the diseases that took hold of so many. For a people very acquainted with early death, one might think we'd be more comfortable with it, more savvy. That we'd turn into Buddhists, get on the eightfold path and not react to life. No such luck.

And finally, we arrive at the American Names. We did not interact with these people. To them, we were dog shit. These are the Blue Bloods, the Mayflower class, but in L.A. this was mostly the Hollywood crowd. Doctor to the stars, say. The only respect I felt from these people was out of cold hard cash ambition—which wasn't respect but clever manipulation. They'd look askance at me and see that one day I would need a facelift or a divorce.

Shirin, my little sister, lived in Houston in a McMansion she thought was the White House, pretending she mattered. But even in the beginning, I saw the truth, and I adjusted to it. We rented a ranch-style house in the flats of Beverly Hills, on a street as wide as any I'd seen, those skinny palm trees grazing the white clouds. A kitchen with painted yellow cabinets. I fell asleep with Bita during her naptimes. She, over my arm, limp and wet because she was a drooler. I played with her. Tickled her. Dressed her in white ruffly outfits like a snowflake machine or marshmallow sandwich on Wonder Bread anchored by white leather sandals. I paraded her down the street. Americans ogled this beautiful tan, prim child, maybe confused at the obvious clash of this Middle Eastern beauty dressed up like a vintage French doll.

Nounou came to me in visions now. I forced myself not to directly challenge her. No "Why did you strangle yourself knowing your granddaughter would find you?" No "Why didn't you tell me about what the Great Warrior did to your husband?" No. I was raised to treat my elders like gods. Sure, I ignored that when it came to Elizabeth, but not with Nounou. Always in her black dress, hovering, advising.

THE PERSIANS

In America, I had no family to visit. I walked down the wide boulevards of Beverly Hills, like a rare tumbleweed, and nobody knew who I was. I could strike up a conversation with anybody if I wanted to.

Marta, a Venezuelan girl with stringy hair and dimples, came to work for me, to help with Bita. All I ever saw her drink was chocolate milk made with Nesquik from that yellow plastic tub. Never water from the tap, a suspected poison. Rose lived in the housekeeper quarters so Marta took the pool house with its private kitchenette. Teymour imagined this pool house would welcome relatives from Iran, but no relatives had yet arrived. We weren't sure they ever would.

But really, I don't know why I hired her. I didn't want to share Bita. I didn't want anyone to take her, especially not Marta from Venezuela. I wanted to give my child the very best, which in theory was me. For a time I even convinced myself Marta, with her chocolate milk mustache and her imitation Jordache jeans, would steal Bita and charge us ransom. I woke myself up all night dreaming of this, scenarios of how I would locate Bita down a dusty, littered side street off Pico Boulevard in a shopping cart, still my marshmallow.

Nounou died the day after I dreamed she would. This did not bode well for my tendency to invent life-and-death situations. So, like I did on Big Dog's bed, I shut my eyes tight, pushed against my ears. I held in my shit. When I thought of something bad, truly bad, like Bita not giggling in the shopping cart but stone-cold dead, this is what I did. I squeezed, pushed, and tightened around my orifices. But nothing changed.

In the early mornings, to fight it all, I started going on hikes in the Santa Monica Mountains. Nobody told me to do this—I visited no psychics or snake charmers, no soothsayers. I didn't say, "What should I do to feel better, Doctor?" Did I do it to pretend I was in actual

243

Tehran, not New Tehran? Prancing around in the Alborz Mountains? Maybe I did.

I brought Marta and Bita along because I didn't trust Marta to be off the mountain with my one and only. I took one of those school backpacks I found in the stationery supply racks at Sav-on with squishy cartoon dinosaurs, cut out four holes, and stuffed Bita, who was finally talking, inside. She wore a straw hat with a brim decorated with purple cloth petunias. I made Marta carry her like a sherpa. We went straight to the top of Will Rogers Park. It was always so dry in the chaparral, like it would set itself on fire. This was the extent of my rebellion—to take to the hills without Teymour's knowledge or approval.

Hiking through the dry scented trails, Marta grew sweaty and tired. We stopped under shade and opened my bag. I poured a full bottle of Evian over our three angelic faces. I hoped Bita wouldn't drown. Mother Earth was *in*, so to speak—this was Los Angeles in the 1980s—and I passed out a couple avocado-and-sprouts sandwiches on whole wheat. I spooned Marta's homemade baby food of plantains and squash into Bita's mouth. Ate a carob bar. I thought of Nounou's baby birds, Marta's ulterior motives, and squeezed my sphincter.

Marta thanked me profusely but I knew she wanted to kill me for not bringing something with pork or cheese, and really I couldn't blame her. She took her Evian bottle, which was filled with chocolate milk, out of the backpack we had Bita squirming in and guzzled the whole thing. Bita smiled her little toothy smile, and I thought: How is it that we are here deserted in this town? With no family. No culture. Just me and her and Marta. A husband who mostly hid in his office trying to put himself on a map that didn't want him. A dead grandmother's ghost who shook her head at me. I tried to look on the bright side. To adapt. Join the local tennis club. Brush my teeth with Aquafresh, the red, white, and blue colors I thought would work their way into my brain.

THE PERSIANS

The problem was still I resisted talking to Americans. I didn't want to know them. I didn't want to know their ways. What was I scared of? Who else but an American could blow up the world with a finger and still pretend to be good? They thought they were better than us. And why? Their beloved Constitution, which fooled them into thinking they lived in a democracy. Sure, some voted, but for who? What choice was there really?

A few years later, with Bita in school, I met the mothers of her classmates. The Parents' Association, they called themselves. They knew everything about everything and each other; they had no private lives, no secrets. These mothers and their ankle-length prairie skirts—it was like entering a self-imposed regime of oppression with them. They didn't know that we'd just fought against covering ourselves, and I'm sure they didn't care. Shirin urged me to get involved and network, increase my visibility, but I couldn't be like that.

These women did not approve of me. To school events, Girl Scout meetings, I wore Armani suits. Drove a shiny black Porsche. Sure, it was an act—an armor, a misguided attempt to show them what type of person I was, that I was worthy. I laughed at their beige and brown Volvo station wagons. It took me years to understand their fish stickers. What if I'd responded in kind? Koranic script on the bumper? Let them run the carpools. They wouldn't let me drive their children, anyway—complained five tiny kids in a Porsche was unsafe. Never mind they each weighed fifty pounds. Children can be crammed into a car. They're tiny and tough. Elizabeth drove us without seatbelts, threatened to shove us out the door when we misbehaved. Children can handle nearly anything. I did. What good were these American mothers doing creating childhoods that looked nothing like real life? Of course, maybe I had handled too much.

No matter, I thought back then. I didn't care. I was too proud. They could have their carpools, their troop meetings and handmade

Mother's Day gifts—although I did collect Bita's in a special drawer in our bedroom. I was not like these women. I gave up after failing to appease them with a bake sale contribution or two—some French petits fours I picked up from Café Luna, which they didn't appreciate because they weren't made from a Betty Crocker box. They didn't even know what to call them, pronouncing them *E-clairs*. After that, I pretended I didn't hear them when they approached. Sammy, they cried out, thinking they were being cute, not knowing that they hurt me. Were they also angry at life but better at hiding it?

I grew up not expecting my mother to know anything about me. In fact, I didn't want her to know anything about me. And suddenly, these children were coming home from school with letters inviting us to yet another parent-teacher meeting with the goal of learning more about them. I wasn't sure how to handle it. I wanted to know more about my child, sure. She peed her pants when nervous and secretly touched herself in the bath when she thought I wasn't looking. But the teachers wouldn't tell me anything important like that.

AFTER NINE YEARS IN Los Angeles, finally Elizabeth and Daddy visited from Iran. I didn't invite them. By then, I had distanced myself from my family. I let Shirin handle them from Texas—she badgered Elizabeth but in the end was the dutiful daughter. Still, they came to L.A. probably because I was the eldest. Well, Nader was, but no one took him seriously. I had no sympathy for their stories of bombings or Saddam; they'd had the ability to leave like we did, but chose to stay. This was a year before Daddy, who was almost a hundred years old and still put on his wool newsboy for his daily walk, died of prostate cancer in the crowded agony of a Tehran hospital. "But they have the cleanest rooms you've seen," Elizabeth kept saying. "They bring kabobs to your bed."

For the occasion, I kicked my precious Marta out of the pool house. I couldn't ask how long they planned on staying—that was not a question I could even imply. It could be two weeks or the rest of our lives.

"See, I told you we would have family here and would need this space," Teymour said. We had recently purchased the house we'd rented for so long.

"One visit every decade is not a reason for space," I said. "You should know that."

"It will become more often," he offered, his face strange with his new plastic glasses.

"Who wants that? At least your family insists on staying at a hotel."

Marta refused to share a room with Rose, the maid. But said she'd sleep on Bita's floor if I brought in a mattress. Out of pure desperation I accepted this deal.

Shirin was angry our parents were coming to Los Angeles and not Houston, even though she had been the favorite all my life, always heaped with such praise. Wasn't that enough? But it's true she was the only one who served them. And my guess was that Shirin was more angry that Niaz, at sixteen years old, was refusing to come. Supposedly she was busy with school.

Still, Shirin agreed to help me play host in California. Our brother, Nader, whom I couldn't call "Nate," found me embarrassing with my foreignness, which I exaggerated around him. He was joining us for dinner our parents' first night. I only saw him on special occasions— a particular Nowruz or birthday.

"Please, Nounou," I called up to the sky the day of their arrival, "help me through this." No answer. Bita, who was selling Girl Scout Cookies around the neighborhood with Marta, came home and saw me talking to the sky.

She laughed. "Mom! Why do you always talk with your head up like that? You look weird."

247

"Do not show your grandmother you are selling things door-to-door. She will kill herself," I said and pulled at her hand.

She looked at me, puzzled. "I don't care. We made a hundred fifty-four dollars."

I glared at her.

"Why don't you join next time? Maybe you'd like it."

I watched Bita as she held Marta's hand and then let Marta brush her hair with her own yellow plastic brush and put away the leftover cookies in the cabinet. Marta, who if one squinted, could be mistaken for me.

FOR FOUR WEEKS, I served them as if I was born to serve. I did it not for them, but for Nounou. In her honor. I believed one day she'd admit to me that Daddy had done his best, that she was wrong to kill herself, that no child should find her grandmother with a lamp cord twisted around her neck.

Carefully, I unwrapped brown packages of meat on our marble kitchen countertop, slipped them into large glass bowls, powdered them with turmeric, tossed around onions in olive oil with mint, then once satisfied, I called in Rose. While Elizabeth and Daddy snacked on the pistachios they smuggled into Los Angeles, and Teymour pretended he had too much work to come home any earlier than usual, I supervised Rose in the cooking of elaborate Persian stews.

Elizabeth somehow looked younger. Perhaps it was the weight she lost with so many years of aerobics, declining dessert, the steady smoking of cigarettes. But war was the best diet, Elizabeth always said. She went on and on about Niaz. "You should thank me every day, Shirin. The children there have much more discipline. She will be Iran's future. Mark my words."

Shirin meanwhile had grown Texan. Frosted Vanna White hair.

Teal eyeshadow, padded shoulders, more in line with the cake decoration style of her preteen years than how she dressed before we left Iran. Together we all did the regular rounds: spoke of the diseases every Iranian we knew had contracted in the last nine years: diabetes, cataracts, cancer. People who died was always the favorite topic. Followed by divorce and bankruptcy. The hard work a rare few were doing, the amassing of university degrees, the Ponzi schemes, what was the point—Khomeini will be overthrown and then we leave all this behind and resume our old lives. The money we gave up. Properties in Iran, ours and our friends, now occupied by the dirty mullahs. We talked about the time lost without talking about the time lost.

I was starting to wonder if the return would ever come. "One, two, three, no tradebacks," Bita would shout. Was that America for us?

"You are in touch with the important people here? The government?" Elizabeth said. We sat in the living room before dinner.

"For what?" I said. "Paying our taxes? Of course; they throw you in prison otherwise. It's not like Iran—it's not a bribe. Otherwise, no. They don't know we exist. Why would they?"

"We are a significant family in Iran. Very important, very respected. They should be happy to have you here. Make sure you are happy with them. You meet them. You ask questions."

Shirin, Nader, and I all laughed. It was a rare union.

"Nasreen says at least Los Angeles is one thing. The Iranians here are proper people." Elizabeth smirked. "Not as proper as New York but—"

"Well"—Shirin put out her cigarette—"in Houston they're not liars. No pretense even of culture. No LACMA PACMA to suck up to, no exiled black-tie Iranians making committees when all they really want is to bet on horses. They make money and they buy shit. Good enough for me. Culture's just a way to distract us from seeing life is hell."

"Maybe one day you'll want that distraction," I said.

"Never," she said.

"Who cares what the Persians are like. Here? There?" Nader said, leaning back on our sofa, legs spread wide, his ridiculous wallet chain hanging out of his back pocket. When I looked at him I still saw the boy who enjoyed punching me in the face before school.

"I'm glad you've found people at your level, Nader joon," Shirin said. "So tell me"—she looked at Elizabeth—"why didn't you let Niaz come with you? The truth."

Elizabeth raised her eyebrow and shrugged, adjusted her Chanel suit. "You know how young people are. Exams. Projects. How should I know?"

"You know what they say in America? Nerd alert," Nader laughed. "That's what you get for leaving her in Iran."

Shirin rolled her eyes. "I don't believe you, Mommy. She's not busy. She just doesn't want to see me. That child never accepted me as her mother. Because of you. I saw a TV program on baby gorillas. Sometimes a child doesn't take, and it is not the mother's fault. She's lucky she hasn't been eaten without a mother to protect her."

"Shirin, I really don't think it's like that," I said, stepping in. "She doesn't know better. I'm sure she'd want to be with you." I turned to Elizabeth. "You should have brought her. It's not right."

Bita and her cousin Mo walked in. "It's not dinnertime yet. Go play, children," Elizabeth said, shooing them. "The big people are talking."

"Listen to your grandmother," I said.

"We're not little," Bita said.

"Doesn't matter."

"We'll just go eat a box of Girl Scout Cookies. You can't stop us."

"Fine, fine," I said. "Just go."

Elizabeth looked like she'd smelled bad cheese. "These children. You let her rule you. Why don't you spank her? Teach her a lesson."

Bita's eyes grew wide. I shook my head. "No, baby. Just go. Please."

Mo, who looked like he was in a man costume with his gelled-back hair, said, "That's corporal punishment. That's not allowed here."

"Mommy, he's right. We don't do that here," Nader said.

I raised my eyebrow at them both. "Cookies. Go," I said to Bita and Mo. I tapped Bita forward. She turned and swatted her hand back in my direction, then pushed open the swinging door to the kitchen and they slipped out.

"So you know something about that too," Elizabeth said, smiling at me and then Shirin. "Daughters hating their mothers. It's inescapable."

"She doesn't hate me," I said and felt my finger hooking onto the curve of a bead, pulling on my necklace. Before I could realize what was happening, I heard a pop. Pearls tumbling all around me, rolling down my lap, hitting my leather-clad feet, and resting on the carpet under the coffee table and between the legs of the armchairs next to me.

How hard had I pulled? I held the bare string in my hand.

Elizabeth laughed hysterically. Shirin made a face at her and gave me a long blink. *Stay there*, her face said to me. She lowered herself onto the rug, onto her hands and knees. She crawled around and picked up the beads, in that big hair and high heels. She wasn't so bad, I thought. By being the primary daughter, she made it possible for me to focus on my family. These were acts of generosity.

"Thank you, sister," I said.

"Oh please, it's nothing," Shirin said from the floor. "You saved me from Mommy's rages enough when we were children," she whispered in English, depositing a handful of beads into my cupped palms.

Elizabeth would go home soon enough, I reminded myself. The Revolution gave me that. I started to relax.

I wanted to press Elizabeth more on Niaz, give something back to Shirin, but I knew she wouldn't admit any fault.

After Shirin went back to Texas, I threw Elizabeth and Daddy to the doctors. Put them in the back of Teymour's Mercedes, fastened their seatbelts, inched over the road. To CT scans, endoscopies, colonoscopies. They held hands and smiled together the entire time, these crazy old people. Then off to freezing cold pharmacies to hoard years' worth of prescription pills for hypothyroidism, cholesterol, high blood pressure, sleeplessness. Bottles jumbled around in my bag sounding like one of those lottery ball machines on TV. After all we had been through, they were still alive.

"Why was it you never had time for us when we were kids," I asked Elizabeth one day while having tea in our living room with Daddy. "What was so important?"

"Oh, you know your mother then was the life of the party," Daddy said.

"What parents paid attention to their kids back then, Seema? You know better than to ask such a silly question," she said. Of course she didn't like to be reminded that Daddy had taken me to buy my first bra. Give in where it doesn't matter, Nounou advised. What would I get for this accumulation of points for all the times I gave in?

A YEAR PASSED AND Daddy died. We couldn't go to Iran to see his body—too much trouble awaited. We could be thrown in jail. They could have our names on a list. The mullahs had executed other Great Warrior relatives. They didn't care about an old woman like Elizabeth, but what about us? Maybe we liked to think we were important to the regime. That we still bothered them, kept them shaking. If we ever did.

I pictured Daddy lying in Nounou's loft. A family in brown washing him. No children or grandchildren to say goodbye. A blue stone under his tongue. With his death was the end of an entire way of being. The kind of hope he had for Iran all my childhood. His righting of wrongs. His secrets.

Then, like magic, I met an Iranian named Darya. She called herself an interior designer. She had big, sexy hips and wore skintight yellow skirts and blazers with shoulder pads. She stuck out in places. She hated this and was always starving herself as if it was just a matter of matter. Fixated on the undulation of her hips. She wanted a straight line from torso to thigh—like a man or child. In department store dressing rooms together, she would pinch her outer thighs. "All I need is to get rid of this, and that," she said grabbing at her legs, her stomach, "and all the men will be after me. I'll be rich and famous." Her resolve was intoxicating. And just when I needed something to take my mind off Daddy, she was standing in front of me. I loved her immediately.

Darya was eight years younger than me. No kids. She told me to enroll in Santa Monica College and take interior design classes. I did what she said. I sat in classes with pimply kids. I studied balance and harmony. She took me to parties in midcentury modern houses shelved into mountains. A year later, suddenly she was done with interior design. It was a "rich woman's hobby." She was making fun of me when she said this. She would squint her eyes, tilt her head, and put her arm through mine and tell me to go on a long walk with her. To Century City, to Beverly Drive. Pointed out all the houses she wanted. The joke was on me.

Darya moved on to making jam. Preserves. Bonne Maman with the red gingham lid was the rage in supermarkets. "Let's make it sexy," she said. "We call it Confiture Rivas." She rolled her R's. Only Iranians would know rivas was just the word for rhubarb. For six months, I stood in front of a pot stirring. Use your new design skills to design a label. I did. A sketch of Darya, with her big black sunglasses and sexy hips, holding a wooden spoon. Go to these markets and ask them to place their orders. Nobody bit. Soon Darya stopped returning my calls.

Bita was now a teenager, hair dyed pink, in torn-up fishnet tights and babydoll dresses and I knew she was sleeping with those boys with droopy pants, always looking at them out of the corners of her eyes at Century City, the Third Street Promenade, thinking I didn't notice. They had floppy hair, a single silver hoop earring, smooth cheeks. Names like Justin or Derek. God help her.

A few years after, I met Roxana Riazi. Iranian, too, long flowing skirts, tailored shirts buttoned to the top, chunky glasses. Everyone knew her as RoRo or Chef RoRo. RoRo was opening a restaurant on La Cienega. It would be Persian food but with a French flair. "Of course your little jam business failed. You need to offer them something new! Not just a flashy package," she'd said. So I followed her dream and worked for her. Instead of rice, there would be frisée salad. Instead of cooked tomatoes, fresh juicy heirlooms she found in a secret specialty market. No lavash bread, only baguette. It took off. Iranian Francophiles loved it. We even attracted American Names looking for exotic food, catered Christmas parties where I dressed as sexy Mrs. Claus and fed married women saffron pheasant canapés.

I learned knife skills, cut my fingers chopping onions. I have the scars from sloppy stitches. Before we found a location, I drove my black Porsche all around town, writing down the phone numbers under FOR RENT signs in shop windows. I cosigned her restaurant lease. Worked the kitchen, making rosewater crème brûlées and turmeric chicken paillards. I shopped at all the restaurant supply shops—bought basting brushes, meat cleavers, commercial-grade plastic vats for storing our famous bitter orange sumac dijon vinaigrette. I mocked up business cards.

Then RoRo fired me. Just like that. No discussion. She sent a typed letter to our house, on letterhead I designed. I found it one morning, opening the mail in my silk nightgown, puffy pink eye mask still on my forehead. She wrote, "Dear Seema, We must go our separate ways. This is my life's work. Not yours. Friendship is not an opportunity." And on and on. I ripped it to shreds. I stopped cooking.

Teymour had nothing helpful to tell me. "It'll be fine, darling, you'll get over it."

Does it count when someone briefly expands your life but then narrows it? Still, even dead, I wonder: Did they ever think of me? My drawings, my sauce?

I was getting it all wrong, again and again.

TEN YEARS WENT BY. During this time, we bought a bigger house. Bita grew up. After college, she moved to New York. Teymour and I remained in Los Angeles. I went through the motions. But I still had my pleasures. My midweek walks in the mountains. My cappuccino dates with certain Persian women. Favorite parking spots. Favorite bookstores. An attempt to learn the clarinet without a teacher. An agreement with Teymour to focus on us.

My favorite place in the entire house was our master shower. It was as big as a small room. Beautiful clay-colored handmade tile. Built-in shelves housed a collection of my favorite potions and lotions, oils, hair treatments. It smelled like a hotel spa, the very best ones.

One afternoon, as I rubbed the soap over my breasts, I hit a snag. A bump. What is that? I dared think it, and so it became.

Immediately, I felt weak. Dizzy. Forgotten. Daddy, was this my heritage, your parting gift? What I would be remembered for. I stood there, under the hot rain. Staring at my left breast. Okay. Just breathe. A girl of such late blooming wouldn't face this so early.

Right?

I ran my fingers over again and there in the top right quadrant: hardness. An M&M in a bowl of oatmeal. I held my hand over the spot and pressed hard. Through the implant even. It popped up between my fingers. Like one of those games with the mallet Bita used to play. Whac-A-Mole was it?

And still—an M&M.

My body burned.

I was suddenly sixteen again and had finally gotten my period, my breasts more than the little sunflower seeds they'd once been. Now I was embarrassed because their sharp outlines poked beneath my white school shirts. Daddy had gotten me my first sanitary pads and now he took me to the bra shop. Daddy. Not Elizabeth. We left with a bag of underwire bras fit for a more well-developed woman but I didn't care. On the way home, the state radio blared. In that formal language of official Persian, the announcer said Robert F. Kennedy, famous brother, was shot dead.

"Daddy! Bobby Kennedy!" I heard my younger voice ring.

The state radio was normally boring. Court ceremonies, the Shah's coronation, praising a new economic dawn. But—this? Another leader in America killed too young—that is what the announcer said—just like his older brother the president who was also murdered, and more recently the Reverend Martin Luther King Jr.

"They're starting to sound like us with their assassinations. I thought the Americans had a handle on peaceful government. I thought we had something to learn from them," Daddy said.

"How could they just kill him? They don't like his ideas—is that all?"

"Usually it doesn't take even that. It's enough to have power," Daddy said.

At the time, that sounded like the most exciting thing in the world. To put one's life at risk for power, that upfront possibility of death. The beginning of a love affair. One that was never consummated.

And now, I would really never amount to anything. All that dreaming for nothing. Delayed puberty and a late interest in boys for nothing—didn't help me become more accomplished. Didn't keep me alive any longer.

In the steamed-up shower, my head grew black and ambitious. I yelled—more like brayed. Kicked the glass wall of the shower, *bang*, watched it shake, shudder. What if I was imagining it? Giving myself a nightmare, a test.

That's what this was. A wake-up call. A second chance. I dunked my head, pelted myself with water. Wake up! I closed my eyes, and in the dark I returned my finger to the place, fresh, anew.

Still there. The M&M. A rock. Ice.

How did you miss it? You fool.

I must have felt it a thousand times that afternoon. I didn't know what I was feeling at the end, like when reading a word too many times. Dripping wet, I got out of the shower and called Teymour. My hand shook. His answering machine picked up. Of course he wasn't at the office. He was now buying and selling commercial property in the San Fernando Valley. As well as operating his tea business with Houman. He was probably just driving around, inspecting strip malls for obvious signs of absentee ownership, sweaty on his leather seat. I wondered what he did when he got bored. I knew what he used to do. Enough women—friends they considered themselves—had called me after spotting him walking out of various establishments. After I confronted him, he promised to stop. Said he was sorry. Still, I loved him. Who else was I supposed to love? Those glasses, that face. Now I lay on the bed naked. My body made a wet spot like a filled-in chalk outline. As I lay dying, I fell asleep dreaming of Teymour's cock gripped by a dexterous hand with sharp pink talons.

At six o'clock, I went downstairs and sat in the hallway by the door. Marta was in Venezuela for a month—when Bita no longer needed a nanny, I had asked Marta to stay and help around the house. Rose only came once a week for a bigger clean.

The door jiggled open and Teymour stepped in. "Hi, darling, what are you doing here?" he said.

"Feel this," I said and pointed to the place. I opened my robe, shaking some more.

He smiled, thinking I wanted sex. Idiot. I placed his hand on me. It was like an electric shock the way his arm flew away. "I forgot something in the car, hold on," he coughed out. Patted my shoulder.

"It's fine, isn't it?" I said.

"What?" He did not look me in the eye. "You have too much time on your hands. It's nothing."

He walked back out.

TEYMOUR TOOK THE DAY off from making money. Then the next day, and the next. But there was no need. It took weeks to understand the situation with any medical certainty. Nobody wants to admit it unless they have to. By then, I'd lain in bed so long my ass felt numb and my legs buckled when I stood. When the doctors finally said it was too late for a cure, I couldn't cry. Of course it was going to be me.

Teymour sent Marta home for good. "We haven't needed her for years, Seema."

"I hate you," I said to Teymour. "Marta. Take all the Nesquiks. The Evians too. The Ritz. The Fig Newtons." I wrapped my arms around her.

"I will take care of us," Teymour insisted.

Nounou joon hadn't appeared to me in years. I stopped throwing sunflower seeds into the sky. I stopped trying to find her by singing her songs in the backyard. Did she know this would happen? How unfair that I didn't want to die and I was dying. She wanted to die and yet she stayed up there in her attic room talking to me for years. She had to twist a lamp cord around her neck at last.

The doctors said I should stay comfortable. They gave me whatever I asked for, in whatever doses. That's never a good sign.

When Bita flew in from New York and brought me beautiful flowers—white lilies in a huge vase—I said, "Do I need more of a reminder? Did you bring me my coffin too?"

I remembered something Elizabeth said that time she was in L.A.: "At least in America, the doctors pretend your life is important. In Iran, nobody thinks any one life matters. People give children away like they're nothing. Your great-uncle gave your other great-uncle a son because he didn't have one. Here, they'd put you in jail. Here, they pretend to want me to live forever."

She was wrong about that. So wrong.

LET'S GO FOR A hike, I told Teymour, three months in. He now followed my every whim. He focused on me. Bita joined. She had taken a summer job in L.A. so she could be home. I couldn't walk far. I marveled at the breeze that knew nothing of my ordeal. The air sweeping across the land, brushing, caressing, I thought how much like death was the wind. It gave without caring. Back in bed, I called for Nounou, thinking that finally she'd come to me. But nothing. I closed my eyes. Sitting in the backseat of Elizabeth's big green car as a child, I'd dream I was running alongside, doing flips. A little sprite.

One morning, Bita brought me chicken broth that Teymour had made although I could not eat. I learned there was such a thing as too skinny. I wanted to tell Darya this, wherever she was. Bita placed the soup on the table. I told her, "Let me tell you a story."

She curled up next to me in bed.

"When I was a kid, I had this dream. Have I told you about it?" I said.

She smiled and shook her head. "I'm not sure."

"I lived in a cave, in the mountains in Iran."

"This is a dream, right?"

"I had no brothers or sisters."

"You killed them off?" Bita said.

"It was just me, Elizabeth, and Ali Lufti."

"Ali Lufti? That boy she had a crush on? Where was Baba Roshani?"

"Just listen. I never knew Ali Lufti, so I imagined him, like a Western hero with a cowboy hat and dusty boots. John Wayne."

Bita laughed.

"We cooked the animals we killed over a fire. Rabbits. Elk. We masked ourselves when we heard an engine or hooves on the bridge, then we'd run out and swing knives. We stole their food, meat, tea. Their wine. My hands were dark and rough like Ali Lufti's from cutting trees and hunting quail. Can you imagine? Can you imagine such a life? Free of all societal responsibility. In the woods, no laws, doing whatever we wanted to survive."

"I guess that's kind of romantic. But Maman Elizabeth. She's too fussy to live like that."

"In this dream whatever stops her in life has evaporated. This is the real her. And she loves me so much. You know that this dream could still come true—the spirit of it? I told you our dreams aren't indiscriminate."

"She loves you in real life," Bita insisted and stretched out her arms and legs. I didn't remember them being this long. This beautiful. Elastic. I envied her, and not for the obvious reasons. Part of her beauty was in her knowing she was being watched and performing as if she didn't know. She was clever like her Auntie Shirin.

"That's a pretty cool dream, but Maman Elizabeth and the eggplant is my favorite story." She yawned. "I feel bad for her. She was so alone. Her sisters were so mean."

"But it's funny," I said.

"I don't know. It makes me think of you," she said.

"Why?"

She shrugged. Her brown eyes finally fit her face. They had always been so big they looked unreal, the way they moved. I knew this had been because her face was still growing. Later they would sink into her bones and slowly they would fade. I remembered Nounou's eyes, how she asked me where the color went. I was glad I wouldn't see that in Bita. Perfect, the promise not hemmed. It's cruel, the overkill we are given in the beginning.

"Have you told her about all this?" she said.

"What do you think?"

I felt Bita shift in the bed, leaning away from me.

"Stay and let me hold you."

She sighed, expressing fake annoyance underlined with the real, which itself was a mask for pain. Nobody wanted to deal with this. "Okay," she said and held still.

Look what you did with your life, I told myself. *This is it.* I knew Nounou, wherever she was, agreed. I wish I had been friends with those mothers in Bita's class. That I had praised Teymour for how he took care of us, how he provided. That I called Nader and invited him over. I thought for the first time, maybe all those women who discarded me—maybe they saw my faults. They saw me better than I saw myself: they knew I didn't really love them, not with any pure heart.

I wish I hadn't taught Bita so much about grooming. Then I remembered the saleslady who sold me my first bras, the way she told me my boobs were not just for me so I better take care of them. I failed them—I failed them all. The lampshade, the cord, sound of a running bath, horsey smell of her closed bedroom. I opened my eyes and put my face in Bita's hair. I smelled its youthful musk, heavy with want. "Go out. Be with your friends. Enjoy yourself. Enjoy your life," I said. I squeezed her. See, I was one of those advice-givers, telling others how to live.

A WEEK BEFORE I died, I picked up the phone and called Elizabeth. I did not tell her. I called her "Mommy." She laughed, accused me of being drunk. "I love you," I said. I sounded twisted, unfamiliar, as if asking a question. Elizabeth just blew it off. I wondered if later she would remember and wonder at the truth of it. Whether she'd believe it, whether it was something she'd think of when she was one day dying.

I stopped taking the medicine slowing tumor growth. I stopped eating. I asked Teymour for the morphine: all of it in one dose in the biggest syringe on the planet. He kissed me. I don't want to describe this anymore. It was terrible, and yet it was simple. My lamp cord. My poison swirled into wine. It felt like nothing, and it felt like joy. I was the lucky one.

Bita sat next to me, held my hands. Teymour at the other end of the bed, holding my feet. What else is needed in life besides this? The people you love being with you as you leave? We are at the mercy of so much outside our power. We cried together, the three of us. I let them kiss me all over my face and my arms and my legs. I let them love me.

The day I died, December 15, 2004, I quit having dreams. I saw Nounou again. Not like the hundreds of times I knew she was just a figment, transparent, something I invented to keep me company. Or the way she was in my memories—solitary, feeding birds, washing my hair. No. This Nounou—I could have touched her. She was young and proud, her dress billowing at the waist, her cheeks full and rosy, her eyes dark with fury, eating her seeds in the cloudless sky. This was before she left the North. This was before the long end. She handed me a seed and I took it. She loved me despite my great-grandfather, the Great Warrior. I saw how she could have existed, how I could have existed. We disappeared, yet again.

There was a time we were never here.

NIAZ

AFTER HEARING THE NEWS of Seema's death, Maman Elizabeth didn't emerge from her bedroom for thirty days. I brought her soup and burnt toast, strong dark tea, weak light tea, British biscuits, Perrier-financed Iranian mineral water, clean pajamas and underwear, face cream, hand cream, toothpaste, *I Love Lucy* VHS tapes, lavender growing in a pot, and a small watering can. She always hated plants but tastes might change in crisis.

Feet are a window. So I massaged her feet, used Nivea from the blue tin. I read black-market fashion magazines to her in the lamplight.

Even though they barely spoke, it was as if now, in her death, Seema was Maman Elizabeth's reason for life. "I know why," Maman Elizabeth said. "Homesickness. Or sickness from her home. America does nobody good. It kills all. Never go there. Please. Promise me, Niaz. Never go to America."

Bita told us it was cancer, and Maman Elizabeth became convinced the cancer was coming for her next. At first she expressed normal concern but then she was dialing her doctor, demanding that he tell her if she was to die soon, too, insisting on the worst, practically begging for it. Soon she'd make me take her to monthly breast exams and blood tests, require weekly assurances with my fingers on her breasts that this or that lump wasn't a time bomb.

"I can't go to any funeral," she said. "It is unnatural to lose one's own child. I cannot bear it."

"You might regret that one day," I said.

She shrugged. I couldn't go without her. How would I do that? So instead I did what I could. I built a shrine to Seema in a corner of Maman Elizabeth's living room. On a low table, pink rose petals floating in water in a glass bowl—this represented time passing. It supported a safe crossing when we held it up over the head of a traveler, so why not now? Next to this, I added turmeric in crumbling pyramids— the bright twin suns of California and Iran. And also, my first village. A broken mirror propped against the wall—the duplicity that was core to our family. I knelt before this shrine and prayed. What did I want for us now that one more of us was gone? I looked into the mirror, the way it splintered the bowl of petals, the turmeric, my own face.

IT'S BEEN OVER ONE year since Seema's death. The shrine long cleared away. Even if I could throw a party, at thirty-three, I wouldn't want to. There comes a day when a person is too old for such a lifestyle, and those who continue appear increasingly tragic. Pathetic people who cannot accept the passing of time. How long can a petal float before it drowns?

I work as an architectural assistant—a job deemed suitable for a woman. Our structures, our homes are one of the few things that save us. I live in a prerevolutionary building made of bricks fronted by a curved, embellished wood door. I wear pencil skirts and tidy white button-up shirts under my manteau. In the small office behind closed doors, women take off their scarves and bare their skin and hair. This is illegal. Every morning when this happens, the unraveling as I call it, I watch the four women I work with and it is like an epiphany, discovering a waterfall during a walk in the woods, witnessing a secret smile. The men pretend not to notice, but I take pleasure in it, better than any party. There is beauty in small but radical exposures. I remember the women at Kian's—those long-haired revolutionaries.

I keep my weight low with a home treadmill and an exactitude concerning calories. The mandatory covering is revealing itself to be a sham and an agent of materialism and cartoonish sexuality. At least in Tehran, anything that can be seen or imagined under the scarf is blown up, made ten times as prominent. It's even more important to have impeccable nails, skin, a frizzless hairline, perfect breasts, and a tiny waist that can't be hidden no matter what. Without makeup, a veil makes me look hideous, like an angry boy. Every woman gets this message. Along with the school-age shaming of the female body, it is nearly impossible to be a well-adjusted woman.

What's wrong with a small life? Do we yearn for bigness because we made up manlike gods? What if our gods instead had been animals or rocks?

ONE AFTERNOON AT TEA, Elizabeth begs me to come with her to New York. It has been over fifteen years since her last trip to America.

"Didn't you tell me never to go to America? That America kills?" But, I admit I am curious. What would I do in a place like that? The movies, the skyscrapers, wind in my hair. Bita and Shirin.

"We need to see your mother. She needs our help. What's she doing in New York without Houman?"

"You have no power here. Less power there. But, okay, tell me, why should *I* go to see the woman who left me so easily?" I say. "I am not of her. She's nobody to me."

Elizabeth puts down her glass of tea on the round glass dining table.

"Don't say that. She loves you. Maybe," she pauses. "It's possible that she didn't completely let go of you so easily."

"What are you talking about?" I groan. "Just stop."

"Maybe she didn't want to leave you behind in the first place." She shrugs. "Maybe she kept trying to bring you to America."

I narrow my eyes.

"Don't go crazy, but okay, it's possible I told them you wanted to stay with me. It was so long ago, Niaz joon; it was a difficult time. I think you did want to be with me, didn't you? We were so close."

I cross my arms, stare at the place between her penciled-in eyebrows.

"Khob, I don't remember anymore," she continues. "But you were better off here, with your own culture. Still are."

"You remember what's convenient to you. So why are you telling me this now?" I look straight into her eyes.

"Na kheir!" she says, shaking her head. "You know me better, Niaz joon." She reaches her hand out. I lean away from her as much as I can, my back pushing into the chair.

I make an effort to sound calm. "You are telling me that all this time—twenty-seven years!—I have believed that my mother abandoned me, that she wanted me to stay in Iran with you, that she didn't want me, that she didn't care. And now you are telling me you told her I wanted to stay? You didn't bother to inform me sooner?"

She shrugs. "The first few years. Sure. Who saved you so many times here?"

"I wouldn't have needed to be saved in Houston."

"Shirin didn't try hard enough, Niaz. If I were her, I would have asked more questions. I would have pulled out the truth. I would have made you come to me."

I laugh. "I started to hate her. She probably felt that. Why would she have wanted someone who hated her?"

"Because she's your mother," Elizabeth says.

"How many times did you tell her that I wanted to stay?" My voice now loud.

When I stand, Elizabeth looks small and meek. Something I could squash with my foot. "Well, is it really that important, Niaz?"

"You horrible woman," I say. "How could you? I always thought that having me here gave you a chance to be better than you were with your own children, that somehow you could redeem yourself with me. Even though you barely paid any attention to me. I felt bad for you. But no. How could you think there was any way to redeem yourself when you started with a lie? A lie that has made me feel unwanted my whole life. You love nobody. Not even yourself. I feel sorry for you."

I pick up my glass with a tight grip, smash it on the table as hard as I can. Glass and tea hit her carpet. Her precious silk carpet. Tiny shards pierce my palm.

"Niaz!" Elizabeth screams. "Don't."

"Why not?" I say, my fist pressing against the table. "And now you conveniently tell me this interesting little piece of family history because you need a travel companion, because you're too old and frail and stupid to go to America by yourself? Is that it?"

"No. No."

"Yes, that is it. And you didn't even think it mattered. Not everybody is as heartless as you, Elizabeth joon." Although my hand is bleeding I don't feel it. On the glass table, red drops swim in tea.

Elizabeth shakes her head. "Please don't say these things." A tear falls onto her cheek. How it got past her mascara I can't understand. She's probably not wearing her usual amount. I've never seen her cry before. Not even when Seema died. "I'm sorry," she says very quietly, almost so I can't hear. Like she can't bear to hear it herself. She looks down at her hands.

"I'm not your toy. I'm a person," I say. Elizabeth is silent. I feel a bit of guilt for how I have spoken to her. "Why do you want to get involved with all the chaos over there anyways?" I ask.

She looks up. The storm has passed. She smiles at me. "Niaz joon. Sit down, please." She hands me a box of tissues. "You should see the doctor for that. It could get infected."

I sit.

"I don't like to say this part but you've forced me. There's a chance I may never see my children again in this life. I know Shirin won't come here. Nader wouldn't even know how to. Don't you want to see Shirin?"

EVENTUALLY I AGREE TO go. With the help of my computer, I look up Kian. My lanky deer who moved to America. The one I loved but never told. The one who, unlike my mother or father, was my childhood. He is an adjunct professor of Film Studies in America's capital. For so long, I've refused to look him up.

I write Bita an email and tell her that we will be visiting. In the last few months we've been talking more often, she asking me questions about life in Iran. I told her the story of my arrest in 2002, which she had never heard about. "How did I not know that?" she asked. "Maybe we try to protect you"—I answered, but only half-believed it—"besides, since when do you care so much?" Then she asked me to tell her more about the charity I started. I told her, "You Americans can just give money to something and move on with your lives. Here you have to give away your life or you've done shit."

BITA

THE DEAN OF THE law school, Anthony Hiller, was an important man. We huddled up in his office as if we were friends. It was a nice office; sconce lighting, wainscoting, all sending signals. A mahogany desk, nearly bare as the most important desks are. Sign this. Announce that. It had been a long time since he had to think like a newcomer. He sat with his refined hands origamied together.

Despite this posture, nearly every personal item was an antithesis to the office or its forebears, a protest, a rebuke. Hawaiian leis hung down the wall in rainbow order. On his desk, Polynesian figurines of boys playing the guitar, porcelain men in grass skirts. Thoughts arose in me at doubletime, sharp and clear. I imagined him on the beach every holiday, basking under the hot equatorial sun while hopelessly desiring the young hairless men delivering club sandwiches and dry towels. Knowing full well he'd be a stereotype were he to flirt. And so he'd just lie and watch, and when he couldn't bear it any longer, he'd call the towel boys "darling" or "big boy" and wink. He was disappointed by how much he cared about his image. Another kiwi passion guava juice to his brain and he might just pass out on his towel and dream an alternate life of fulfilled urges. Poor Dean Hiller. All lawyers were like this. All had another life they'd rather be living. But they also needed prestige or money or both, at first usually from necessity or expectation, and then just from habit.

For fifty minutes, after quickly scolding me for barely attending class all term, Dean Hiller told me why I'd regret quitting law school. Before that, strange words had come out of my mouth. An unknown power had coursed through my body. No, I had said. No, thank you, Dean. I object. I decline. I renounce. I am through. "Could you simply be in the throes of grieving your mother—do you need to redo the semester?" he asked and I scoffed. Now Dean Hiller enumerated the reasons: entry into an intellectually rigorous profession, the respect of my peers and community, financial stability. Couldn't I see? As a lawyer, I could really make an impact, on the world even. How could some stuff about my relatives have affected me so much that I was rethinking my future, things that didn't seem to bother me before the holidays? This was America—here, we are all individuals.

"That's kind of why I'm leaving, though. I have a mind of my own that you might not understand. But I also don't understand it, and I want to."

Anything he said reinforced my decision, increased my passion.

He read me my admissions essay: "I want to learn to speak the language of justice. By following a path of purpose, I honor our lost dreams." He raised a sharp eyebrow at me.

"I didn't know you kept these," I said, embarrassed that I'd tried so hard to get an emotional response from the admissions officers.

"We keep everything. If you ever find yourself running for public office." He straightened the knot in his tie. Again and again. I don't think he even noticed. "So you agree leaving is insanity?" he said.

"Are you applying the M'Naghten or the Durham test for insanity?

Do you really think I don't understand the nature of my actions? Would I not leave but for a mental illness? I can't be so split in two," I said, nodding towards his lei rainbow.

He frowned. "So I have hobbies. Hobbies are healthy." He looked back at his leis, ran the fingers of his mind through them tenderly.

"Do I put it in writing?" I asked.

"Glad you remember something from contract law." Dean Hiller smirked. He looked at me to see if I would laugh. I didn't. "Well, then, it's settled." He stood, clasping his hands. "If you change your mind, you'll have to reapply. I don't recommend it—the admissions committee doesn't like repeats. Especially those who left on a nonemergency basis. Are you sure you don't have a dying uncle or something? That's probably insensitive, given your mother . . ." He leaned over his desk, held out his hand. "Rethinking your future is not an emergency."

I stood. "That's fine," I said and shook his hand. "No hard feelings."

"Law school isn't about feelings," he said. "The law isn't either."

"Well, sometimes the law is a lie. When we rely on it too heavily, when we feel so important because we practice it, it becomes a way to rationalize our end desires. And then it becomes more about feelings than justice."

THE NEXT MORNING I gave away all my money.

Mom had left me her Valiat money; no one in my family trusted a surviving spouse to not remarry, so she did it to protect me.

I kept a few grand to pay for Starbucks soy vanilla lattes and cover my rent until I got a job. I wasn't crazy. A couple days earlier I gave my building notice and started looking for a more affordable studio in Manhattan, which I knew wouldn't be easy.

I wore my last remaining skirt suit. The oil spill of black coats, shuffling dress shoes. A single person in the backseat of each yellow cab. It could have been me, then me, then me again. Whizzing by. All these people could be me. The yellow of the cabs nearly blinded me. Steam jetted out of a hole in the middle of the asphalt.

This was my city. Not Los Angeles where I was carted around in a Porsche and sat bored in salons, where I slept in Mom's bed with her until she died. Not Tehran where I would look more like everyone else. Here.

If I left New York tomorrow, it would still disappear from me eventually. That was the lesson I was learning about most things, and it wasn't necessarily bad. The light switched green against blue sky. Go, go, go, we all walked, passed bagel shops, bodegas, cobblers, doggy day care. I looked up and the god of blue sky was daring the god of cloud. There was always a winner and a loser. I tried to imagine a Tehran street. Tea shops, dried fruit vendors, a store selling bright modern furniture from Germany or Italy and ancient Iranian embroidered pillows and rugs, genius in the juxtaposition. Streets littered with fallen leaves like soggy cornflakes.

I looked down at my sparkling wrist. Walking fast, I was a honeybee flying to my target. I felt the surge of life. Was this confidence? Or was I possessed, crazy? Diamonds and gold adorned me, rubies red as blood. My mother's jewels. Snatched from a losing side long ago. I wore them all today. Her gold Rolex said 12:45. I pushed my way through the glass revolving door on Fifty-Third Street.

Every office in town was the same. Men making money. Women there to manage them, take notes on steno pads; sometimes they were ball-busting trailblazers in corner offices. But usually not. These were the spaces my parents, Mo's parents, worshipped for their clear superiority in the world of modern moneymaking. As in, what's cleaner than making money out of money? What's the least bloody? When you can't even tell me what a company does. Or is that the bloodiest?

Mo himself was deeply embedded in this world. He called me from his Dubai hotel shaped like the sail of a ship when Niaz wasn't returning his calls. I told him what I was doing. He said, "This is not a game—you're used to nice things. You'll regret this, Bita. This is your inheritance. It's all that is left of your mom."

I laughed. "God, I should hope not. How pathetic would that be?"

Up the elevator and inside the cream-carpeted offices of high-net-worth private banking, the receptionist with hot pink acrylic nails and plenty of lip pencil gave me the bad news. Fred Miller was out, or quit, or never existed. I'd never seen "my" banker, Fred, in person. Phones were ringing at a steady pace throughout the floor, the sounds flying around me. "Fine, whatever, I still need to meet with someone."

"Please have a seat," she said.

After some time she shuffled over and when I stood up she presented to me Ralph Stanley. Ralph, young and cute, his greasy hair slicked back like Mo's, navy suit pressed to perfection, yearning to please. I followed him down a long maze of hallways.

We sat at a conference table in a small beige room with no windows except for the glass looking out into the corridor. Ralph got up and brought over some brochures and shook my hand again like a big lovable dog, lapping me up, and sat back down across from me. His ears were meaty, healthy, his rosy cheeks smooth as if he had just shaved, his brown eyes twinkled. He laughed nervously and tightened his bright red tie when I told him my plan.

After a bunch of throat clearing he said, "We assist many of our clients with their philanthropic planning, and I'd be happy to help. But may I suggest you retain a workable percentage for your personal use? That is, unless you have an account outside our family of institutions. If so, can we suggest transferring the remainder into low-risk investments in-house that will provide you a steady income stream?" His cheeks blushed a deeper red, and his navy-suited arms folded over themselves on the large table. His Montblanc pen was too rich for him. I imagined it was a gift or hand-me-down, but I enjoyed the playacting.

"Sell off all the stocks and bonds. Just leave me five grand," I said.

I could tell how hard he was trying to keep his eyebrows in line. "Of course, then. I will start the paperwork for you immediately."

I began removing the jewelry with a new dexterity. Off my neck, wrist, fingers, ears. I had a couple pieces in my suit pocket. I made a pile then pushed it towards Ralph who watched, mouth agape. Whatever I was with Dean Hiller, I was even more with Ralph. I couldn't wait to tell Patty. Who is this Bita, she might say. I don't even know, I would tell her.

"And these. Sell them and include them in my giving."

He scrunched his eyebrows. "Um, that's not really . . ."

"Look," I said, because I felt his skepticism. I wanted him on my side. Of course I did. "Ralph," I said. "This money is a dream killer in my family. A curse. Money can have bad juju. You've heard of guilty southerners giving away their plantations? It's a bit like that. Can you understand that? But it's also kept me from being honest with myself. Would I have gone to law school if I had to take out a loan and actually pay for it with my future?" I laughed. "No fucking way. Luckily I have education and privilege. And I've realized I don't care that much about things. I won't die hungry, don't worry."

He squinted, like he wasn't sure if he heard me correctly. Then he shook his head and shrugged. "Well, the client is boss," he said. "I'm here to make you happy."

"I know," I said and smiled.

He flipped the page on a legal pad and I saw that his pen was etched with the name Trudy, and he wrote a list. "These are your options," he said. "We could create a separate entity—a trust, or a foundation. That is one path, but there is also an easier route."

"Let's go with easy," I said.

Under this easy path, Ralph Stanley would be my agent, and after we liquidated my investments, any time I was ready to give away money, I would simply call and he'd generate a letter on bank letterhead, send a money order. Easy. I'm not saying doubts didn't flutter in my brain then. I pictured Auntie Shirin throwing watches in the sky. I had doubts, of course I did, but I had to do this. Everything was screaming for it to happen. The money was baggage. A kind of immortality I didn't want. It never really felt like mine anyway.

Ralph Stanley agreed to my wishes. What was the alternative? I knew in this Christian country that a sacrifice of this kind would be respected even if not understood. I handed him the initial list of donations. The obvious recipients: Planned Parenthood. The Audubon Society. The Quakers. All the big names. But also I wrote in Zan Foundation, along with Niaz's details in Iran. I was going to push her back into this work. I didn't believe that she was finished. Ralph said a donation to Iran would take longer—there were restrictions in place. But in a few days, if all went well, my $3 million would be down $600,000. In a few weeks, I'd have only the $5,000.

Three million dollars wasn't much—I was no heiress, no Paris Hilton. But it was enough to let me not think about money and I wanted to think about money. It led me to law school because there was no risk in it—no risk but my time. People blame the rich. Rightly so. But what about the money itself? There's no rich people without money. I was no longer rich. I was becoming part of the solution.

"As for taxes," Ralph said. He had an even gentler voice for explaining complicated financials. It was slower, and smoother, like it was caressing me, lowering me gently into a casket. He tried to tell me something about the taxes owed on such and such amounts.

"Take out any money you need for paying taxes. I don't want my recipients paying taxes."

"So under the tax code there is a charitable deduction," he said.

"Look, Ralph. I trust you. Take care of it."

I stood up and held out my hand. Who did I think I was, Siddhartha in the Hermann Hesse book? It was no longer fashionable to renounce one's possessions. The modern Western scholars didn't count antimaterialism as part of wisdom anymore. But they were wrong. I trusted the old philosophers. And maybe even myself.

I CALLED PATTY ON the way home. Told her what I did.

"But how are you supposed to pay for your life? Have you ever even balanced a checkbook?" she asked. I just laughed and told her I would figure it out.

In my apartment, I took a cold shower. Shirin was in a tizzy getting herself ready for Elizabeth and Niaz's visit.

"Maybe they realize since you and I are both here that it's the best way for all the girls to be together." She still hadn't noticed the disappearance of the majority of my belongings. My closets nearly bare. Collection of expensive perfumes handed in a box to the doorman, Fadi, for his wife and sisters. A piece of extraneous furniture here or there sent away in a van for charity. A mirror. A lamp. I was keeping only what I needed. Shirin would just take her purchases back to Houston or wherever she went next.

Downstairs at the ATM, I hit the buttons, favoring 9's and 0's, and held my hand out for the cash until it beeped like crazy and told me to go away, I had exceeded the daily limit. I tucked the pile into the coat of a young man sleeping against the building. A woman pushing a stroller smiled at me and so I made an ugly face at her to snap her out of it. I wasn't doing this for her.

A FEW DAYS EARLIER, we had met with Patty to discuss the news that the prosecution was refusing to allow a plea. The case was going to trial for sure. So this time, meeting Patty again, when Shirin ordered bloody marys at the fancy diner I didn't stop her.

"We'll have to bring Mommy and Niaz to Aspen now. So get working on that ASAP, Bita."

"It's not a vacation, Auntie."

"I can't leave them in this city alone and god knows how long they're staying."

"What a time for a reunion," I said.

When the drinks arrived, I looked at the tall glasses, red and icy. Large stems of cucumber, celery with their shaggy leaves branching out the top. A rainforest in lava. I took a large sip. The largest I could. The pepper and vodka burned my throat.

"I know you can't officially represent me, but maybe you do the opening statement—is that what it's called? I want my little lawyer-in-training to get some practice in."

"I can't, Auntie. And anyways, it wouldn't make sense anymore."

Shirin shot me a quizzical look as she sipped her drink.

"I quit school."

Patty pushed her leg against mine under the table and Shirin looked up from her drink. Big-eyed.

"Also, I gave all my money away."

Shirin coughed and slammed her drink down on the table. "You what?"

Patty smiled a small smile.

"Mageh divooneh shodi?" Shirin said. She picked up her bloody mary again and downed it. Every extra spicy inch of it. I watched the veins in her neck bulge. "Don't even tell me why, Bita," she said, now wiping her eyes, smearing mascara and eyeshadow. "I know why. It's

278

because you hate us, you have no respect for your family, or what that money meant. We are all that is left. That was all you had left. Now it's nothing? You think you'll be rewarded for this? You are not Bill Gates." She laughed. "It was a pittance, really, to the world. Nobody cares. You think your own grandmother is living like a queen in that tiny apartment—like she couldn't use the money? You'll suffer. And you'll be sorry."

"You're wrong," I said. "It's not like that. Others need it more than me. And her. Can't you help Maman Elizabeth?"

"Oh. She thinks she's being a martyr." Shirin stood. "Your mother would be so disappointed."

"Auntie, why do you care so much? It's my life," I said.

"This is the danger of being born with money. You can think it's not important. Why do you think most of the Persian communists were well off? Not only the Persians. Mao was the son of a rich farmer. Marx's family was upper middle class; they owned vineyards."

I thought of Siddhartha, the Buddha, who was a prince.

Shirin put on her jacket. "A pleasure to see you again, Patricia. Thanks for all your work. I just hope you're not as dumb as my niece. I'll be in touch." She flung her purse over her shoulder and wobbled out.

AUNTIE SHIRIN WAS RIGHT about why I could do what I did. But she was wrong about Mom. She wouldn't be upset with me. Maybe she'd be upset that Ali Lufti was her real father, but for a reason I could respect—she loved Baba Roshani. This money wasn't important to her. Nor was me being in law school. Mom was after something else. When I was eight or nine, I'd watch her flirt with her friends at her large garden parties. She'd laugh over all their voices. I emulated her in my pink bed, my room facing the garden, hosting imaginary parties with my teddy bears, passing out drinks, smoking a tightly rolled-up tissue. At last, I'd pass out, drooling on my pillow, to find that in the morning, Mom snuck into bed with me.

I'd wake up first and watch her. In the early light, blasting so brightly through the thin openings in the blinds, she looked like a child. My child, lit up, heavenly. Even with her makeup and earrings still on, other people's lipstick smeared across her cheek. She breathed and I smelled her, the stink of liquor through her pores—not like the alcohol she forced onto my cuts, but a whiff of something human, animal. I'd wake her up and give her some water, rub her toes as she praised me.

The next afternoon, Shirin made a show of turning away her head, greeting me with her back when I stepped inside the bedroom. I cleared my throat. "I'm moving out, you have a month to find a place to stay, Auntie. Assuming you're not headed back to Houston any time soon?"

She didn't move. I grabbed a few things and left for Patty's on Avenue C, where I had slept the previous night. After Shirin had stormed out of the diner, Patty said, "Well, that went well."

I laughed.

"We might as well finish these," she'd said. Our two bloody marys nearly full, we picked them up and toasted. "To you."

"No," I said. "To you."

"You're doing the taarof thing of not accepting a compliment. Aren't you?"

"That's just a tiny part of taarof." I tipped the drink, took a long sip—the ice melted enough so that what was once harsh was now smooth.

"I like how you dropped those bombs like you were telling her you lost your toothbrush. And don't dispute that."

I smiled. "What do I tell her now?"

"Nothing. Give her space. Stay at my place. I'm not letting her murder you in your sleep. I mean, you know you need to find a job, right? This is serious, Bita. It's not just a fun game."

"I know. I'm not stupid." I took another sip.

THREE DAYS LATER I was washing dishes in Patty's kitchen, which she actually used for cooking. And now I did, too, at least for basics like tomato pasta. Patty was in New Jersey checking on her parents. She told me I could stay with her as long as I needed. My phone rang.

"Mageh misheh?" Shirin said—pulling back the handset to exhale cigarette smoke, I could tell. These were the first words she spoke to me since the diner. "This has gone far enough. Who do you think you are telling me to leave? I'm taking over your lease and you are permitted to stay on the couch. And that's final."

"I'm glad you like the place, Auntie, but I'm not staying there. You need to call the landlord and negotiate that yourself."

"Your grandmother and Niaz are arriving tomorrow night—the stupid travel agent has them making two layovers—Amsterdam, then Paris, before JFK—so she'll be exhausted. I booked them into the best hotel I could find at such late notice. But I cannot deal with them alone, Bita. You have to help me. The queen will come to New York for a whiff of an old flame set free—I know that is her real reason for visiting. Never once did she go to Houston. He's more important than me? How am I supposed to face that lying wretch who let me live my life in a complete void about who I am? The only thing that gives me any ounce of sympathy for her is that your children aren't supposed to die before you, no matter what you think of them. No matter how much they don't attend to you. And then there's Niaz. My daughter who hates me. I don't even know how to talk to her on the phone. What will I do when she is standing in front of me? Bita, you owe me at least your time."

"Auntie, when did I say I wouldn't see Maman Elizabeth and Niaz? I never said that."

"You were right, I don't give a shit about what you do with your life. Look—I don't even want to talk about what you did. You're lucky your mom wasn't successful, because if she was, then you'd probably be a junkie."

"Okay, good," I said. I didn't tell her that in a sense she was right. At my last appointment with Jamie, she'd said, "You say you went to law school to make your family proud, to have their respect. And that your mom never lived up to her potential. That she failed. Do you think there's a connection?" Of course—some part of me wanted to make up for her wasted life.

Shirin continued: "Nasreen, the big mouth, keeps telling everyone Mommy has become such a slob. Letting her apartment go to rot. Smelly fridge, dustballs as big as mountains. Oil stains on her manteau. She wears all her jewelry all at once as if that will make her look elegant but it makes her look like a museum. 'Why is she behaving like this?' Nasreen said on the phone to me, full of glee."

"The so-called friends are spreading this nonsense all over Tehran—keeping an eye on her like she's some kind of degenerate. Head full of white hair. She is wasting away because she is old and doesn't have the money to look like a wax mannequin. The first thing to go is looks, appearances. Then the mind. And in the midst of this, five clients have dropped me. I can't afford Mommy making us look worse than we do."

"We?" I said.

"And now this so-called best friend, who herself is nearly dead, is snooping where she has no business. That's what concerns me."

"Snooping? I don't understand. She's just reporting what she sees as a friend."

Shirin snorted. "Oh please! Sounds like Mommy hasn't defended herself. How could she not care what they're saying about her? Maybe she shouldn't live alone anymore. I thought that Niaz would at least take some care of her. She should come live with me."

"Did you tell her this?"

"Of course not. What if I want to kill her after two days?"

TWO DAYS LATER, MAMAN Elizabeth rode in a taxicab with Shirin, zooming downtown. Shirin had swooped in and rescued her like a pelican dipping its mouth into the ocean. Apart from a few items, they'd left her suitcase and everything in it at the Hotel Maurice. The hotel managers were sending it all down for her, free of charge, once they eliminated the risk of contamination. Niaz had disappeared to D.C. straight from JFK without telling anyone her plans.

"Bedbugs, Bita! Bedbugs!" was the voicemail I received. "She's moving in," Auntie Shirin screamed into the receiver. "I'm giving her your room. Well, my room. She's in a state. I need your help. Please. We're already here, but fix the apartment quick. I assume you've fired your cleaner, though I've never seen anyone here. And I think some of your furniture is missing—maybe your cleaner ran off with some? Anyways, I'm taking Mommy sightseeing to stall her. Prada Mahda, that sort of thing. Ugh, she's back; I have to go. Do this for me, please Bita. We haven't even talked about anything big. But I have a plan. I'm going to tell her about my trial after I confront her about her disaster of a life—she'll be on the defensive. She won't even have the nerve to be upset at my little thing."

I'd never heard Shirin more desperate. I don't think she'd ever used the word please with me. Maybe that small shift is why I complied.

Back at the apartment, I put the sheets in the wash and remade the bed with clean ones. I Lysoled whatever I could put my hands on, sprayed the different bottles lying around, and scrubbed with paper towels. I didn't mind cleaning—it wasn't this terrible thing, it even felt good. Still, the bed looked lumpy, like a joke.

Even in a dwindling apartment, there was stuff to contend with. I hid prescription bottles, recycled empty wine bottles, and threw away broken glasses. I swept stray black hairs, dead skin, used cotton pads black with makeup Shirin seemed to shed like a bird with feathers. I filled three large trash bags.

Three hours later, Shirin burst into the apartment. She tossed a handful of shopping bags at my feet. "New sheets and towels. Go wash them. Please. I'm having a dressing table and an armoire delivered in a couple hours."

I walked past her and peered out the door.

"I'm here, darling," Maman Elizabeth said, still in the hallway. Holding on to the wall, breathing hard. She held out her other hand, a big shopping bag with long handles woven through her fingers. I rushed out and took her arm, brought her inside. She was bony and smaller than I remembered—maybe five feet. And she moved with tiny steps, like a princess doll, like a person who never had to get any-where fast.

Inside, I found myself bowing like an idiot.

"No, no I am trying to give you this." She shook the bag at me. I saw the dark spots on her hand that I loved on older people.

"Oh. Of course, sorry," I said in my bad Persian. I wanted to kiss her or hug her or something. Her hair was not white—it was a beauti-ful caramel color and was set around her face in smooth fine waves. As she handed me the bag, she tottered towards the kitchenette with its all-white appliances and counters, the big opening that connected it to the breakfast bar and the living room—the feature Shirin had scoffed at when I moved here because how was I ever supposed to have guests over if they could see the kitchen, smell the food cooking.

"Shirin," she called from near the fridge. "Make me tea. Where's your samovar?" She scanned my stovetop.

Shirin laughed at her question. "Hold your horses, Mommy."

Maybe she would hug me later. The paper bag was heavier than it looked.

"Open it, air it out. Bita, you have grown up," Maman Elizabeth said, smiling. Shirin rustled with the kitchen cabinets. "Where are all your teacups and saucers?"

"I was a little girl last time you were here," I said.

She laughed. "Impossible."

At the dining table, I tipped over the bag. A black felt hat and large leather purse, big black sunglasses. New clothing with tags attached slipping out of tissue paper. Inside the hat, a big rock-heavy bundle wrapped in dozens of hotel bar napkins, *Hotel Maurice* in curlicue gold script, all held together with a plain rubber band.

"What's this?" I poked my fingers over the package. It was hard and lumpy. I squeezed, and pointy things jabbed me.

"Those are Mommy's jewels, plus some insurance. And souvenirs. Give me."

I used my fingers like a claw machine to pass her the bundle.

"Not with your bare hands!" Shirin shrieked. "You could get bedbugs."

I sighed and released the bundle back onto the table.

"Here." Shirin sprayed a green bottle all over my hands and arms. It smelled like spearmint and lighter fluid. "I'm just being careful. I disinfected everything in the bag with the hottest setting on the hotel blowdryer. I nearly set the room on fire. Mommy, sit, sit." She motioned Maman Elizabeth to the leopard print couch.

Shirin's eyes glowed catlike under the dining table light fixture. She pulled on blue disposable gloves and ripped open the Hotel Maurice tissue jumble. Inside, delicate stones and rocks glittered. Also, tiny silver teaspoons, mini liquor bottles, a petite crystal bowl, and a porcelain ashtray with a Hotel Maurice crest in blue in the center. She gave it all a few spritzes.

"Here, Mommy." The pile of jewelry draped over her hand like wet noodles. "Your pride and joy. Thank god Bendel's wasn't crowded. She needed everything, Bita. I had to buy her a bra so she's supported until Monday."

"Stop being vulgar," Maman Elizabeth said. "Let's forget about all this." She took the jewels into her lap, unbuckled her purse, which Shirin had also just handed her, and swept them into the blackness. "It's finished. Khob, where's my tea?"

"Mommy, I'll get you tea and then we talk. Properly talk." Shirin returned to the kitchen.

Maman Elizabeth raised an eyebrow, gave me a look.

I smiled. "This reminds me," I said. From a cabinet where the stereo used to go, I removed a cushioned cloth bag, pale yellow covered in small roses. It had probably once been white. "Here." I sat next to her.

"What's this?"

"They're yours. Mom had them."

Shirin came out with a mug, its palm tree image faded to a crooked line. "I know this bag. I'm surprised you didn't just dump these too."

"These weren't mine to give away," I said.

Maman Elizabeth pressed her fingers onto the bag and pulled at the center's pink button. It opened like an envelope. She turned it upside down on the sofa. More jewels spilled out. They were even shinier, finer. A necklace made of three chains of diamonds joining together at the ends. Rings of large colored stones. A golden cuff with rubies, emeralds, and diamonds in a lattice. A tiger brooch with emerald eyes. I pictured her piling all this on when she was back in Iran, all at once, in her crumbling smelly apartment.

"You never made Seema give these back to you?" Shirin said.

"My yellow diamonds." Maman Elizabeth stroked the tiger. "I knew they were safe."

Also on the sofa lay a miniature envelope. I had carefully opened and resealed it. She tore the top right off and revealed the curl of black hair tucked into a yellowed paper.

"What is that?" I said.

"Nothing," she said and put it in the jacket of her ancient Chanel suit, which I guess she'd already had fumigated.

"You know what else I found in Mom's things?" I took out a button I'd stuck into my jeans pocket. I spoke in English: "It says 'Reagan~Bush in '80' across the top, with 'Let's Make America Great Again' on the bottom." The two men's faces were nearly touching in the middle like in a *New York Times* wedding announcement. I wanted to give it to Ali Lufti.

"What a silly slogan. America was never great," Shirin said. "Mommy, your tea." She nodded towards a coffee table she must have bought to replace the one I gave away. Maman Elizabeth leaned forward.

"I'm shocked Mom voted for Reagan."

"It wasn't politics," Shirin said. "She was a Marxist at heart." She smirked. "But look at him."

I looked at Ronald Reagan's shining, smiling eyes, his white teeth.

"Cowboys, the West, open spaces, prairies. What a hunk. This is what L.A. does to a person, even if they won't admit it. Smoke and mirrors. I mean, look at you even, confused about what matters."

I laughed.

She narrowed her eyes at Maman Elizabeth. "You've had some tea, enough sleep. Now let's talk, Mommy." Sitting opposite us, she crossed her leg dramatically over the other. "Is there something you want to tell me?"

Elizabeth shook her head. "I have nothing to do with Niaz. She is her own woman."

"I'm not talking about Niaz. I'm talking about why you're here. Is it really just because you miss your family?"

"Well, sure."

Shirin's face was changing color. "You are my mother," she said. "I know I need to respect my elders but—Bita, fetch me a cigarette?" She looked to me as if in agony.

I pulled a cigarette from her pack on the coffee table, lit it for her, and sat back down. I wanted her to calm down a bit.

As Shirin let out a plume of smoke, Maman Elizabeth sipped her tea, then returned her mug to the table. "Shirin joon, daughter, I know what you're trying to say. You actually think that my dear Niaz would not tell me something so important as your recent meetings with Ali Lufti and what has come out of them? You think she'd let me come here and just be eaten by a wolf like you? Are you crazy? Why did you go behind my back and meet with him like that. How dare you? Why didn't you just ask me?"

So much for being on the defensive.

"Niaz told you?" Shirin said.

Elizabeth laughed. "You are just like me. Deceptive to the core."

"I'm not like you, Mommy. I never would have had sex with my chauffeur's son," Shirin sniffed.

"Oh, but you'd be a prostitute for an Aspen police officer?"

Shirin looked at me. "Bita, I am going to kill you."

I held my hands up and shook my head.

"It doesn't matter. I don't care about other people's affairs, Shirin. I don't even care if you accepted money from this man. We women spend so much on our looks, on our clothes. Would it kill a man to give us a monetary show of his appreciation? I know you don't take your worth lightly so I am sure you demanded a nice high price. But next time, think about your name, your business, your family's future. Don't go down a path you can't recover from."

"Hah!" Shirin said. "You sound just like Ali Lufti. I can't believe this. What was the price for Mommy—a three-night stand and you were willing to throw us out the window?"

"Is that what I've done?"

Shirin shrugged. "Well. Not exactly that. Not yet. But everyone is talking about you letting yourself go."

"Bita joon, does your grandmother look anything less than elegant to you? Isn't she an old woman who sometimes has more important things on her mind than hair color?"

I nodded. "Of course, Maman Elizabeth."

"What about Daddy? He was a good husband to you. He was a good father. And look at me: I'm whatever a female bastard is. How am I supposed to live with myself?"

"Roshani was okay at both, Shirin. None of us were perfect. But am I sorry for my affair, for you and your siblings? What would that look like? The same can't be said about your trial. Look, Shirin, you can't make this into a joke. Niaz told me they might return you to Iran."

"Just a tiny chance."

"You have to take this seriously. Lie if you have to. You have to fight with everything you have. You don't want to live there."

Shirin nodded. "Who says I'm not? Offer your grandmother something to eat," she said to me, stamping out her cigarette in a bowl. "I knew you'd change the subject as soon as you could."

"What is Niaz doing in D.C.?" I said, heading to the kitchen, with another change of subject.

"Don't ask," said Maman Elizabeth.

"One of these?" I held out a pizza pocket box across the breakfast bar.

"Don't insult her," Shirin said.

"Yes please, I'm starving. Feed your dear grandmother before she dies of disappointment *and* hunger," Maman Elizabeth said.

When I came back with the warmed pocket on a paper towel, she had put her old wandering jewels away.

"Where's the plate, Bita?" Shirin asked.

Maman Elizabeth dug a book out of her giant purse.

"Here, Bita," she said, holding it out. "I have something for you too. I can't think of anyone else in this family who might actually read it. Niaz did around your age."

I passed her the pizza pocket and took the book. It was old, burgundy leather, with gold edges. Inside there was a black-and-white photograph I had seen before. A man in a fez hat: my great-great-grandfather, the great man and the murderer. Then the title page, which is the same as what I saw embossed on the front cover but with a subtitle: *Choking the Great Lion: The Persians.*

"It's the story of your family. And others during that time. Written by an American," she laughed. "He wasn't perfect, but he was ours." She nodded towards the book.

I ran my thumb along the edge of the pages and stopped in the middle where there was a whole section of glossy black-and-white photographs. Groups of men. Individual men. Men when they were boys. Men when they were old. "What about the women? The women are forgotten," I said.

"Mommy," Shirin said, ignoring me as usual—I guess forgetting me too. "As angry as I am with you, we will make appointments to get you to all the doctors—make sure you're not about to die. And we'll get your hair and nails looking perfect. I'm no monster. Then I'll arrange a meeting with Ali."

Maman Elizabeth frowned and palmed her halo of hair. "He's really not why I'm here."

"Yeah, right." Shirin laughed.

ELIZABETH

WHY WAS SHE STILL alive and not full of malignant tumors or bursting arteries? Because she had unfinished work to do. The body holds; it is a mystery for who or what. Afterwards, she envisioned disease digging into her like curious, savage moles. Starving, ready to end her.

When Elizabeth had sex with Ali that first time, she knew they'd have a child together. To mark the event, she cut off a lock of his hair, tucked it into her blouse. See, she was built to pull out hairs, to dream. And then came the next time, and the next. Just after Seema was born, Ali went ahead and married another woman. It was time to end things, but they continued. After she birthed the third, Shirin, Elizabeth and Ali stopped seeing each other. Saeed Roshani never suspected infidelity, despite none of his children having his famous blue eyes.

Then came the endless and undivided years of marriage and motherhood. During one of those boring days in one of those boring years, Baba surprised Elizabeth at home. With Roshani away at work, Baba secretly promised to give her all his land when he died, all fifty thousand acres that were still his. Did he think he could bring this favorite daughter back to him? Sometimes she tried to imagine that remote land, all those miles of dust, from their modest home in the wealthy enclave of Shemroon, which was nothing as grand as her childhood estate and a speck of dirt compared to Baba's acres. Still, determined, Elizabeth made do. Dressed in the newest fashions, and leaving Roshani at home, she soon became a fixture at all the best Tehran parties. When she'd return drunk, she'd let Roshani have sex with her. It was easier that way.

In 1960, when Shirin, her youngest, was five years old, after writing and not sending many hateful letters to Ali's bride, Elizabeth invited Parvaneh for tea. Maybe she wanted to keep track of Ali. Maybe she wanted to keep Parvaneh, the enemy, close. This woman, if she knew the truth, could ruin Elizabeth's entire life in a single conversation. After they had tea, after declining Elizabeth's crystal bowl full of the most exquisite gaz, this Parvaneh said to Elizabeth, "Thank you for your hospitality but my husband does not like to be reminded of those years with your family. His father has spent his entire life in the service of those who treat him as property. How can we trust that you don't see my husband as such?" And then she was gone.

Soon after this meeting, Elizabeth made her first new painting in seventeen years. Painted Ali to see if her body still desired his. She used the green paintbrush of her youth, found in a box hidden in the back of her closet, long and thin, splattered with dried paint. When she began to tingle at just the first line of his chin, she learned that her body remembered, and so she continued. Then she touched herself—for the first time in as many years—initially with the end of the same paintbrush. So inspired was she by the powers of this green brush that, despite her mistrust of still lifes and landscapes, she eventually painted it, stretched across a table on its side with her pencils and other brushes fanned out behind in a chipped drinking glass. For the first time, she saw that a still life could hold all the depth of a portrait. That it could reveal and not just avoid or hide.

Elizabeth found herself wanting Ali more and more. Every time she dressed his children, coddled them, ignored them, hated them, laughed at them, refused to teach them or speak of anything serious with them—fearing that they would become like Ali, some kind of thinker or philosopher who would grow too good for her and then discard her in frustration—she knew. Even as she filled up Nader's head with talk of fighting boys at school, Seema with cake and sweets and silly schoolyard games, Shirin with dolls and dresses and ideas of romantic trysts, she understood there was a piece of these children, all three, that wanted, that needed their real father. Even if they didn't know it. Something was missing. And likewise, a piece of herself needed him. She thought, how horrible it was to make a secret child—how horrible this infinite, invisible tie!

Today, forty years later, she was an old woman. Eighty or eighty-one. What did it matter, who could remember? When she remembered her early years, in Baba's house and then the years with young children, she thought, what a silly girl! How unable to navigate life. What did Ali ever have to do with her soul? She put aside this desire of Ali Lufti long ago. It was an old book she had shelved. Useless. Worn. She stopped listening to stories of his goings-about. No man had a hold on her anymore. She didn't stop painting—she just stopped painting him.

Yes, yes, she traveled after all these years to New York, but only on her terms. She wanted to see her family. She knew Shirin was in trouble even before she found out about this court case, this drama. How far they had fallen—but not just Shirin. Did anyone have dignity still? And maybe she wanted to see Ali too. Couldn't she be curious?

Luckily the grandchildren were grown. Gone was the requirement to buy or pinch or kiss or cook. With a small child, she might reluctantly have shared her collection of miniature Korans, the black-and-white photographs with scalloped edges, or, god forbid, her adolescent paintings of family, acting like the child might care about her lonely girlhood. Thank god they were past that age. Those squirmy nosy phlegmy years evanesced.

She didn't have to pretend now that the bond was anything other than them wanting her money, her value. They didn't want her, not a real her. Progeny—children and grandchildren—were, like in the horror movies she loved to watch, vampires. It was the natural order. She wouldn't begrudge or deny it. "I told you, children aren't worth it," Elizabeth had said to Seema once when a small Bita had fought with her. They turn on you the instant they learn to talk. They turn on you again when they learn to find love elsewhere. But a week before she died, Seema called and said, "I love you." Elizabeth didn't believe it then, but she nearly believed it now, not because she said it, but because Seema had spared her; she'd kept from Elizabeth that she was dying. Let it be a surprise. That was an act of love, if anything was.

Elizabeth had packed her suitcase for New York with her best outfits. All vintage now. Giorgio Armani suits Seema had smuggled into Iran using a distant cousin as mule. Valentino dress. Calvin Klein sweaters. The jewel of her suitcase was the new Chanel flats, now nearly ten years old but with nowhere good enough to go still never worn, from Shirin who had bought them at Neiman Marcus in Dallas of all places.

She would dream about Neiman Marcus—the Beverly Hills one Seema paraded her through on that trip years ago. Especially when her mind was uncooperative and showed her images of a desiccated liver, a stomach teeming with fungus and red with flames, an empty bed—it was all on its way. At "Neiman's" as Seema called it, with its rows of well-labeled French and Italian designs in a sweeping frigid room, beige carpets, hardly a person. The petroleum smell of plastic wrapping and tang of fresh leather and wool. Occasionally an elderly woman pushed in a wheelchair by her caretaker. A wife of a near-billionaire with her spoiled children coasting the aisles. Dressing rooms the size of her childhood bedroom. Tall women in severe shoulder-padded suits offering perfume samples on silver trays. Heaven. If she could only die there.

Elizabeth today was shrunken, but her breasts remained large. She was not the glamour queen of the early 1990s, after all the bombings and sirens and Roshani's death, even after the government had seized most of her lands—from a princess to a widow calling up for groceries from a worn-out Tehran apartment with rusted pipes but still zapping men with her smile. It was decades since she'd taken cans of lentil soup or ash-e-reshteh in each hand and bounced around their big family house, inventing aerobics. She'd never even heard of that Jane Fonda woman. Elizabeth Valiat, the first Jane Fonda! Maybe for that, her looks lasted longer than most. She also theorized that unexpressed desire kept her young—of course this was her "unfinished work" as she usually liked to call it to minimize the emotion. It rose inside her, smoothing out her skin from the inside, as if she were a peach sitting in a bowl untouched inside the cool, dark refrigerator. She had not had enough. She suspected her Shirin was the same—at fifty, still raging, waiting for her chance.

Their disappointment was what saved them.

Packing for the trip, Elizabeth had looked at herself in the mirror in her small bathroom. The mirror couldn't hurt her now; she was too old. She fastened her girdle to test whether she'd bring it with her. She used to have her maid, or even the children's nanny, help with the hooks. Shirin, once her fingers developed the strength, would assemble it, appreciation in her eyes. Now there was no one to turn to at home—Niaz over fifteen minutes away and with a life of her own—so Elizabeth had to stretch her arms back, farther than they enjoyed reaching. Staring at her reflection, it looked like a bandage for a vast wound. Underneath was a cave of secrets, a womb that produced three babies with a man who, since eighteen, was not hers. She could not say, Ali, can you bring home a chicken? That is what she wanted to say, after all these years. A thing like that.

She was kidding herself about being through with him. There were moments sure, but who was she trying to fool? It was obvious. Anyone could see. She could hardly breathe. The girdle was too tight. She removed it and, hunching, stuffed it in the plastic trash bin. She opened the cabinet under the sink and, bending low, rummaged at the back for the unopened pack of cigarettes. She'd quit ten years prior on Doctor Borzadeh's orders, but he died earlier than expected, what did he know? Besides, she's lived long enough to enjoy what she enjoys. She peeled the wrapper with its golden lead and flipped open the top. Even that sound was a pleasure. She stuck a cigarette to her mouth, her dry lip catching, lit the tip. Ahhhhh. Now, dizzy and warm, she was living. The second her mind went to a backlit X-ray of blackened lungs, she flung at it the sweeping frigid rooms of Neiman Marcus.

Nasreen and Elizabeth's other so-called friends had it right. Elizabeth knew she had become a mess. Did they know why? Without Parvaneh, the truth had no reason to hide. All the truths. She would have to speak with Ali. Elizabeth fired her maid who dusted like a wrecking ball, breaking a glass teacup every other week—but it had gone on like that for years and she'd never said a word. Elizabeth stopped eating. This was the first time emotions stole her appetite. She refused to play cards. In fact, she tossed her favorite KEM deck with the red and blue peacocks out the window, watching the cards fly about in the air. She watched later as small children fought over the cards down below in the murderous street.

She had decided that day to piece herself together. Be a mother, a grandmother, god forbid eventually a great-grandmother. She looked over what she'd packed in her suitcase. What nonsense it all was. Clothes she'd saved for special occasions, but there just hadn't been any. Elizabeth could finally have Ali Lufti, but she was too old. Just as she was too old to cry over a wrinkle. Was that her final act—seeing Ali? Please god, let it not be so. In New York, she would cut any lingering mucousy string of feeling. While she'd insisted to Niaz her philosophy of Accept and Move On, she had been the worst at following it. From now on that would change.

The day before their flight to New York, Elizabeth dyed her hair. She'd spent thousands of hours of her life at the hair salon. Like fastening her girdle, now she did it herself—the typical Iranian woman's color, honey caramel. As she painted her hair, adorned herself, she had a sense of her artist self. To paint herself into her vision of herself. This was not falseness—embellishing her hair and her face with color was her true nature. Her freedom. She filled up her cosmetics case with favorite creams, makeup, and her pink curlers. All nearly forgotten. Any instinct to hoard these delicacies had vanished.

Elizabeth was so elegant she didn't need more than a head of well-styled hair and a pair of heels to walk correctly. She didn't need pearls or Chanel—but of course, Chanel was nice. No. It was in the still slender shape of her fingers, the way that when she cared she sat up straight and proud, how her smile always seemed half as big as it might be. She required the smallest amount of makeup—a bit of blush and lipstick, a slash of mascara. Even now. Nasreen and the others didn't appreciate her inherent charm. Her sisters—especially Katti—were blind to it. But Baba saw it. Ali too. So did Roshani. It was even true of her nose. Large noses were now in vogue in Hollywood. On her bootlegs she watched Angelica Huston, that coltlike Uma Thurman. Elizabeth was ahead of her time.

"WE'RE STILL GOING, AREN'T we?" Niaz said, the night before the big journey.

"Yes. You need to see your mother." After Elizabeth's confession, Niaz, thank god, made no more mention of Elizabeth's lies.

"What if I want stay in America?" Niaz asked.

"Don't get your hopes up. Visiting America is like going to the circus. It's not real."

"Do you think she'll be awful to me?"

Elizabeth shrugged. Niaz with those uncertain eyes. As a child she'd sit next to Elizabeth, let her brush her hair. But then she'd run off to her room. Once Kian entered the picture that was it, even after he left. Only once did Niaz truly open herself up to Elizabeth, the night Niaz drugged her. "This drug is the only thing I have worth living for," Niaz said, loving the high and the suppressed appetite. Elizabeth laughed thinking of her soliloquy on food. "People who don't enjoy food don't know how to live," she'd said. "To enjoy a creamy dessert is the highest purpose." Elizabeth was at her most motherly in this moment. What was this drug that made her also want to share unlike ever before? She told her granddaughter about Ali Lufti, what they'd done. "In and out, in and out, five years of that with Roshani, something had to be done. But with Ali, we wanted it so much that there was an energy in the air, I tell you, an energy that entered my vagina and his penis and made babies." After that night it was Elizabeth who pushed Niaz away, she knew.

Niaz sitting across the table from Elizabeth pouted. "Well, maybe a circus is what I need. Iran is never changing."

"Your concept of time is a baby's," Elizabeth said as she leaned back in her chair. "Mountains take millions of years to crumble."

"Maybe I'm more American that way," Niaz said and laughed. "Aren't you excited, though? You might see that time has stopped or reversed—gone back on itself with you and Ali meeting again. All those years might vanish."

"Nonsense," Elizabeth said. She crossed her arms. "Do you know how many years I spent taking care of one old man? I have no interest in doing it again."

Still, Elizabeth prepared herself.

THEY SPENT A DAY waiting in lines. The old woman and her granddaughter. The granddaughter carried more than her share of bags, her knuckles aching. The old woman complained to anyone who listened. Swollen ankles, lack of courtesy in the employees, putrid fecal smells in the airport lounge, the Morse code flicker of the airplane's reading light. She couldn't help her insistence, and she didn't want to. Otherwise, the world would think everything was correct. The world couldn't think that. She needed to press against its bag of problems, failures—so it would hear, take note, do better.

This is what she didn't do enough as a young woman. She didn't fight. She received and refrained. Ali wasn't as her mind wished. His uncouthness, boldness. She retreated. She didn't have an honest conversation with him about what she wanted, about what was bothering her and why. How she wasn't sure yet what she wanted in life. She didn't know how to say these things then.

Somewhere between Paris and New York, Elizabeth hummed as Niaz pulled open the foil on the airplane dinner. "Eat this instead." Elizabeth took out a jar of sunflower and pumpkin seeds in their shells. "You don't need to take what they give you. Demand what you want. Do the same with your mother when you see her."

AFTER LANDING, NIAZ VANISHED straightaway for the train to D.C. to see Kian.

Elizabeth was met by Shirin who looked just as she had in L.A. nearly twenty years ago, although she had traded in her hairspray for oils.

"I don't know why I let you come," Shirin said after initiating her big talk. "I can barely look at you, Mommy. The chauffeur's son? I thought he was your silly crush. Well, now you have to talk to him. It can't just be my problem. I want to see you squirm."

Elizabeth thought of admitting outright that, yes, she wanted to see him. That she'd started dreaming of him again. But she couldn't. They sat together at Bita's apartment, drinking weak American tea. Now apparently Shirin's apartment because Bita had lost her mind. Bita sat next to her on the sofa staring at her like she was a new species of domesticated animal.

"At least you could have turned it into something glamorous—look at your Elizabeth Taylor and that construction worker! Did you see the wedding photos? Michael Jackson gave his house for it. Valentino dressed her."

"They met in an alcoholics center and they divorced."

"That's not the point. You should have told everyone when Parvaneh was alive so she'd look like the fool and not you."

Elizabeth found she didn't have much to say. By telling Shirin about their affair, it was like Ali had taken her voice, but she wouldn't allow for her silence to continue. "People have been gossiping about us your whole life. You've just been too in your own world. Yes, I will speak to him, but let me get situated first. I want to get adjusted to this American way of life."

"You'll never get used to it here, Mommy. This is not your life."

Shirin was right. There was no boy to bring up the groceries or give her a lift whenever she needed one. No sense of ownership in the streets, even if she didn't really own much anymore. She couldn't look into the eyes of a stranger and expect that he had tasted her favorite foods, visited her most loved sites.

"Maman Elizabeth, tell me how it's different over there," Bita said in that atrocious Persian of hers.

Elizabeth felt like drawing her. She still made art sometimes, and though her eyes weren't as sharp, she thought there was more depth to her work now. She couldn't quite place Bita in the pantheon of her family. Maybe because Bita resembled her father and not a Valiat. She had dark coloring but with rounder, daintier features. A tabby cat, not a tiger.

"It would be my pleasure," Elizabeth said and reached out and patted her arm.

ON HER THIRD DAY in America, Ali Lufti invited Elizabeth, Shirin, and Bita to his home via letter. It took longer than Elizabeth expected. Bita read the letter, which was typewritten and started with "Dear Khanoum Valiat and her beautiful daughter and granddaughter: May it please you to indulge Ali Lufti with the pleasure of your company."

"He's no longer the cave-dwelling bandit," Shirin said.

"A what?" Elizabeth said, sitting at the dining table finishing her solitaire game.

"Seema used to talk about him like he was a Robin Hood and came out of his lair in a mask to steal food and wine, to share with the other forest people," Shirin said.

"She told you about that?" Bita said. "I thought that was a dream she only told me about."

"No, no! Seema loved to tell me stories like that. After Nounou died, we'd sneak up to the empty attic and she'd whisper these strange tales in the dark. Ali and Mommy were a runaway couple in the woods, with Seema as their only child, all dressed in tattered rags."

Elizabeth laughed, gathered up her cards. "Hardly." Yet in this moment, she saw him as he was then. Inside her, there was also something of her youth, standing on steps to the house, watching him sit on a tree branch. It was easier to think of a thing like this than wonder why Seema had invented such fairy tales.

"What would Seema think of us now? Mommy, you haven't quite addressed that Bita has tossed away her inheritance like an empty bottle of perfume. Abandoned law school at the same time. What are you waiting for?"

Elizabeth looked up. She clapped her hands together. "Well, of course she is an idiot. But what was it really paying for? You think this is living out her destiny? This tasteless apartment, these nonsense books?" She gestured to the stack of red and black law books—to her, just books. "We are so far from what we think we are in our minds, you and me. If you would have told me when I was a child that *this* would be the fate of my granddaughter, I would have said that you were the biggest liar I ever met. My granddaughter would be conversant in five languages, a skilled painter and pianist, adored by all the best men in Tehran. But, so what now? What good did my version do me? I ruined my own life. Let her do what she wants. Who cares about the money. Look—now at least I know she's not catering to me because she wants my inheritance, wants something out of me. She's a rare bird, this granddaughter of mine."

Shirin and Bita stared at her, silent. Since arriving in New York Elizabeth decided no more rigid rules, A.M.O. included. Maybe any philosophy was the wrong philosophy.

ALI LUFTI OPENED THE door to the three women, the barefoot maid nowhere to be seen. Shirin immediately started removing one Louboutin with the heel of the other, scratching the leather.

Elizabeth looked around for a place to sit to remove her shoes. When Bita told her that Ali insisted on bare feet in the apartment, she made sure to have not one but two pedicures.

Ali Lufti waved them off. "Not to worry, my dear. I've been too protected. Bacteria is good for the immune system. I'm watching Dr. Oz on *Oprah*. You know him? A Turk! Did you know that there are friendly bacteria?"

"How civilized," Shirin said and slipped her shoes back on. She flowed into the hallway, giving Ali quick air-kisses. Bita did the same.

Elizabeth took off her shoes anyway. Her feet were too pretty to keep gagged inside this leather. The polish, an opalescent peach, shone through her sheer stockings.

"Well well well," Ali said and smiled.

He glanced at her toes and she was pleased. The jacket of her Chanel suit was staying on too. "Agha Lufti," Elizabeth said, still near the entrance. "I hear you tell our business to my children." They approached and gave each other two air-kisses.

"Elizabeth"—he held her by the shoulders—"now don't start this with games. Look at us. Just look." He stepped backwards, reaching out his hands. Elizabeth raised her eyebrow and smiled. She tensed her toes. As they stared at each other, she didn't know what to say.

"So," Shirin said, returning to hover over them. She rubbed her hands together. "Let's get this reunion started. Are we in hell yet? Let's go sit." Shirin held both by the arm and walked them towards the large living room. Elizabeth had pictured a space furnished with lush fabrics, a table full of sweets and fruit and crystal. As they walked farther inside, she saw that she was correct. Except for the many maps.

"If you two want Shirin and me to leave, we're happy to," Bita said.

Shirin turned and glared at her.

"No, no," Elizabeth said. "You stay. Right, Ali joon?"

"Of course. Follow me." Ali led the way to a smaller more intimate study, adorned with the same sweet delicacies, and offered the women places to sit.

Shirin picked a sofa and before it was exactly appropriate to do so she helped herself to a gaz—most likely arranged in the bowl by Parvaneh—and started to untwist its crinkly wrapper, crossing her shiny muscular legs. Was this illicit gaz made in Iran, or a lesser American-made product?

"Well, Ali joon, you've come a long way from sitting in Maman's special chair in the courtyard. Trying to upset me by going where you were not allowed," Elizabeth said, seated across from Ali.

"Your mother was never nice to you," he said. "I never understood why you defended her."

"Mothers don't need to be nice, they have enough to concern themselves with," Elizabeth said, at first a message to Shirin, though then she considered the logic of her words. This was not true, but what she'd been taught. To expect nothing but still defend. Deep inside, Elizabeth did know that a mother's job was to love her children.

"No, I suppose they don't," he said. "Although I've heard you have taken care of your granddaughter. Saved her from much trouble."

She avoided Shirin's eyes. "Hardly," Elizabeth said.

"Sometimes affection skips a generation," Shirin said.

Ali raised his eyebrow at Shirin.

Elizabeth thought of Seema and Nounou, how they cuddled in bed, shameless.

Bita rose from her corner chair. "Why don't we go for a walk, Auntie?"

"Why?" Shirin said.

"Just come."

"Fine." Shirin floated upwards as if Bita had magnetic pull.

"We'll be back in a couple hours," Bita said.

"A couple?" Shirin said. "Isn't that a century for them?"

Bita grabbed Shirin's arm. Ali kissed them on their cheeks and walked them out.

When Ali returned he was loosened. He was wearing a tweed sportscoat, and in it his shoulders were softer.

"It's not good to get everything one wants," Elizabeth said, finally unwrapping a gaz herself. Ali sat down right next to her. Their legs touched. She quickly moved hers away, then felt a sting of regret.

"No?" Ali said, turning sideways to face her.

"It's a false goal. There's always dissatisfaction. It's better to choose one's disappointments." Elizabeth took a breath. "Well, that's what I told myself." She paused. "I threw my best playing cards out the window when I found out about Parvaneh Khanoum's death. I'm so sorry."

"Thank you, Elizabeth joon, I am grateful to you. But why would you do that?" Ali smiled. He offered her a tea in a beautiful glass cup that reminded her of a painting of a white swan. She held the cup delicately to protect the swan in her mind and drew the tea to her mouth. Her eyes were arranging his face into brushstrokes, geometric planes. Lines and contours. A circle, what she saw first. She saw the hollowed-out cheeks of the young man she slept with. She saw the man he was now. She liked these eyes best—they were smaller, and so more humble—but also more open, honest. He looked more like her now. Isn't that what they say about couples? But they aren't one. Or do we all look alike in old age, like babies do, except this time with big ears, paper-thin skin. What nice symmetry.

"Tell me, Elizabeth. Why did you throw them out?" Ali smiled, and the lines that made his wrinkles smiled all together, like a folding fan. His eyes flashed with the fire she lit in the woods that day.

"Fear. I knew the time had come. Maybe hope," she said finally.

Ali's smile did not waver.

"You see, I loved you."

305

"But only in theory," he said.

"I thought about it too much."

"Don't lie," Ali said.

"I was so young. We both were. I didn't realize it but I was just waiting for something to let me run back to Baba and Maman. That's what the chair was. An excuse. I didn't really care. I was too scared. Nobody did what we were doing then."

"We were doomed," Ali said.

"I let myself find things wrong with you because I was afraid you would stop loving me one day. I knew Maman would never speak to me again if I married you, and Baba would have been forced to follow. Nobody ever loved me unconditionally. Why should you? Who was I, even?" Elizabeth shrugged. These things that happened over sixty years ago were so far away it felt like describing a movie. However, the distance made it easier to talk. She had put the black curl in her jacket pocket and felt a warm spot where it pressed against her.

Ali stared into her eyes. She stared back.

"You're wrong. We were not doomed," Elizabeth continued. "I just needed to have been brave. It was all or nothing."

"It could have been something in the middle," Ali said.

"And look at how you have turned out. Better than us. At least you've improved the lot of your descendants compared to where you came from. Shirin tells me you have a lot of important friends here." She shook her head and laughed. "Despite how badly they treated me, my mother and sisters, I had always thought: at least I am a Valiat. None of that matters anymore."

Ali nodded. "Well. They're my descendants too. The poor dear ones. Your children are my children." He smiled shyly. "Elizabeth, you were brave. A married upper-class woman knocking on the door of an outspoken upstart with her driver looking on? You are brave. I couldn't have lived in Iran like you all these years. What you must see. The dogma of ayatollahs on top of everything. Our Iran lost." A telephone on the graceful side table next to him rang and he lifted the receiver. "Much appreciated, yes, much obliged. We will be ready. No, just me and the lady." He cleared his throat and she watched Ali in profile. His strong face and jaw, his Adam's apple. He still had so much hair for a man his age, and that persistent stubble.

There was that terrible time when she couldn't draw Ali. When his teeth turned yellow and brown, like urine and feces, and rather than draw him like that she put down her brush. Kept it down for nearly twenty years.

And now, she was expecting unbearable sadness. This was what she had really feared about coming to New York. That face-to-face, she'd see her indisputable mistake. She could not trick herself anymore if he were right there, elbows touching. *We don't learn what we need to learn in time*, she imagined saying. *Time doesn't move at the right speed.*

But, as she waited for this sadness, she didn't feel it. Instead, she was happy and relaxed, maybe for the first time in her life. Is this what it means to make your destiny instead of meet it? She did not have to come here and speak to him. It had not been required of her. She could have just stayed in her little apartment in Tehran and pretended that her time with Ali had belonged to somebody else. Or else she did not have to speak to Ali with such honesty. The expected thing would have been to keep it all inside. At that, she was an expert.

A maid walked into the room with a tray of tiny egg salad sandwiches arranged into a flower, dusted with chopped dill. Elizabeth bowed her head. Ali served her, traded her teacup for a plate.

"Show me your teeth," she said and bit into the soft bread.

Ali's laughter was deep and alive and spread across the room with its still furniture and huge drapery. Then he smiled a beautiful smile and held it, again. His teeth were not the white of his youth, real or imagined—not sparkling and clear. They were not the yellow and brown of their worst days together. They were a subtle off-white, pleasing, clean. The teeth of a man who had eaten his way through a whole lifetime and who still, miraculously, cared for his mouth. Elizabeth imagined him in his bathroom at night gently flossing both sides of each and every tooth.

"You really got back at me, didn't you?" Elizabeth, feeling so light, picked up an Hermès ashtray and examined it. In the center, a man in a turquoise suit held a rifle and marched along elephants, horses, and tigers decorated like carousel animals. It was a silly frivolous party, a circus. She smelled the ashtray—immaculate like dish soap.

"I was going to do this either way. It was inevitable. Without political power, without a seat at the table—or even hope of it—what is there but money? You know that."

Elizabeth said, "I still would have resented you. Maybe Baba was right to disapprove. But you know, I'm giving up his lands however I can—I've finally hired a good lawyer to help. Why do I need to keep them if I don't want them? History? You know our history. My dear crazy granddaughter has done something similar. I tried to love the lands, but I can't. They're a curse. You know, maybe if I didn't have these acres, I would have just left Iran. Been with my children all along. Maybe it kept me there, the fear of the mullahs stealing it. Except I do need the money. At least a portion of it."

"It can be a curse, although my ancestors would say the opposite of wealth. Perhaps that's made my thinking lazy. But, Elizabeth, you wouldn't have been you. Who knows who you would be." He still had her empty glass between his legs, holding it steady. "What does the family think?"

"They know nothing of it. I want to sell but even if the mullahs don't block it, and we bribe the right ones, they'll still try to pocket most of the money. What do I do? It's worth millions."

"Could you sell to your sisters? If you hate them still, you can pass the curse along."

"Those monsters." Elizabeth laughed. "They couldn't afford it. Besides they're all dead except Katti, and she'll be dead soon enough."

"Just give it to your children," he said, placing the glass on the table. "Our children. With the right heart, it won't hurt them. Give them something of Iran."

"Can you imagine Shirin having to go to court in front of an Islamic Republic judge? She doesn't have the right fear of them—they'll throw her in jail as soon as she talks back. Maybe I just burn the deeds—burn them in the woods. Spend my final years in one of the empty shacks."

Ali poured more tea into her glass. "Why don't you let me buy it. Privately. Just give me your bank account number and I'll send a wire. You won't have to think of it again. If we need to, we can do the deal in the Swiss banks and you can pass it to our children one day. As I will with the land—I'll make sure it goes to their names."

"Ali joon." Elizabeth's eyes widened. "What would you want with this land? Would you even go to Iran to see it? Well, I mean, you know it from years ago, sure."

"I'll do it for my baba. He wouldn't believe his eyes. A chauffeur's son with thousands of acres. The Great Warrior's acres, no less."

Elizabeth smiled. "You know, your baba became my baba's greatest confidant in his later years—I guess all those hours in a car together were bound to lead to conversation. Baba trusted no one else. Their friendship is what started it, gave my baba the idea of leaving the lands to me. . . . Okay. They're yours. I'm not too proud for this. I can give you the maps, you like maps—I paid for new ones. Thousands of people work on it. You'll have to deal with them. They can hate you now."

Ali held out his hand. They shook. "I'll go to Iran if I think they won't kill me," he said.

"Baba said one day I'd thank him for giving me this land." They stopped shaking, but their hands did not part. She felt his warm flesh. Her hand, her whole arm was dissolving but into something stronger, bigger. Brimming with feeling.

After a moment, Elizabeth asked, "So you really think your uncle, my driver, knew about us?"

"Everyone knew," Ali Lufti said. "At least the older ones. They just loved us enough to keep the secret."

"Not Roshani, he didn't suspect," Elizabeth said.

"That I don't know either way," he said. "Did you notice Shirin looks just like me? That Lufti charm."

Elizabeth watched Ali's dark twinkling eyes as he smiled. His head of silver curls. He was pleased to have these new children in his life, Shirin and Bita. She said, "Let's play a game. Remove your clothes."

Ali raised his eyebrow.

"Look, she's gone. Do it so I can imagine this was my house. That you were my husband. If you were mine, you could walk around without your trousers on. I might get annoyed with your smell. Or, I'd love even that."

Ali stood up and shut the door. He turned around. "Okay, let's pretend." He walked back to Elizabeth, then unbuttoned his trousers. They dropped to his ankles and he sat back down with the puddle of gray swimming at his feet. Elizabeth nodded so that Ali knew to continue. He removed his shoes and socks, his shirt, so that soon he sat in just his white undershirt and briefs.

She expected him to neatly fold everything but she was pleased to see that he left it all in a messy pile on the rug. Ali's legs were the same legs that had wrapped around her years ago. Still shaped with muscle.

"Your legs haven't aged."

"Your vision has," Ali said.

"Let me smell you," she said.

Ali stretched back on the baroque sofa, widened his arms until they stretched out along the top of the wood filigree. He angled his neck towards her.

"Not there," she said and held him by the shoulders. She lowered herself down in front of him—this was not easy at her age, even using him for balance. Her knees gave out on the way to the floor. She sat flustered for a moment, smoothing her skirt. She cleared her throat. Clutching his legs, she kneeled—thankfully there was a luxuriously thick carpet under the massive silk Isfahani rug with its intricate Shah Abbasi flowers. Elizabeth felt her knees sink down and leaned towards him, lifted his undershirt, and put her nose in his chest. She let the white fur swallow her face. Like a mohair sweater, she rubbed her cheeks on it. As Ali exhaled, she heard the rattling in his chest. She then lowered down until she was level with his knees, his underwear. He flinched but held still. She hadn't smelled him in fifty years. She inhaled and, sure enough, it was him. The same but more. Leafy trees, decomposing vegetables, mushrooms, coffee, cheese. Less milk, less sugar. She rubbed the outsides of his thighs. She breathed in again.

"Imagine us married," she said and looked up at him.

Ali squeezed her shoulders. Suddenly she was a girl with a love of looking at faces, especially his. She thought of wasted minutes, moments she had missed with him. Driving with children in the backseat, arriving arm in arm to an evening soiree, two people facing each other, heads on pillows. There she was, daydreaming again. Couldn't she stop? The black curl burned her skin. He was actually here. Now. Now that she was eighty. Now she was three hundred and four. Where did the time keep going? She rested her cheek on his legs, real legs, but her mind skipped years, bounced around decades, forwards, backwards.

She indicated a desire to rise, and he helped her return to his side, heaving her steadily onto the tufted middle of the ornate sofa, its silk jacquard a salve. Looking into his eyes, she could tell that there was

311

no part of him that wasn't here. He lifted her hands and held them together, then he leaned forward and started to give her quick kisses like jumping bugs. His warm breath on her face.

"Oh, Elizabeth. My strange love." He kissed her on her lips gently. Their eighty-year-old tongues had lived through decades of war and revolution, kept so many secrets safe, and now look at them. Still pink, still wet, still warm. Swirls of desire pulled them towards each other. She felt light-headed, everything tingled. Like she could pass out. What was the point of this? What did she want with this very real man in front of her?

Elizabeth looked him straight in the eyes. Back in Iran, she would throw out the old paints. The old pictures she drew of Ali. She would get rid of it all. Everything. That's how she'd do it. To stop escaping the present. It wasn't happening just because she was old and had too many memories saved. It was like this when she was a teenage girl and dreamed of the wizard touching her. Or as a young mother, plotting revenge against Ali's wife, writing her letters only to toss them into the trash. Scheming. Drawing, too, was just a way to dream. As always, drawing was the problem—back to that old theory. Her drawing made her focus too much on the surface—like a smile, like teeth, or else pulled her into a world of fantasy leaving her ultimately always alone. She wanted to be here—she wanted to experience the present moment. She wanted to know herself now.

But no. No. Dreaming was not the problem. Elizabeth kissed him back, squeezed his hands hard. Deep inside this very moment, she knew the truth: reality only ever gripped her because of the depth of her dreaming. Pining without telling anyone. Painting. Loving. All the same. This was her. The story of a nose. A story of creation. Ali Lufti wasn't Ali Lufti without Elizabeth. Elizabeth wasn't Elizabeth without her art.

Ali watched her in her daydream. Elizabeth was still the same. And they were together again. He and the young artist who had drawn that picture of him and dropped it into his hand, one of the many she nearly set on fire in her strange attempt to either erase him or bring him to her. The picture he'd kept wherever he lived, tucked in a bottom drawer or inside an old boot.

Don't let me die just yet. Don't make this my final act. "Does this room have a key?" she said, her hands on his shirt.

Ali went over to the door and locked it. Dimmed the lights. She laughed. She didn't know what to do with herself. "Hurry," she said.

He slipped off her Chanel jacket, unbuttoned her blouse. She removed her skirt. Thankfully she wore no girdle. They lay down side by side, allowed their bodies to pull together. It was the natural order, this. Them. She turned her hips onto his. They groaned in pain and pleasure. But more than anything else, what made it extraordinary was that Elizabeth was entirely present. No dreaming. No drifting off. At eighty years old, thousands of miles from home, in a dazzling apartment in New York City, he became her anchor to a world she wanted to live in. Maybe it was just a beginning.

SHIRIN

NOW THAT I KNEW Ali Lufti was my father I really got to evaluating what kind of a man he was. Sure, it was maddening that the peasant-chauffeur forbidden from marrying Mommy grew up and became a homegrown boy wonder, then a self-made Bobby Kennedy, admired all across the land, or at least the philosophical corners of Tehran, one of the most politically thoughtful men of his generation. And then finally, somewhere between these two lands he struck it rich—don't ask me how, I still didn't understand. Now richer than Mommy ever was—the kind of man even Baba Valiat would let marry his favorite daughter as long as he concealed his origins. Ali had cut ties with most of the Persians we knew back home and lived among people with reduced information: Iranians who became rich in America as well as the lesser American blue bloods of Manhattan's Upper East Side, drinking scotch on the rocks, fingertips blackened by the *Financial Times*, wearing blue blazers with gold buttons like how I used to dress my Mo. Ali spends his weekends playing golf in the Hamptons, acting like some kind of princely sage to the WASP wives of Maidstone Lane by way of Park Avenue. Mommy didn't know the extent of this rise until her visit.

Did I respect him? I don't know. He was a pretty run-of-the-mill millionaire.

I went to a stupid Starbucks to wait out the time Mommy was with him. Bita had gone to meet Patty and I told her I would remain near in case Mommy needed to be rescued. But Mo and Houman each called me—they couldn't leave me to drink my cappuccino in peace—and they both wanted to talk about the trial. Of course. After telling me for ten minutes about the Copenhagen hotel he was staying at and the Michelin-Star dinner he had involving foraged weeds, Mo said: "Don't you want to be able to travel freely like me? Don't put your freedom in jeopardy. Do everything the lawyers tell you. Mom, you're too old to be playing games like this." I hung up on him without even telling him my opinions on Copenhagen. Houman, I let him talk to me for a while. It was almost like the old days, him trying to make me laugh about stupid things. He put on the dumb voices of Popeye and Olive Oyl. I laughed, I admit it. He liked to think of us as them—a sweet brute and a damsel. But then I grew mad, remembering those New York Persians and their finance husbands. Did he really think tea bags were going to do the trick?

After three hours, I collected Mommy from Ali's apartment and her cheeks were pink. Her stockings sloppy, bunched at the ankles.

"Oh great," I griped, helping her into the cab.

Mommy shook her head. "Shirin, stop it. Take me home."

A FEW DAYS LATER, as if from the dead, Niaz rose. "I have a young woman here for you, Miss Shirin," Fadi the doorman said on the phone. I never thought I'd see her. I had a feeling of wanting to hide on the ceiling, crawl into a hole—strange for me because I've never wanted to be invisible. What was she doing to me and I hadn't even shared air with her yet?

315

"At last," Mommy squealed and clasped her bejeweled hands together, sitting on Bita's leopard sofa. "We can all be together."

I looked up at the ceiling. "You forgot about your other children? Seema, did you hear that?"

A minute later the young woman—well, she wasn't that young—stood in the doorway. There she was.

I guess I could see myself in her face, but mostly I saw my sister. My sister who I had lost for good.

I thought I'd lost Niaz too. Seema looked like me if you took an eraser and softened everything up—the hair, the eyelashes and eyebrows, the nose. Made it less sharp. Then to get Niaz, as I was examining her as she waited in the doorway, I'd say that you needed to start with Seema and elongate the face. Then add those Houman eyes—giving nothing away, seeming to accept everything. My long-lost daughter. But, god, was she a beauty.

I stood on the other side of the threshold, hands on hips, a foot from her face for the first time in twenty-seven years. Niaz held her dirty duffel bag up to me.

"Niaz! You look like one of those trees on Pahlavi Street," I said. "Too thin, ready to fall over."

"Valiasr Street," Niaz said. "It's been Valiasr for decades."

"Whatever." I snatched her bag and threw it behind me. "Pahlavi Street is better. What's Valiasr, something from the Koran? Come in, come in. Why are you just standing there? How's your boyfriend? He was that important that you postponed seeing me by another week? Was it worth it?"

Niaz looked at me, raised her eyebrow. "Khob. This is my welcome? Until now, you didn't invite me."

"What are you, a vampire? Never mind. Does a mother have to invite her own daughter? Come, come." I pulled her inside and held her—it was not a natural hug. We were mismatched pieces in a puzzle.

I positioned her in front of me and took her in some more. It was clear she distrusted me. But I'd made sure to provide for her. I had a perfect childhood in Iran, and she had one too.

She seemed to be examining her surroundings, like a neighbor cat who slipped in unnoticed, wanting to memorize the nearest exits, points of safety. Sure, fine, maybe she wasn't that thin. I was overreacting—I was used to larger American people now. Supersized meals. She was just petite, let's say. I was already getting used to it.

"Give your Maman Elizabeth a kiss," Mommy cooed.

"I didn't see him," she said, sitting next to Mommy, who drew her in and rubbed her shoulder.

"Why not? What have you been doing then?"

Without answering, she looked down at her feet. I remember Seema doing exactly this when Mommy questioned her.

"Never mind," I said. "Let me take a better look at you. Spread out your arms. I don't even know you." She stayed still. I sat on the small chair opposite and shook my head. Took a big gulp of my wine. "I can't help it. Just look at me a few moments and don't say a word. This is almost too much to bear. My daughter is here."

Niaz had the face of an angel, she did. So solemn. Bita came out of the bathroom in her towel.

"Finally, Bita, you've extracted yourself. Your cousin." I outstretched my arm, wine sloshing. "Ta-da!" I tried to smile.

Bita, nearly naked, looking like teenage Bita, as if transforming herself into something more pure for the sake of Niaz. She shrieked and ran to hug Niaz. I rolled my eyes. They held each other like they were best friends, Bita still dripping. Mumbling affectionate nothings. Was I jealous? Maybe. They sat down with Mommy in between them, Mommy holding both of their hands and smiling like a pig in shit.

"Khob," I said, after some time, the only one now standing. "But really, Niaz. Why did it take you so long if you weren't with your boyfriend?" Niaz looked at Bita then back at me. "Fine. You three be comfortable. I'm going to get chips and dips and cigarettes from downstairs. Mommy, you take your vitamins. She's not dying on my watch, girls. Do you need anything? Any requests? At least tell me that."

"Nothing," Bita said.

"Of course." I narrowed my eyes. "Mommy, what about you? I'm going for you, you know."

She shook her head.

"Niaz?"

"Can I come?" she said, quiet like a mouse.

"You want to come?" I put my hand on my hip. "Okay. Sure."

She followed me like my shadow. I wanted to reach out to her, grab her, and attach her to my body. Start it all over. "I'm glad you're here, honey," I said at the elevator bank. It felt pathetic to use a word like honey, but I meant it. I pressed the down button for the elevator and it glowed.

"Thank you."

"For what?" I squinted, and hearing no movement from within, punched the button again. I shivered. "It's cold in here, isn't it?"

Again, she looked down at her feet. "Yes, it is cold."

I rubbed my arms. As we stood there on the hallway carpet, her eyes remained on her feet like they were talking to her. "You're just like Seema. It's driving me crazy. Eye contact."

She looked straight into my eyes and smiled. "Maybe we can all go to L.A.—I'd like to visit her grave."

"Oh, come on, Niaz. You don't remember her."

"Of course I do. She was so gentle with me."

"You really look like her," I said. "But she was not some magical little sprite. She was dark." Did my sister know these family secrets we were uncovering? Surely she knew things she didn't trust me with.

"Stupid elevator," I said and kicked the metal door so hard it rang. "Well, this is America. What do you think?"

"It's different," she said.

The elevator doors closed on another level, then the sudden shooting upwards, the soft mechanical whistle. I closed my eyes when the sound stopped and we waited in the moment before the doors were to open.

"But I like New York so far," she went on. "Have you called Baba recently? He and Mo are worried. They call me every day. They want you to come home."

"Of course they do. Don't worry—I talked to your dad just a few days ago. Since when do you concern yourself with us?"

She twisted her mouth. "You've been here two months already? You must really like it. Maybe you can convince Baba to move here. When I was walking from Penn Station, I kept looking up at the sky. The buildings are so beautiful. New York makes you look up. Same with Tehran, except there my eyes look for the mountains. For escape."

"You walked all the way here?" I asked.

"Why wouldn't I? Are we in a rush?"

"Where is this damn elevator? Gah." I pounded the door. I heard the doors open on another floor. "Is our floor invisible?" I looked in her face. The elevator dinged and finally the clunky golden doors opened. A woman with a walker, two couples in suits, a water deliveryman with a giant jug hoisted over his shoulder. A clown car. I looked at Niaz and we smiled at each other and both stepped back. The doors shut again.

"I give up," I said. Leaning against the wall near the elevator doors, I bent my knees until my ass nearly touched the floor and then straightened my legs. "Sit," I pointed at the wall opposite me, my Louboutin boots gleaming under the dim light. Niaz drifted downwards and sat too.

"Niaz joon. It's so lucky you joined us finally. And you'll love a nice trip to Aspen. We leave in three days. I want to spend some time with you there, once we get through the nasty stuff."

"Of course. That's why we're here."

I shook my head. "Mommy is here for Ali," I said.

"I think it's more complicated than that," she said. "Is Aspen like a village?" she asked. "I'd love to see an American village."

I laughed. "You'll see one alright."

BITA

"**I HAVE A BAD** feeling about Aspen," I told Patty. I'd let myself into her apartment since now I had keys. I sat down on her couch, the one I've been sleeping on, folded my legs under me. Patty served us cups of coffee in big white mugs.

Sitting on the other end of the couch, notebook on her lap, mug in hand, she nodded. "I get it. Your bad feeling. Shirin is a loose cannon and I don't think she can actually imagine things not going her way. No matter how much prep we do with her. No matter what she says to us. She is the classic self-sabotaging defendant."

"I'm worried she'll be distracted with Maman Elizabeth and Niaz being here. What if she has a fight with one of them before the trial?"

"When we get to Aspen, I'll sit her down and get her focused. Go through everything and tell her the best way for her to keep the peace in the family is to just beat this completely. How else can we get her to just behave?"

"Lobotomy?" I said.

"Ha. How you feeling about all the other stuff?"

"The other stuff?"

Patty tipped her head back so it touched the top of the sofa and looked at the ceiling instead of me while she spoke. "You know. No school, no money. No mother. Sorry. You have a lot of other stuff."

I stared at her chin. "I think I'm okay. I saw a place in Flatbush that looks doable—the roommates seem cool. One bathroom for five people. I guess that's fine? I gave my résumé to all the restaurants and bars near it in case they need a hostess or something."

She lifted her head. "Bita," she said, "one bathroom for five people is going to be pretty different from your usual standard of living. Has that sunk in?"

"I'm not sure it has," I admitted.

"You're a bit like your aunt. You can't imagine things not going your way either. People have emergencies, sudden needs. What if you can't find work for a while? What if you're in an accident? If you thought like that, you'd have held on to that money. At least more than a couple months' worth of rent."

"I don't know if I even have that much," I said. "But I'll be fine."

"You know, maybe that's the key to getting Shirin to be truly single-minded about winning this trial—her standard of living. Didn't you say she makes the majority of money for her and Houman?"

"A good portion of it, yes, for sure."

"And she has several clients who have dropped her? Her idea of wowing the New York Persians doesn't seem to have panned out. Maybe we take her to Flatbush. Let her see how normal people live. How she might have to live if she loses everything. Get her assistants on the phone and have them tell her how many events she needs to plan this year to keep her current lifestyle. Let's scare some sense into her."

"That's a great idea." I sipped my coffee. "It'll be an interesting field trip."

I WAS HAVING FUN planning and plotting with Patty. But as the trial date got closer, I wished what we were doing was actually just for fun. A game. I didn't want to admit it to Patty, but it had always felt a bit like a game. Had giving away my money been like a game to me too—had Patty known? Is that why people couldn't understand it? The money was Monopoly money. Is life a Monopoly life?

SHIRIN

NIAZ'S FIRST EVENING I took the family out for dinner to that diner Bita loves. I ordered everyone cosmos. I even made Mommy drink. Niaz and Bita talked incessantly, Niaz telling stories about her Blue Rooms and her New Intimacy salons.

"Did you get your idea for being a party planner from Niaz?" Bita asked me like she caught me in some trap.

"Ha!" I said. "You think I was paying much attention to what Niaz was doing?"

"That's not something to brag about, Auntie," Bita said and went back to her conversation with Niaz.

Mommy shook her head at me, sloshing around her martini glass, even though I should be the one shaking my head at her. Bita's probably had enough of me. I'd been with her two months, and even I was getting sick of me. "I just want Aspen to be done," Bita said when I asked why whenever I said anything she acted like I'd given her an electric shock.

The next morning, I booked all five of us in for mani-pedis at a salon near Bita's. We didn't have the time to go uptown to a proper hotel salon but Bita insisted this was just as good. "How hard is it to cut a cuticle?" she said. "My treat!" I announced and even convinced Patty to join. That way maybe Bita would be occupied with someone other than Niaz and I could actually have a conversation with my own daughter.

We sat in a private room in the back normally used for bachelorette parties. "This is like a bachelorette party, isn't it?" I joked. The cream fake leather chairs were arranged in a circle, the yellow tubs for our feet practically touching one another. We were the dainty figure of a daisy from above. We were so close that we could hold hands if we wanted. The girls—I call them girls because they were all at least twenty years younger than me—brought us flutes of cheap champagne and little French pastries that looked like jewels. I nodded and the girls got to work. Soaking, sloughing, filing, shaping. I know I was supposed to find it relaxing, but it was too fussy to be relaxing—not like lying on a waxing table. The girls sat on little black stools at our feet and later they'd all move to our hands. I thought of synchronized swimmers and smiled.

"Patty, you can get a navy or gray color, don't worry," I said. "It doesn't have to be girly. The men do manicures now, too, you're in good company."

"Auntie!" Bita said, but Patty laughed. She was on my side, this one.

"Isn't this wonderful? We can relax a bit before the big trip." I let out a sigh. I was good at pretending. I stretched out my arms and yawned. My girl, with her lavender eyeshadow and thin blond hair, gripped my leg, I guess to make sure I didn't fall out of the chair. "I'm fine I'm fine," I said to the top of her head.

Bita and Patty were deep in conversation—talking about my case or who knows what—and Mommy appeared to be napping, so I turned to Niaz and said the first thing that occurred to me. "So, Niaz. You haven't told me why you never visited before. Isn't this the most natural thing?" I gestured at our daisy. "A daughter with her mother? What kept you, Niaz joon? Didn't you know you were always welcome?"

Niaz looked at me without speaking. Did I say too much? I was trying to be soft, empathetic, as they say.

"Basteh," Mommy said, waking up. "Don't antagonize her about this. Not now. Let's just enjoy the pampering."

"How is this antagonizing? We are having a lovely time together, aren't we? Do you do this in Iran, Niaz? With your friends? I don't even know who they might be."

"Not this, but similar," Niaz said, motioning to the champagne flute in her hand.

I looked at Mommy. "Maybe the question is more for you. Now that you are so honest and open with me. Sleeping with my real father. A new lease on life practically. Why didn't you insist that she come here and visit her mother before now?"

Mommy turned her gaze from me and looked at Niaz.

"Look. It's not like we've been on great terms," Niaz said. "But I am here now."

I nodded. "No, I suppose not. You've always hated me."

"No, I—" Niaz said.

"Shirin," Elizabeth interrupted. "I need to tell you something—"

"No, no," Niaz said firmly to Mommy. "There's nothing to say. Let's just move forward. It's finished."

"Na kheir," Elizabeth said. "It's necessary, Niaz. She needs to know. Shirin, I've already told Niaz this." She breathed heavily. "You're right, it is time for me to be honest with everyone about everything." Mommy proceeded to tell me that for the last twenty-seven years she has lied to me about my last day in Iran. About Niaz wanting to stay by her side. Niaz had not asked for anything of the kind, she had just come to say goodbye or god knows what a six-year-old might want when she runs to her grandmother's with her doll. "Niaz didn't want to stay that day," Elizabeth said. "I lied to you. Then I lied to her too. I told her that you asked me to keep her. I didn't want everyone to leave." Her bird voice sounded cooked.

The champagne flute to my left was empty. So was the one to my right. They were all watching me in silence. I didn't know what to say or do. It was like we were strapped into our seats on a spaceship headed straight for hell and I knew there was no getting off. There was no eject button, and no more alcohol in reach. The girls were at our feet massaging them. I asked one to go and refill our drinks.

When I finally responded, I said quietly, "Niaz, you had that low an opinion of me? You thought I didn't want you?" Hurt, angry, I didn't even want to look at Mommy.

"I was six. I believed what I was told. And then you never sent for me. You didn't want me."

"So you really never asked to stay," I murmured. I finally turned to Mommy, who looked away. Was she telling us this because she was so near death now and she knew it? Was this her ploy to die feeling innocent? As much as I wanted to scream at her, I felt a pang of guilt. Not for that last day in Iran. No, that last day was not my fault. Mommy lied to me, an outright lie, and I believed her. I kept talking to Niaz.

"Remember how you didn't like to talk to me on the phone on Sundays? You'd barely tell me anything about your life," I said.

She nodded.

"And then I started to hate calling. I always felt like I was talking to the ghost of you. Now I understand why."

She looked at me silently.

"Weren't you happy there? Aren't you happy you stayed?"

"It's all I know," she said.

"You wouldn't have liked life in America back in the eighties."

Niaz shrugged. "Iran was death back then. It still is."

I took a deep breath and smiled with an idea. "Niaz, why don't you come live here now? Maybe I'll stay here in New York, too—I'm going to rent Bita's apartment either way. It would be interesting for you. Unlike Houston—you would have hated Houston. What do you need to stay in Iran for? Haven't you had enough? We can start over together." What a joke I was, trying to put a bow on a pile of garbage.

Niaz smiled back, but it was a look of pity. My daughter. What have I done? I went on, "I was younger that day than you are now. And look at you, you are still a child."

"You were young," she said.

"At least you had a much more interesting life than Mo." I laughed. "But really. Look at him. You'll see him. He's wonderful, but my god, is he shallow. Predictable. He's nothing like you. You, you have more to you. Be grateful for that." I looked around. Nobody was amused.

"I am grateful for my life," Niaz said.

Maybe it *had* been up to me to bring her to Houston. To insist on her departure.

Even from the very beginning, that first day. Even with Mommy's lie. "I never thought it would go on for so long. We thought it would just be a few months," I said.

Niaz nodded.

I was still making excuse after excuse. Didn't I know even then, despite the confusion and rushing and my anger and hurt at a six-year-old, didn't I know deep down that Niaz would have wanted to join us? If not immediately, then at least after a few weeks? Every child needs their parents. Then why didn't I insist? Was I stubborn? Of course I was stubborn. I am stubborn. But also, was I selfish? Something new struck me—and maybe with her sitting in front of me I felt it more. Right now, as we sat there in that stupid flower formation, rainbow hues on our toenails, there was nothing left of me in Iran. Mommy and Niaz were both here. We were all out. But back then, and even now, did I want something of me in Iran? A real part of me. Is that why I am not that bothered by Patricia's threats that I might be sent back? Maybe I thought that Niaz being there meant that I wasn't really gone, had never really left. Not fully. What a beautiful explanation in a way, something to tell a shrink if I believed in that self-pity crap, but was it true? Was it really me that day on the plane with Seema who needed the hug, who needed to cry? Who needed a sister. And then, maybe this was more true and more damning—was it just easier to leave her? I mean, we had a lot to figure out in America. It was easier with just one child. One responsibility. Did I just convince myself it was what she wanted so I'd feel better?

Even if any of this was true in the slightest, it sounded ridiculous. How could I ever tell Niaz these thoughts? "Mommy, you should have sent her to me," I said because for now this was more reasonable to say.

Mommy nodded. I looked down at my fingernails. What stupid nails these were. I didn't even want them to refresh my polish. I was ready to go and lie down.

"Shirin joon," Patricia said.

"Yes, Patricia joon?" I smiled as brightly as I could.

"Do you want me to take you back to the apartment?"

BACK THEN I HAD convinced myself that I was unfit to raise a daughter. That I had been spared. A boy was easy. Mo accepted everything I told him; he ate his bites of gruel, he wore the sailor suits I laid out on his bed. Only later did he pick dumb girlfriends who just gazed at him with admiring eyes for reasons like he can shout numbers across a trading floor. Never did he disagree with me. But who has more of my spirit locked inside them? Is this the difference between a daughter and a son?

Was it too late now?

The next morning I got up from the sofa—usually I find sleeping on a sofa disgusting but what choice did I have—and woke Niaz and Mommy. "We have to pack for tomorrow," I said and clapped my hands. I really did want them to see Aspen. Even if I had a court date there. Even with all this regret. I had a reel in my head that played an apology from the judge, the cop, and sometimes the mayor too. I would accept graciously.

Mommy, in her dressing gown, smiled and said, "Sure, but packing will be easy. Let's enjoy this day."

I rolled my eyes but complied. We let Mommy take us for brunch on the Upper East Side. "This is more my scene," Mommy said between the taxi and the restaurant entrance, smiling at groups of older women strolling by, some in visors and sports outfits, others in Saint Laurent and Ferragamo. At brunch, none of us mentioned anything about our talk yesterday, or Ali, or even the case. We spoke instead of trends in plastic surgery, vitamins, and fashion. Mommy and I agreed that Sophia Loren was the perfect woman. It was all so pleasant. Maybe that was what we needed between us—some truth telling.

When Mommy and I got back to the apartment to pack I poured her some tea. Niaz had already thrown her stuff into her dirty duffel bag so she went over to Patty's with Bita. "Do you remember our family trips when I was a kid? That's what this feels like," I said. Being stupid and sentimental, I was remembering the Caspian where for generations our family went on holiday in the summer. Our big family trips north of Tehran. Cousins, aunts, uncles, grandparents.

"Except then you weren't potentially going to prison," Mommy said with a sneer.

"Don't worry. I won't be," I said and grabbed the suitcase I'd tucked into Bita's hallway closet. In those Caspian years, I would bring every dress I owned. My one pair of sandals. My one bathing suit, all white. "Remember I met Houman on one of those trips?" I said.

"Is he meeting us in Aspen?" she asked.

"Of course not. What good would he do?" The summer I met Houman he drew over my bathing suit in black marker. A comic strip about the two of us all over my stomach and ass. You see, us Iranians are mythmakers, romantics you might say. We love to love our lovers. Layla and Majnun. Yusuf and Zulaikha. Shirin and Farhad. It's always the same. Houman drew a lusty boy falling over a princess in the sand, the waves eating him, the sea and its monster. I stole a clean bathing suit from Narges, my cousin with hairy thighs, who stayed fully robed. What good would a person like Houman do in a criminal court?

Mommy held up a pair of shoes I had bought her years ago but they looked brand-new. "Will there be an occasion to wear these? And you should call him at least. You don't want him to turn on you now, Shirin," Mommy said.

"He wouldn't dare," I said.

Back then, we filled leather crates passed down for a hundred years. Green ones with golden buckles. One car was just for luggage. Children in another. Adults rode in the newest, best car, which went the fastest because Mommy drove. She'd turn and lose us for miles. Once there, the old people wouldn't so much as look at their young. The help—who rode in our jalopies—gave us what we needed. We moved to our own schedule. Days at the beach, climbing rocks. Fried by the sun. I don't know what the old people did. They played cards. They smoked. Listened to their songs. But who cared? We didn't. How was I supposed to be a mother with adults like these?

When Bita and Niaz joined us later, I called for pizza.

"Bita, come here and play Rami with your grandmother," Mommy said, tapping the spot next to her at the table, deck of cards in her other hand.

I raised an eyebrow. "Look at this, Mommy the family woman!"

"Shirin, I've always loved playing cards. It has nothing to do with family. Tell her, Niaz."

I joined Niaz at the sofa. "Niaz, how do you even walk past these mullahs all the time. Do you make faces when they turn their heads? I know they have all the money. The mullahs, the revolutionary guards. It was always about money and power," I said.

"I fantasize about running past one and toppling his turban," Niaz said.

"That's Islamophobic, Niaz," Bita said, holding cards Mommy passed to her.

"No, it's not. That's bullshit. Fucking with the warden of my prison isn't discrimination. They'll use the cloak of religion to get this reaction from people like you."

"People like me?" Bita asked.

"You with your Western liberal perspective. You want to be so tolerant of everyone that you can't make distinctions."

"Of course I can," she said. "That also just seems childish. Toppling a turban."

"I would applaud it," Mommy said. "You should see how they torment us."

"They're authoritarians; they deserve it," Niaz said annoyed, and stood up from the sofa. "I need to shower."

"Go now before the pizza arrives," I said. "I ordered real Neapolitan pizza. Better than in Italy." I turned to Bita. "You know, I think how could these Italians, the Italians of today, be the descendants of Michelangelo and Leonardo da Vinci? Look at them with their football fanaticism, the ridiculous eyeglasses, old men eating ice cream cones. But you know what I say? It is there. Under the layers. Just like for us, the great ancient Persians."

She smiled like I'd said something more amusing than I realized.

But I was trying to make her smile. "What, Bita? Go give her a towel," I said. "Quick."

When Bita returned, she sat back down next to Maman Elizabeth. They continued their game.

And I continued talking: "Lately I've been thinking of Nounou. At least she said, 'I won't be a fool any longer, I won't be a joke.' They all died to relieve themselves, our family. Nounou, the Great Warrior, Seema. I don't want that. I don't want to have to kill myself to stop being a joke."

"Mom didn't kill herself," Bita said.

"Are you sure?" I said. "Neglecting oneself can lead to death too. But fine, you're probably right."

"Shirin," Mommy snapped. "Stop it. We all know it was America."

Bita narrowed her eyes at me. "If you want to be less of a joke, then you should think more before you speak. Actually speak less, Auntie. That would be the best thing. And maybe consider why you feel the need to distract yourself by causing a scene everywhere you go. The thing you seem to be the most scared of is not having everyone's attention at all times. Why is that? Are you worried you'll have to face your own shortcomings if nobody's watching?"

"Oh, look at you," I said. "Maybe you're right. I talk too much. Others should talk more for a change. But shortcomings? Hah! Just stop it, Bita. I've been wanting to ask you, what are you going to do now that you're a pauper?"

"Well, if you really want to know, I'm writing a book about a Persian family."

"Oh really? About us?" I raised my eyebrow. "You know, usually money comes in handy if you're planning on being a starving artist," I said. "Haven't you noticed that's what people do—the ancestors give them money and then the freeloader lives as they please? They redeem the family, or so they think. But they don't just throw out the money."

"Well, I did," she said.

"You sure did," I said. "You want your own version of hardship. Is that it? You'll regret it."

"Leave her alone, Shirin," Mommy said. "She will make us proud. Smarts have skipped a generation in this family."

"Oh please. She wishes," I laughed. "Of course this trip to Aspen is on the house. But don't count on it forever, Bita joon. Maybe it'll be your last time there. Let's go and be a real family for once. A nice family. Let's enjoy ourselves. Talk about the trees and the coffee. Like normal people."

"You mean you're not going to get wasted and buy everything you see?" Bita said. "This could be interesting."

I laughed. "Idiot."

BITA

THE MORNING BEFORE OUR flight, which would leave that afternoon, we all took a taxi van to Flatbush. Me, Niaz, Shirin, Elizabeth, and Patty. I could see Shirin's face drop as we rose over the East River. "Why would you ever leave Manhattan, Bita?" she asked. Patty who was sitting next to me pinched my thigh. I held in my laughter.

We stood outside the walk-up and greeted the super, a small bald man in a navy jumpsuit, who was going to let us see the place. The roommates were all out.

"This isn't even New York!" Shirin said.

"Oh god, Shirin, come on," I said.

I turned and saw that Maman Elizabeth was stepping over a pile of discarded clothing and crinkling her nose. "Even Tehran is cleaner than this."

"No it's not," Niaz said. "You just don't go anywhere."

I laughed. We walked up the stairs, Shirin complaining about the smells. "What is this, rotten eggs?" In Persian she said, "Bita, you can't live here. This is not appropriate for a girl of your upbringing!"

"Khob," Elizabeth said in front of the peeling blue painted door.

"Is it safe? That is what matters. Even I know the young ones like to live in filth these days. They aren't like us, Shirin. Look at Niaz."

"I don't live in filth!" Niaz said. "Just because I don't want mirrors and gold on everything, or French antiques!"

"Auntie," I said, "if you're not careful and lose the trial or any more of your clients, you might have to live somewhere like this."

"Stop, stop! Don't say that. I mean, what is the cost of this dump?" Shirin whispered as we walked through the long dark hallway littered with art projects and salvaged metal.

"For the whole apartment, probably five thousand a month," Patty said and winked at me.

"What! No?"

"Shirin, this is a middle-class neighborhood in one of the most expensive cities in the world. So if you don't get an acquittal—" Patty said.

"I'm kind of a fan of this bathtub in the kitchen," I said, lifting the counter to expose the cracked porcelain tub. "That's fun. I could cook dinner and take a bath all at once."

"Was that a rat? Or—" Shirin screamed. "Did you see that?"

When I turned to look, a flash of boxer short and scruffy leg disappeared around the corner.

"Probably," Patty said.

"Bita joon, you cannot live in this rat-infested, bathtub-heavy, flat-bushy apartment with strange undressed men. Your mother would die a second death. And I am never setting foot in Brooklyn again."

SHIRIN

BEFORE SUNSET, WE BOARDED the plane. I carried Mommy's bag. We were a beautiful set. Me, Mommy, Niaz, Bita. Elegant, dramatic eyes, big brown hair. The Ivanka sisters Bita was not-so-secretly jealous of could eat shit. Even Mommy was at her best—maybe some sex was the jump start she needed. The night before, she did her hair in curlers. This morning she made her eyes like ancient Egyptian royalty— I couldn't show her to the judge like this, however, because the whole insulting "baby be my Cleopatra for the night" was part of my legal defense. I couldn't have Cleopatra for a mother. At least she wore her Chanel flats. If I had seen us in the terminal, if I looked up from my *Us Weekly*, some schlubby American tourist with a McFlurry on my mind, I would have thought we were untouchable.

Of course there was Patty too. She rounded us out; we needed her. She was the friend, the assistant, the person with the tickets and itineraries. Don't tell me you don't notice that person in the paparazzi photos. These figures of American royalty are nothing without their outsider-insider who holds it all together. Patty could be our Seema, too, in a way, how she obviously loves Bita. I mean, to put up with Bita, it has to be love, who else could deal with that drivel. She took care of Bita in school and supported her when she decided to quit—just like I know Seema would have.

I wanted to drink on the flight but I was too tired and we still had to switch planes halfway there. It had nothing to do with what Bita had said. Why should it? *You're not going to get wasted and buy everything you see?* Yet I could do it—be strict with myself. Live a life of glory. Be a star. Why not? When the cabin lights turned off, I focused on our big machine pushing its way through the thin air.

WE CHECKED INTO OUR usual Aspen hotel. Four rooms on the third floor. I took 3E again, but this time no Houman, although when I checked the red-blinking telephone he had already left me three voicemails begging me to do everything I could to secure a not guilty verdict and to please come home. Same old story. Even without him, I brought the green felt and the cards. Instead of cocaine, I brought vitamins. But, in my heart of hearts I did wonder, what the hell were we going to do here if not party and shop? What does any visitor do in Aspen? We could eat, but how much crepe and raclette and gimmicky sushi could I take?

The next morning was March 20, the first day of spring. Nowruz, in fact. The ancient Zoroastrian holiday Persians have been celebrating for millennia in Iran, even in defiance of the Islamic Republic. Niaz reminded our group of the day, unfortunately. Nothing could stop a Persian, a certain kind, from wanting to leap over a bonfire or wear new clothes. I hated Nowruz because it was nothing here. Nobody cared, or understood what it was really about—darkness, evil, and cleansing ourselves each year because evil always returns.

They all came into my room after breakfast. Of course my room was a sort of gathering place; I was their leader, after all. Their commander. Their G.W., you could say. At least my room was the biggest so it didn't disturb me too much to have them taking up space. "Sit, sit," I said, fluffing pillows.

Niaz, Mommy, Bita, and Patty all sat on the dueling sofas.

I offered them the minibar. They declined. How long was that going to last?

"We need a goldfish and sabzeh, somagh, and samanu," Niaz said.

"Where are we supposed to get that? This is not Tehran and it's not even Tehrangeles," I said. "These people don't know what a Persian is besides a cat."

"I'll see what I can find. Niaz, you come with me. Bita, you too," Mommy said. "It has to be ready before 11:27 or it's too late."

"Like any of us can feel the exact second we're leaning towards the sun again?" I said and handed Mommy my worst credit card in case she lost it.

It was a different Aspen in March. The Texans and fur were minimized. There were some young couples on their first getaway—all lips and hips, there were groups of single girlfriends on the prowl. Compared to Christmastime it was like walking into the Library of Congress. This really is our Caspian, I supposed. We are mountain people, after all. We do this to emulate something we once had.

"Well," I said as they got up to leave. "Patty, you stay with me and we talk business?"

Patty looked like a boy. I was growing to love this about her. She didn't care about wearing makeup, showing the V of her cleavage, the shape of her waist and hips, blowdried hair, fake lashes. Today she wore toddler dungarees with tan boots and a wool cap. A paperboy crossed with lumberjack. She had these naturally rosy cheeks and expressive eyes like a baby's.

As Patty watched, I pulled on my Louboutin boots, my long Prada coat. I needed a break from my relatives, and I was glad it was just me and this practical stranger. I preferred strangers. We went down to the lobby lounge, which was dead. Nobody needs a thirty-dollar piece of toast when it's sunny out. I ordered us club sandwiches wrapped in lettuce, extra pickles and mustard, no mayo. I rummaged around my leather shopper for the court documents, as well as a full description of events I had typed out on Bita's computer a few weeks earlier, and handed the various folded papers to Patty. "Bita said I should give you all this in case you're missing anything before I make an appearance at the court."

"It's not called making an appearance, Shirin," Patty said. "You can't be fashionably late." She created a single stack and looked through the papers.

"Fine," I said.

As she read, I leaned back and studied the room. Waiters, a few scattered guests, the bottom of the wood staircase that whirled up to the mezzanine. The fireplace behind us unlit and empty. Nobody was at the big black grand piano. John Denver's "Take Me Home, Country Roads" played on the speakers. Next I'm sure it would be Bob Marley. Earlier, Dolly Parton.

Patty looked up. "Yeah, I have all these," she said and handed them back. "This shouldn't be too hard, Shirin. We should be able to get it entirely cleared. You don't want to lose your business. You don't want to have to live in a kind of squalor like Bita's new place. You don't want to have to go back to Iran. I may not even need to rely on the entrapment defense because you weren't really trying to sell sex. You're fine as long as they believe you were joking. Let's focus again on what you need to say. Why were you flirting with this police officer?"

"He was cute. I was mad at my idiot husband. I don't know why. Why does anyone do anything?" I drank the coffee in front of me. It was cold and sour. "Wait, I didn't order this."

"Yeah, that's not ours."

"Yeck." I spat into the cup. "Excuse me. Waiter! Garçon!" I called.

340

A young boy arrived in a navy uniform. "I just drank this unidentified liquid. Clean this up, please; this is a health hazard."

He apologized profusely enough so I let him go. A minute later he returned with two brimming flutes of champagne. "A small token."

"Small indeed," I said and raised my eyebrow. "But twist my arm." The sweet boy looked like a young Val Kilmer with that wonderful long jawline. He walked away, and I thought he'd trip over his feet he was so flummoxed.

"Okay. Let's keep going. Did you ask him to pay you for a sex act?" Patty said, picking up her drink.

"Sex act—what a funny way of talking. Of course not. He wanted to be my sheik for the evening. I was insulted. He was stupid and as you say racist."

"Not 'as you say.'"

"Fine. He was racist. I was angry, and so I insulted him back. I never intended for him to give me money in exchange for sex. That is not the person I am. Do we really need to go through this again? I know what I'm doing."

AFTER SETTING UP THE Nowruz display, the Haft-Seen, which literally means "seven S's" for our Western looky-loos, something I hadn't done since Mo was a little boy, Mommy insisted we jump over fire even though that was supposed to happen last Tuesday. What a distraction Ali Lufti was for this to slip her mind. "We need a renewal. Especially you, Shirin. A purging of your past, a stepping into a clear future, free of damage and chaos." The others agreed, even Patty who had no idea what we were talking about. Mommy set up a pathetic candle on the floor of my hotel room and made us all jump over it as she chanted *sorkhi-ye to az man, zardi-ye man az to*, let your redness be mine, my paleness be yours. Then we ate a big baked fish dinner at the hotel restaurant. They cooked it just for us, plated over herbed rice. Mommy said it was fine and that was all that mattered.

The next morning, I sat in bed and drank my coffee. Today was court day. The first full day of spring. I told the rest—besides Patty—to sleep in, stay home. I didn't want their clouds of wishy-washiness misting over me.

Patty and I walked to the Aspen Superior Court. The air was fresh, barely any smell of fumes. Everyone was walking, for god's sake! I looked at the big mountain to my right. The snow was beginning to melt, brown patches showing through. I thought of myself up there that day, throwing around the jewelry like a sprinkler. It had felt like freedom. It really had. What did those snow angels take home that day? What sad loser gave his wife the emerald necklace and claimed he bought it for her himself? Good for him.

We passed by the infamous jewelry store. "Don't ever go in there," I said to Patty. "They don't know a thing about creating a fantasy. Jewelry should never be in the hands of people like that."

"No ma'am," she said.

"I like you," I said.

She smiled. We stood at a light. I imagined Bita going into the bank in New York and giving up her money. Waiting for the suited man to raise his eyebrows, to convince her otherwise. Why couldn't he discourage her—those men, the purest capitalists? Mo couldn't either.

And then there she was, approaching the courthouse from the other side, practically arm in arm with Niaz and Mommy, taunting me. "Shirin," Patty said quietly. "I asked your family to come as character witnesses. If we're given the opportunity—"

"You're joking. They'll fuck it up. They have nothing nice to say about me." Air-kisses as they joined us.

"Auntie, how are you feeling? Just do what Patty and I have been saying. Then we can see about getting this expunged and you'll go back to doing what you do best—throwing parties and not being in jail. Please." Bita smiled at Patty like a big dope.

"Niaz, what do you think?" I said. "You've been in jail. What's a little jail time in Aspen? This is no Evin Prison." I let out a hoot.

She shook her head. "Don't disrespect those prisoners. What's wrong with you? It's disgusting, Mom."

"Oh, this Mom again!" I yelled. "Don't push me, Niaz! Not today."

"Look, Mommy or Shirin or whatever you want to be called. You're lucky to be where you are. You've proven your point."

"Saket, Niaz," I said.

"Shirin, really," Mommy said. "Think of your business. Your husband. And your dignity. Think of what you came from. You're better than this."

"And I just want to remind you for the last time, this is not a joke," Bita chimed in.

"Okay, I've had more than enough of all of you. Go sit in the back and don't look at me. Don't even breathe. I don't want to know you're there. Patty, let's go."

We left them outside and went through security. A woman in uniform slid a big gray wand up and down our bodies like a lint roller. The way they do at the airport, but in this environment I felt like a real criminal again. A jailbird, that's what I was! That night in jail, I was one of three accused prostitutes. The others were, I could tell, suspicious of me. They were young, and I could picture them in their shiny vinyl platform boots. I was their deranged mother, or fine, even grandmother—they looked sixteen, seventeen. Twelve. They whispered about me. They laughed the way I laugh at others.

We had front row seats behind the wooden gate. The Denver lawyer sat down with us as a formality. There was shuffling and papers exchanged; I had no idea what it all was. I smelled cologne, wood polish, and mixed sweat. Out of the corner of my eye I saw Niaz, Bita, and Mommy walk in, and I tried to put them out of my mind. Why did I ask them to come to Aspen in the first place? I needed nobody but my Patricia, in her suit and bolo tie looking ridiculous and vaguely Colora-dan. My little smarty-pants has a plan even I don't know about.

The judge entered, and an usher or some low-level officer hollered "All rise." So we did. The judge sat down and we followed. A man in a messy suit with a clipboard and a pencil behind his ear spoke with the usher. There was a series of other cases. DUIs, traffic tickets, indecent exposure. Sad people approached the bench and spoke with the judge. A pink-faced man with a stubby nose and white-blond dreadlocks down to his ankles, no shoes and an orange loincloth around his waist. What was his crime, allegedly?

Finally, the man with the clipboard said, "Next is People versus Shey-reen Jay-vaughn." Like I was some cowgirl. Stevie Ray Vaughan's sister. I laughed loudly. Patty shook her head no and motioned for me to go through the gate and sit at the empty table. She sat to my right, the Denver guy next to her. I peeked behind me and saw Bita looking like she'd seen a ghost.

"Your Honor," Patty said.

He nodded. The suits all exchanged some secret language and I let them give their sermons without focusing much on the specifics. It wasn't of consequence to me, the legal mumbo jumbo. Well, it was of course, but it wouldn't help me to worry about it. That's why I hired my lesbian angel.

As they spoke, I stared at the judge with his white mustache and black robe, his cowboy hat of which I could tell he was proud. A little slice of personality. He looked like a Western mullah with that cos-tume. I'm sure, like his Iranian counterpart, he thought he was blessed with greater moral faculties so that he could tell me, a woman he didn't know—would never know—how I could or couldn't flirt. I bet a part of him wanted to chop off my hand, sever my boobs for making his man in blue look bad. Or I was going too far—I'm sure Niaz would tell me I can't compare the two. She'd probably be right. If enough of these cowboy judges wanted to stone us for living a little, they would. We learned that in 1979.

I heard the door open behind me. Then, I saw him.

My cop. He was a pretty cop, I have to admit. Two other cops were with him, but one was a woman—surely part of the show. As he swung open the wooden gate, I swear he smiled at me. His grin was just like that night, leaning across the cocktail table, complimenting my eyes. Now, he went to the People's table, and I watched his big, muscular ass, which a part of me wanted to kick.

This made me think of Houman. He had left me ten voicemails since we arrived and I still hadn't returned a single call. But was he so annoying and clueless that I should completely ignore him? Sure, he was preposterous. But he had a spirit. I don't know. He excited me with his talk sometimes, I admit. When we had sex, he was gentle, the big bear. God, how he wanted to love me, if only I let him.

My cop sat down next to a man who'd been speaking, the Aspen assistant district attorney or whatever. He was bald and outwardly confident with a shiny watch.

Patty looked over. She put her hand on my arm and rubbed it, but I swatted her away. You don't show weakness before these people. That's rule number one.

"Relax," she whispered. I turned away from her.

I tried to understand what the judge was doing, flipping through documents, asking the clipboard man questions. Then the lawyers took turns arguing again. It's not worth repeating. We all know the story.

When I was called to give my testimony, I swore to tell the truth but with everything in my brain crossed. I sat in the booth. I knew what I was supposed to say.

"No, of course I didn't mean to hurt the police officer," I said when the prosecutor asked about the drink I allegedly threw. "Ask anybody. I wouldn't hurt a mouse. It slipped from my hand. I had just applied hand lotion. A very expensive one. Maybe one drop of watered-down martini touched his finger."

After that, I don't know what it was. The judge and his holier-than-thou look. The way they always got it wrong about women—they should be thanking these prostitutes for coming within five inches of their dicks. But is that why I said what I said? Was it catharsis? Showing off? The first day of spring—a new day? Or simply preempting a punishment I deserved? Really, I don't know what did it. It wasn't my pauper niece or my lying mother, my dead sister or my newfound daughter, I don't think. Though something clicked—who my family was, who I know we are, the gossip, those former friends at Mezzaluna, my business—maybe none of that mattered and I needed to take a stand. Say *fuck it*. Sure, maybe it would be better in a good, fair, decent world, if I did what I was told and spared Elizabeth the embarrassment, Bita and Patty the disappointment, gave Niaz a responsible parent. Sure. But this was not a good, fair, decent world. If the courtroom had a face, after I spoke, it would be one with its mouth hanging open.

"Your Honor," I said looking at the judge even though I was answering the prosecutor's question. "In the immediate seconds before I spoke those fateful words on the evening of December 23, 2005— 'Okay, honey, I can be your Princess Jasmine, but it's gonna cost you. Gimme fifty Gs'—I wanted to know what it was like to be a prostitute for the night. Just one evening of having sex for money. Of doing exactly as I pleased. And this cop"—I pointed to the man in blue—"my cop, gave me the opening, the opportunity. Why does anyone do anything? Well, I wanted to do it for me. Maybe if I wasn't feeling so low I wouldn't have done any of it. I wouldn't be humiliating myself like this in the first place. But there are a million reasons for every thing;

which is the most important? So, yes, I wanted to be a whore for the night." I paused and listened to the whispers travel like wind. "One detail my dear cop forgot to mention in his little report was that I also offered him cocaine."

"Objection, your Honor," Patty begged throughout my speech and shouted other legal-sounding phrases, but I didn't slow down and instead I raised my voice to let them know there was no stopping me.

From the back of the room, the last row of pews, Bita shouted, "Auntie, no! What are you doing?"

"Mom, stop!" Niaz yelled. I sneered.

Patty stood and argued. "She's not making sense, your Honor, she is having a mental breakdown. Regardless of everything she's said, this was still entrapment. If the officer hadn't insulted her in a racialized way, she never would have brought up money. He induced her! And what's more, at this very moment, my client is undergoing several major family crises—we cannot accept this testimony. Just look to the evidence. We need a recess. I need to speak with my client."

I shook my head. Maybe this is why I went with a complete newbie lawyer in the first place. I didn't want anyone to get in my way.

Given my various unprovoked admissions, the judge disagreed with Patty, declaring that I had acted of my own will with no inducement. I was not pushed into anything. Patty argued with him some more until the judge banged his gavel. Just like on television. But to be fair to her, she had lost before she even fastened that bolo tie.

Verdict: guilty. And given the new admission involving a Schedule II drug, court adjourned until tomorrow at which point I'd receive my sentence. The judge scratched the back of his neck. I wasn't worried—I didn't actually do anything, just attempted, and we all know America is more about doing than thinking.

The usher told us we were excused. As we stood to leave, I saw my cop. He was staring at me. Of course he was. Probably thinking, how could I be real? But I won. I felt him walking behind me, and I lifted the edge of my dress a few inches and then let it drop. If he saw that, he would be happy forever.

Patty seemed to be on the verge of tears as she whispered that she needed to deal with some of the paperwork and to go ahead without her. Outside the courthouse, the sky was blue, the clouds slight feathers. I waited for my entourage, unable to hide my smile. Despite it all, I felt relief, like I was reborn.

"What the hell was that performance? Why are you smiling? This is no cause for celebration," Bita said. "You understand you're going back to jail? Patty is in there pleading with the prosecutor not to pursue a charge related to the cocaine."

Mommy shook her head at me. "You really did it this time, didn't you. Didn't even consider your family. What will you tell Houman?"

"So are they going to deport her to Iran?" Niaz asked our little ex-lawyer Bita.

"I don't know. She's very lucky he didn't find her guilty of assaulting the police officer, but the prostitution conviction means immigration can definitely cause her some trouble now," Bita said and turned to me. "You just felt like it? *This* made you feel free?" she asked.

"Trust me. I told the truth. Without mushing it. It's a victory. And look at us. You're all still here," I said.

BITA BOOKED US THE biggest, best table at the mezzanine lounge. I specified to her the kind I wanted: round, a tight fit, but room for extra men. She wasn't going to do it until I threatened to go out and proposition another policeman. Back in my room, I showered and changed for the evening. I called Houman and he didn't pick up. Maybe he heard what I did. If so, then Marty and Tony heard, too, and word has probably spread to my clients, or whatever ones I have left. The apartment in Brooklyn—it wasn't so bad, was it? I could make anything work, a little razzle-dazzle, a couple candles. I'd call Houman again later.

At the lounge, small groups were gathered, talking quietly. Like a good girl, Bita, who was sitting with Mommy and Niaz, had laid the table with my green felt. KEM cards in stacks. A bottle of champagne in a silver bowl on ice. I pointed at the flower centerpiece. "Put these on another table," I said to Bita. "We are going to need all this space." When we both sat down, I watched the three of them and smiled because they'd all made an effort to look their best. Patty was still upstairs apparently.

The waiter circled our table with the champagne bottle, angled just enough to fill our flutes. Mommy was berating Bita for not knowing how to play Pasur. "This is your heritage, Bita. Next you'll tell me you can't play backgammon."

"She grew up here. You can't blame her," I said. "Not entirely."

For a while I let Mommy teach Bita the rules—"You just make eleven, is that so hard? But no, not like that, silly girl"—while Niaz and I drank up and laughed about Iran. How women look meaner in those black chadors—a good thing in this world. The men in Iran and their short sleeve shirts, so vulnerable and soft. Ahmadinejad's ill-fitting suits. Xerxes slapping the ocean. The drama of being an Iranian. It was almost a moment to remember.

Mommy shuffled the cards. As she was dealing, four cards to each of us and four face up in the middle to form the pool, and I rubbed my hands over the soft felt, I saw an old man's thick hand passing out cards by dropping them into the air—the cards flowing down to the exact right spots directly in front of their players, descending like Persian script. Like birds. It was Daddy. My father. My real one or my fake one, I didn't know. All these stories of relatives, ancestors, heroes. But these empires, my friend, were long dead. All that mattered was us. The people we have. Real life. And look at how much I have fucked it up. Looking to the past instead of what was in front of my face. Oh, Seema, if only you could see me now. Hah!

Even before the Revolution this started—this need to be admired, without giving anyone a chance to truly love me. Or to truly love back. And I could blame it on Mommy, I could blame it on political forces, but I am the one who left my daughter behind. What was I upset about when I threw those fistfuls of jewels across the sky—not being loved, or feeling loved. Isn't that what I was always looking for—even through my confusion?

I could barely look at the women in my family they were so beautiful. When would we ever sit like this in one place again? I lowered my gaze and examined my four cards and the pool in the middle of the green.

SEEMA

NOW I AM DEAD-DEAD.

Not alive-dead like before, not in that in between place. I have reached my true afterlife, my final home. Not an empty country, but one with others like me. A kingdom with its own skies and oceans. Not a paradise, and not a hell—like nothing I'd imagined. None of that worrying and endless repeating of the past. I am released forever. My family on Earth has come together, they have held me, held us. I know this.

For someone so fascinated with death, I didn't see my own coming. Now I spend my days with Nounou. We've moved beyond eating sunflower seeds. We don't question each other about the past. She doesn't wash me like when I was a child. I'm always clean now. She's younger than me.

The age you are in eternity is the age you were the happiest. Isn't that a nice touch? So, in the end, all that focus on antiaging cream is meaningless; you'll be your favorite age forever. For me, it's when Bita was a baby. When I'd go into the mountains of Mulholland with Marta and her chocolate milk.

I wake up each morning and splash water on my face. I think, this is my water. The water I was born to drink, and died to drink. Me, in this new soul body—this body that is not flesh, but spirit. Not made of tissue—more like living dust. I wake up and I only consider the day as it happens. I'm taking a walk. I'm picking berries. And so on.

I knew I was getting closer to dead-dead because my stories were getting narrower—there were only five or six I would recount. It had once been hundreds. Like a never-ending movie. I longed for the day when I'd have only one story. And then when I'd have none.

I could have been Bita or Shirin or Elizabeth or Niaz. That I was me only mattered for a short time. In the true afterlife, there are no facts. It is the opposite of life. It is freedom. One of the stories I told myself up to the very end was the one of my death. How I got cancer and I didn't stop it fast enough and whether that was partly my fault. Maybe—I used to think I was ready to die as soon as I gave birth to Bita, like an octopus mother, but that my body persisted beyond that moment. My dreams were never more vivid or monstrous. I contained two brains—mine and Bita's, and even after her birth, I had the trace of her brain inside me for a while. Some would say Bita created me—not the other way.

ANOTHER STORY WAS ABOUT my mother. How she was not a good mother to me. And how I was not a good mother to Bita. That she, in turn, will not be a good mother to her children if she chooses to have any. There are good mothers in the world and bad mothers—the sides are chosen long ago. Nothing changes it. No books, no experts.

But wasn't I a good mother? A good sister? I wasn't ready to die after I gave birth to Bita. No. It was with her that I became a sun, that

I became a person worth revolving around. Mother. Giver of love. Of course I could have been better, but that isn't important.

Earth itself is the only perfect mother. That is my last story. Of Earth and ultimate mothers. I look up at the sky, beyond Nounou's house and the surrounding hills. There are layers—pink and orange nearest the sun, then lavender milk, then a creamy perfect blue.

NIAZ

I SIT NEXT TO Shirin in Aspen and I feel her though our bodies don't touch. It's clear we're related, both elegant with a flair for drama. My flair is more internal. Maybe inside, she burns like me. In a way, we're both born leaders. Sure, I'm quiet, sometimes unassuming, but I've never followed anybody else in my life, not even my own mother to America. No wonder we both descended from the Great Warrior.

The carpet is lush. The workers are dressed impeccably, all in perfect pressed navy suits. There is the threat of possibility. Anybody might check into the hotel tonight. A movie star, a royal. Everyone working or dining is primed for it. Me too. It's as if we're being observed by a god who will decide if this hotel, if we, are good enough for such a reward. The workers on their best behavior. Little do we know how special each of us already is.

Maman Elizabeth is shuffling the cards. She is lulling herself into a daze, her body slouching, grinding into the seat. Patty is not here so we're all speaking Persian. Except for Bita. She can barely put together a sentence.

"Are you comfortable, Maman Elizabeth?" I ask.

She nods without looking up, her eyes on her flexing and releasing hands.

"It's interesting that they call Aspen Mountain Ajax," I say. "Do you know the story of Ajax?"

Shirin smiles in amusement. "Oh, my wise educated daughter."

"Tell us," Bita says and swirls her wine.

"Do you want me to say it in English?" I say. "Maman Elizabeth, is that okay?"

"I speak English, what are you saying?" she says in Persian.

"You're sure?"

She shoos me. The gold bands wrapped around her wrist and various fingers shine in the dim light.

"So, Ajax was a hero in Greek mythology. He gained great glory on the battlefields. At the end of the Trojan War, there was a dispute over the magical armor of Achilles who had been killed by Paris. The fight is between Ajax and Odysseus, but they agree to resolve it through arguing their case rather than bloodshed. Odysseus is the better orator, and the judges award him the armor. Some say dishonestly because Odysseus had help from Athena, the goddess of wisdom and war. Ajax is very angry. And so he sticks his sword into his chest and kills himself." I raise a sword made of air. I look around at their faces, feeling for a response.

"Wow," Shirin says and pulls out a cigarette from her purse. She lights it and exhales. I look around—will she be forced to put it out? "We are the children of Ajax. We are Ajax," she says and motions impaling herself with its lit end.

"Exactly," Maman Elizabeth laughs. "Better to be dead."

"I don't accept that," Bita says. "Why did he do it? Why not just get over it? Deal with it. I don't think that's the whole story."

"People are stubborn. Greedy. Don't you know that by now?" Shirin asks. "Anyways, where's your little friend?

355

Our eyes flash onto Bita and the empty chair next to her.

"I'll go and get her," Bita says. "I'm sure she's still looking at the court papers. She said there's maybe wiggle room, something to negotiate."

"I don't want that. I'm fine with jail time," Shirin says. "Just go get her. We need a fifth person to watch us play. To be the fan." Shirin laughs and drinks her wine. Bita has gotten the hang of the card game—I'm her partner against Shirin and Maman Elizabeth.

"Don't peek at my hand while I'm gone, you little cheater," Bita says to Shirin and walks off.

The place fills up. The men look well-fed, the women under. Same at upscale restaurants everywhere. The men are red-faced, jovial, satisfied bulldogs. The women nervous, trembling chihuahuas.

I'm getting drunk. It's my third glass. Niaz, slow it down. The room is alive, bright with talking—the voices like from a Western movie.

"Look at that stupid-looking group of tourists," Shirin says. She nods her head at the table next to us. A tall, thick man in a black suit and large purple tie is the center of attention. He's lapping it up. He reminds me not exactly of a bulldog but of a pig—with a pinkish face and wispy sand-colored hair that looks carefully combed over his head to hide baldness but instead draws my attention to it. I imagine a little curly tail poking out of his trousers, sometimes getting crushed by the back of his seat, making him grimace. He's talking over everybody even though he has a very undignified voice—like the ones in movies I've seen: *Taxi Driver*, Mafia ones. He's all mouth and eyebrows, pursing his lips when he speaks, his neck disappearing into his shoulders. The rest of the table is similarly clothed men and a few blond women with perky breasts squashed in tight dresses wearing so much makeup it is impossible to know if they are thirty or thirteen. They rarely talk, but when I hear a voice, one sounds like a little Slavic urchin.

"Who do they think they are, flying in from some low-rate city and acting like some kind of big shots. Or maybe just some Denver crime boss?" Shirin says.

The waiter comes with our fresh round of drinks and caviar, not Iranian caviar, which he apologized for earlier, just the unbanned Russian kind. I put down my empty glass and start on the new one. "Who is that slob holding court over there?" Shirin says.

The waiter smiles. "You don't know him, ma'am?"

"Don't ma'am me. I could be your lover."

"Um."

"I don't want to be, but I could," Shirin says, rolling her eyes. She has so many messages to give with that eye rolling. This time it's mock sexy.

"Of course. I apologize." He looks down at his tray and then back at Shirin. He whispers, "He's that millionaire from New York. The real estate guy."

"Oh! That asshole," she says loudly.

"Enjoy your beverages, miss." The waiter bows his head, excusing himself.

"So good of you to join us," Shirin says as Bita returns with Patty. "Did you see who's at the next table?"

"Shirin, good news," Patty says without looking over. "They're not considering the new cocaine revelation at all."

Shirin claps her hands. "My genius, thank you." She clears her throat. "But have you looked?"

"Oh god," Bita says glancing over her shoulder.

I watch my official mother continue on about our neighbors. I represent something lost to her. Youth, ambition, the gristle it took to form me. The mother wanes haggard, anemic—but I don't see it when I look at Shirin who hides it well. Women are good at this, they've had to be. It's like this with the world, the universe, everything expanding and fading. Not just mother loss. With each year, we are further

357

from god, Mohammad, Jesus, Moses, Vashti, Buddha, Shakespeare, Homer, Boudica, sheela na gigs, Hafez, Joan of Arc, truth, whoever, a more pure language. An early human spirit that was more true. I wish I could get there, but I know I can't. The things people care about now—pink rhinestone cell phones, Brangelina, a TV show with some idiots stranded on an island again—make it worse. America, everyone's reviled and worshipped center of the universe. I am drunk.

I watch her—my mother figure, my nonmother. Did I split off from her but take the best parts? Left her garish, pathetic. I just want her to say I'm sorry. I made a mistake. I should have insisted on you. I love you. Will she ever say that?

I need the toilet. Now Shirin is joking with the defenseless hostess about the rich man next door. These Americans, even Shirin now, are so amused by nobodies—in Iran a real estate millionaire would not be a person to look at.

Past the chandeliers and clattering of glasses and dishes—I find a line for the bathroom, well, a line of one. The woman in front is old, hunched, and doesn't turn back to acknowledge me. It's dark in this corner; they have forgotten to light it or it's a matter of ambiance. The piggish tycoon is making his way over. He stands behind me.

I turn. "Go ahead. There's nobody in there," I say and nod at the men's room with my best pretend smile.

He sticks out his chest and pats his belly. "Oh, that's great, because you know." He laughs.

I roll my eyes. But he doesn't see. The door to the men's room reels him in. I expect him to ignore one bodily urge for another—to place his belly against my back, whisper into my ear so heavily with vapor I can only guess he's talking dirty. His shirt front sweaty and warm against me. I'd pipe up with "excuse me," keeping the mood light, not making a scene, while he tells me to take it easy, and moves even closer, grabbing, pushing.

But none of that happens. I'm standing alone in the hallway fantasizing about this pig when he exits the men's room and winks. I smile— what else can I do? Is it because of my sexy dress and being seen nearly naked by such a man in such a place—as if I'm in a Hollywood movie? No roosari, no roopoosh. It is a vulnerability but also a power to be unveiled—a power because my curious desires, whatever their causes, are making themselves known to me. I think of the bearded man at the Tehran jail.

It never would have worked with Kian. It was best that I never entered the restaurant. I stared at him for twenty minutes through the glass. He was no longer the boy with the long gangly neck. His chest was broad, his arms strong. But worse, we had become too different. Not too different to be family, but too different to be lovers. Sitting face-to-face would have been a cruelty, at least to myself. It would have opened a box I wish I hadn't. I checked into a hotel, saw the sights, cried in the white bed.

Back at the table, the women are talking. I'm the only one who has grown up forced to cover her body in public under risk of imprisonment, flogging, or death; who knows what it is like to be furniture. It's made me different. I want to share this observation with the table but I don't know how. I don't even know how to tell them how I feel in this very second, let alone how I've felt my whole life.

I drink an entire glass of water, and before I finish the waiter is untwisting the top of a new bottle.

One day there will be another revolution and I'll be ready. I am ready. The repression, the silencing of our hearts cannot last. The Islamic Republic cannot live forever. I know it is up to women. Will these women be ready, too? Or will the pigs have their way?

When Bita asked why Ajax didn't just get over it, I didn't know the answer. I thought, well, he was a fool. But later, I will look up the story. What I didn't remember is that Ajax didn't kill himself because he didn't get what he wanted. He killed himself in shame. When he lost, he flew into a rage. Athena cast a spell on him. She clouded his mind, and Ajax, seeing just shapes, killed innocent cows and sheep thinking that they were the Greek army. When his mind cleared, he felt shame—killing all those animals—and so he killed himself. Even though it wasn't entirely his fault. Better to be dead than ashamed. We are the children of Ajax.

"Doesn't this place remind you so much of Tehran in the old days?" Shirin says to the whole table. She is passing around chunks of bread that she has buttered.

We have all forgotten about the cards, which are now spread all over the table, red and blue flags.

"Yes, it's beautiful," Elizabeth says and chews.

I want to say that I don't see it. It's not like Tehran at all. This place—Aspen—is nothing like I could have imagined. Sure, visually it is what I expected. Everything big and clean. The streets, buildings, the people. Gleaming. I laugh because all this time I was told Americans were dirty. But in Iran, there is an understanding that there is something more important deep below the surface—it runs through everything. It's thousands of years old, older than Islam. Here, there's a resignation that, in the end, it's what you can see—and hear, smell, taste, and touch—that matters, that makes a difference. It's the only part anyone can trust, so you better make it shine. I don't mean this in the usual insulting way; I mean this seriously, without judgment, with love. I do not know who has it right.

But then, what good would it do to argue? This is Shirin's opinion, and if it helps her then let it. Let her think she is re-creating Tehran.

"Now it's too Persian," Shirin says. "We come by the thousands in December. It's disgusting. You can't even say anything behind anyone's back." She laughs.

"But L.A.'s like Tehran, too, isn't it?" I say. "Why is it that all these

Persians left but keep looking for Tehran. Isn't it better to just let go? Do you know why I didn't see my old boyfriend Kian in D.C.?"

"Finally she speaks about it!" Shirin says. "The big mystery!"

"You really didn't see him?" Bita asks. "I thought you were being private by saying that."

"No. What would be the point? Bita, I am different from you. But we are linked together. With Kian it's not the same. His life is here and I will never understand it as he will never understand mine."

"Can it be that different in Iran? People drive on roads. Fruits are sweet. Nights are dark," Bita muses, swirling her wine again.

I light a cigarette. The waitstaff is so permissive. "That's nice and poetic but just further proof," I say.

"Well, then I guess it's good that I'm giving half a million dollars to your Zan Foundation," she says.

"You've what? That doesn't exist anymore. Why would you do that?"

"I told the banker to give it to you to help women's causes in Iran. Since I can't do it. And you can."

I didn't know what to say. This act of hers—giving away so much money. It was shocking for me. I'd left that old Zan Foundation work behind me. If not for Elizabeth, checking in on her, I'd be moving to a smaller town or a village by now, to have a quieter life. Less surveillance, more freedom. I want to ride a horse. I want to climb the mountains.

"Aren't you going to say something, Niaz? At least she's done one good thing for us with that money," Shirin says.

"Yes, thank you," I say. "Maybe that's what I need. A push."

Patty smiles and puts her arm around Bita.

"Na kheir," Maman Elizabeth says. "Niaz will not put herself at risk again like that. It's enough."

"I'll be careful. I'll talk to some people and make sure I don't do anything they can question. It's fine."

"If they want to question you, Niaz joon, they will find a way. Please, my god, don't take the money. I know you better than you know yourself. You'll go overboard."

"Mommy, if she wants to help, don't get in her way," Shirin says. "My daughter is a trailblazer, I've always known it."

"Shirin, this does not concern you," Elizabeth says.

"Oh!" Shirin says. "My own daughter doesn't concern me?"

"Auntie, listen," Bita says, leaning over the green felt. "It's been a long day. For once in our lives can we just enjoy the time that we have together? Just think, what would my mom want for us? She told me to enjoy my life. Let's enjoy life."

"Fine," she says. "You're right. For Seema." Shirin raises her wineglass. "She loved the mountains. Remember her Mulholland hikes? Her cross-country skiing here?"

"I thought she wasted her life and that I needed to make up for it," Bita says. "But she didn't waste it. She loved us. I wouldn't have done the things I've done without her influence."

Elizabeth nods. "I believe Seema is happy we're together. She's protected now. I used to dismiss the old ways. You remember, Shirin? Nounou taught you: we have to give the deceased our strength and support until they're accepted into the world of the dead?"

"You really buy that?" Shirin says.

I look for the bottle of water and refill my glass. I have a mother, I do. For the first time in my life, I want very simply to be here with her. I really do. I am surprising myself. But I can't stay long if I can help people back home. How could I? Right then I wish that Bita hadn't done it. So I wouldn't feel this debt. But, Niaz, what would you do in America? Don't be ridiculous. You don't get a small life after all.

I turn to Bita. "Remember how you didn't used to know Iran was mountainous. If you went there, if you went to the Alborz mountains and you saw what they looked like. If you walked on them, touched them, your body would know, your bones would know you began there. I hope you'll come see us some day."

Bita smiles. "Thank you, Niaz."

Shirin looks over at me intently. "So you are going back?"

"Yes, now it's my turn to leave," I say. "I was starting to think I might want to stay here with you, like you asked me back in New York. But I can't."

"The tables have turned," Shirin says and looks down at her hands.

Maman Elizabeth picks up a knife and hits the side of her wineglass several times. The entire room, the diners, the waitstaff, all freeze for an instant.

Patty looks around, gestures to indicate people should move on. It's nothing, her hand says. The commotion of the room begins anew.

"Thank you, Patty," Elizabeth says in English. She stares at all of us, as solemn as I've ever seen her. She switches back to Persian: "Look. Niaz, I'm glad you're with your mother. It's time. But let's get this clear. All this is my fault. Why we have to meet here like strangers. No, don't interrupt me, Niaz," she says after I try to give her a private look. "My secrets, my affair with Ali, they hurt everyone. Even you, dear Niaz. My second chance—pfff. Maybe I wouldn't have needed that. And what—I was supposed to be okay with losing all of you at once?" She shakes her head. "Do you see how hard it is for me to show emotion? Especially with you people. This kind of talk was easier with Ali. Three glasses of wine and still this." She pauses. "You see, secrets are powerful. They hurt you. They hurt me too." She looks into her wineglass, clear and still. "And now I think—maybe they're the reason for how I was. Distant, alone. How I am, even now. The very things I've feared. Secrets, not art. But why would you care about that?" She clears her throat and looks up. "At least no more secrets."

"But Maman Elizabeth, we're not strangers," Bita says.

"Good speech, Mommy," Shirin says, cocking her head. "What I can't understand is, even though your precious Ali Lufti fathered all of us, you still hated being our mother. Couldn't you have seen us as a gift?"

Maman Elizabeth picks up her napkin and dabs her eyes. "I wish I had, Shirin. But I didn't have these tools you have. The luxury of such thinking. I had myself. And this unexplainable feeling that everything was wrong. How could I see you were a gift?"

WE SIT AT THE table. We've been drinking and talking and playing cards for what feels like hours. The rest of the room has disappeared. The sounds faded into a gentle fuzz. The table with the bulldogs and chihuahuas, the pig too distracted to assault me, the bad music over the speakers, all the clinking and the footfall of waiters crossing the room trying not to trip over themselves. Even the shouting I can't hear but can imagine in the bright, busy kitchen with the sweating cooks.

I watch each face at the table, each a face like my own. Everything softened. Mother, grandmother, cousin, friend. Maybe I am home—a home of the heart if not this place. I smile at them, they smile back. I close my eyes. A silent spirit snakes between us, wraps around our ankles and onto the next woman in the circle. The way you can hardly know anything about a person, but also know everything. Blood, history, empire, ghosts.

Shirin crosses her legs and uncrosses them, again and again. She wears a cashmere sweater with pearls sitting along the collar that are somehow not matronly but sexy—the pearls are sinuous and shiny and loop around her neck twice. She is looking around the room, waiting for someone. Not the royal or the movie star. Her mother has just given her both a daughter and a father. She is waiting for herself. She is near.

"Why didn't you want me?" I say when she smiles at me. The question that's lived inside me since I was six.

Shirin shakes her head. Her eyes are wet. Her face is not hard. The truth is near the surface, closer than it's been in our family's history. She lays her hand out on the table, palm up.

Bita holds Patty's thigh under the table. There is freedom in her gestures. And risk, fear. A fresh path. Who cares that she doesn't know Iran the same way I do. She is learning something new. I watch her lean over and kiss Patty.

ELIZABETH

ELIZABETH IS TIRED. SHE doesn't like listening to English, even though she pretends she doesn't mind, so she plays games in her head. She takes out her watercolors and paints the mountain in the night sky, and below it, the women talking inside in a circle. They are playing cards, and she thinks of the way they pose their hands. It is their relationship to the mountain that matters. The painting is neither a pure landscape, nor a pure portrait. There is a sense of human time versus Earth time. The particular mountain isn't important—it could be Ajax. Alborz. A mountain in hell. One in heaven.

When Elizabeth came to New York she wanted to show them who she was. Did she succeed? Will she do it even more now? If bravery required less than ideal circumstances to grow, maybe those circumstances weren't entirely so bad. A young love, a settled marriage and house, a second motherhood, and now this. But Elizabeth still has time—this wasn't her final act either. There is more to do, to be. Beyond Ali. Beyond them. Could she invent this way of being anew? Like she invented aerobics. Like she invented an escape from her limited sphere. Maybe she doesn't need luxurious tools. She is an artist after all.

THE PERSIANS

Elizabeth thinks of her favorite painting, which similarly is neither pure still life, nor pure portrait. This one she can touch—the painting of her green paintbrush. That brush that revealed so much about her—more than any rendering of a face, even her nose. The brush was her tool for so much of life, was her. That specific brush, and the unspecific ones. Even in the painting, the brush was not alone. She will show this painting to Ali when he comes to visit—this green paintbrush with its pencils and other brushes, the chipped glass—and see if he can see her in it. A work in progress. Familiar laughter, tumble of voices. She's back in the room, in this hotel, this country, and looks around at these women, works in progress too. But will he also see Seema, Shirin, Niaz, and Bita in her paintings? She sees them, who sit around the green felt table, fingers glittering. Born into loss—but who isn't?

ACKNOWLEDGMENTS

Thank you first to Emma Paterson, my agent, who I'm convinced I was fated to meet, for your unerring sensitivity, tremendous care, and endless wisdom.

Thank you to my editors, Kishani Widyaratna and Kara Watson, you helped me make the book better, more affecting in every way imaginable, and you did so with humanity, intelligence, and humor.

Thank you to so many others at Scribner and 4th Estate, especially Nan Graham, Joie Asuquo, Kassandra Engel, Colleen Nuccio, Liz Byer, Nicola Webb, Hope Butler, Patrick Hargadon, and Eliza Plowden. Thank you also to Monica MacSwan, Lisa Baker, Anna Hall, and Lesley Thorne from Aitken Alexander, as well as Thomas Tebbe from Piper Verlag, Katharina Martl, and everyone who is giving the book homes in other languages.

Thank you to *McSweeney's Quarterly*, *Kenyon Review*, *Idaho Review*, and the Pushcart Prize for recognizing my short fiction, which is what I did for a very long time before I got the nerve to try something longer.

Thank you to my teachers, especially Edan Lepucki, Lou Mathews, and Jim Krusoe. You helped me with the confidence and the craft when all I had was just a feeling that this was what I wanted to do with my time.

Thank you to my mother, Maryam Mahloudji; my sister, Sally Mahloudji; my grandmother, Victoria Khalatbari; and my father, Farhad Mahloudji, who is no longer with us, but whose gentle spirit is always with me and whose love for books has shaped me deeply.

Thank you to my dear friends and relatives who have inspired me along the way. I won't be able to name everyone here, but thank you especially to the following. You make life feel more like a journey meant to be on together, more like I think it is supposed to be: Janet Frishberg, Dina Nayeri, Sara Soudavar, Brittany Kesselman, Jen Welsh, Mina Orak, Josephine De Haan, Deanna Fei, Vali Mahlouji, Ameneh Mahloudji, Michael Krug, Jeremy Lent, Ari Zeldin, Karen Ma, Sam Leader, Darri Farr, Jen Kushner, Allison Devers, Anittah Patrick, Jessica Sanders, Marisa Matarazzo, Ted Huffman, Elena Oxman, Abdi Nazemian, Lila Nazemian, Lilly Ladjevardi, Ronit Kirchman, Ed Park, Zadie Smith, Kate Thorman, Soo Hugh, the GWA, Blake Hazard, Stephen Brower, Rena Croshere, Shaparak Rahimi, Peter Kolovos, and Alexis Soloski.

When my children are old enough to read this book (we are still negotiating the exact age), I hope that they will read it and feel encouraged that it is always possible to reinvent oneself, even long after it feels much too late, if even the notion itself feels like a pure flight of fancy. Please never stop playing, my darlings. This book would not be possible without the love that you have given to me, which has made it more possible for me to love myself. Because writing a novel, most of the time, is also an act of love. Thank you Dahlia Anise Mahloudji Krug and Juliette Saffron Mahloudji Krug, always and forever.

ACKNOWLEDGMENTS

And finally, thank you to Zachary Krug, my husband, the father of my children, and my biggest fan, who doesn't even need to read my words to love what I write. Thank you for always believing in me and doing everything you can so that I can live the life of both a mother and a writer. More than anything else, thank you for loving me.